As she was speaking there was a terrifying scream, as a stick of bombs came hurtling through space. In that split second, expecting death, they fell into each other's arms. The explosion deafened them. The house seemed to jump in the air and then subside.

Silence.

She still grasped his shoulders. Then she relaxed.

'Well,' he drawled, 'that one didn't have our names on it after all.' He did not let her go, and with his arms still holding her she felt shy.

'I'm very glad you're here,' she suddenly said.

'Me too. You okay?'

'Perfectly.'

She was conscious of how close he was; she could see his dark eyelashes which curled like a girl's, and smell a faint scent of eau-de-cologne and clean skin. Her hair brushed his face. He let his arms drop at last . . .

Sisters

SUZANNE GOODWIN

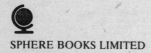

SPHERE BOOKS LIMITED

First published in Great Britain by
Severn House Ltd 1985
Copyright © 1985 by Suzanne Goodwin
Published by Sphere Books Ltd 1985
27 Wrights Lane, London W8 5TZ
Reprinted 1985, 1987

Set in Caledonia

Printed and bound in Great Britain by
Collins, Glasgow

Part I

Chapter One

The air raid warning came early, it was scarcely half past six, and the girl walking down the road quickened her step and muttered, 'Damn.' The siren rose and fell, rose and fell, wailing like the Irish banshee which people believe is a prophecy of death. The message moaned across the great lightless city, one district starting it, another picking it up and sending it onwards until the whole world seemed to echo. At last it groaned its way into silence.

Philippa walked fast but she did not run. The blitz had been on over London now for two months, and nobody ran during the raids. It was considered a sign of panic. The street lamp in the distance, shedding a ghostly glow round its base, faintly showed her that she was almost home.

As she stopped at the gate of the house, a figure in uniform emerged out of the dark. A thin ray of torchlight explored the painted name on the gatepost.

'Are you looking for St Helen's?' she asked.

'Why, yes I am.'

Overhead an ominous noise had started. It grew steadily louder, sounding like a swarm of giant bees. There was a distant muffled shudder of an explosion.

'If you want Doctor Tyrrell, I'm afraid he's at the hospital.'

'Oh, I'm not a patient. I just dropped by.'

'Well, whoever you are,' she replied curtly, 'don't you think we would be better indoors?'

'If you say so, Ma'am.'

Philippa led the way up the short gravel drive towards the dim shape of a large house. She unlocked the front door.

They plunged into a black cave. When the door was safely shut, she switched on the light. They were standing in an old-fashioned entrance hall. The visitor looked about curiously. There was a good deal of dark panelling, a heavy-looking staircase with carved banisters, a grandfather clock in a corner, its face showing the sun and moon. A Tudor chest against the wall was large enough to hold two people. There were Persian rugs on the floor, which was tiled in patterns of black, white and brown stars.

While the stranger examined the house, Philippa looked at him and saw a tall olive-skinned young man, in very new RAF uniform. He had taken off his cap and he had thick dark hair. Catching her eye, he smiled.

'Barny Duval. Glad to know you. Dixon, he's the English Intelligence officer in our squadron, told me his father knows Doctor Tyrrell. They belong to the same club. When he knew I was coming to London he said what about calling around to say hello. He mentioned that the doctor had some daughters. Which are you, ma'am?'

'Philippa. The middle one. There are three of us.'

She thought him too friendly too soon.

He turned towards her and she saw a badge on his sleeve, of an eagle, one claw clasping arrows, the other an olive branch. Above the badge were the letters E.S.

'Eagle Squadron,' he said.

'I thought you were a Canadian.'

'We have some of them, but no. I'm a Yank.'

There was a deafening roar of gunfire.

'*About time*!' exclaimed Philippa suddenly.

'The guns, you mean?'

'I should think I do. There wasn't one when the blitz started in September. Not a single one. There we were, sitting ducks, while they flew over dropping their bombs wherever they liked. It made us sick. Now we're putting up a show. The bigger the guns, the more we like it.'

Another, nearer explosion made the house quake.

'Don't you prefer to shelter?' said the young man. 'Have you one of those what-do-you-call-its in the garden? Or we could go to the subway, I guess, but it's quite a way.'

'Oh, we don't shelter in the Underground! We've got one in the house. Let's go.'

She led the way into a room which, like the hall when they had first entered the house, was an extent of blackness, every window muffled by thick curtains pulled to exclude even a pinprick of light. Philippa's father had twice been fined for blackout infringements, both times it had been the fault of his daughters. Now he demanded blackout perfection.

4

'Wait a minute.'

She disappeared, appearing a moment later silhouetted in the open doorway of a further room. Barny Duval crossed what was apparently a drawing room filled with chairs, footstools and other traps for blundering strangers. He followed her into what turned out to be a large billiard room. She had lit a lamp which was on the floor under the billiard table.

'The family shelter,' she said, with a sort of flourish. 'My father fixed it up at the beginning of the war. Idiots that we were, we couldn't believe it would ever be used. It was quite a family joke. But my sister Trix and I did paint the double ceiling. It's made of corrugated iron.'

She pointed upwards, at a sheet of corrugated iron fixed to the ceiling and supported at each corner of the room by a stout wooden post. The iron was painted a glossy dark green.

Like the hall and the unlit drawing room, the billiard room was spacious. It was panelled from the floor to about five feet up the wall and above the panelling was a line of early nineteenth-century sporting cartoons, grotesque figures boxing or fencing. There was a rack of billiard cues, big leather chairs, a smell of cigars. The place was old-fashioned and prosperous.

Philippa crawled under the table and politely patted a cushion for her visitor. The floor was arranged as neatly as the interior of a tent, with mattresses and pillows, cushions and folded rugs. The lamp stood on a tray, with cups and saucers and a silver ashtray. There were books, copies of *Vogue*, and a pack of cards.

He crouched his six foot one and crawled in beside her.

She had decided that social conversation was necessary. After all this man was a stranger and an American. She remarked brightly that it was good, wasn't it, not to be shivering in an Anderson shelter at the bottom of the garden. A girl friend had found three inches of water in hers last week: she had been sharing the shelter with a family of toads.

He undid the button of his breast pocket and offered her an American cigarette. She refused.

'May I?'

'Of course,' she said, still the hostess.

Although she was the English girl making polite talk to set her visitor at ease in ludicrous circumstances, Philippa saw rather resentfully that there really was no need. She would have preferred him to be miserably shy, but he wasn't. Here she was, in her own home, on the floor under a table with a strange man. But all he did was hunch up his long legs, lean back and look at her through the cigarette smoke.

The noise of the blitz went on, the giant bees droning, the explosions thumping. There went the guns again.

'Ah,' said Barny Duval, 'now that's a Bofors. And that – ' listening carefully, 'must be a 4.5.'

'My father says Londoners can recognize sixteen different noises in the blitz now. The various guns. Warden's whistles, warnings, different kinds of bombs. Falling shrapnel too. The other night when he was coming back from the hospital, a great lump of shrapnel fell on his head.'

'Was he badly hurt?'

'He had on his tin helmet. The only time he forgot it, he said it felt like being a crab without its shell. The shrapnel bounced off the tin hat and he found it in the gutter and brought it home. It was still warm.'

Barny looked at this matter-of-fact girl. She was pretty but not beautiful. Her eyes, wide apart, were grey and had a charming candid expression. Her mouth was large and when she smiled – but she hadn't done much of that – she looked very young. Her hair was brownish with copper lights, it was smooth and curled behind her ears. She looked so English. And yet there was something he couldn't exactly define which reminded him of the girls back home. She might be stiff and hostessy, but she had an independent carefree kind of look. But there the resemblance ended. In place of the frills and wide belts and glamorous gew-gaws worn by American girls, his blitz companion was in a brown sweater and skirt. At least she wore silk stockings; but her shoes were as heavy and low-heeled as a man's.

'My younger sister Trix is going to be furious when I tell her that somebody from Eagle Squadron called and she wasn't here,' remarked Philippa. 'She's out as usual. Dancing.'

'Is she a dancer?'

She burst out laughing.

'She's very good, but only on the dance floor at Grosvenor House.'

'But surely she comes home before the raids?'

'Not Trix. She has friends who live on the ground floor of nice solid blocks of flats. She rings them and goes there, and sleeps on the sofa of whoever-it-is.'

6

'Not in the subway?'

'You haven't met Trix.'

'Sounds as if I'd like to.'

They were silent for a moment. The blitz was in full swing.

'It was kind of you to ask me in. I feel very guilty at imposing on you like this.' Her social manner was very slightly wearing off, but he still felt it necessary to say that.

'We're always glad to meet friends of friends, Pilot Officer.'

'Oh, hell. Can't you manage Barny? Pilot Officer's such a mouthful and I haven't been in this uniform too long.'

'How long?'

'Well . . . four months. We landed in Southampton in August. Since then we've just been sitting around waiting to get trained. And becoming very frustrated.'

'I think it's wonderful, you coming here to England,' she said suddenly in a warmer voice.

'If we were in the States, I'd say "shucks".'

They looked at each other in a friendly way. They were huddled under the table, while an orchestra of destruction went on across the sprawling darkness of the city. Everywhere in London people were doing the same thing. They crouched in damp concrete shelters in the garden; they sat under the stairs or in cellars; on the crowded platforms in the Underground, or under the kitchen table, listening to the blitz which had been going on night after night for the last nine weeks. Doctor Tyrrell was right, people had become experts now at the different instruments of the orchestra. They knew the bark of the Bofors, the big-mouthed roar of the 4.5. They could tell when a bomb rushing earthwards was a thousand-pounder, they knew the light scattering noise of fire bombs, the rattle of machine-guns, the drone of enemy bombers. They listened and identified the sounds with a kind of stoic acceptance.

Philippa found herself grateful for this American's company. The family's old servant, Miggs, was down in the cellar of the house. She went there every night before the alert sounded, remarking that she liked her own company. Philippa never offered to join her and was often alone during the blitz, for her sister was always out and their father on duty at the hospital. She preferred a companion, even if he was a stranger. He also happened to be part of the thing she admired most in the world – the Royal Air Force.

7

From the start of the war she had fallen in love with flyers, as many English girls had done. This feeling had grown passionate now that the Battle of Britain was on. Philippa looked at pilots across the street, or in buses, or in restaurants, with eyes full of stars. She was like Desdemona, and loved them for the dangers they had passed.

She glanced at her companion. His face was thin and hawkish, his nose slightly aquiline, his dark hair fell in a lock on his forehead. There was something Latin about his looks. She had only known one American before in her life, a girl at her finishing school in Brussels. She, too, had seemed romantic to Philippa.

There was a louder burst of gunfire.

'Hotting up,' said Barny.

'Shall I make tea? I usually do.'

'Let me make it for you.'

'Gallant. But you'd never find anything in the kitchen. I sometimes can't either. Miggsy puts things in the oddest places. The tea is in the jar marked Rice, and the sugar in another marked Ginger. The biscuits, if we have any, are hidden. She does it to annoy because she knows it teases.'

'Is Miggsy another sister?'

'Gracious, no. She's our old nanny who has turned into an inefficient sort of housekeeper. She's been with the family forever.'

'Like a Mammy in Louisiana.'

'Oh, I know about them, I saw *Gone With the Wind*! But that was Georgia, wasn't it? Miggsy isn't a bit like a Southern Mammy. I wish she were. She was my grandfather's gardener's daughter, if you follow? She's quite old. She was my father's nurse and he inherited her. When the parents married and came here to Kensington, Miggsy came too. When we were born, she was our nanny. Now she has a stab at the housekeeping. She also calls herself the doctor's secretary. That's a laugh.'

He was looking at her with attention, and she saw with surprise that he was rather shocked, either by what she had said or her manner or both.

'Your family must love her, I guess,' he said, sounding very American.

'I'm afraid we don't. She can be very annoying. Specially when she deliberately lets the boiler go out before Trix and I have a bath. Miggsy doesn't approve of more than one bath a fortnight, she says it takes away the natural oils of the skin. But there she is. Miggs. Part of our lives. She's all we've got now. We used to have two maids as well before the war, but they vanished into the ATS.'

'Does the old lady live here?'

It was the first time in her life Philippa had heard Miggs so described.

'Oh, yes. She's in the cellar at present. It's quite snug and dry and my father had it whitewashed. She goes off there every night, taking the wireless and an enormous old rug and a thermos of tea.'

'Brave of her to stay in the blitz.'

'She's as tough as old boots.'

'I think,' he said, 'that *you* aren't as tough as you pretend.'

She raised her eyebrows. Were American girls really like Scarlett O'Hara's Southern girl friends, either ninnies or pretending to be? Did they pay lip-service to the obvious sanctimonious opinions, to match a man's idea of a tender, sensitive, vulnerable woman who must be protected?

She returned to the subject of tea.

'The bombs don't sound too close. I do long for tea – '

As she was speaking there was a terrifying scream, as a stick of bombs came hurtling through space. In that split second, expecting death, they fell into each other's arms. The explosion deafened them. The house seemed to jump in the air and then subside.

Silence.

She still grasped his shoulders. Then she relaxed.

'Well,' he drawled, 'that one didn't have our names on it after all.' He did not let her go, and with his arms still holding her she felt shy.

'I'm very glad you're here,' she suddenly said.

'Me too. You okay?'

'Perfectly.'

She was conscious of how close he was; she could see his dark eyelashes which curled like a girl's, and smell a faint scent of eau-de-cologne and clean skin. Her hair brushed his face. He let his arms drop at last, and she leaned back, tugging at a cushion.

'You're very beautiful.'

Philippa went scarlet.

9

'Hell, I've made you blush. You must know you're beautiful. A heap of guys have told you so before now . . . there are freckles on the bridge of your nose.'

She managed a laugh.

'Seven.'

'You counted them.'

'No, it was my sister Trix. She said that I must get rid of them. She bought some expensive stuff at Harrods before make-up disappeared from the shops. She used to rub it on my nose every day for a week. It didn't have the slightest effect. She was more disappointed than I was. She's the family's beauty expert.'

'You talk about her a lot.'

'So would you if you met her.'

'But isn't there another sister?'

'Yes, the married one. Elaine. She's with her husband at present. He's in the Royal Naval Voluntary Reserve, and he's got some leave.'

He nodded, indicating a kindly interest; he was very polite. He lit another cigarette and sat smoking and staring into space; unselfconscious, easy. It was odd to be here on the floor with this foreigner. It was rather fascinating to realise that she knew absolutely nothing about him; it gave him a kind of power in her thoughts. He came from the country she knew only from the cinema, and about which she had hazy ideas based on Hollywood. It was a land of the rich, the frivolous and the glamorous, where girls in white satin nightdresses were stranded in situations which could not offend the strictest Puritan. Everything American was foreign to Philippa. But this man wore English uniform.

'There isn't a moon tonight,' he said, after a pause. 'Moonlight helps.'

'The enemy?'

'No, no, the fighters. The idea of a bomber's moon is quite wrong, it ought to be called a hunter's moon, a fighter's moon.'

'Have you been in a fight, Barny?'

'Wish I could say yes. But no, we're still hanging around, supposed to be training. And God, there's one hell of a lot to learn.'

Suddenly he tensed. They both heard the sound outside the house, an extraordinary noise, plop, plop, plop, plop, as if somebody were dropping a thousand tennis balls. No explosions followed.

'What on earth – ' began Philippa, when there was a thunderous hammering at the front door. A voice yelled,

'Warden here! Warden here! Open up, your house is on fire!'

They threw themselves out from under the table and pelted to the front door. A man in blue uniform, wearing a tin hat, said quickly, 'Thank God you're here. There's a fire at the back. Look sharp.'

Not stopping to say more, he rushed back into the road. Out in the dark there was fire everywhere.

'I must get Miggs,' shouted Philippa, but just then a bent figure in a dressing-gown appeared at the top of the cellar steps.

The old woman said, 'I've seen it. It's the conservatory. You take the sand. I'll get water.'

She hurried to the kitchen.

Philippa grabbed a bucket of sand which had stood in the corner of the hall since the war began. She and Barny ran down the front steps. The blacked-out night was transformed. Small brilliant fires burned fiercely all down the road, and figures silhouetted in the dazzling orange flames were hurrying to quench them. An extraordinary sound broke out from road and gardens, as men and women put out the incendiaries with earth or water. It was laughter. The bombs fell like hail, weighing little, and burst into flames the moment they hit the ground. One girl contemptuously kicked a flaming bomb into the gutter.

Philippa and Barny ran round the corner of the house as a soldier appeared from nowhere, carrying a stirrup pump.

'Water?'

'We've got a tank.'

The conservatory, tinder-dry from the hot summer, was already burning with a roar, the sparks flying upwards like fireworks. Barny and the soldier began to pump, Philippa rushed forward to fling her sand into the flames.

'Hell!'

The sand was caked solid. Dashing to a flower bed, she dug the sand out with her nails, filled the bucket with earth and returned to throw it on the fire. Miggs came out of the kitchen door bent under the weight of an enormous iron kettle. Barny took it from her as if it were a feather. Protecting their faces, the men advanced into the smoke to seize deckchairs and mats which they threw on to the grass.

The leaping flames lit the garden as if it were Guy Fawkes'

night, throwing fantastic shadows. The smoke was choking. But after some minutes of pumping the water and dousing with earth, Miggs and Philippa hurrying to the kitchen and back over and over again and the tank providing a steady stream, the fire at last began to hiss.

'That's more like it,' grunted the soldier, wiping his face with a blackened hand. 'I'll go next door.'

He ran off towards the garden wall and a reddish gloom from a neighbouring house.

Miggs passed Barny a final kettle of water which he threw on smouldering windowsills. The old woman, hands on hips, looked at the smoking mess.

Barny said to Philippa, 'Shall we go too?'

A high wall separated St Helen's from the next house which had been empty since the war. Barny called, 'Let me give you a leg up,' but Philippa went over the wall like a bird.

The garden of the empty house shone with glittering fires on flower beds, lawns, and the steps by the French windows. There was a smash of glass as the soldier broke a window to go indoors – he'd seen a fire on the roof.

Earth quenched fires, as water did, but Philippa found a quicker way, she used a dustbin lid. She and Barny ran from fire to fire until there was nothing left but smoke and the smouldering ashes. The wardens' whistles had begun to blow again in the street – a fresh rain of incendiaries was falling, each bomb bursting into flames as it fell. The road was still crowded with helpers. Somebody shouted to Barny, as he pushed a ladder against the empty house.

At last it was over. The whistles were silent, the figures in dressing-gowns had melted away, every fire was out. Philippa put down her dustbin lid, and stood by the ladder, which Barny and the soldier were shinning down. The sky over towards the West End was stained dark red.

'We put up a good show, didn't we?' said the soldier, grinning. He loped away into the dark.

The front door of St Helen's was open.

'Where's the old lady?'

'Don't worry about her. She'll be back in her lair drinking tea. Tea! We need it!'

Slamming the front door, they went into the kitchen, and Philippa put on the light. The room was big and old-fashioned, like the rest of the house, the floor tiled, and a coke boiler in the corner. The curtains were closely drawn, or they would have shown a first-rate view of the burnt conservatory.

Philippa made the tea and found about half a glass of brandy in a dusty bottle high up in the pantry. She divided it fairly, pouring it into the two cups. Then she sat on the table and looked at her legs. She sighed.

'Ruined.'

The precious, gleaming silk stockings were a mass of ladders through which her muddy legs showed. Her face was as black as a sweep's, her jersey filthy, her skirt, torn with jumping over the wall, was smeared with earth and smuts. Barny's uniform was as bad.

'Heroine.'

'Hero.'

'We make a fine pair.'

They drank the tea, refilling the pot and examined the brandy bottle for a few final drops. Carrying the tea tray to the billiard room, they crawled back under the table and settled down like birds in a nest. Guns still barked but the bombs were far off.

'Wish I could take you out for some champagne. And to dance.'

'I feel the same. I want to celebrate. But we'd never clean ourselves up, we need baths! And your uniform's really awful, Barny. We'd never get the muck off it.'

'Suppose you're right. Pity.'

He looked at her and added, 'My leave lasts until two o'clock tomorrow. What are you doing for lunch?'

'A sandwich and fund-raising. I write endless letters begging for cash for a children's hospital.'

'Could you stop begging long enough to eat lunch with me?'

'I don't know . . . yes, I think so.'

'That's nice. And what about breakfast before you go to work?'

'But we'll be having it here. You're staying, aren't you?'

'Somehow I feel I should scram. Your father – '

'He wouldn't mind.' Her voice said the opposite.

'I'd mind you spending the night with a strange man if you were mine. Come to think of it – I wish you *were* mine.'

He took her in his arms.

Philippa had wanted him to do that. She had kept thinking about it, imagining what it would be like if he kissed her. She

13

had found herself looking at his mouth, the lips firm and the bottom lip full. Now, as he closed his arms round her she gave a kind of sigh as she shut her eyes. She snuggled closer, giving and receiving passionate, exploring kisses. How beautiful he tasted, she thought. Her mind began to blur, she could no longer think, she could only feel. He shifted and lay on top of her, covering her with his weight and pushing her down into the cushions. He was heavy, and she was excited by the sensation of being crushed by the weight of a man. Between kisses he made choking sounds, half exclamations.

'Christ, you're so – oh, God!' He began to pull up her sweater, and putting his hands into her brassiere, he exposed one of her breasts. She came spinning back to earth.

'No. Please. No.'

When she gasped, 'No' he pushed her naked breast ridiculously back into the lace cup, resembling a man putting a peach into a paper bag. He pulled down her sweater. Philippa had never been half seduced before, and thought he would move away from her. But he did not. He still held her, looking down into her face.

'So you won't let me make love to you. You don't want us to.'

'But I do. Dreadfully. It's just that I never have.'

He rubbed his face against hers, scratching her skin.

'Then I guess you shouldn't.'

Her body throbbed, she felt giddy, she wanted to be kissed again.

'It's your fault I behave badly, you're such a luscious female.'

'I wish we *could*.' Her sorrowful look confused him. He ached for this brave foreign girl.

There was the sudden loud noise of a slammed door.

'Damn. That must be my father.'

Guilty as a schoolboy, Barny slicked back his hair and buttoned the filthy uniform jacket. Philippa pulled down her skirt. We might be in an old-fashioned French farce, she thought. They were sitting well apart when the billiard room door opened.

'Philippa?'

Her father's voice was hoarse.

'I'm here, Father. Trix hasn't come home but this is Pilot Officer Duval who came to help with the fire.'

Her father, in coat and tin hat and holding his doctor's bag,

14

stared down at them. Barny crawled out from under the table and politely introduced himself. Doctor Tyrrell did not reply. He went out, saying – which part of the house was burnt?

A moment later he put his face round the door again.

'Where in God's name is Miggs?'

'Safely back in the basement, sir. A wonderful old lady at helping put out a fire.'

Doctor Tyrrell grunted and disappeared.

Putting out his hand, Barny pulled Philippa to her feet. He thought how tired the pretty face looked under its smears and smuts.

'You could use some sleep. I must get weaving. Philippa - mind if I call you Flip?'

'My sisters do.'

'I'll join them. See you for lunch, then. The Ritz at one-fifteen okay?'

'Goodness, how extravagant.'

'You belong in places like that.'

He briefly kissed her, picked up his cap, turned to look at her for a moment, and left. She heard the front door close.

She crawled back under the table, covering herself with the rugs. Her father did not return – she heard him going up the stairs, and coming down again to his study. It, too, had an iron ceiling.

Lying open-eyed, she listened to the blitz. Was Barny safe in the dangerous streets? Where was he going, she had never asked him.

The All Clear did not sound until dawn.

Chapter Two

When Philippa came downstairs, bathed and dressed in neat working clothes, Miggs was in the morning room. The old nurse wore a hectic puce and green apron over her grey skirt and blouse, and stood with arms folded looking out of the window. She gestured in the direction of the conservatory.

In daylight the scene of last night's fiery drama had become a blackened mess against a background of leafless winter trees.

'The doctor's only just seen it properly. Stood starin' at it for ten minutes, then in he came and carried on somethin' shockin'.'

Miggs dropped her *g's* like a member of some aristocratic hunting set.

'I suppose it was shock, Miggs.'

The old woman snorted. 'He sees forty times worse every night. Some of the things he tells me, and he doesn't say much, mind, always reserved, your father, they make my hair curl. Anyway he was lucky last night; if you and that young chap hadn't looked sharp, the whole house would have burned up and me in it. I told him. He doesn't listen.'

Migg's manner of speaking about her employer was anything but respectful.

Her real name was Ada Margaret Higgins but nobody called her anything but Miggs. She had grown up in the gardener's cottage of the Sussex manor where Philippa's father was born. At seventeen she had been employed as nurse to the little Tyrrell boy. Theo had been Migg's only love affair. He had been good-looking, with sparkling blue eyes. He loved music and Miggs could play the piano. The little child in spotless white, or dressed like a sailor in imitation of the Royal children, would sit in a trance under the nursery piano while Miggs thumped away at *Floradora*. She read to him and he knew every old rhyme by heart. 'I saw three ships come sailing by, sailing by' Theo chanted, and Miggs put her arms round him and hugged him until he couldn't breathe. She waited on him like a slave, spoiled him dreadfully and never said a cross word to him. When he was a grown man and became engaged to be married, it did not occur either to Theo or to Miggs that she would not accompany him to his new home.

In her youth her back had been injured and she had something of a hump. She was as small as a child, stoutish, solid, and although in her seventies she moved niftily. She had a mole on one side of her cheek the size of a half-crown, and wicked little hazel eyes. When children first saw her she frightened them, she looked so like a witch. But after two minutes they were on her knee, giggling. So perhaps she was a white witch. Children and animals and Theo loved Miggs.

Her passion for Theo had altered, she no longer thought him perfect and often criticised him to his face – the only woman in his life who got away with that. She was possessive. She had been kind enough to Mary, Theo's wife and mother of the three girls, but Mary treated Miggs gingerly. She was not strong, and was glad of Miggs's sturdy presence while the children were young.

The three Tyrrell girls, Elaine, Philippa and finally Trix were all cared for by Miggs, but she never gave them her heart. She bossed them about and complained about them to their father. They enjoyed her when they were very small, but by the time they were old enough to go to school they were glad to be out of her way. There was no fun in having an old nanny if you weren't spoiled, and Miggs's reaction to a new frock was 'handsome is as handsome does', or to a good school report, 'think yourself clever now, do you?'. Elaine sometimes said that Miggs was jealous.

When the Tyrrell girls grew up, Miggs suddenly transformed herself. Theo's receptionist was leaving to be married. His Kensington practice was busy and he needed a girl at the desk in the hall, to answer the telephone, show the patients into the waiting room and send out the monthly bills. He was interviewing girls for the job and had not made up his mind who would suit him when Miggs appeared. She wore a white starched coat over her miniature humpy body. She'd bought it in the medical department of the Army and Navy stores. It had bone buttons and cufflinks, and she had had to take up the hem which had touched the ground.

Theo was staggered. If there was an argument about his old nurse's plan, the family never heard about it. He gave Miggs the job. The two young housemaids working at St Helen's were delighted. Miggs would now have no time to order them about.

Since the war and the disappearance of the maids, Miggs transformed herself again. She remained receptionist, but was also housekeeper, cook and housemaid. Sketchy at all her duties, she was dead keen at answering the telephone.

'Sleep all right, Miss Philippa?' asked Miggs, leaving her scrutiny of the burnt conservatory with reluctance and going out of the room to fetch the tea.

'Yes, thank you, Miggs. Did you?'

The old woman returned with the teapot covered with a green knitted tea-cosy which she had made. It was hideous but the Tyrrells never dared to say so.

'Like a top. Never slept so well as I do in my shelter.' That was how she described the cellar. 'It's bone dry. I don't mind the noise either. Funny when I think in peacetime that gramophone in Mrs Next Door's garden on summer nights kept me awake till all hours. Just shows.'

She began to pour the tea, looked up and said, 'Ah, there you are.'

Doctor Tyrrell came in, carrying *The Times* and looking his usual spotless self. Nobody, thought Philippa, looked as clean as her father did. He wore old-fashioned checked tweeds, some of his suits were years old, but perfect in cut and of quality which never seemed to wear out. His cream-coloured silk shirts were washed and ironed by Miggs: he had a clean one every morning, blitz or no blitz. Philippa's mother used to say he was a dandy. But if his appearance was perfect, his expression was not. He looked very disagreeable.

The gas fire roared, as it did now since the blitz began, sending out a feeble warmth. Theo took his place with his back to what little comfort it gave.

In the winter of 1940, the second of the war, food was scarce, but he expected his breakfast formally served in the morning room where he and his family had breakfasted every day for the last twenty years.

'I suppose the damage is worse than you feared, Father,' said Philippa diplomatically. Miggs gave her a sardonic look, knowing what she was up to.

'No, it isn't. But the mess must be tidied up, it can't be left like that. It will be rebuilt eventually.'

'Eventually?' echoed Miggs.

'Yes. When the war is over. In the meantime, it must be cleared up.'

'Not much point, is there?'

Such a question from his daughters would have received a very cutting reply, but the doctor was reasonable when talking to his old nurse. He treated her as an equal.

'When it has rained and the dust has settled, it may be possible to get somebody to remove the worst,' he said.

Philippa was amused and faintly annoyed. Who but her father would suggest tidying up war damage in the middle of the blitz? Tomorrow St Helen's might be rubble.

'One of Trix's boyfriends might help when on leave,' she said unwisely, getting the inevitable.

'Where is your sister?'

He asked the question almost daily. Philippa wondered why he bothered. Trix was always out. During the day she met her friends, went shopping, and saw the latest Bing Crosby films. By six o'clock she was dancing in the big ballroom at Grosvenor House, which was packed with officers and their girls.

And, as Philippa had told Barny Duval, her young sister now had a network of useful London friends with safe ground floor flats where she could stay the night.

'She's probably with the Parkers at St Mary Abbott's Court. Their flat's facing the garden. They never go to a shelter.'

'Did she telephone?'

'Perhaps she couldn't get through.'

Looking down his nose, he returned to *The Times*. Trix's behaviour displeased him but he never bothered to quarrel with her.

Miggs, arms folded, regarded the newspaper behind which he had hidden.

'While you were out lookin' at the damage, I hope you remembered it was Miss Philippa who saved the house.'

She marched out, returning with a rack of symbolically burnt toast.

Miggs only said this to annoy; she knew he would never admit owing anything to one of his children. He groped for toast and marmalade, and when he was finally forced to put down the paper to pass his teacup, Miggs filled it in silence. She never sat

19

with the family at meal times, but remained on her feet, a humpy, aproned butler.

Philippa glanced anxiously at her father wondering if the fire had given him a shock. Perhaps, while on his way back from the hospital an air-raid warden had told him that St Helen's had been hit. He'd looked so alarmed when he burst into the billiard room last night. Had he thought she, Trix and Miggs had been killed? He was out in the blitz every night now. Bodies covered with sheets and laid out in gardens were a usual sight to him.

But Theo did not look shocked. His face was closed as it usually was, as if he had slammed it shut. He was a spare, shortish man, over sixty and aging well. His face resembled the famous head of Julius Caesar, he had the same strong bones, furrowed cheeks, determined jaw, and thin unrepentant lips. His hair had been fair but now it was sparse and white. He retained the fresh colour of fair-skinned people but his eyes, once blue and eloquent, were bloodshot. He had a certain air and Philippa had seen him being gallant with women. Her elder sister Elaine said he needed and despised them.

It was a year since Mary, Theo's wife for thirty years and mother of his daughters, had died. She was the only woman he ever loved and throughout his marriage he stayed faithful, although he was far more highly sexed than she. Sometimes he had been rude to her when his medical friends came to dine. He ignored her or frowned if she ventured an opinion. But he did the same with Philippa and Trix, although not with Elaine. Mary did not seem hurt by her husband's behaviour, but Elaine told her sisters that the way their father sometimes treated their mother made her sick.

'But he loves her!' protested Philippa.

'You really are,' declared Elaine, 'hopelessly sentimental.'

The family laughed over this trait. Philippa saw people in a rosy light. They forgot that this view of hers included themselves. In her girlhood Philippa accepted their verdict, but since her mother's death Philippa often asked herself if sentimental was another word for being right. Her father *had* loved her mother. He was an autocrat in the Victorian tradition but he had married for love.

The Tyrrells had lived at St Helen's, a large nineteenth-

20

century house in d'Abernon Road, Kensington, since Theo and Mary were first married. It was near Addison Road and Holland Road, a leafy pleasant district. The houses had large gardens. Theo's father had bought him the practice before the Great War, and it had been a measure of Theo's taste for grandeur that he moved into St Helen's when he and Mary had no children and were not particularly well off. Theo had served in the Artillery during the war, was wounded and invalided out. He was one of the lucky ones.

Mary Tyrrell's parents were wealthy Quakers in the Midlands, she was accustomed to spacious houses and good living, but she always said St Helen's was too big. It had a study and a billiard room, a library which Theo used as his surgery, a dining room with French windows, a drawing room, a morning room and seven bedrooms. The kitchen quarters had been built for a large and comforting staff. It was a house which possessed its own authority – it required to be well run.

Like other massive rambling Kensington houses within walking distance of the gilded gates of Holland House, St Helen's had been built during the pre-Raphaelite period. Its owner, a Jeremiah Armstrong, had been a friend of the artists who settled in the district like flocks of peacocks during the 1860s. Lord Leighton made his house into a Persian paradise. G.F.Watts, bearded and nearly fifty, had a tall house with a vast studio. He married a ravishing seventeen-year-old Ellen Terry and brought her home there; the redheaded beauty didn't stay long.

Jeremiah had been a bad poet and a worse painter but he loved art and his artist friends and built a house to be near them. St Helen's was his creation. His taste had chosen the tiles patterned with yellow pansies round the drawing room fireplace, the carved mantelpiece of oak leaves and acorns. The handsome staircase was straight from a Victorian painting of *The Taming of the Shrew*. In the garden was a sundial which bore the motto '*Pereunt et Imputantur.*' 'The hours pass and are numbered against us,' translated Theo to his children. 'You should remember that.' A bronze Guinevere, none too well sculpted and covered in verdigris, still stood in her ivy-clad alcove. The garden was quite large, with pleasant high brick walls against which Mary had trained pears and peaches. The house needed its three servants.

But if St Helen's meant work, staff in the 1920s and 30s was cheap. The cleaning and coal carrying, grate polishing and cooking were done by two girls from St Ethelreda's orphanage. The girls came to the Tyrrells in two's for company. Every few years Theo and Mary drove to an orphanage in a distant London suburb, to be allotted two orphans who had reached the working age – about sixteen. The girls arrived at St Helen's with cardboard suitcases filled with stout uniforms. They were invariably so shy they were in a permanent blush. They stayed for three or four years, and then left for better wages, and back Theo and Mary would go on another orphan-foraging expedition.

Mary, with her Quaker upbringing, took her maids' welfare seriously. She saw that they joined the Girl Guides, which meant there was somewhere pleasant where they spent their half-day a week off. She chose their best uniforms, brown poplin, with coffee coloured lace collars and aprons. On the maids' birthdays the Tyrrell daughters gave them embroidered best aprons and caps threaded with velvet ribbon, and tins of Palm toffee. The girls liked their new aprons, but they loved the banana toffee.

Mary was a gentle soul. She was at home with her maids, and taught them to cook well. Sometimes when Philippa came into the kitchen, she heard her mother's slow voice, 'No, no, Alice, don't be so impatient. Cooking needs all the time in the world.' Mary laughed more with the maids than with her husband and children.

But despite Theo's impatient, authoritarian ways and distinct lack of generosity over money, Mary was serene. Her round face looked girlish, even in middle-age. Her nose was a little snub blob and her eyes were pretty. She wore her grey hair coiled in a knot on the top of her head.

Inherited money began to arrive, in slices of varying thickness, at St Helen's. Uncles died. So did a wealthy godfather of Mary's. On the death of her Quaker father, Mary actually became wealthy. She did not expect her money to be at her own disposal, but to do Theo justice he never suggested she should do what she did, which was to have the entire income paid into his bank.

Elaine was twenty at the time of her mother's inheritance. She was a girl of commonsense. She was small, the shortest and most valiant of the Tyrrell girls, with a straight nose, rather fixed blue eyes, a matter-of-fact voice, rather flat, never loud. She was as stylish as *Vogue*, where she worked.

'Mother, you are surely keeping some of Grandfather's money for yourself?'

'Oh no, dear, that is your father's business.'

'It is *not* Pa's business! The money is yours. Grandfather left it to you. Why not keep it? Or at least,' she finished severely, 'some of it.'

Her mother wore a smile which showed that nothing was going to move her. She prided herself on her strength of mind.

'Mother, can't you even write a cheque?'

'I've never done such a thing, why should I begin now? What matters is that my dear father left me his portrait and his books and the family Bible. And there's his gold watch, as well. Do you remember how you loved it when you were little?'

Elaine repeated the conversation to Philippa, who declared their mother was right and what mattered were the portraits and the watch. Elaine raised her eyebrows. Philippa was as hopeless as their mother.

Money had never been plentiful in the Tyrrell family when the girls were young; it hadn't been easy to afford the boarding school fees. Neither of the elder girls went to university, although they wanted to do so. Theo said he could not afford it, and since they were bound to marry, what was the point?

Both girls had jobs. Elaine managed to work at *Vogue*. She liked it very much, was fascinated by the photographers and models and journalists, and above all by the style. Philippa's job was dreary – she was a typist at Vickers Armstrong in Victoria Street, working in a huge room with sixty other girls. An elderly gorgon sat on a raised platform, dishing out the work and watching to see if anyone was wasting time.

'What is the point?' said Philippa to her family. 'There just isn't enough work to go round. I *asked* for some. And last week I read the whole of *Martin Chuzzlewit*, sitting at my desk.'

The girls – Elaine to begin with – had a number of boyfriends, the sons of friends. Men ran after Elaine but she did not fall in love. She was pretty and beautifully dressed, her connection with *Vogue* formed her tastes, she was bright and carefree. But Mary began to worry when her attractive eldest daughter did not find a husband by the time she was twenty-two. Mary believed that if girls did not marry when very young, they would land up on the shelf. Other girls, fresher and sweeter, were at their heels. 'I dislike,' said Mary, 'an old bride.' When she spoke anxiously of Elaine's single state to Theo, he said Elaine had a head on her shoulders. Mary could comfort herself with the certainty that Elaine would not do anything foolish. She'd be as sensible over getting married as she was about everything else.

He would not have said that about Philippa. Four years younger than Elaine she began to fall in love at sixteen, and continued to topple in and out of love like a child learning to walk, tottering a step, then collapsing, then scrambling to its feet again. She was hopelessly romantic.

Elaine introduced her to a number of young men and took her to dances. They drove out to the country to swim at newly opened road houses. They punted at Wargrave, or piled into open cars to go to the Aldershot Tattoo. In garden party clothes and white gloves, they accompanied their parents to Trix's Speech Day. Trix was now a leggy untidy teenager, outclassed in everything academic; she won the prize for gymnastics.

'Golly, what a relief,' hissed Trix to Philippa, 'I'm bottom at everything else.'

To celebrate the New Year, Elaine and Philippa went to the Chelsea Arts Ball. Elaine had a friend whose parents had a box, and she and Philippa had been invited.

The girls had a great deal of fun hiring their costumes at Nathans. They chose crinolines with enormous hoops sewn into linen petticoats, which swayed so much they were difficult to control. They carried fans, and Elaine wore a bonnet with a pale blue satin bow under her chin.

When they arrived inside the Albert Hall, they felt they were walking into an enormous jungle. Wherever they looked were hundreds of the strangest creatures; hectically coloured, feathered and crested, there were macaws and butterflies, parrots and orchids, walking orange trees, Rajahs and tigers. The girls were entranced. Clowns went by, and ballerinas. Black-clad Hamlets winked at them, and demons blew them kisses. At a corner they collided with a living Oxo cube. There was no need for introductions, everybody talked to everybody.

Just before midnight Elaine and Philippa were in their box watching the scene on the ballroom floor below. The students had built a series of huge cars, a different car for each College, and were dragging them in procession. There were towers of flowers, palaces of cardboard, geometric creations, planets, ships. Girls in costume posed perilously high among rockets and fountains. Teams of boys pushed and pulled the cars to applause. At last the procession wobbled to a halt. Twelve o'clock had come, and balloons hidden in nets high up in the dome of the hall came floating down in thick multicoloured cascades. At the same moment everybody moved in a wave to the cars, and began to pull them to pieces. They wrenched down their own work which had taken them weeks to make, they pulled out chunks of painted cardboard and trampled on it. In a few moments the bright fantasies were gone, destroyed like houses swallowed up in hell.

As Elaine, half amused and half shocked by the mayhem, swayed out of the box she walked straight into her future.

'I'm most fearfully sorry! I'm a clumsy fool,' exclaimed a young man who had nearly knocked her over. 'Are you all right? What can I do? Shall I go down on my knees? Give me a task to prove my repentance, I beg!'

He was dressed as a sailor, with broad collar and trousers tight across the hips, a sailor's hat on the back of his head. He was tall and thin and dark and had a quick way of talking.

Elaine refused everything but the apology.

'Could we dance?' he asked. 'I saw you just now, you know. I was in all that scramble in the ballroom and I looked up and there you were in the box. I thought – I must find out who she is. Do you mind?'

When she knew him better she learned that was an expression of his. He would buy her flowers and say 'do you mind?' And he called girls lilies.

'You're the prettiest lily here,' he said.

He introduced himself. His name was Miles St Aird. They found they had a few – not many – mutual friends.

When he laughed, Miles St Aird seemed as if he really meant it and as if his laughter came from the heart. He was quick and casual, his narrow figure was graceful and his grey eyes were expressive and rather beautiful. He stayed with her all the evening, and when they parted he wrote her telephone number on his wrist in ink.

She thought she would never see him again. People said that sort of thing always happened at the Chelsea Arts. But he telephoned her the next day.

25

They began to meet a great deal. She thought him very attractive. She was stirred by his chaste goodnight kisses. When they parted late at night after dancing somewhere expensive – Miles never took her anywhere but to fashionable places – Elaine sat down at her dressing table, to cream her face and brush her hair. She wondered why she felt sad. She never saw him go without a feeling of loss.

He liked to give her things. A box came from Moyses Stevens containing three tiny white orchids. The scrawled card said, did she mind? Why did the flowers make her cry? She was being, she thought, as silly as Philippa.

The scare of war, strong, terrifying during the previous year, had faded. At least it did so for Elaine who forgot politics and fell in love. But Miles did not ask her to marry him, as all her other young men did. She had had, so far, six proposals. She always became very nervous when she knew a proposal was in the air. And was inevitably sick.

'But how do you manage?' asked Philippa with some curiosity.

Elaine laughed and made a face.

'When I know for certain that whoever it is is going to ask me, I begin to feel really queasy, exactly like on a Channel steamer when it's rough. Then, just before I absolutely *know* they're going to say it, I say will they forgive me for a second and I dash off to the ladies. Then I am really sick. It always gives me a colour, and when I get back I suppose I look fine. Then he pops the question and then I'm very nice and say, no.'

None of this happened to Miles. What was more, he had not done that other essential thing, introduced her to his family.

During the summer he stayed in London, in a cousin's flat in Sloane Street – his parents lived in the Cotswolds near Woodstock. Miles was working for his accountants' examinations, and at weekends he went sailing at Itchenor.

'You must learn to crew, Elaine, I'll begin by teaching you your knots.'

'Oh help!'

They were in Hyde Park. It was spring and they were sitting on a bench facing the Serpentine. Miles produced some string from his pocket and taught her the difference between a granny and a reef knot.

One of Elaine's elderly aunts lived at Bosham, so it was possible for her to go down at weekends, to sail with Miles in his

Sharpie in Chichester harbour. She spent her nights in blessed chastity in her aunt's spare bedroom.

Elaine liked doing things well, and soon became Miles' useful crew. They won two or three races in the Regatta.

Miles had joined the Royal Naval Voluntary Reserve, and after leaving the office on weekends he trained on HMS *President* moored near Blackfriars.

'There'll be a war this year,' he said briskly, 'So I shall be ahead when we're all called up.'

'There *won't* be a war. Don't let's talk about it.'

'But we must, sweetie. London will be bombed flat, you know, so you and your family will have to leave beforehand. They will send over bombers in five-minute waves until there's nothing left but smoking ruins.'

He was twenty-three and couldn't keep a note of Wellsian drama out of his voice.

'But Hitler's only threatening,' she said. Her voice quavered.

'Oh poppet, I've upset you, what a pig I am. But now that I've joined the RNVR and we do seem to be making plans I thought we ought to be engaged. Would you mind?'

That had been Miles' proposal.

Philippa never forgot Elaine's face when she told her the news. It had been ecstatic. It had been almost terrible, Philippa thought, to look at such happiness. When she thought of it, she remembered that while Elaine had stood there with her swimming eyes and heartbreaking bliss, Fats Waller had been singing 'Honeysuckle Rose'.

The past, the peaceful past, had been filled with music. The gramophone at St Helen's, sometimes muffled by a cushion so as not to disturb patients in the waiting room, was on at all hours. Fred Astaire. Bing Crosby. Fats Waller. And Miles' favourite, which was 'Plenty of money and you-hoo-hoo, Say baby what I wouldn't do-hoo-hoo.'

Philippa had a lot of admirers now. When she came home on hot summer nights, after dancing with some young man, they would jump into a taxi as closed and intimate as a hansom cab, the window at the back the size of a coffee saucer.

'Drive round the park, please.'

Accustomed to the order, the driver set off slowly into the dim and leafy park. And boy and girl fell into each other's arms to kiss until they were breathless. The boys never put their hands down

27

Philippa's low-cut evening dresses, or up her clinging satin skirts. It was never anything but lips-shut kisses. But their hearts thudded against each other.

Eventually the taxi stopped at the gate of St Helen's and the young man 'saw her to the door'. Standing in the porch they kissed again, pressing close their flushed youthful faces.

'Darling, darling, you're so sweet.'

They finally parted and Philippa yawned her way up the stairs. Moonlight slanted through a stained glass window and threw blue and yellow lozenges on the stairway.

In her room, her hair was untidy and the little wreath of gardenias was squashed and turning brown. Her lips were bruised. Philippa stripped off her white evening dress and left it on the floor. She and Elaine never wore any other colour but white in the evening. Their dresses were picked up and taken to the cleaners by Miggs on the following morning; no white evening dress was worn twice.

Summer was hot. People walked slowly in the parks under the elm trees, and sheep browsed there. It was a pastoral.

Those days were dead. They had resembled the elaborate cakes of icing sugar, confectioners' architecture created in the turreted shapes of the Houses of Parliament or the intricacies of the Eiffel Tower; elaborate, breakable, sweet. But the war had come like hammering rain and they had melted and vanished for ever.

Chapter Three

As Philippa left for work on the morning after the fire, the telephone rang.

'Flip?' said a metallic little voice, 'it's me.'

'Are you all right, Trix?'

'Of course I am. I'm with Jenny. I've told you, the flat's below ground. Could you ask Miggsy to rustle up something horrible for supper tonight? Unfortunately I've got to be home to finish making my dress. Oh, guess what. I picked up two Free Frenchmen on the bus. They're coming to lunch on Sunday.'

Philippa wasn't listening. She said that the house had been hit last night by fire bombs.

'Oh God! Is my room okay?'

'Aren't you going to ask if *we* are okay?'

'If you weren't, you wouldn't be answering the telephone, stoopid.'

Philippa grimaced, and briefly described the fire. When she rang off, picked up her handbag and leather gas-mask case and slung both over her shoulder, she was not even annoyed. It was always like that with Trix.

D'Abernon Road was a mess. Rain had worsened the quenched fires, the pavements and roadway were littered with heaped earth and the blackened remains of bombs, which also lay in the gutters. At the bus stop, a crowd of people waited. They were tired and pale, but there was a glitter in their faces, a leftover light from danger.

'Came down like rain in the docks, it did,' said a woman in a mackintosh, 'My hubby's in the brigade. The warehouses, tea and rum they were, burned something horrible. The barrels exploded like a second load of bombs. He said the tea burned as fierce as paint does, and the smell! Fair made him choke – all sweet and mucky and getting into your throat.'

Other people joined in with tales of destruction.

'Molotov cocktail on the roof.'

'Crater fifteen feet across.'

'Lamb and Flag pub's gone. Six people killed.'

'They say over three thousand incendiaries fell in ten minutes.'

When the bus lumbered up, everybody climbed on board and stood squeezed like sardines. Philippa looked out of the window at the panorama which each day changed for the worse. Houses were sliced through as if by a giant carving knife – one house standing, its neighbour collapsed in rubble of bricks and burned wood. Blast never had the same effect twice. One house had only the top rooms remaining, the rest a blackened hollow. In another, an attic bedroom was exposed, high up, untouched, with rose-patterned wallpaper and dresses and coats still hanging on a rail. In the next room a bath precariously hung from a half-destroyed wall.

Even in the bus the blitz smell was strong, a mixture of escaping gas, burning, and the bitter stink of high explosive. Pavements were covered with broken glass, and the workers on their way to offices picked a path through the glass, lifting their feet delicately like wading birds.

Rich houses or poor were identical after being bombed. Wealth and class had divided them but in their ruins they were the same. In the grey light of morning Philippa saw the remains of so many homes, the fireplaces round which people had gathered, mirrors which used to reflect happy faces, beds which had known love.

At Knightsbridge she edged her way out of the bus and went down the steps to the Underground, it was the quickest way to work. Closed streets, diversions, flaming gas jets and yawning craters made any bus journey hours long.

Swept down the escalator, she entered the Londoners' new catacombs.

The government had forbidden people to shelter in the Underground, but since the blitz began the usually docile English had ignored that. They simply moved into the Underground and took it over, it was their equivalent of the Tyrrells' billiard table. After two months of nightly bombing, the underworld kingdom was becoming organized. There were rows of neat bunks in many stations and the platforms smelled of antiseptic. Most of the shelterers were gone at six in the morning when the All Clear sounded; they were queuing in the evening for their places well before the siren went. They brought

30

blankets and pillows. There was clean water, bucket lavatories in decent corners, a good deal of Jeyes Fluid. They settled down on the platforms, accustomed to the trains roaring by. They listened to the wireless when it was possible, made Cockney jokes and hot drinks. There were sing-songs and even a lending library. After nights in the Underground, people did find lice in their hair occasionally. But so did the well-born Wrens. One Wren whose father was an earl had stayed the night at St Helen's recently and had shouted at Philippa from the bathroom, 'I'm smearing my head with paraffin. Then I'll wrap it in a towel and leave the little things to die the death. Sorry if I stink.'

In Philippa's train compartment now there were a number of Scottish soldiers, their rugged faces full of wonder as they looked at London's underworld.

Her journey ended at Holborn. She came up the escalator among workers flowing like a river into Kingsway. There was so much glass in the street that it was hard to walk – scarcely a window remained in the office buildings, doors had burst off, and in one crater in the road was the remains of a burned-out car. As she made her slow progress, the morning was full of the noise of glass being swept from the pavements, and the sound of windows being knocked out for safety.

She no longer worked in the typing pool at Vickers Armstrong. After Elaine's wartime marriage, Mary Tyrrell became ill. She did not recover but faded slowly; Philippa gave up her job and helped Miggs to nurse her. Mary died early in 1940.

Theo took his wife's death very hard. He was stricken and lonely and often angry. Philippa wanted to join one of the women's services, all her friends were doing so, but felt she couldn't leave her father. He gave no sign that he needed her.

'He needs a bit of time. Later on, you can leave him to me. Dessay you want to get into uniform.'

'I suppose I do.'

'Quite right. Very edifyin'.'

'But even when Father feels better, Miggsy, what about my leaving Trix?'

'Do you think *she* needs any of us?'

During her mother's illness, Philippa had worked at home for a few hours each week on the thankless task of trying to raise money for a down-at-heel hospital. The lady who gave her the job was a Quaker friend of her mother's, Mrs Jane Alwynne.

31

After Mary's death, Mrs Alwynne took it for granted that Philippa would work for her full time. So Philippa agreed, still feeling out-of-date that she was not a Waaf or a Wren. It was as if by remaining a civilian she missed the essential heart of the war.

Mrs Alwynne's offices were in Chicheley Buildings in a narrow street at the back of the Law Courts. The buildings, fifty years old, were a fantasy of orange-red brick, with turrets and a set of gargoyles for spitting out the rain. Every morning when she turned the corner, Philippa wondered whether Chicheley Buildings had survived. This morning they had – and there they were, rising out of a sea of broken glass, hideous as ever.

Before the war, prosperous insurance companies and small businesses had occupied Chicheley Buildings, but most of those were closed now. Mrs Alwynne, persuasive with landlords, had a set of rooms for which she paid almost nothing. Her rooms were lofty, with red Turkish carpets and bookcases and open fireplaces. When the blitz did not prevent her, a charwoman came from Hackney to light the fires, staggering up the stairs with buckets of coal.

This morning – no fire and no charwoman. Also no Mrs Alwynne, which meant peace. Philippa kept on her coat and sat down to work in the ice-cold room. Her desk was as old as the buildings, with a worn green leather top and brass-handled drawers patterned with swallows. She began to type letters to possible benefactors . . . but her thoughts were on Barny Duval. She kept remembering just how it had felt when he pressed her heavily down on the floor and kissed her.

At one o'clock she arrived, early, at the Ritz. She had only been to the hotel once, when her father gave a party for Elaine's twenty-first birthday. The place made Philippa feel shy. She was wearing her only winter coat, dark brown with a velvet collar, and a little hat with a blue feather. A woman in the entrance hall went by, swathed in fox furs. Philippa felt shyer still.

The Ritz was very Frenchified with its gilt and marble, and a little fountain playing in a basin. No wonder, thought Philippa, that Trix used Ritzy as an adjective.

Barny, also early, sat at a table which was too small for him, long legs stretched. He sprang up.

'On time. Few dames are.'

She couldn't help laughing.

He ordered champagne but the waiter sadly told him that

today there was only sherry; much Philippa cared. She would not have noticed if they'd drunk watery cocoa. But Barny was not in a trance as she was, and chatted to the waiter, saying he'd heard a rumour in the Squadron that the Ritz chef 'had gotten hold of some onions and lemons?' He must, he said, come and have a meal here soon while the supply lasted.

When the waiter had gone, Barny looked at her.

'Shall we eat here next leave? Seems like a nice idea. Do you know what, Flip. I've been thinking about our fire dousing. You sure went fast over that wall.'

'But my poor stockings! I had to throw them away. My second to last pair.'

'I thought of that too. I'll get my sister to send you some.'

It was the first time Philippa heard the authentic voice of American generosity. She did not know that was what it was; she thought her companion impulsive and kind, and didn't really believe he meant what he said. But that same voice, filled with the beautiful love of giving, was to speak in the years to come to English people, who would be as surprised and affected by it as she.

'How did your father react to you saving his house?'

'Oh, he didn't admit it. That's not his way.'

'I don't understand.'

'He'd hate to think a *woman* stopped the house from burning down. In any case, it wasn't me, it was you. After the war we'll put up a plaque. B.Duval, Eagle Squadron, saved this house during the London blitz, November 1940. We'll have your crest, the eagle and the E.S. What's Barny for?'

'Not for anything. I have one hell of a name. Jean Louis Desmond Duval, can you beat it? The first two are from some French ancestors my mother was proud of. I've been Barny since school. Not sure why.'

The waiter brought sandwiches on a silver salver, cut into mouthfuls inadequate for a big American.

Philippa said she had been thinking – they'd spent all those hours together, and she still knew almost nothing about him. Just that he came from Louisiana and had arrived last August. Could he begin at the beginning? She wanted to hear everything. About his home and his family and his childhood and being a pilot and coming to England. Everything.

'Sure you really want to hear all that?'

It was a rhetorical question because she looked at him so eagerly, and perhaps he just wanted her to repeat it all again. He described the country that he came from – a land of great heat, where the enormous live oaks grew, festooned with Spanish moss hanging in ghostly draperies. Louisiana had great swamps, and forests of huge cypresses, prairies of soggy grass from which hummocks of trees rose like islands. White herons lived in the swamps, and egrets, and snakes. The cane-brake rattler was the swamps' most dangerous creature, it could grow over eight feet long . . .

Both his parents were dead. She gave a little gasp when he said that. Yes, Barny agreed, it had been terrible but 'you get to bear things'. His family owned a timber business and three years ago his parents had been out in a motor boat, looking at the flooding river. The boat struck a submerged log and sank in minutes. Both were drowned.

'That isn't why I came over, Flip. I'd hate for you to think it was a kind of desperate getting away from it all.' He had been in love with flying since a child. Planes excited him. 'I must have read every darned book about the aces of the Great War before I was twelve. And the movies, I'd seen those over and over. *Hell's Angels* was the best.'

His father hoped he would work in the family business, but after he left college, Barny learned to fly. He joined a civilian air line flying freight from one State to another. When his parents died, his sister Mary Lou and her husband had taken over the firm.

'Then your war started, Flip. I thought – that's where I want to be. We aren't allowed to enlist for your war in the US, so I had to slip over the Canadian border. And here I am.'

He looked at his watch.

'Damnation. We've only gotten ten minutes left.'

Without thinking, she leaned forward and took his wrist to look at the time. His watch, wafer thin, was gold and on a crocodile strap. She pushed back his blue uniform cuff to glance at it, and his arm, covered with fine dark hair, was exposed. Barny put his other hand up and pressed hers very hard.

'I've got to see you next leave. Okay?'

'Okay.'

They walked in silence through the gilded rooms. At the doors he paused.

34

'Not allowed to kiss dames when I'm in uniform.'

He bent and kissed her.

'See you real soon.'

They parted in the cold dirty London afternoon.

Philippa returned to the Temple and climbed the stairs to her office: the lift had been out of order for months. The charwoman, hours late, had lit a smoky fire. Sitting down, Philippa looked vaguely at the work she had left an hour and a half ago. The afternoon rang with silence – no cars went by in the street. She shut her eyes. She felt as if she were at the top of a steep hill. It was a hill which had haunted her since girlhood although she did not know why; it had curved down from the gates of her boarding school in Devonshire, a steep incline in a road which dropped steadily until it reached the sea front. In her thoughts she had returned many times to the top of that hill, wondering what would happen if she began to run. Now her thoughts moved downwards, slowly, faster, until she could not stop. Her ghostly self, heart hammering, breath gasping, ran and ran, hurtling down faster and faster until she was thrown into the ocean of love.

After the night of the fire and her next day meeting with Barny, Philippa's life returned to its pattern of dull work by day and the nightly blitz. St Helen's shuddered as the bombs came down. London grew more and more chaotic. One crater in Piccadilly was so huge that ten people fell into it, with consequent broken limbs. Food grew ever scarcer. At night the streets were empty and the sky burned.

One person showing no sign of the strain was the youngest member of the Tyrrell family. Trix, just eighteen, was enjoying the arrival of foreign troops in London. She went to parties at night where, in the phrase of the day, 'we just ignored the blitz socially.' She went to lunches. She went to films. And her conversation had become international.

'Guess what, Flip, I danced with a Pole and he turned out to be a prince. He asked the band to play a mazurka. They didn't know how.'

'Two New Zealanders took me to lunch at Grosvenor House. The grill room's been re-named, it's the Shelter restaurant now. Wizard food.'

'If a boy rings called Ian, he's in the Black Watch and tell him I *need* to see him before he's posted.'

Philippa was amused by her young sister. She was also impressed for Trix had become a rare thing – she was a beauty.

Mary Tyrrell had been reading *Henry Esmond* when she was pregnant for the third time, and she decided if the child was another girl she would name her Beatrix. Trix detested her name from an early age. At school they called her Beaty and she loathed that too. Two years before the war, when she was an unremarkable fifteen, she had marched into the St Helen's garden one Sunday afternoon when the family were having tea.

'In future,' she announced, 'I shall be known as Trix.'

Everybody looked up. Her father said sarcastically, 'In future I shall be known as Horatio Bottomley.'

Elaine and Philippa giggled. Mary smiled.

Trix looked stony. 'You may as well all get used to it. I shan't answer to any other name.'

'No good speaking to me,' said Theo, 'if I am not addressed as Doctor Bottomley.'

Trix walked off.

Within a week the family had given in. It was too annoying to call her or speak to her and to get no reply.

In just the way that she made up her mind to change her name, Trix decided to be beautiful. She was sixteen when the transformation began. She was naturally slim, with long legs, but her shortish hair was mousy, her nails dirty and bitten, and the clothes her mother chose for her were simply dull. Trix washed her hair in camomile and touched it up with something else: it turned a silvery blonde. She grew it long in imitation of Hollywood stars. Nature had given her a thick-textured skin: somehow she made it look like the petals of a gardenia. She had the short straight Tyrrell nose and eyes the colour of black treacle. When she began to alter the way she looked, the men began to stare. Now, two years later, she was every serviceman's dream.

Pictures of girls looking like Trix were cut from magazines and pinned in army messes and steamy canteens. She was glued inside army lorries, in the cockpits of planes and the cabins of ships. She was painted on the whitewashed walls of army huts. A girl with Trix's face and figure and hair was the phantom goddess who travelled with the pilots and their impish gremlins in the upper air, and ploughed the Arctic seas, and wavered in desert heats. She stood in the dreams of the men fighting a war.

Philippa admired her young sister more than Elaine did. She thought it wonderful that Trix had turned herself from a leggy schoolgirl who sucked sweets and failed exams into a beauty. Trix had invented herself, a 1940 self. She not only made her hair into moonlight and painted her exquisite face, she also painted her legs, using dark sun-tan lotion and drawing a thick straight seam down the back with an eyebrow pencil. Her skin was smooth and silky, and her naked legs looked exactly as if they were clad in silk stockings.

It was Saturday morning. Theo had gone to the hospital early. Somewhere in the depth of the house was the familiar noise, a dull rattling thunder, which was Miggs filling the kitchen boiler. Philippa wandered into Trix's bedroom.

'Good, I can fit your dress,' said Trix.

The room, like its occupant, was much altered from its 1930s appearance. Trix had painted all the antique furniture white and covered her dressing table with stiff pink taffeta. There were some misty photographs of herself and a litter of large and small photographs, framed and unframed, of men in uniform. These were signed 'My love, darling, Peter'. 'Forever, Pat'. And 'Yours till hell freezes, Jack'. On the wall was a flat vase filled with ivy and yellow roses. Trix was always being given flowers.

She knelt down and began to pin Philippa into a dress made of Parma-violet wool which she'd found in her mother's trunk.

'You'll look lovely,' she said encouragingly.

The front door bell rang.

'Bother and blow, that's my two french A's, Quick, Flip. Get dressed. You know that I can't manage a word of French.'

Leaving Philippa still pinned, she skipped out and Philippa heard her at the top of the stairs calling, 'Bonjour!'

The gramophone began at once, and Fats Waller sang 'Honeysuckle Rose'. The music reminded Philippa of Elaine when she had first fallen in love. And love reminded Philippa of Barny. She was not sure why she had said nothing about him to Trix – she wanted to keep him a secret. When she heard the planes at night, the stutter of machine-gun fire, and thought of the fighter pilots up there in the dark, she had such a pain in her heart. *He* would soon be flying up there. She remembered a poem about an RAF pilot, 'keeping your station in the sky: solitary cunning star.'

'Here she is,' cried Trix, through the music, 'come and show your paces, Flip. In French.'

Philippa and the two A's smiled politely at each other.

Trix's nickname was apt, the French visitors shared the same first-name initial, they were Alain and Alexandre. But that was all they shared except their nationality. Alain was not in uniform but wore a shabby jersey and baggy old trousers. He was pasty-faced and spectacled. Alexandre was short, scarcely five foot eight, but he had drama. His black curling hair shone, his skin was swarthy, he burned with life, and when he laughed he had a mass of gold teeth. He wore navy blue French uniform, with a cape thrown over one shoulder and fastened with a gilt chain.

Philippa launched into her finishing-school French. Both men looked relieved and pleased.

'*C'est une perle!*' cried Alexandre.

'*C'est vrai,*' agreed Alain.

Trix re-wound the gramophone and put on a record she liked. 'Oh Johnnie, Oh Johnnie, How you can Love.'

'The two A's have brought us a pressie,' she said, 'Look, Flip.' She held up two beer bottles.

'How kind of them,' said Philippa, who detested beer.

'Stoopid,' said Trix, laughing, 'Wait and see.'

When Alexandre poured out, the bottles were full of burgundy.

'Nothing remarkable, from our canteen and alas, cold from being carried through the streets,' one of the visitors murmured in French.

'Tell him he is wonderful. Shall we save some for Pa? Perhaps not. It'll improve our horrible lunch. Miggs says all she can manage is veggie pie. Ugh.'

During the meal eaten by the Frenchmen without surprise, which Philippa thought particularly courteous, Trix bombarded the two men with questions. Philippa had to translate these, together with their replies. They were at present in what was called the Centre d'Acceuil in Kensington. When they mentioned the house, the sisters knew it. It was a big rambling old place in a large garden, where an elderly patient of their father's had lived until her death. Men arriving in England from Europe, the two A's explained, were brought to London and taken straight to the Centre for questioning. How did they come to England? asked Trix, fascinated. It seemed they had rowed across the Channel in an open boat.

38

'It was fortunate that I have the rudiments of navigation,' said Alain. 'With Alexandre in charge, we would have lost our way and rowed straight back to France. He knows nothing of the sea.'

'Do you?'

'Of course. I am a Breton.'

After freezing nights and danger from enemy planes, mercifully more intent on getting to London than on machine-gunning a small boat, they had beached at a seaside village in Kent.

'As we put foot on shore we were seized by English soldiers, sure we were spies. Then to the Centre for a litany of questions. And now – here we are.'

The girls looked at the men in awe. It was hard to grasp the fact that they had been so recently in the heart of darkness.

'Was the escape exciting?' asked Trix. Philippa translated.

They shrugged.

'Explain to your sister, mademoiselle, that we are forbidden to speak. We may not tell of the weather or how many stones there were on the beach,' said Alexandre.

'Or the name of the rowing boat,' said Alain.

'Or how much Breton sugar Alain brought in a sack.'

'Or how we must throw it overboard for the weevils are eating it.'

'Or how they put me in this uniform of the French Air Force and never have I been in an aeroplane.'

They grinned as they described the many extraordinary questions they had had to answer at the Centre. Alain was made to describe his childhood, the name of his school and of the teachers ('some I forgot'), details of his village. In what square was the War Memorial? Was it the bronze figure of a poilu or the statue of a mourning woman? Or both? During the interrogation he became angry. He had not faced danger and the sea to answer questions of such idiocy. Was he a guide book?

The intelligence officer was soothing.

'Do not upset yourself. Last week we had two doctors here in the French Medical Corps. One was not a doctor. The other was not French.'

Alexandre, longing to burst in while Alain held the girls' attention, then described his questioning. It had lasted four hours longer than Alain's. He had been asked about his life in South America (he would tell them of this later!), and when he had obligingly launched into stories of Buenos Aires they

39

suddenly switched to his Burgundy childhood. Had he any family remaining there? He had visited the village early in 1940. By train or coach? When Alexandre said 'train' the officer gave a satisfied grunt. 'If you had said by coach, you would go to prison. There is no coach to that village.'

After the unappetising lunch, the four returned to the drawing room where Alexandre and Trix danced the rumba. 'Tell your sister she dances like the girls in Rio.' Alain sat with Philippa, and spoke of Brittany. He did not mention the Occupation.

As dusk fell, Alexandre gave a sigh.

'Soon will come the Alert and then we are commanded to run home like good little boys.'

Shortly afterwards the siren wailed. The two men kissed the girls' hands, thanked them, begged to be allowed to come again.

Trix showered invitations like confetti. They must come any time! All the time!

When they were gone, she looked at Philippa mischievously.

'If I told you what Alexandre hissed in my ear while we were dancing, you'd have a pink fit.'

For once, that night she was home and joined Philippa under the billiard table. The girls arranged their heavy coats and scarves, gas masks and handbags within reach in case the house was hit.

'If there is a bomb and we have time, or suppose it's an unexploded one, what'll you take with you? All I need is my biggest bottle of *Moment Suprême*.'

'I shall take an extra pair of outdoor shoes,' said Philippa perversely.

One night after an intensive blitz, when Theo returned he found Miggs in the hall. She was sitting wrapped in her voluminous old rug.

'All Clear's gone, Doctor, thought you'd like a cuppa.'

The sight of the bent figure huddled in a chair, like other old people dazed after being dug out of their homes, affected him. While she was making tea he said, 'If these bombardments continue –'

'They'll go on for months. The milkman says the government's preparin' for it. Cardboard coffins, thousands of 'em, and now they're opening up the old Plague pits for burial grounds.'

Miggs had not changed from the days when her favourite

story, read to him as a child, was one in which the old witch fattened up the children to eat them.

But he was not to be sidetracked and said seriously, 'I think you should be evacuated, Miggs, there is no need for you to remain in London. Nor, for that matter, Miss Philippa and Miss Beatrix. All three of you can go to our cousins in Devon.'

Miggs slowly began to saw off the top of a cottage loaf.

'You and the girls could leave today or tomorrow. The trains are pretty appalling, but at least they get there. You'll be comfortable on the farm. When Cousin Anny wrote to me she said there's no shortage of milk, eggs or poultry.'

He gave her a smile which very faintly reminded her of the child she used to love a long time ago.

'Well, Miggs?'

'Not a chance, Doctor. You're not goin' to get rid of me so easily. Miss Philippa won't go either. She wouldn't budge. As for young T – Miss Beatrix, can you see her on a farm? Bombs are better than bein' bored to death.'

Theo tried to persuade her, but he might as well have saved his breath. He mentioned the matter to his daughters – they were as adamant. It did not occur either to them, or to Miggs, that it would be a weight off his shoulders if they left London. Miggs said it was her duty to look after the doctor. She did not add that she hated the country, despite being born there. Philippa refused to leave her work; Trix just laughed.

The blitz provided something that suited Miggs. Drama. She read every column of the *Daily Mail* each morning, listened to the news bulletin on the wireless, and was up-to-the-minute in the triumphs of the RAF. 'We bagged forty last night,' she would announce, as if giving the cricket score, 'They only got three of ours.'

The growing food shortages also interested her. She enjoyed announcing that this or that had vanished from the shops. The family's four ration books were in her ancient leather handbag, and it was Miggs who queued for the minute weekly rations of bacon, sugar, butter and meat. The only ration she resented was tea, a measly two ounces each for a week. She cut open the tea packets with a pair of scissors as carefully as a surgeon performing an operation; it was to make sure not a single tea leaf was hidden in the folds of the paper. The Ministry of Food's instructions: 'One spoon per person and none for the pot' annoyed her. She detested orders.

Theo was anxious about her; he was fond of her. He was too busy during the day at the hospital or attending his patients at home, and at night helping to care for the wounded and writing the pathetic certificates for the dead, to realize that he was blessed by Miggs remaining at St Helen's. Philippa knew it. 'What should we do without you, Miggsy?'

'Starve, I shouldn't wonder,' said Miggs, making a hideous grimace. She had just put a spoonful of golden syrup into her tea to replace sugar – the tea turned black and tasted disgusting.

Miggs went to Shepherds Bush for the family's food. She said the smart Kensington shopkeepers were bribed.

'Saw a woman in a skunk coat puttin' a pound note on the counter at John Buckle's. The man gave her a whole tin of salmon.'

But she had her triumphs. Rice had disappeared from the shops but a packet found its way into her shopping basket, and so did a tin of sardines. She queued for fish, the one unrationed food, and chatted to the women ahead and behind her. She waited two hours for a piece of salt cod. Once she'd tried whalemeat. After cooking it and gingerly forking herself a piece, she spat it out and threw the rest into the dustbin. It had tasted like cod-liver oil. After this experiment she said severely to Theo, 'Don't you be too proud, next time a patient offers you a chicken.'

Theo *had* been too proud, and wondered how the devil she knew. It did not occur to his honourable soul that she listened at doors.

Sidling through the big old house, moving fast to answer the telephone ahead of the girls, donning her white overall as Receptionist, her purple apron as cook, Miggs ran St Helen's. She was like the man at the ship's wheel. She steered, looked at the compass, saw her crew was fed if only on salt cod. Sometimes, standing on the bridge, she raised her eyes heavenwards and saw fire.

When Mary Tyrrell had been alive, Miggs' sense of what was proper kept her in check; she respectfully called her The Mistress while dodging the duties Mary tried to give her. But now that The Mistress was dead, and Elaine married and away, Miggs had the reins firmly in her gnarled old hands.

Philippa sometimes resented her but was too kind or too craven to do anything about it. Recently, though, Miggs had a new kind of charm for her – she had met Barny. Philippa had still not mentioned Barny at all to her sister. She felt she could not bear to listen to the old repetitious teasing, or hear the worn out word 'sentimental'. She had merely told Trix that a soldier had helped with the fire. Trix, her head full of conquests and clothes, had asked no questions.

Very early one morning Philippa came into the kitchen. Miggs, at present in her role of witch, was stirring the boiler with a misshapen poker.

'Dratted fire won't burn. Got it into its head to go out. Too early for breakfast, lady. The kettle doesn't boil for the askin'.'

'I don't mind, Miggs. I only got up because I was awake. I didn't sleep very well last night.'

'So we gather.'

Philippa sat down near the boiler, she was cold. She stared at the split through which the coke dimly glowed.

'How'd you meet that American chap, Miss Philippa?'

The girl gave a start.

'Nice lookin' fellow,' said Miggs. 'Friend of yours?'

'No, he called round by chance. Someone in his Squadron knows Pa and gave him the address, so round he came. You know how casual Americans are.'

'Can't say I do. Eagle Squadron, is he?'

'Yes. He came to England in August.'

'I've been readin' about them in the *Mail*. Young American chaps who say they don't feel neutral and come here to join the RAF. Very edifyin'.'

She stirred the boiler, and added, 'Tell you what, Miss Philippa. Just you keep that young chap to yourself.'

She looked straight at Philippa, hoping what she said would go home.

Nobody knew more about the family and its doings than Miggs. She watched the present with fascination and had an utter disinterest in the past. When Philippa had been young, it had seemed to the romantically-minded girl that somewhere in her old nurse's memory there must be a vision still, a living vision of a golden Victorian and Edwardian England. It was as if Miggs had a treasure hidden away in a kind of Monte Cristo's cave. But when she eagerly asked Miggs, all she was given was an impatient laugh. Miggs couldn't remember a thing worth talking about. And in time Philippa saw that Miggs's sharp little eyes were fixed in her head so that they couldn't, and wouldn't, swivel backwards.

Just now, Miggs approved of Trix whom she saw as a goer and no mistake. The girl had been a trial when she was a child, and she never did a stroke of work at school. But now she certainly knew how to make the young chaps jump. In her youth, ugly though she had been, Miggs had had sex appeal. She had been a flirt. She had treated men as if they were the enemy to be vanquished, and that was what Trix did now.

But Philippa was another kettle of fish entirely. Miggs didn't use the old 'sentimental' cliché any more, but she still thought it was true. She had seen the girl falling in and out of love, eyes like stars one week and all red the next. She was just the sort, thought Miggs, to get herself hurt. Philippa had a silly look on her face when she mentioned that American chap. Miggs felt it only kind to warn her that with men, it was wise not to share.

At the start of December, one evening before the Alert began wailing, the telephone rang. Philippa answered it and Miggs, for once arriving too late, said, 'If it's a patient, let me have it.' She stood openly listening.

'May I speak to Philippa Tyrrell, if you please.'

'Barny!'

Feeling herself blushing, Philippa gestured crossly to Miggs to go away. Miggs raised her eyebrows and went back to the kitchen. They talked for a moment or two, and Philippa waited, tensed for an invitation. The Warning began just then.

'Better get under the billiard table, Flip. I can hear that clearly. Look, I can't stop, there's a goddammed lecture starting and we're working fit to bust. I called up to say I hope to hit town soon. When I do, can we meet?'

'That would be lovely.'

'I think so too.'

'Oh, Barny – ' anything for another word, 'how *are* you?'

'Missing you.'

She put down the receiver. The guns were barking like giant dogs and she heard the drone of planes. I suppose I must shelter under that beastly table, she thought. It was no good suggesting she should join Miggs in the cellar, for Miggs preferred it to herself and had turned it into a sort of private flat.

Alone during a blitz, Philippa was alternately frightened and bored. The stupid thing was that she had been asked out tonight by an ex-boyfriend of hers who had wanted to take her dancing to Hatchetts, one of Trix's favourite places, smart, and below ground. Why had she refused? She knew why. She had been hoping for that one meaningless telephone call.

She turned towards the drawing room in search of her book, like every other girl in London she was reading *Barchester Towers*, when her father's study door opened.

'I didn't know you were home, Pa.'

'How many times have I told you to call me Father.'

'Sorry,' she said automatically.

The lamplight behind him made a halo round his balding head. His face was in shadow. He was not standing as erect as he usually did.

'Would you like a glass of sherry? Only one. The bottle won't run to more.'

The invitation took her by surprise. As if in celebration the guns shook the house.

'Hope I'm not called out tonight,' he said, yawning. 'The Mobile Squad have my number, so I daresay I will be. Working is better than lying quaking in bed, I suppose.'

'Pooh. You never quake.'

'Of course I do and so does everybody else.'

Except Trix, thought Philippa.

He fetched the decanter and they went into the billiard room. Ignoring the shelter-table, he sat in a high-backed chair. She sat opposite him. He did look tired. The lines in his face were cut deep.

'It's Christmas in less than two weeks,' he said, handing her the glass. 'Miggs asked what I intend to do about it. Her old friend Stutfield who supplied us with poultry has finally shut up shop and left London.'

'That must be why she keeps giving us salt cod like dried flannel. Not too festive for Christmas.'

'A patient offered me a turkey.'

He looked pleased at her astonishment.

'By the by, your sister telephoned. Miles has been posted. She's been with him on leave in Oxfordshire and her in-laws asked her to remain. I said it was a good idea, but Elaine won't

hear of it. She is coming home. And bringing,' he said solemnly
'a Christmas pudding.'

Philippa murmured appreciation, looking at him gratefully.
People always looked at him like that when he decided to be
pleasant. He took it as his due.

They talked of the previous night's blitz, and Theo, approachable because he'd decided to be, said that two houses had been
hit in the North End Road.

'We managed to pull out an old couple. Poor things, they
looked like two bedraggled old birds, so thin and small and
covered with dust from head to foot. They were quite calm when
we pulled them out. Talked as if nothing had happened.'

'That sounds like a miracle.'

'No. Just shock. Reaction sets in later.'

He said how strange he found doctoring now, compared to the
last war. He couldn't get used to civilians being killed.

'Odd. I just can't,' he said and put down his glass. 'You must
get some sleep, Philippa. And so must I – until the telephone or
the front door bell rings.'

She lay among the cushions, scarcely conscious of the din
outside. She was thinking of love. On her way home from work
tonight London had seemed full of lovers. Couples whispering in
the bus. A sailor and his girl in the Underground staring at each
other. Even in d'Abernon Road in the blackout she hadn't been
able to get away from love. She had passed a couple locked in an
embrace. She thought of Barny. Her father was right. Reaction
set in later.

46

Chapter Four

When the train stopped at Oxford it was already so crammed that Elaine thought she would never manage to get in. But four soldiers had thrown open the door, stretched out their arms and laughingly dragged her into the corridor. When the train door was safely slammed and the train started, two of the soldiers squeezed themselves into the lavatory where they sat on the floor, so that Elaine could at least stand upright in the corridor. Despite the gallant gesture, she could scarcely breathe, squashed between their two companions, both made gigantic by back packs, bulging pouches, kitbags and rifles. The pair whistled in a melancholy way, and when they caught her eye, winked.

Elaine, like young wives all over England, was on her way home because her husband was going overseas.

She and Miles St Aird, engaged during the summer of 1939, had married the week after war was declared, by special licence in St Barnabas's church in Kensington. The marriage, a few months earlier, would have been an affair of white satin and four hundred guests. Now it was hurried, disorganised and in the dark. Miles had been at Devonport Barracks and was granted compassionate leave. He was five hours late for the ceremony, by which time daylight was gone and the blacked-out church lit by a few wavering candles. Most of the dozen guests, alarmed by the new blackout, had left. Miles' parents stayed. They were scarcely what Miggs called 'forthcomin'.' In their upper-class way, they made the occasion even more uncomfortable than it was. They did not approve of the match.

The St Airds had been quite hospitable when Miles first took Elaine to their Oxfordshire home; he did not introduce her to them until after he had proposed. The pleasant manner of her future in-laws had altered after she met them two or three times. Later she had the suspicion, turning into a certainty, that they had believed she was rich. They thought their son had wisely chosen to fall in love where there was money.

47

When they realised the truth they cooled. Miles did not seem to notice, and stayed his enchanting self both to his parents and to her. But Elaine knew she was being patronized.

Miles took his new life in the Navy with lively amusement. The spoiled only son of an aristocratic family, he learned to do his own washing, darn his socks, and cook the appalling greasy food which was served to the Lower Deck. With other enthusiastic beginners, he acquired the knack of scrubbing the collar of his uniform to make it look faded. This implied that he had been a sailor for years.

After months at sea, he was eventually picked out as what was called 'officer material'. He was sent home for the course which would turn him into a sub-lieutenant, at the officers' establishment called King Alfred, on the front at Brighton.

When Elaine was allowed to be near him, she went to stay at hotels, or took two-roomed flats. She lived for a while in Brighton and in Portsmouth. But when he was sent to places which were out of bounds to civilians, she returned home. Leaves were all spent at Shelton, the St Aird's family home. Elaine longed for his leaves, but when the precious time arrived she swung between joy and the nervous irritation of sharing him. On their last morning together they walked in the Shelton woods. He kissed her. Oh, how she loved him. He was everything she worshipped. Simply seeing his figure at a distance turned her bones to water. Even his faults allured her. He was restless and easily bored, and his standards particularly about women, were tiresomely high. He despised girls who looked tatty, as he called it. He admired style and a look of money, and had chosen a girl with much of the first and none of the second. His snobbery, which she detested in his parents, only made her smile.

'I wish you'd stay here at Shelton after I've gone. They want you to,' he said, pressing her close.

'Oh, darling. I can't cower in the country for the duration.'

'My mother would be delighted if you'd cower, sweetie. Not that she would call it that.'

'She's very kind,' lied Elaine, 'but I do miss the family. I'd like to be with them. You won't worry about me in the blitz, will you? We can't both worry, me about you at sea, and you about me in London.'

Miles grinned. He was young and adventurous, and he said

the blitz sounded exciting. When the talk was of the fighter pilots in the Battle of Britain, he said, 'If I wasn't in the Navy, I'd choose the RAF and fly.'

Now he was gone. And Elaine was on her way back to London. Thinking about Miles hurt her heart, so she made a mental effort not to long for him. She stared resolutely out of the train window. Since the danger of invasion, every name of every station and village, every signpost, had been removed in England. The stations which went by now had no names. It was a journey into nowhere.

When the train finally sighed itself to a stop, it was pitch dark.

'Waterloo? Must be, I suppose,' said one of the whistling soldiers.

The crowds poured out on to a platform, seeming to know their way by instinct. Everything was black and echoing and smelling of acrid train smoke. Gleams of torchlight bobbed here and there.

A disembodied voice rang round the station, 'An air raid has sounded. An air raid has sounded. Members of His Majesty's Forces must, repeat must, proceed at once to shelters. Passengers are advised to do the same.'

'We gotter go but *you* can take it or leave it, see?' said one of her soldier friends, clanking beside her.

Elaine decided to leave it. At last she made her way through the uniformed figures, tin hats, kit bags and suitcases, to the outside of the station. Torches showed the shapes of waiting taxis.

'Sure you want to have a go?' said a driver, 'You could go by Underground to High Street Ken.'

'I'll be quicker with you.'

'We live in hopes.'

As the cab set off into the obscurity he called over his shoulder, 'Sorry, miss, you must open the windows. Better to freeze than be cut with broken glass. Play for safety.'

The icy wind blew in as Elaine looked from the open window, at first seeing nothing. Then her eyes grew used to the dark and she realized there was a moon. Its bluish radiance shone down on the wounded face of London, the collapsed houses turned into rubble which resembled mountain shale. The blitz smell filled the taxi. Barriers had closed many streets and the rest were almost empty of traffic. But the driver stopped at every traffic light, circles of black with a tiny green or red cross in the centre just like a hot cross bun.

At Hyde Park Corner she saw the dim shapes of buses and heard gunfire. Once the driver pulled the cab to a stop and she was poised, ready to throw herself on the floor.

'All right. False alarm. Thought I heard a bomb.'

The journey took a long time but at last they drew up at St Helen's and Elaine paid him and thanked him. He tipped his cap in a Cockney salute and drove away – to stop at every traffic light across the battlefield of London.

'Anybody home?' called Elaine, shutting the front door behind her.

The drawing room door opened, and her father's grim face broke into a smile. She allowed herself to be kissed, offering her cheek. She did that with everybody but Miles.

'Good to have you back, Elaine.'

They stood taking each other in, for she had been away for weeks. Both pairs of eyes, one bright, one bloodshot, examined the other. Theo thought his favourite child looked well, which was his way of describing the blossoming which came from Miles' lovemaking. Before her marriage she had merely been prettyish. Now her skin glowed, her eyes seemed to swim, her whole expression was relaxed, gentle and sweet. Miles had all her love, her absorbed love, and when she saw her father worn and tired, she felt guilty. It was as if that other violent sexual love were a kind of sin.

Asking her with abrupt courtesy about the journey, he took her into the drawing room. The wireless was on, the music growing loud, then soft, then loud again as it always did in a raid.

'The girls are out and Miggs is in the cellar. Would you like some tea? I could cut you a sandwich.'

Elaine would not allow him to do anything for her. She went into the kitchen to look for something to eat. All she found was bread, margarine and meat paste. She had brought her own packet of tea.

Returning to the drawing room she sat down with her tray. He looked at her, raising his eyebrows as if for news. Of what? thought Elaine. She could not tell him her heart was heavy because her husband had gone, that thinking of him reduced her to a jelly and that it took all her character not to cry. Nobody talked to her father about emotion, nobody in the family, that was. In St Helen's, such things were underground, powerful secret rivers which were deep and dangerous and must never be spoken of. Her parents had been like that about sex, and it had affected her in a way.

She could have told him how she disliked the St Airds, that would amuse him for he did not like them either. She decided not to. He looked so tired. She thought he missed their mother more instead of less. Apparently Philippa and Trix were no help.

Her calm presence had a relaxing effect on Theo, and to her he was approachable. He only rarely spoke to Philippa about his work, he sensed a tenseness in her and too much emotion. He certainly would not condescend to talk to Trix. But now he described his work with the hospital's Mobile Squad, whose job it was to go to a house which had been hit and in which wardens reported that people were trapped. The squad joined the police at the rescue. Last night a big old house had had a direct hit and was still smoking when the team arrived. The police had heard somebody's voice in the wreckage. The squad began to dig.

The house, near Addison Road, had been four storeys high, and digging in mountains of brick and smoking wood they had needed to shore up a wall before they could get closer to the eerie sound of a voice. It took hours to make a tunnel into the ruins; then two men wriggled down it inch by inch with Theo following them. The voice grew closer. It was a child sobbing. They reached her at last, a little girl scarcely seven years old. Theo gave her an injection. Her parents lay nearby, both dead. The child, mercifully now unconscious, was pulled to safety. She was not even bruised.

'Well,' he said, 'one child saved. Many of those we dig out die in our arms. Who was it who said that courage is the willingness to die quietly?'

In the days before Christmas, Elaine looked at her family with new eyes. Perhaps, she thought, one must go away to be able to do that. Her father was overstrained. Philippa seemed drawn and quiet, and Trix, lacking in any daughterly concern, was out the entire time. Miggs was at her most tiresome. Meals did not have to be quite so disgusting, but Miggs served them with an air bordering on triumph, as if it showed patriotism to eat food which choked you.

Elaine did not feel there was anything she could do for Theo. She turned her attention to Philippa. Their mother used to describe her second daughter as 'going about like a ship in full sail', but Philippa had lost that proud bearing. On the morning after Elaine's arrival, she came into her room with morning tea and sat on the bed.

She poured the tea and talked of this and that. Of Trix and the two Frenchmen, Trix and a New Zealand pilot. Trix refused to do any war work. 'She says,' said Philippa, dryly, 'she is not strong.' Philippa said nothing about herself. Her usually candid face, with the flicks of dark hair in two crescents on her cheeks, was closed. Was there a man in her sister's life, wondered Elaine, and was the romance going badly? Perhaps he did not want to marry her.

Elaine's ideas about love were formed in her teens in the 1930s. There were rigid rules. Going to bed with a man before he married you was wrong. It was (to quote Miles) second rate. There were labels for such girls, they were shop-worn, tarty and immoral. Elaine had known a few and disliked them. She thought there was something hectic and disturbing about them.

Well brought-up girls stayed virgins until the wedding day, and their pure white satin was both a symbol and a truth.

There was also a thing called honour. When Miles had fallen in love with her during the last peacetime summer, when they sailed at Itchenor, danced at Hurlingham, and kissed each other so passionately goodnight, she expected him to propose. When she had to wait for that, it worried her. But of course he asked her in the end. He behaved as young men of the educated classes had done for hundreds of years. They did not swear in front of girls whom they respected, they stood up when they entered a room, they always paid for everything. And there were no seductions. There were also accepted ways of behaving in smaller things. Girls were given chocolates and flowers. Never anything very expensive.

Less than twenty-four hours after arriving home, Elaine's rules were shattered.

'Hello, Sis,' cried Trix when she eventually arrived back. She gave Elaine a riotous welcome. 'I had a stroke of luck last night.'

Elaine was in the drawing room by a small coal fire, knitting a sweater for Miles. Her lap was full of navy blue wool. Trix, looking radiant in short skirts and a pale sweater with 'TT' embroidered on the shoulder, waved something in a braceleted hand.

Elaine looked up vaguely and returned to her knitting.

'Did you win a raffle or something?'

'No, stoopid! Look properly.'

Trix rustled something in front of her – something which looked like two large pieces of tissue paper. Two £5 notes.

Elaine sat up as if scalded.

'Where on earth – '

'Andy, my New Zealander, gave them to me. I've got two New Zealanders, Bob and Andy, and Andy's going on ops now, so he said would I buy myself something special.'

She fanned herself with the notes.

'Do you mean you took *money* from this man?'

It was Trix's turn to be surprised.

'Of course. He's so generous, a real poppet. Last week he gave me the cash for my new nail varnish. It has a naughty name. It's called "The Night Afterwards".'

A desperate struggle was going on in Elaine. How long had her sister behaved in this disgusting way?

'I think it very unattractive for a man to give you money, and more for you to accept it,' she said, sounding cooler than she felt. 'Don't do it again. Wait until your friend is on leave, and then if he wants to, he can take you to choose a present.'

Trix giggled. Elaine, she said, must not be stuffy. Hadn't she heard there was a war on? She did hope and pray Elaine wasn't turning into one of the old folks already. Not waiting for an answer, she whisked out. She left the house soon afterwards, bound for Harrods, a shop Philippa called Trix's spiritual home.

When her sister had gone, the telephone rang and Elaine, with Miles always in her thoughts, ran out into the hall. But Miggs, who moved with the speed of lightning when she wished to, had already seized the telephone.

'Western 6468, Doctor Tyrrell's residence,' chanted Miggs, her voice retaining an echo of the old Sussex lilt. 'Ah yes, Mrs Renshawe. How is he?'

She listened and nodded. 'Just keep him warm and give him barley water and beef tea. No, no aspirins.'

Elaine returned to her knitting and her thoughts.

One way and another, St Helen's seemed to be running down, and Miggs was certainly one of the culprits. The rooms were none too clean. The only household enthusiasm the old nurse had shown recently was to damp down the boiler and prevent the girls from having a bath. And now she had the impertinence to dish out medical advice on the telephone. Mild though the advice was, it was quite wrong of her, and Theo would have a fit if he knew.

Miggs hobbled into the drawing room later, to announce that she had got hold of a Christmas tree. The greengrocer was sending a boy round with it. She waited for congratulations with a faint air of triumph. Miggs had a maddening trick of making it impossible for anyone to criticise her.

But in spite of her anxiety over the family, Elaine had an effect. She seemed to bring unity back to the house. Miggs did some cleaning and – when Elaine was about – gave no more doctorly advice to patients. Trix did not wave illicit money any more, but offered to make the mince pies. She did not say where she had obtained the mincemeat and Elaine preferred not to enquire. Philippa, two days before the Christmas holiday, climbed the ladder to the attic to fetch down the Christmas boxes.

She carried them into the drawing room, blowing the dust from them, and put them down on the floor in front of Elaine who was squatting on the hearthrug.

It was not yet blackout time and the curtains had not been pulled. Outside the windows was the December afternoon, misty and mysterious. Moisture hung on bare branches. It was almost like peacetime.

Elaine began to untie the strings round three large and ancient hat boxes which had once contained Mary's Ascot hats. For as long as the girls could remember, the boxes had been used to store the decorations for the Christmas tree.

'Nice to open them again – we haven't looked at them since war broke out, have we?' said Elaine, undoing the first tissue-papered packet. She glanced at her sister in a friendly way, and felt a stab of annoyance. What was the matter with Philippa? She herself had Miles away at sea, God knows where; what could Philippa have to worry over compared with that?

'Here's the glass teapot,' said Elaine, 'and the glass Father Christmas with the cotton Mother tied round his neck. And the lovely bluebird.'

'He's lost his beak.'

'You broke it. Quarrelling with Trix.'

'How many ages ago was that?' said Philippa sharply. The floor was beginning to be covered with purple and blue globes, with red bells and artificial holly wreaths, long strands of metallic-smelling tinsel, tiny Aladdin's lamps, paper chains, and a paper cherub glued to a circle of white spun glass.

'Old Mrs Hetreed gave *me* that,' said Philippa.

The door opened. It was Miggs.

'Miss Elaine. Telegraph boy.'

Philippa saw the colour drain from her sister's face.

At the door a boy in post office uniform was rifling through a sheaf of orange envelopes.

'Mrs St Aird?'

Elaine put out her hand.

Miggs stood and looked at Elaine, who stared back at her. Their eyes went to the envelope in Elaine's cold hand.

Everything she feared and dreaded, every terror which haunted her and which had to be fought before it tore her to pieces, came pressing and hovering about her. She could scarcely open the envelope.

> *Happy Happy Christmas, my darling,*
> *thinking of you non stop will*
> *Chanel Five do love and kisses MILES.*

Trix had invited a small international gathering of troops for Christmas dinner. Her father usually disliked visitors, he called them 'strangers', but he seemed reconciled to the prospect of patriotic entertaining. Everybody in London had been in search of turkeys, and when the bird from the grateful patient arrived at St Helen's, there was general rejoicing. It was a handsome turkey and weighed eighteen pounds.

Elaine set up the tree in the drawing room and decorated it with every glittering bauble and tinsel strand from the Ascot hat boxes. The tree stood by the window and even when the blackout curtains were drawn, a slight draught made the tinsel shiver. Trix announced that there would be the two Frenchmen, a Polish officer called Jan Something and maybe her New Zealander.

55

'Why don't you ask somebody, too?' Elaine said to Philippa. Trix replied for her.

'Oh, Flip can't ask anyone of her own! She'll have her hands full coping with the two A's. Don't encourage her to skip her responsibilities. The Fighting French *need* her. She can speak French.'

'And why can't you, miss?' demanded her father, coming into the room at the end of the conversation.

'Pa! Sorry, Father. You know I didn't go to finishing school although I begged on bended knees.'

'War broke out.'

'Only the phoney war. Lots of girls got to Paris before the Occupation and then escaped in the nick of time,' said Trix, waving her hand, 'If I'd been in Paris singing for the troops I'd be able to speak French like a native by now.'

Theo did not deign to reply to a silly child talking nonsense, but Philippa laughed.

The dining room was to be used for Christmas dinner; it would be the first time a meal had been served there since Elaine had been away. Dining rooms, family silver, serving dishes (not food dumped on plates in the kitchen) were part of Elaine's civilizing effect. Miggs was now dusting the house every morning, Philippa cleaned the knives and forks, and Trix spent part of her ill-gotten ten pounds on a centrepiece for the table. It was made of tinsel and silver ribbon and miniature crackers. She also paid too much for a single branch of mistletoe which she tied to the lamp in the hall.

'Did you know that in France you must take a berry off every time you get kissed?'

Nobody answered that.

On Christmas morning Theo took his daughters to church, and Miggs was left in charge of the meal. She preferred Evensong. By the time the family returned, the house was filled with the unfamiliar smell of roasting turkey.

The two Frenchmen arrived first. Alain had at last been allowed his khaki, which was as thick as a blanket and so harsh and hairy to the touch that Trix, patting his arm, gave a scream. Alexandre was loth to take off his navy blue cloak which swung with Ruritanian gallantry. Both men had their arms full of beer bottles.

Nobody was better company than Theo when he wished to be,

and after some glasses of Centre d'Acceuil burgundy he was positively benign to the two A's, while all three talked of the progress of the war. But Trix put on the gramophone and dragged Alexandre away to dance. Later the front door bell rang again and Trix, abandoning him, dashed to answer it. She shared Miggs' passion for the telephone and the door.

Through the brown paper strips glued to the stained glass of the door, she saw another figure in uniform. It was a young man in RAF blue with a New Zealand flash on his shoulder.

'Merry Christmas, Bob!'

'These are for you, beautiful.'

He piled her arms with parcels, and then kissed her laughing face.

Trix hastily put down the parcels, stood on tiptoe, and pulled a berry off the mistletoe.

Like the majority of Trix's friends, the New Zealand pilot was conventionally handsome and not more than twenty-two. Theo was hospitable to him, but it was the Frenchmen who interested him more. He liked their politeness and their realism.

'Our companions bore us, *Monsieur le Docteur*. *Dieu*, how they bore us.'

'The forms we had to fill in, you would not believe.'

'Giving us these uniforms, imagine! Why is Alain in khaki and myself in Air Force blue? He cannot march a step and I have never entered a plane.'

'And how may we apologise for the quality of this wine?'

The meal was voted the best dinner that anyone could remember. When it was over everyone listened to the Empire Broadcast on the wireless, which followed the King's speech, and finished with the bells of Coventry Cathedral and Polish troops singing carols.

'That reminds me, where is Jan!' suddenly exclaimed Trix.

'Poles are so unreliable,' said New Zealand Bob, 'And *not* the favourites of our squadron.'

'We do not like them either,' said Alexandre.

'Have they not something of a reputation as lady killers?' said Theo, mellow with burgundy.

There were loud denials from the men, and Trix, appealed to, refused to give a verdict.

The party went on into the afternoon. Tea was served, with a dry eggless cake topped by a red candle, and for supper there were turkey sandwiches. Alain carved. When he, Trix and Elaine helped to get the supper, he took out an extraordinary knife which he wore in his belt. It had a horn handle, its blade was chased, it was short and heavy and very sharp. Theo came into the kitchen and remarked on it.

'That is a very unusual knife,' he said.

Alain lifted it by the blade and balanced it.

'Yes. It is a good knife. It throws well,' he said, and lunged as if to send it hurling through the air.

It grew dark, and the blackout curtains were pulled, but no wailing sounded over London. The Frenchmen could stay at ease by the fire, instead of grumbling back to headquarters.

'I reckon,' said Bob, 'it's a truce.'

It was. It lasted all that night, and the whole of the next day, and very strange it seemed. People spoke to each other in the street about it.

'Wasn't there a Christmas truce in the last war? Didn't the German soldiers and the Tommies meet in No Man's Land?'

'Think it'll last?'

When the second night of Christmas came, and there was still no sound of the banshees, no guns, no shuddering explosions, people in d'Abernon Road came out of their houses to look up at the sky.

'Where have they got to?' asked one of Theo's neighbours.

Theo was also looking up at the clear stars. Apart from being sickened at the death of civilians, his attitude to the blitz was one of intense curiosity.

'I daresay they are standing round their Christmas trees, singing *Stille Nacht*,' he said.

'Funny buggers.'

During the second night without bombs, the telephone rang. Trix was out and Miggs put her head round the door.

'Chap for you, Miss Philippa.'

Blushing scarlet, Philippa went out into the hall, closing the door behind her. Her heart was pounding. Weeks had gone by without a word, and she had thought of Barny and imagined he was dead.

'It's your pal in the Eagles,' said the American voice she had longed for. 'How are you fixed for tonight?'

'Do you mean now?'

'Sure. Have you eaten? Have you got a date? I just hit town, I'm at the Wings Club in Curzon Street.'

'I'd love to see you.'

'That's my girl. Grab a taxi.'

Still red-faced, Philippa returned to the drawing room.

'I've been asked out tonight.'

'How nice,' said Elaine mildly, 'anyone I know?'

Her manner was undemanding and kind. She always told the family whom she was meeting and where, rather like a man emptying his pocket of small change. Trix was the same. She reeled off the hotel or restaurant she was going to, and a litany of nicknames and countries, the two A's, Bob, my Canadian, my Pole.

'Only somebody in the RAF,' said Philippa. She did not know why it was that she couldn't bear to say.

It was cold and black and blessedly peaceful when Philippa left the house. The sky was thick with stars, and when she turned into Kensington High Street, the tiny crosses of the traffic lights were like smaller stars fallen to earth. She found a taxi which drove her to Curzon Street.

The Wings Club was in a very large old brick house overgrown with ivy, in a cobbled cul-de-sac. Before the war the house had only come alive during the London season. For four short months it echoed with dance music. Crimson carpets were unrolled across the cobbles, and girls in billowing tulle dresses arrived for debutantes' dances.

The door was answered by a smart RAF corporal who saluted her and said in an American voice, would she sign the visitors' book, if you please, ma'am?

The hall, which smelled of American cigarettes, was hung with dark over-varnished landscapes. It was also draped with the Stars and Stripes flag. There was a Christmas tree ten feet high hung with coloured parcels – for whom? Through an open door she heard the jingle of a jazz piano, and as she followed the corporal, some men in uniform came out of the room, talking and laughing boisterously. They were slightly drunk, and seemed oddly un-English in spite of the RAF blue with wings on the tunic.

In an overfurnished room with an open fire was Barny. He sprang up.

'I should have come to get you, I've been kicking myself. It's so good to see you, Flip. I'd like for you to meet Chuck.'

59

A man who had also stood up shook her hand. Chuck was younger than Barny and seemed scarcely more than a schoolboy. He had a fresh open face, a frank smile and hair much brilliantined. It sprang up on his forehead in a ridge. His accent was not as slow as Barny's.

'Proud to know you. Shall I get the drinks, Barny? Does Flip like rye?'

English girls did not drink whisky, but Philippa accepted it with a smile and left most of it.

They all sat down and the young men talked of the truce. It wouldn't last but it was welcome, wasn't it? He and Chuck were sure glad to get some leave. They felt they deserved a break.

'Boy. Do we,' said Chuck. 'We get so browned off, that's the English expression isn't it? To think how I imagined the moment I got here we'd be operational. Of course Barny has hundreds of hours in the air to his credit,' he went on admiringly, 'and I've only got thirty-five. I said I had fifty when I enlisted.'

He talked of how he and Barny had met on the ship coming to England, and of their disappointment at still being grounded. They'd come over to see action, hadn't they?

Like Trix's two Frenchmen, the young men had come from different worlds, sharing only their nationality. Chuck was from the smallest of the states, Rhode Island. He had been to Brown University, and to his family's disapproval had learned to fly . . . and left for Canada.

'If you knew Rhode Island you wouldn't be surprised,' drawled Barny. 'Rhode Island is the last place you'd go for a good time.'

Chuck disagreed. There were all kinds of pleasures there. The coast was fine for sailing, he'd managed a sixteen-footer when he was twelve years old. There was an English tradition in his home state, he told Philippa. It was a fine place. True, he'd left home. But that was because he couldn't resist what was going on over here. He'd always been in love with speed, had driven a motor cycle on a speedway before he joined the flying club, and – well – here he was rarin' to go.

'Barny and I both read all those books about flying in the Great War. Richthoven, Guynemer, all those guys. I guess I knew the air battles over France like other boys know the

60

gunbattles in the Wild West. So we came to England. The English seem glad to have us. Any man who can fly and wants to fight is welcome.'

'Except that we haven't done much of the first or damn near any of the second,' said Barny.

Philippa, listening to them talking, felt a thrill go through her. To all young women in England that winter, the RAF pilots had an extraordinary and painful glamour. People lay under bombardment in fear of their lives, but these young men rode the winds. They engaged, night after night, in deadly combat. They were heroic. Her eyes shone. What did it matter if they had not yet started to fight? They wore on their breasts the ominous silver wings.

The trio went into the dining room to have supper. During dinner, turkey and an unfamiliar cranberry sauce, she listened to them talking about their training. Chuck complained that they were making no progress and might as well be sitting at the corner drugstore. What use were they to the RAF? Finally they had gone to the CO in desperation to ask when they could start being trained.

Barny grimaced at the story naively told. It wasn't that simple, he said. The only instructors were pilots who were actually fighting – how had they time to teach?

'They go out at daybreak, return to base to refuel, then out they go again, day after day, night after night,' he said, 'They're dead beat. One guy who was supposed to be our instructor came back yesterday from France, went to sleep while eating his breakfast and waiting for his plane to be refuelled, was woken up by his engineer, and went off to fly again. Like a man moving in his sleep.'

'While we,' said Chuck, 'sit around fresh as daisies.'

They described the man who commanded the Eagle Squadron. He was an Englishman, a great flyer, who'd been until recently in the Battle of Britain. He could make a tactical report sound like a thrilling adventure story. But, there were a lot of buts. He was too keen on discipline. He made the Eagles stand up any time he came into a room. He insisted that they must learn how to salute smartly, that their uniform must be perfect and – to crown it all – that they must have a soldierly bearing, whatever in hell that meant. They had not come to England for such stuff.

Philippa wondered if she should spring ignorantly to the defence of their commander, but before she spoke Barny went on with the story.

'My pal here won't admit that our CO has some awful job,' he said. 'We aren't trained. We're wild with impatience. All we want is to get up there and win some glory. No, Chuck, don't interrupt! We're undisciplined, Flip. That guy has got to turn us into a fighting unit somehow. He has to cope with men like Tex who is a wild cowboy and has the idea that you just hop in a plane and have a go at the Jerrie, just as you would in a scrap on the ranch. If you did, you'd be shot down in ten minutes.'

But at last, Barny said, the CO was getting the time to lead them in the air. He was flying with them. During the last week they'd had fulltime training and what was more were finding out just how much there was to learn. They had to discover the way to make a plane do whatever they wanted. They must treat it as an extension of their own bodies, so that it instantly obeyed them. They must learn to make it twist and weave, to drop like a stone, to rise like a swallow. Pushing their coffee cups aside, they used their hands to illustrate what they were saying. When Philippa knew many pilots, she found that they all used their hands to describe flying, flattening and curving their hands like birds, swooping, rising, falling.

'We've got to learn how to stand a plane on its nose,' Chuck put it, 'or climb so high the thing is hanging on its propellers.'

They told her of studying detailed maps, of aerial photography, artillery shoots, long distance reconnaissance, air to ground Morse. The technicalities fascinated her. The jazz piano had started again, the dining room had emptied. She could have sat forever with the two young men. Finally Chuck looked at his watch and exclaimed that he must go. He was meeting some English friends 'on the other side of town'. He gripped Philippa's hand when he said goodbye, smiling as if they had been friends for years.

Barny and Philippa walked back to the room where they had sat before dinner. It was empty except for a pilot and a girl in a corner, talking in low voices. The music played on, but the door was half closed, the sound muffled.

'Chuck makes me feel old,' Barny said. 'Even the States that we come from are so different.'

He rubbed his nose.

'It isn't good to be old right now,' he said.

'We English are very old.'

He looked at her with eyes as dark as Trix's, but the quality of their glance was different, not fixed and brilliant, but tender.

'I've been thinking a lot about you. Every time the radio says a raid on London, I pray to God it isn't near St Helen's.'

'And all the time I'm safely tucked up under the billiard table and the corrugated iron ceiling!'

'So I'm not to worry,' he said, as if at a loss when faced by female courage.

They talked, then, of Chuck. He said that his friend's excitement about flying bothered him. Not that they were not all of them excited, but Chuck seemed uncontrolled.

'He swears that it is the *idea* which fires his imagination, and that he's perfectly cool in the air. I suppose I must believe him. He doesn't like discipline, though, he's worse than I am, and it certainly bugs me. The trouble with the Eagles is that we're just a bunch of American individualists. Flip? How do you find us?'

'I like you.'

'You do, don't you?'

It was long past eleven but there was still no Alert. Barny talked idly, his long legs stretched out, as relaxed as if they had been at a pre-war dance. Philippa's heart was full. If it had been before the war, how could she ever have met this man? Everything about him stirred her. His slow accent, his manner so much more gallant than her own countrymen's, his loose-limbed ease, even the exotic smell of his cigarettes. He came from a land where a single State was so large that you could lose the whole of England inside it. The animals and birds of Barny's country were different from those she knew, and so were the trees, the swamps, the snakes, the very air. She was physically conscious of him. Of his thick hair and the shape of his mouth. She wanted to step inside that male body, think with that mind, speak with that accent, learn to fly, risk her life.

She was laughing at something he said when he touched her.

'I want to kiss you.'

She stopped laughing.

'Come to my room. Just for a while.'

They went out to the hall, and up the staircase. She felt as if every person who saw them, a group of men in the hall, a maid in the corridor, knew where Barny was taking her. But nobody looked or paid the least attention. She was still in an agony of nervous embarrassment.

His room was on the top floor, very small and cramped, with a sloping ceiling.

'This one is a bad bet in the raids. That's why it's vacant. It's tough to get a room here unless you book in advance, and how can we know when we'll get leave? The only vacancies are always right up here. But it doesn't matter tonight, does it? Not while the Germans are trucing.'

'Do you really think they are?'

Her voice was forced.

'Honey, if the planes were coming, they'd be here by now.'

The room was as bare as a cell; nothing but a bed under a white quilt, a dressing table, a looking glass, an empty grate. On the mantelpiece was a candle in a china candlestick, with a box of matches. An expensive looking suitcase was in the corner and a clean blue shirt on the chest of drawers. It was just a room.

He moved over to her, narrowing his eyes, and put his arms round her. They stood, bodies touching, and he rocked her to and fro, and began to kiss her, forcing her lips with his tongue and exploring her mouth and running his tongue along her teeth. When she opened her eyes, she saw his pale face, eyes shut, wearing an expression as if in pain. She wanted him.

'Beautiful. Beautiful. Shall we lie down?'

Knowing that she shouldn't, she let him lead her to the bed where he lifted her and laid her down, and then shifted from being beside her, and lay on top of her as he had done that other time, his mouth on hers. He put his hand down her dress, found her breast and caught the nipple between two fingers, moving it to and fro. Still pressing her down and thrusting against her, he pulled up her skirts.

'Barny, oh Barny. I can't.'

He had been lost and dazed and intent, and he came slowly to himself. He stopped moving.

'Can't you?'

Because she was refusing him, she pressed closer.

'It's what I told you. I have never made love.'

He took his hand from her nipple and rolled off so that she was no longer lying underneath him. Sitting up, he gave a shudder.

'You must go.'

'Must I?'

He did not reply. Philippa could hear his thoughts as if he spoke them aloud. What do you expect? That you can stay here and I'll go on kissing you when I know I can't have you? Do you imagine I'm going on with such a farce? Yet she could break the horrible silence between them so easily, and change the shuddering expression on his face. She could throw a torch into the cold embers and light a fire fiercer than she had ever known – simply by telling him to untie her virgin knot. She couldn't do it.

He picked up her coat and put it round her shoulders. She leaned back to press against him, but he moved away. They went down the staircase and the corporal at the door said he would find a taxi. Barny politely waited with her. Neither of them spoke.

'Cab's here, sir,' said the corporal, returning.

Barny walked out into the street, opened the taxi door in the dark.

'Goodnight, Barny. Thank you for a lovely evening.'

There was no reply.

She cried as she was driven home.

Chapter Five

Early in February Elaine finally decided that she could not stay another month at St Helen's without doing some kind of war work. The half life, brought on by the blitz in a mixture of fear and boredom very like Philippa's, did not satisfy her. As her father said, human beings could get used to anything. There was nothing useful in simply putting up with the blitz like everybody else.

There had been the great fire of London at the end of December, after which the Fire Guard had been started. Elaine took her turn like most Londoners at sitting on rooftops in the freezing night, staring at the sky and waiting for the bombers to rain down incendiaries. But they hadn't done so again in d'Abernon Road. There were now a number of efficient local people fire-watching, and Elaine and Philippa were only needed about once in ten days. Somehow Trix was not asked.

What Elaine wanted was a job that would swallow up her time and tire her out and give her a feeling of belonging to the war. She wanted to be a Wren. But there was always the wild chance that Miles would get unexpected leave. If she were in uniform, that could be difficult. When she thought of him in the Atlantic, she was frightened by images of the terrible sea. She clung to an idea she had had which comforted her. Perhaps on his next leave she might succeed in becoming pregnant.

Meanwhile she was at St Helen's, keeping her father company when he was in, and bearing Miggs' appalling food. One evening after a dinner consisting mainly of potatoes, Theo was driven by disgust to take her into his study and give them both a strong gin and tonic. They listened to the guns.

Elaine looked tentatively at him. She knew although she did not approve of it that she was his favourite. Yet it was difficult to talk to him about herself. He was a man who thought people should solve their own problems. She rather respected his selfishness. After all, his three daughters were adults. His life was one of dedication, he risked it nightly in the streets. Why shouldn't he be free of the weight of his family? She was surprised when he suddenly remarked that she ought to get a job.

'I quite agree,' she said brightly.

'Do you remember a patient of mine, Captain Pendleton? Friend of your mother's family? He's by way of being a colonel in the War Office now. He called round to see me yesterday and asked me to dine. I couldn't accept, of course. We talked a little about you girls. He mentioned that the department he is connected with is very short of staff.'

'Which department is that, Father?' She had not yet recovered from the rare experience of her father interesting himself in her life, apart from smiling at family chat.

'MI5.'

She burst out laughing.

'Not the Secret Service!'

'Those ridiculous names from the *Boys' Own Paper*. Pendleton is in Counter Intelligence. Apparently a large section has been evacuated to the country and they're in dire need of secretaries. He actually remembered you went to secretarial school. Fellows in that sort of work train their memories, I suppose. Well? Does it appeal?'

She did not know what to say. In her own fashion she had a streak of the Tyrrell impulsiveness, as Philippa and Trix had, but she could control hers. Yet it was there in her nature, a dog straining at a leash. Working for the Secret Service did sound fascinating and unlikely. She had no idea what the work might be, and guessed that in spite of its alluring sound, it could turn out to be monotonous. Yet all the same, it *was* secret. The dog tugged at the leash.

Her father was looking at her affectionately. It had occurred to him once or twice lately that he did not do much for his daughters, apart from providing a home, and the small allowance from their mother's money. It pleased him to help her.

'I'd like to meet the colonel if he'll see me,' she said.

'Well done!'

When Elaine told Philippa about the possibility of the job Philippa merely nodded absently. She seemed, thought Elaine, to have lost her generosity. She had also lost weight and omitted to wash her hair. Her sister's gloom, Elaine had noticed, dated from the Christmas night when she had had a telephone call, and gone out with some man whose name she had carefully not mentioned. It was since then that there had been dark rings under her eyes.

What happened, wondered Elaine uneasily. She thought of the old rules that used to hedge young girls with safety. Blessed rules, where were they now? You might as well expect a wicker fence to keep back a tidal wave. Her sisters lived in a city teeming with men in uniform, strangers, foreigners whom their father had never met. The girls picked them up on the top of buses. The idea that Philippa had been seduced remained in Elaine's thoughts like a splinter she could not dig out. But she did not know what to do, nor how to ask Philippa about it.

Since it was clearly impossible to help her because Philippa wanted nothing but to be left alone to wallow, Elaine concentrated on herself.

Her father, still pleased at the rare sensation of helping one of his children, arranged for her to meet the colonel at a club in St James'. When Elaine arrived he was waiting for her in the hall and she recognized him. He was big and white-haired, with burly shoulders and a manner in which grandness was mixed with a somewhat lecherous gallantry. He took her into the enormous stuffy lounge where elderly gentlemen dozed, and talked to her in a low voice. He asked her a question or two in a perfunctory way. Then he told her that he would arrange an interview for her at MI5's country headquarters.

'Your shorthand and typing are still in good shape, of course,' said the colonel in a tone expecting the answer yes. 'Your father told me you are very speedy.'

He gave her a flirtatious look.

She returned it with a pleasant smile.

'I haven't done any secretarial work since I married, Colonel.'

'Skills like that don't rust, they never rust. And they're mighty useful to a young woman. There's a dearth, a positive desert of good secretaries in our department, Mrs St Aird. You'll be the most welcome applicant in Oxfordshire.'

Elaine's heart gave a dive. Oxfordshire! Where her in-laws lived.

There was no getting out of it now. The colonel went on to say that he would make the necessary telephone calls, and she

68

would be interviewed tomorrow. Desert or no desert, his manner said plainly that he had done her a favour. Elaine found it necessary to look deeply grateful.

Very early the following morning she arrived at Paddington. The February day was so dark that it seemed as if daylight was never going to come; the streets were dim with fog and the station was worse. Elaine found herself again in a packed and dirty train filled with troops and civilians. The train was nearly half an hour late before leaving Paddington, and she kept looking nervously at her watch. At last it started. The morning grew slightly lighter as she watched the suburbs going by, with long rows of houses in which there were gaps like missing teeth. Some streets seemed to have totally disappeared into a mass of fallen masonry. When the dreary streets and ruins were left behind, the countryside was misty and damp, the glimpses of the river grey and sad. She remembered going to Henley Regatta with Miles one summer day, and saw in an inward vision the jostling punts and bright dresses, hats wreathed in flowers, strawberries – and Miles' sweet laughing face.

Dragging herself out of the past, she looked round the compartment – she had been fortunate this time to have a seat. Everybody looked shabby and tired except for the soldiers. Pasted up on the wall were the instructions which were in every train compartment now, the target for a good many wartime jokes:

If an air raid occurs while you are on the train:
1. Do *not* attempt to leave the train if it stops away from a station, unless requested by the guard to do so. You are safer where you are.
2. Pull down the blinds, day or night, as a protection against flying glass.
3. If room is available, lie down on the floor.

It was the last instruction that made people laugh. Elaine recalled Miggs' account of a visit to her niece in Sussex. It had been at the start of the Battle of Britain, and the train had been attacked by an enemy plane which dived down and gave a burst of machine-gun fire. Everyone in the compartment scrambled down on to the floor. Miggs was in the bottom layer, with a stout girl of fifteen lying on top of her.

'I shoved her out of the way and crawled back to my seat. I'd rather be shot than squashed alive any day.'

The train was late when it drew up at Oxford. Elaine, joining the crowd leaving the platform, wondered if she would be met. The colonel had said a car would be waiting. Well, if it isn't I shall simply have to go home, she thought. She had no idea where MI5 was situated, and how could one ask? Even the idea was comic. At least, she thought, I look good if I do manage to get the interview. She had dressed with care, choosing her expensive suit, made for her in Savile Row before the war; it was in Glen Urquhart checks, tiny squares of brown and black on white, with a faint blue stripe. She wore a small brown hat tipped over her eyes, a blue sweater she had knitted herself, and Miles' diamond naval crown on her lapel. The day was cold and she had slung her camelhair coat round her shoulders.

As she came out of the station she heard a car hoot twice, and a thin bright-looking girl at the wheel of a Morris wound down the window.

'Are you looking for somebody?' she asked.

'Well – yes. I'm being met. Or I thought I was.'

'Could you identify yourself? Sorry, we have to ask.'

Elaine gave her name, address and – always thorough – produced a letter to prove it.

'Okay. I thought you were you. Hop in.'

The driver introduced herself as Marjorie Flower and drove off into misty deserted Oxford.

'Ah. There's the Keble bus,' she remarked, slowing down at a traffic light. There was a bus waiting outside the college, and about a dozen young women were climbing on board. Every single one was dressed like Elaine. There were a dozen Glen Urquhart tweeds, a dozen plain sweaters, and even at a distance Elaine could spot a dozen lapels pinned with badges of the Forces.

Marjorie passed the bus and drove on.

'I suppose they didn't tell you where we're going?'

Elaine, thoroughly put out by the girls' clothes, turned to her companion to reply. Marjorie Flower was thin and humorous, with a triangular face, a Robin Hood hat with a long feather, and the identical tweeds.

'We're off like the Keble gang to Blenheim. The palace, you know. Seat of the noble Marlboroughs.'

Elaine stared.

'How very extraordinary.'

'Isn't it? Not that it feels like a palace, as you'll see. Who recommended you, by the way?'

'Colonel Pendleton.'

Marjorie laughed. 'I always think he's like the major in the poem – the scarlet one who sends us over the top.'

The girls, like people playing a game of cards, put facts down for examination. They found that Marjorie's cousin Dick Polglaze had trained at Devonport with Miles. Marjorie was married, her husband was a doctor in the Army in the Far East. She had a small daughter whom her mother was looking after. 'That is Ma's war work. Which means I can have a job. I live at home with the parents now. Don't we all?'

She remarked that Blenheim might be thirsting for secretaries, but the fact still remained that only influence got you in.

'Everyone has to be recommended somehow. One of my friends was taken on because her aunt was having an affair with an MI5 officer.'

Elaine smiled somewhat frostily.

'Using influence always seems wrong to me.'

'Oh, I disagree. My father was in Crosse and Blackwell's and when we were children he used to bring us back enormous glass jars of sweets, like the ones you see in sweet shop windows. Samples. Influence is like that. Something special you only get by knowing somebody. Jobs in MI5 are the jars of sweeties. Not that the Blenheim jobs are any great shakes, the work is quite hard. But the food, believe it or not, is delicious. And the Duke's daughters serve behind the counter.'

Marjorie laughed when Elaine mentioned the Glen Urquhart tweeds.

'It's our uniform, isn't it?'

The car slowed down at two elaborate stone pillars standing on either side of tall open gates. In the distance Elaine saw the palace. In the thin winter mist it seemed to float.

'Are you nervous about the interview?'

'I suppose I am a bit.'

'Don't be. They need dogsbodies. And there is the morning busful of them.'

The Keble bus had rumbled up behind them and stopped, and the flock of girls jumped out and began to ascend a flight of steps

71

to the palace. Marjorie and Elaine followed. Through great doors, they entered an enormous hall, lofty as a cathedral. In this place dukes had sometimes welcomed kings. Carpets like lakes of crimson had been thrown down to warm the marble floors, and exotic trees had stood about, blossoming and scented and bringing the winter indoors. Now the hall was filled with metal filing cabinets. Shabby, scarred and scratched, they were piled one on top of the other until they formed entire pillars, the highest almsot reaching the ceiling. It would be impossible to get at the top ones, thought Elaine, without a fireman's ladder.

The day outside was chill, but the palace was like a tomb, with an intense, penetrating, arctic quality of cold. All the girls wore boots and thick woollen stockings. Elaine shivered and pulled on her coat.

Like water into dry earth, the Keble girls began to disappear. Some went down passages on the ground floor, and others through double doors. Marjorie took Elaine up a staircase, along two or three corridors, and finally deposited her in a room containing nothing but four kitchen chairs. The window was uncurtained. The walls were covered with yellow damask.

Blowing into her woollen gloves, Marjorie said she would come back to collect her after the interview. She wished her luck.

Alone, Elaine went to the window and looked out. Below lay a cobbled courtyard overlooked by high palace windows. The courtyard was crammed with hideous army huts.

'Mrs St Aird?'

A dark woman with a face of an eagle stood in the doorway. She beckoned Elaine to follow her into an office next door. She sat at a table and indicated yet another kitchen chair. The room was marginally warmer than the rest of the palace, a little fire burned in a large marble fireplace. On the walls were portraits of sexy-looking men and women who gazed scornfully down at Elaine with worldly eighteenth century faces.

The dark woman picked up some papers and glanced at them.

'Recommended by Charles Pendleton. And you're Claire St Aird's daughter-in-law, I gather.'

She looked up with approval. Elaine thought her pleasant and alarming. Her glossy dark hair was coiled in a bun at the nape of her neck, not a tendril out of place. Her face was unlined and experienced, and looked as if it was scrubbed daily with Lifebuoy soap.

The questions she asked Elaine about her previous work were brief. She seemed pleased at her total ignorance of MI5.

'You can start at once, Mrs St Aird. Now, let me see. You're with your family in London at present. Many of our girls have digs at Keble. I'm afraid they complain a good deal. Particularly if there is any snow, as they have to cross the quad to have a bath. I've told them, surely it is worth the journey. However. We have a bus which passes quite close to Shelton. I imagine you will find it much more convenient to live with your parents-in-law?'

The eagle regarded her benevolently. Elaine saw she was not going to escape the St Airds.

Marjorie fetched her when the interview was over. She said mischievously, 'I bet she didn't once ask about your shorthand speed. When she saw me, I said I couldn't remember mine and she said We Will Call it a Hundred. Isn't she like a hospital matron?'

'I thought a headmistress.'

'Interchangeable.'

The girls went through green baize doors, crossed store rooms filled with more filing cabinets, and eventually out at the back of the palace, and into the stables. They were given an excellent lunch, mostly of vegetables but cooked with inspiration.

When Elaine was on the train on her way back to London, the thought that she was now being forced to live with Miles' parents hit her with its full force. How infinitely would she have preferred Keble's snowy quadrangles.

She did not, and could not, like the St Airds. Miles's father was a man who always reminded her of a duke in a Shakespeare play, expecting homage and giving nothing in return. But it was not her father-in-law who was the problem, it was Miles' mother. After the first welcoming meetings when she had clearly believed Elaine was bringing money into the family, Lady St Aird had become very cold. It was perfectly obvious that she did not like or admire Elaine, who was chilled and depressed by that. The irony was that she knew very well the St Aird's wouldn't hesitate when she asked if she could live at Shelton. 'Of course,' they would say. She was family. And when Miles knew that she was going to live there, he would be delighted, touched and happy. He loved his parents, Shelton, and above all, Elaine. He was convinced that they would suit each other wonderfully.

73

A raid had started by the time Elaine arrived at St Helen's. Both her sisters were out, and Miggs was in the cellar. Tired and depressed, she went into the kitchen and sat down, listening to the ground shudder with explosions, the strange whistlings, the guns. She thought of Blenheim floating in the cold mist. Of Miles in a ship plunging in the icy seas. Oh, this war, this war. It did not only kill people, and reduce poor homes to smoking ruins. It destroyed everything. Lovers were dragged apart. Families divided. It even took away a place where your thoughts could be at rest. A person could hide in the deepest Underground, she thought, or hurry to the loneliest part of the country. There was no shelter anywhere.

When Elaine left for her new job in Oxfordshire, Trix made a sudden dragonfly dart in the direction of Philippa. It had not escaped her black eyes that her second sister was depressed. Trix diagnosed love. She had seen the sickness too many times not to know the signs as accurately as her father recognized the measles. Trix had already coaxed Philippa to come out dancing once or twice, and the occasions had been a moderate success. She now decided that it was high time something was done about Philippa's appearance. She would find time to make her a party dress.

Trix was always busy, in and out of the house, whisking to the telephone ahead of Miggs calling, 'It will be for me,' and now also occupied with what she called her war effort.

Wrapped up against the cold, she dug up her mother's herbacious border, throwing away the plants in their winter sleep, and preparing the ground to sow vegetables. She had visited the local nursery, collected a good deal of information, and bought some stakes from the nurseryman. They were to be for beans.

'We will have fresh vegetables all next summer. So good for our skins,' she told Philippa. 'And the man is finding me a special rose bush. He says the flowers have a really strong scent. He said, "It'll do well for you, miss. I can see you're the sort whose roses always come out."'

As well as sewing for Philippa, Trix was making herself a dress copied from *Vogue*. It was of grey flannel, with white stripes as thick as if they had been drawn with chalk.

74

'Jan, my Pole, gave me the money – he's gorgeous. So gallant,' she said, neatly sewing.

Philippa raised her eyebrows but said nothing. She did not approve of Trix, but she had spoiled her since she was born.

Trix bit off her cotton.

'You are feeling ropey, aren't you?'

It was the RAF's now universal word.

'I'm perfectly okay.'

'Don't pretend, stoopid. I know you. The trouble with you is that you don't go around enough. You quite liked it when we went to Hatchett's, didn't you? Well, there are lots of boys about and we can get them to take us to movies at weekends, and then in the evenings – the blitz *really* isn't too bad, is it? – we'll go dancing. But we must do something about your clothes.'

Like a horse led to a high jump, Philippa was dragged along to her bedroom where Trix opened the wardrobe and threw all the clothes on the bed, commenting on each dress.

'Old-fashioned. That waist! Poor you. Let's give this one to Miggsy.'

The dresses lay in a heap, looking just what they were. Old clothes. Philippa could not think of a way to refuse Trix's offer to brighten her up. When had she refused Trix anything? Her little sister had been six years old when Philippa saved her pocket money to buy her an outsized teddy bear that her parents had thought unsuitably big. When Trix was eleven, Philippa did her homework and went to watch her riding in the Row. Elaine and Mary Tyrrell, never Theo, were interested enough. But Philippa was the fairy godmother.

Now Trix had apparently decided it was her turn. She spent unselfish hours remodelling her sister's dresses, spent money given to her by 'her' Canadian, Pole or New Zealander on knitting wool, burgundy and ice blue. Philippa must, she commanded, knit herself a sweater, half one colour, half the other, buttoning down the back. It would be *very* smart.

With Elaine away again, Philippa's life was altered by Trix. She was taken about, still resembling the horse led by a pert little girl. There were foursomes, and whoever the two men were who made up the party, they were admirers of Trix. While she danced with one, the other would order Philippa a drink, (she had never left so many rums and limes in her life) and watch Trix dancing.

'Isn't she a whizzer? What a girl,' the young man would wistfully say. Philippa agreed. While her sister danced she drew all men's eyes, seeming to have a light round her. Philippa watched too; she did not mind her sister being adored.

Her own boyfriends from the past had disappeared one by one. They never telephoned when they were on leave; or, if they did, they never took her out more than once. She discovered that if your mind is on another man, your male companion knows that by instinct. Was it the opposite of a mating scent? Men did not ask her out any more.

She knew it was ridiculous to have fallen in love with Barny Duval. She had met him three times in her life. But she could not see him in perspective at a distance, only close and out of proportion. He had come here with a few other men, scarcely fifty of them, to fight for England. She thought him one of the most romantic and reckless men in the world. Soon, perhaps now, he would be in the dark air over France or London or the sea – what was the RAF slang – 'dicing with death'. The words were flippant and true. Pilots did gamble with the dark opponent. Danger excited her. It made Barney sexually alluring and somehow unreal. When she had lain with him she had felt she was in the arms of a god. But she was a virgin and believed you must marry before you lie naked with a man. So she had lost him.

Her eyes were clouded with desire and sadness. She did not know how it was that she remained in love. She travelled to the Temple through the mess of bombed London, she worked, she went home to be pounced on by Trix. She sat in smoky ballrooms in the company of men who wanted her sister. She stayed miserably, passionately in love. She thought of Barny all the time. She thought of the country he had come from, about which she had such hazy ideas – of its swamps and rushing rivers, its orange groves and its huge deserts never as dry as her unhappy heart.

It had been her own decision not to make love. If they met again, and were embracing on a bed in the same way, would she behave differently? She had found that all the solemn warnings of the past against the lust of men had never mentioned how much a girl might want a man. I know that everything I want is wrong, she thought. I should never have him in my arms. Wanting him can only bring me pain. And even that he didn't

76

care for me. And yet – and yet – how he haunted her imagination. But I have never done it, couldn't he understand that, she thought. If you won't let a man have you, does he always leave you? Does it have to be so? Perhaps American girls sleep with their boyfriends. And if they won't, you are no good to them. That's a thought. No good.

One night when the blitz was slight, and she was not out with Trix, Philippa lay under the billiard room table, and lit the lamp, and wrote to him. It was a short enough letter, full of clichés. How was he? What news? Her own was slight, nothing much was happening except the blitz. Would he read what the letter did not say? She posted it to the Eagle Club, with 'Please forward, urgent.' on the envelope.

For weeks she hoped. She listened for the telephone, and ran to the front door to the postman. She had a hundred disappointments. Trix noticed. Kind-heartedly, she said nothing.

Philippa was not the only member of the Tyrrell family to be gloomy that 1941 spring. Theo was leading the most exhausting period of his life at an age when he should be slowing down. If Miggs took her daily queuing for fish and the steady reduction of unrationed food, with a grim, amused philosophy, Theo took his work with nervous determination. He was not as tough as he liked to think himself. The blitz showed no sign of abating; blast and collapsing houses and broken glass caused most of the casualities, but there was also the terrible danger of fire. Firemen on the top of ladders faced infernos. Injuries were terrible.

Although he worked part of every day at the hospital, and fitted in his private patients when he could, he was ready at any time of the night to go out with the rescue parties. He delivered a baby in a kitchen, with the warden holding a torch to shine on the mother while Theo, in rubber apron and tin helmet, stitched her up. Like every doctor, he had a carapace which protected him when he had to cope with the dying or the dead. But he never managed not to suffer when the patient was a child. Returning to St Helen's in the blitzed dawns, he was often in pain.

To add to a doctor's anxieties, there now began what the newspapers called 'the great drift homewards' of evacuated children and their mothers. 'Leave the children where they are!' shouted a government poster, with a Hitler figure in the background hissing 'Take them back'. Hundreds of thousands ignored the warning and poured back into London.

Short of sleep, working beyond his physical capabilities for his age, he confided in nobody. His favourite child was gone. He did have a sentiment which he never admitted was love for his old nurse, but Miggs was not the devoted slave she used to be. She looked at him sardonically. It seemed a long time since he had been admired. There was nobody in his family to talk to. Philippa was too like her mother, soft and sentimental. As for Beatrix, she was his child and must live at home if she chose. But he had never had a sensible conversation with her in his life.

He was unexpectedly involved in his two daughters' social life when the two Frenchmen from the Centre d'Acceuil reappeared.

'Guess who's turned up,' announced Trix to Philippa one evening. She looked at her sister's closed face and said, 'Ah well, no point in asking, it would bore you to answer. My two A's are here again. I thought they'd been posted. They've been away on some ghastly course, very hush hush. I met them in Kensington High Street. Alexandre was swinging along like something out of the *Prisoner of Zenda*, and poor Alain plodded with him, all dumpy. I told them to come round. If Pa's out, we can raid his study. My jewel-case key fits his drink cupboard. The luck! And I know his patients bring him black market gin.'

'He'd have a fit.'

'It's patriotic to entertain the Fighting French.'

Trix, who had been sitting on the arm of the sofa, jumped up and peered at herself in the glass over the mantelpiece. She frowned. She was her most severe critic.

'I do wonder if Miggsy can manage to give us all something to eat, don't you?'

'I suppose that means you want me to ask.'

'Oh Flip, would you? She's not mad keen on me just now. I used all her beastly butter ration for a cake for my Pole when he came to tea. He loves sweet things.'

Trix laughed at the old joke.

Philippa went to the kitchen. She found that Miggs was out of her disguise as doctor's receptionist – the starched coat hung on a hook behind the door. The boiler was well damped down, and Miggs, in her hideous puce apron, was peeling potatoes. She was watched by the unblinking gaze of a large ginger cat.

'Miggs! Where did that come from?'

"Tisn't a that. 'Tis a he.'

'Is he from over the road? Or the people at the corner?'

'Nobody's seen him before in their lives. Not the milkman. Nobody.'

The cat's green eyes were glued on Miggs.

'Outside the kitchen window all day yesterday he was. I was washin' up and there he was. Glarin'. I told him to get off with it. Half-hour later, back again. Starin' fit to bust. No sign last night when I went off to my shelter. This mornin', blow me down, back again in the pourin' rain. More than a body could stand, so I let him in.'

'But Miggs, you're not thinking –'

'Not thinkin' anythin', Miss Philippa. His fur was soppin'.'

Philippa felt bound to say that her father disliked cats.

'The doctor isn't goin' to know.'

Philippa did not argue. She wondered how a cat as large as this one was going to be concealed. But Miggs, it was only too obvious, had made up her mind. Philippa tentatively mentioned lunch for the Free French visitors.

Miggs held up a potato.

'Got some carrots and a heel of cheese. I'll make a veggie pie.'

'Poor things, they probably get that at barracks.'

Miggs sniffed.

'They *are* fighting with us, Miggsy.'

'Didn't see much of them at Dunkirk.'

'You know very well these Frenchmen came over to join us, risking their lives. We ought to welcome them. But veggie pie I suppose it will have to be.'

As Philippa left the kitchen, the cat began to purr like an engine.

Things did not work out the way Trix had expected. When the front door bell rang, she winked at Philippa and flourished a key. But then the girls heard their father's voice in the hall.

'Bother and blow,' whispered Trix, 'goodbye to the gin.'

The door opened to admit, not two people but four. There were Alexandre and Alain, a strange young woman they had never seen before and – wonder of wonders – Theo. Was he joining the party?

The Frenchmen introduced their companion, they did trust they were not trespassing on the doctor's hospitality? Theo smiled benevolently as they presented Mademoiselle Ghilain. She was a little thing who looked like a bird. She had narrow feet in high-heeled shoes and thin legs and her black hair was as shiny as the wing of a crow. She was dressed in black and white.

Alain explained that Annette was his cousin from Brittany. She had recently arrived.

'I am to work at the Centre,' said Annette, whose accented English was surprisingly good.

Alain explained that many Bretons were now arriving. He said this with sombre pride, and exchanged a look with Annette which seemed tender.

Theo bustled about with glasses, produced the gin – Trix and Philippa did not dare to exchange looks – and the Frenchmen presented their usual beer bottles of burgundy. There was animated talk. Philippa thought it very surprising of her father to remain. He talked a good deal to the French girl, and took her over to the window to show her the burned-out conservatory which had become a kind of Tyrrell landmark.

Trix, always indifferent to bad food, had expansively invited everybody to lunch. Theo and Annette Ghilain, still talking to each other, were not listening. But Alain, who had understood, said to Philippa,

'Could you tell your sister that we hope you will do us the honour of lunching with us?'

'At the Centre?' from Trix, when Philippa had translated, 'What fun.'

'No, no,' put in Alexandre, who never let a conversation continue without taking it over, 'Chez Prunier.'

Trix looked delighted. Philippa was embarrassed. She stammered that it was very, very generous, but was not Prunier's a little . . . she stopped, hoping for rescue. She knew, and so should Trix if she'd given it a moment's thought, that the two men hadn't a penny between them.

'But we have money,' said Alain seriously, looking at her through his spectacles. 'We have saved our pay. And there is some South American money Alexandre has changed.'

'Also,' put in Annette Ghilain who, with Theo, had joined them, 'my cousin has sold his watch.'

Horror from Philippa. Admiring silence from Trix.

Alexandre spread out his hands.

'We have money. We wish to use it up. Money does not

80

belong in the pocket. It must continue to roll. *Monsieur le Docteur*. We trust you will join us?'

Theo, who spoke good French, thanked them very pleasantly but regretted he was due at the hospital. Annette said that she, too, was expected back at the Centre and Theo said he would walk there with her. Annette looked gratified and they left the house together.

Miggs greeted the news that the girls and their visitors were lunching out with 'a good thing too.'

Trix darted up to change, coming down soon afterwards in a new dress she had made from some expensive pink crêpe de chine sheets she had bought in Bond Street. Perched on her head was a tiny hat, with a veil floating behind it like a pennant. She carried suede gloves with gold tassels. Alexandre admiringly watched her descending the stairs, and she jumped the last three steps into his arms. They both burst out laughing. Nobody was better at starting off for an expedition than Trix.

The quartet walked down St James', to stop and admire some potato plants growing in tubs which used to contain bay trees.

'What a marvellous idea,' said Philippa.

'The English have ingenuity,' said polite Alain.

Alexandre thought it a pointless gesture. How many pounds of potatoes would be grown from those? A plateful.

The two A's entered Chez Prunier like fish emptied back into a lake. They argued about the table given to them, studied the menu critically and disapproved of the wine. Everybody treated them with deep respect.

When the meal had been ordered to their satisfaction, they turned their attention to the girls. Their conversation, sentence by sentence, was translated by Philippa for her sister. Or rather, Alexandre's conversation. Alain merely listened with an occasional pointed interruption.

Although he was French, said Alexandre, he was not French. He had left his native land twenty years ago, only returning when war broke out and 'idiot that I was, I thought I would be needed.' He told his story to Trix̄ rather than to Philippa, although Trix only understood the flattering expression in his eyes and the smile that flashed with gold.

His hunting ground, he said, had been South America. He had made and lost three fortunes. He had sold guns in revolutions to both sides, he'd helped a president during a *coup d'état* to escape in a motor boat upriver, where a half drowned forest under the water was more dangerous than enemies. He had been paid in suitcases which were filled to bursting with money, and lost it all in a month on gambling. He had returned to the gun-running and the smuggling, and to the company of the most beautiful women in the world.

'Their beauty,' he said, 'strikes the heart with fear. Their hair is so long and thick you cannot lift its shining weight. Their music forbids you to keep still.'

Trix did not mind such talk: it put her on her mettle.

Alain did not bother to hide the fact that the talk irritated him. Alexandre irritated him, he was a cork you could not keep below the water. But destiny had thrown the men together, and they were friends in spite of the laughable difference in their natures.

'Tell your lovely sister,' said Alexandre, 'that I have made a decision – never to go out with women unless Alain is beside me.'

'You're afraid we'll trap you,' said Trix, pleased.

Alain did not join in the laughter. He looked sombre, and Philippa wondered if he had left a girl in Brittany.

Counting their money to pay what Philippa read, upside down, as a very large bill, the young men declared they could afford a taxi back to Kensington. Trix was squashed between them on the seat. Philippa, offered a uniformed knee by Alexandre, preferred to sit on the folding seat.

The journey home was enlivened by an argument between the men as to which of them spoke the better French.

'The Breton of good education has no accent,' said Alain.

Alexandre scoffed. Why, he could distinctly hear the Breton note in Alain's voice, in the vowels and intonations. Even in the expressions Alain used. He was unmistakably from Brittany. Whereas he, continued Alexandre with a wave of one olive-skinned hand, had originally come from Burgundy, had spoken nothing but Spanish for twenty years, but retained an accent of perfection. His French was pure – not a shadow of regional sound. Speaking like an actor, he began to intone Racine.

'Oh Flip, tell them to stop arguing,' interrupted Trix, 'and what's more, tell them they are not to speak another word of French until we get home. They can jolly well have a stab at English. I shall help them.'

This silenced the dispute, and they obeyed her. There was laughter for the rest of the journey.

Released from the task of turning one language into another and back again, Philippa stared out of the window. A man in RAF blue was walking in Green Park – something in his swinging walk made her stomach turn over. Of course it wasn't Barny. But all the way home she looked into the streets, and three times more saw men in RAF blue, with broad shoulders and a relaxed, easy stride. It was like being haunted.

Chaper Six

Lady St Aird received Elaine at Shelton with her customary cold politeness. Elaine was given Miles' bedroom and dressing room. 'If you wish to invite friends to stay, please do,' said her mother-in-law. She spoke as if she still had a staff of servants.

Shelton was very beautiful and Elaine loved it, despite its owners. It had been built before the time when titled landowners had attacks of glory and meglomania. It was not a building to St Aird importance, but a comfortable Cotswold stone manor set in gardens, with a lake and a little wood. The family had lived there for generations. Before the present Shelton was built there had been a Tudor house on the same land. The remains of the older house, low rose-coloured walls, could be seen in the gardens.

Every day except on Sunday, Elaine travelled to Blenheim and back by bus. She had wanted a job to swallow up her time, and she had certainly found one. But even so, breakfast and dinner at Shelton were meals she did not look forward to, and the company of her mother-in-law on Sundays was something that had to be bravely borne.

Elaine was too much in love with Miles to admit a fault except that he was over-devoted to his parents. Once before they married he had said to her, 'I don't know a woman I would rather spend the day with than my Mama.' Elaine had felt jealous. Miles was also deeply fond of his father, whom he respected and admired.

St Aird was a tall white-haired man, with a well-trimmed beard and a long haggard face. He looked older than his years. He had been born at Shelton, grew up there, and left only when he joined the army in the summer of 1914. He fought bravely, won the MC and in 1916 was badly gassed – which explained his lined face and stooping figure. St Aird's meeting with Claire resembled a musical comedy of the Great War. He met her in the military hospital where he was taken after being gassed; she nursed him. But she refused to marry him until after the war ended: it would have stopped her from nursing.

When he was invalided out of the army, he returned home and began to paint. He had talent, took lessons, and one of the Shelton stables was converted into a roomy studio, given the necessary north light by a large new skylight. For twenty years, apart from occasional trips with Claire to Italy, St Aird painted.

The first time that Miles took Elaine to Shelton – it was after picnicking on the river at Oxford – he told Elaine that unless they bearded St Aird in his den Elaine would not get the chance to meet him. Miles took Elaine round to the stables, knocked at one of the doors and shouted, 'Father? It's me.'

St Aird opened the door and looked down at Elaine. She looked up at him as brightly as a robin, with the same quick inquisitive way of holding her head. He shook her hand and that was all. Miles asked if he might show Elaine some of the paintings. The elderly man pulled a few canvases out; they were stacked with their faces to the wall.

Elaine liked pictures and knew a little about them. She was very surprised by St Aird's. They were all of country subjects. There were winter skies and misty trees, smoky November distances, rooks. There were also rainbows, and tangles of poppies in flowering grass. The paintings had poetry and an instant appeal to the heart.

When she exclaimed over them, St Aird looked dark. She innocently asked if he exhibited at the RA. He said, 'No.'

He made it plain that he disliked talking about his work.

Later Miles told her that his father had never exhibited anywhere. He had once given a picture away – he had not wanted to do that but a relative had insisted. He had not sold a single picture since he began to paint.

'But that's unbelievable. They're lovely! Why not?'

'I don't know, poppet. He's a funny old stick, and they're his pictures. His sister Joan marched into the studio one day and said she wanted to buy one for her godchild's twenty-first. He exploded.' Miles burst out laughing, and added, 'He thinks selling things is vulgar.'

Now that she was living at Shelton, Elaine had become used to her father-in-law and his painting. If she was not meant to admire them or even look at them, that was his business. She was bright and polite, but rarely addressed a remark to him, although she always answered pleasantly if he spoke to her. Like a contrary dog, he occasionally advanced towards her and once actually asked her to the studio to show her a new picture. It was of the same horizon and the same wood in other pictures – but it was bleaker. All she did was to nod. He quite cheered up.

The trouble with Shelton was not her father-in-law, misanthropic, talented and usually invisible. It was Lady St Aird. Elaine tried to like her. She tried hard but she simply could not manage it. She and Claire resembled the queens of two islands, set close to one another but in a sea utterly impassable except to Miles. Only he could navigate it, land on either island and find fresh water there and food and welcome. But without him, the islands stayed within sight of each other and immeasurably distant, the sea between them boiling with whirlpools and monsters.

Elaine was perfectly aware of her mother-in-law's good qualities. Claire was brave. She had nursed right through the 1914-18 war in France, and been wounded by shrapnel. Miles told Elaine that his mother had a livid scar running the length of her left arm, and that was why she always wore long sleeves. Her courage was part of her, like her protuberant pale blue eyes. The photographs in the crested family album – Claire was the daughter of an Earl – showed a blank-faced young beauty under a hat stabbed with a large feather quill. Later the same beauty appeared in ugly 1914 nurse's uniform, and later still there she was on her father's arm in wedding satin.

Now Claire's golden hair was a clouded grey which she still wore in the frizzy style of her youth. Like Queen Mary, she stayed in her period. Her tweeds were old and fine, her jewellery was a choice of heavy yellowish diamonds and strings of large valuable pearls.

Claire's courage did not fade with age. Until the war she had hunted, jumping the highest fences as recklessly as a boy and contemptuous of any other rider who had nerves. Matching her courage was a deep unselfconscious patriotism. People in this war simply got on with the job. But Claire talked of England as of a lover.

Bravery, patriotism, and devotion to Miles were undeniable in Claire. But she was cold and snobbish. Elaine did not mind the coldness so much, she herself could be reserved. But she detested the snobbery. She found it hard to believe that it was possible to be such a snob in the 1940s. Surely nobody could treat such nonsense seriously? But Claire did. She measured

86

people by her dusty, dated old standards, she spoke of The Family as a saint might speak of God. She knew the geneaology of the St Airds by heart, and had hung a painted family tree in the dining room, illuminated with shields and crests. Sometimes when she talked of a cousin or uncle or more distant relative, she reminded Elaine of Miggs. Miggs had a passion for the Royal family which was also very detailed. But Miggs' references, to Princess Victoria or Lady Mary Cambridge, were more exalted.

Claire had no critical faculty about the St Airds. Those whom Elaine occasionally met were nothing very exceptional. Most of them were boring or rather stupid, and all were as snobbish as Claire herself. But she shone at them with her pale eyes, and if the daily woman did not arrive on a day when she was entertaining, she cleaned the silver tea pot herself.

It was late in the spring, and the trees in the huge parkland at Blenheim were budding. Ducks appeared on the lake. At lunchtime, Elaine and Marjorie hurried through their good meal so that they could walk in the sun. In the distance, beyond a group of tall trees, the column of Marlborough's Victory rose against a blue and white sky.

The girls had become friends. Both were optimistic and matter-of-fact and they shared an interest in their work, and the fact that their husbands were serving abroad. Marjorie's humour was an antidote to Claire St Aird.

'My mother-in-law is up to her eyes in the WVS,' Elaine remarked, as they walked in the park, 'She lives in her green uniform. This morning she had breakfast in that hideous hat.'

Marjorie giggled. 'Do you realise the country's packed with girls like us, stuck with their in-laws. In peacetime one only has to see them at Christmas, and then they're improved by all the strong drink. But now! I know I'm lucky living with my own parents, but we have to keep *visiting* Bob's and that's torture. His mother is one of those patient women who complains in a gentle voice and makes you want to swear. And his father's a teacher who turns every conversation into a lecture. You may have the St Airds. How would you like the Old Pretender and the Jacobites?'

Escaping into the park was a brief respite for the girls during their days of grinding work. Over a thousand people now worked for MI5 in the palace. The hordes of girls who tripped up the ducal steps each morning, waving their passes, and clattering down again each evening, had signed the Official Secrets Act. The work was secret and dealt in dangerous matters. Yet the atmosphere at Blenheim made Elaine think of a large school. The senior girls who had worked for MI5 from the start of the war had previously been based at Wormwood Scrubs prison. A cell had been allotted to each girl. They spoke nostalgically of The Scrubs. At Blenheim there was no privacy.

The extraordinary place in which Elaine and Marjorie, and all the scores of girls, found themselves did not feel like a palace at all. Sarah Churchill had called it 'that wild unmerciful house', and there it was, Queen Anne's gift to a hero. Everything about Blenheim was on a gigantic scale. The emblems in stone and in marble, the hundred rooms, the lake and bridge and beech-woods all symbolic of battle and victory, the grounds planted by Capability Brown with avenues of trees to represent the Battle of Blenheim. But the noble rooms were divided up by matchboard partitions and metal files the dun colour of war hid the painted walls. The young women who worked in one of the strangest houses in the world scarcely noticed it.

There was no social life there. All day long the typewriters clattered and the place was full of voices. At night the girls went home on the Oxford bus. On their time off they went to London to see boyfriends or husbands. And the palace was not only unsociable, it was freezing cold. During the chill spring it remained an ice house. Marjorie worked in a hut in the Great Courtyard, and wore three sweaters and two pairs of stockings. The wall by her desk ran with damp.

Elaine's boss was a handsome grizzled ex-lawyer called Paul Goodier, who had been educated in Poland and spoke the language as easily as English. He had caught the formality of Polish people, and always said to Elaine when she gave him her work, 'Thank you *so* much.'

Goodier's section was concerned with the Poles who had come to Britain since war broke out – waves of refugees. He and his officers were on the lookout for enemy agents who could have been planted among the innocent. Elaine typed interviews and reports made from carefully sifted information. The work of spy-seeking was difficult: officers had to be judges of people under suspicion, or of the evidence against them. The curious thing Elaine found was that she could not remember a twentieth of all that she typed from week to week.

'I agree. I'm the same,' said Marjorie blithely.

'I suppose it is our subconscious working. We don't realize it, but we're deliberately making our minds blank because the stuff is secret.'

'Speak for yourself, Elaine. My mind's a blank anyway.'

Elaine worked in the first floor in a room much envied by Marjorie for its small coal fire. It overlooked a pretty terrace where she sometimes saw the Duchess of Marlborough walking up and down in the spring sunshine, pushing a pram. 'That baby,' said Marjorie who was always up-to-the-minute with palace jokes, 'is known as the Duke's war effort.'

Travelling to and from Woodstock, Elaine watched the slow spring begin. She thought of the shrubs in the garden at St Helen's which she had watched budding during her child-hood. She knew the corner where the snowdrops came up first. She missed her family. Telephoning them was unsatis-factory, for Trix was rarely at home and when Elaine did manage to speak to her, her conversation was about young men Elaine had never met. Theo was brief and monosyllabic. Miggs was the same. This left Philippa who was the warmest, but even she was not communicative. Elaine was delighted when Philippa actually rang her one bright evening to say she had some leave due to her and would it be possible to come to Shelton?

'I'd love to stay with you if it's allowed.'

'Lady St Aird said I could ask people. Hold on and I'll check,' said Elaine eagerly.

Claire was in the drawing room, listening to the wireless and knitting the usual sweater in khaki-coloured wool. She knitted or sewed at any time when her work for the WVS, or in the vegetable garden or with the chickens, did not occupy her time. She glanced up.

'My sister Philippa has a few days off from her work for the hospital,' said Elaine, spelling it out because she required Claire's approval. 'Might I ask her to Shelton for a day or two?'

Claire continued to knit so quickly that her body and the chair shook.

'I have told you that you may invite your family or friends at any time.'

She did not add 'except that young sister', whose appearance at the wedding had appalled her. She sometimes wondered how Elaine would take her refusal to receive Beatrix.

It was a relief to Philippa to leave St Helen's and take the Oxford train. She had not heard a word from Barny for nearly three months; it was two and a half since she had written to him. The silence was a knell. She knew she would never see him again. What made it worse was that Jane Alwynne, who knew everything about the RAF through her husband, an air vice marshal, had told her the Eagle Squadron was now operational. The following evening it was on the nine o'clock news.

'The Eagle Squadron took part in a sweep over the French coast, both attacking and successfully beating off the enemy.'

Philippa had left the room and rushed up to her bedroom, despite the blitz. It was terrible to know the Eagles were flying, that Barny by now was probably dead. She knew her feelings were exaggerated and out of proportion – what right had she to feel like a war widow? He had been an incident in the shifting patterns of the war. But there it was, the pain inside her that would not go away.

She enjoyed the few days with Elaine in Oxfordshire. Her sister prevented her from giving in to a gloom which seemed to Philippa to taste like a London fog. Trix's way of cheering her had been to set Philippa's hair in a pageboy bob, produce young men, and wink at her on the dance floor. Elaine merely chatted and smiled and kept her busy. Claire was polite. She had decided that the visitor was quiet and well-mannered, and that her clothes were passable.

The rambling old house was the right place for wartime domesticity. The sisters made jelly from the withered yellowish apples, the last from the autumn crop, which they found in an apple loft. They tried out Ministry of Food recipes, and made a cake with raw carrot, margarine and rum essence. They dug in the kitchen garden and in the evenings they darned the heavy linen sheets embroidered with oversized coronets.

They were restful together. Elaine never looked at her probingly with her gentle blue eyes, and never asked her hurtful questions.

Claire left them alone most of the time. She was much occupied with her WVS work, from peeling buckets full of potatoes to visiting sick young women whose husbands were in the Forces. During the day, when Elaine was at Blenheim, Philippa took the bus to Oxford. She went to the cinema, and browsed in bookshops. One afternoon she spent in the public library, reading about Louisiana in the *Encyclopaedia Britannica*.

Her last afternoon at Shelton was on Sunday. The sisters walked to church, then came home and decided to weed in the kitchen garden. As they came into the house, they heard Claire calling.

'Elaine?' The voice was soft but curiously brusque.

Claire was at her desk in the drawing room.

'Miles telephoned.'

Elaine went as white as a sheet.

'Is he all right?'

'Perfectly. He's in Liverpool. His ship is in for a boiler clean, apparently. He was in a fire raid on the docks last night, he said. Most exciting.'

Elaine was still as pale as death.

'Was his ship hit?'

'I have no idea. He couldn't give any details, of course. He said it was a lot of fun. There's no chance of his getting any leave. But one did not expect it. Well, now. Shall we have tea?'

Philippa said she would get it and left them.

The Shelton kitchens were large enough to cook dinner for thirty people. The floors were of brick, there was a black kitchen range, a scullery with a hand pump for water, a flower room with shelves of vases of every size, age and shape. The Tyrrells still had Miggs, but the St Airds had lost all their servants when war came; Claire encouraged them to join up. Elderly help arrived erratically from the village sometimes.

Philippa laid a silver tray, and made the tea in a silver teapot shaped like an Aladdin's lamp with an ivory handle. At Shelton the Minton china was used every day, and the Georgian sugar tongs, although the sugar ration was down to four ounces a week.

Elaine's cheeks were pink again when she came into the kitchen.

'Oh Flip. If only I'd been here.'

'But he's going to ring again, isn't he?'

'If he can.'

'When?'

'She didn't ask.'

At seven the telephone in the hall rang. The St Airds were changing for dinner, but Elaine and Philippa were already dressed and downstairs. Elaine started violently, and ran.

Philippa heard her sister speak in a voice she had never heard before in her life.

'Miles. My dear one.'

Philippa shut the drawing room door.

Philippa had been glad to go to Shelton for a change of scene and even more glad to see Elaine, but when she came back to London she found that she was not refreshed. The uncanny night silences of the country did not make for peaceful sleep to ears accustomed to the blitz. Philippa had woken more often at Shelton than during the deafening nights under the billiard table. And Elaine's serenity, a kind of settled spirit in her despite her not enjoying Shelton, had made Philippa more aware than ever of her own unhappy heart. Both the still midnight which had lapped round the old house, and Elaine's love for Miles, had disturbed her. She was in love too, but *her* love was absurd. All the way home she planned how she could soon escape into the WAAF.

When Philippa arrived at Chicheley Buildings the next morning, she toiled up the stairs, feeling very nervous. She tried to settle to work, opening a shabby ledger and filling in a few cheques which had arrived since her absence. Poor Princess Victoria Hospital was poor in many ways.

Mrs Alwynne arrived at midday, her arms full of files, followed by an elderly man weighed down with more. Jane had recruited him from the street outside – he had been pounced upon on his way to buy some sandwiches, and looked bewildered.

'Could you place the files on the table? Very civil of you. Many thanks for your kindness.'

He went out hastily, sensing that if he lingered he would be given further duties.

Jane, smiling at Philippa, marched into her office and called to Philippa to bring her book. Philippa thought the time did not look ripe for breaking bad news. But when would there be a time to tell Jane one wished to leave her? Jane Alwynne was a big, fat, wonderfully-bosomed woman with a noble face which would have suited a general. She had coiled grey hair, a straight nose and eyes as bright and sharp as gimlets. Her clothes were expensive, her blouses real silk, her RAF brooch winked with large diamonds.

'I want a word, Philippa – '

'Mrs Alwynne, may I have a word?'

Both spoke at once. They laughed.

'You speak first, child.'

'Oh no, please.'

'Very well. What I have to say is brief enough. Are you considering enlisting in the WAAF?'

Jane was uncanny.

'Ah. I see I am right. You've always had a penchant for flyers. I suppose you have been reading about the WAAF's glamorous jobs, working in the flying control rooms, air ambulances, radio location and so on.'

'They do marvellous work.'

'Certainly they do, I only wish I were in uniform myself. But where would my charities be if I let my heart rule my head? We must stop talking like a recruiting leaflet. I don't want you to leave and I don't think you should.'

'But there must be lots of other people you could get – '

'Nonsense. There is nobody. It was an answer from heaven when you agreed to work here. I have managed to keep you so far, but I know very well you are havering. Now. Let us talk.'

Jane talked. Her voice was youthful and full of vitality, the voice that forced people to give her money. Girls, she said, joined the women's services by the thousand and the recruiting for the WAAF was a runaway success, she had met one of the commandants recently. As for the Wrens, they were turning girls away. There was the ATS, of course. But she knew Philippa cared most for flyers.

'Now, child. You have been in our hospital. You know the straits they are in. Can you in all honesty say they do not need you?'

The Princess Victoria Hospital for Children, in Surrey, had been built in late Victorian times, opened by the old Queen's daughter. It had been a fine hospital then. But the years and lack of money had begun to destroy it. Kitchens were antiquated,

93

Out-Patients in a gloomy basement, lighting in disrepair. There were no dimmed lights in the wards at night, the furniture was old and difficult to clean, the children's cots heavy and nearly worn out, the cumbersome lifts went wrong. Philippa had been shown all these things.

'And you remember Sister's office!' finished Jane.

Taking Philippa to visit the hospital had been Jane's way of binding Philippa to the cause. Jane had many good causes. She fought to keep anyone who unwittingly strayed into her circle of good works.

'Say you'll stay at least for the next few months,' said Jane, fixing her with bright eyes.

Philippa was beaten.

It was true, she thought travelling home, Shelton had done her no good; it had not even strengthened her will against Jane. And after the country, London looked dirtier and more damaged than before she had gone away. When you were here all the time, you were used to the mess and greyness and looming danger. But after looking through windows at lawns and yew hedges, and smelling the green spring, your eyes were different. D'Abernon Road depressed her. And at home the burnt conservatory looked as grim as a gibbet.

Miggs was on the telephone.

'Don't forget to gargle with salt and water three times a day, Miss Bassett.'

Ringing off, she looked at Philippa guardedly.

'Your sister's out with some chap in the Black Watch. The doctor's on his rounds. Had your tea?'

It was as if Philippa had never been away. And there was no letter for her.

She felt restless and jumpy, she did not know why. The old house did not welcome her. Her sisters were not here, her father out, Miggs unwelcoming. She wondered if her nerves meant the usual expectancy of a raid. Perhaps this one will be it. Perhaps we'll be hit. Oh, stop being a fool, she told herself, and went up to have a bath.

Trix's extravagances – where did she get hold of all the things and who paid for them? – filled the bathroom shelves. There were unpatriotically expensive creams, geranium soaps, almost unobtainable shampoos. Philippa had a slow bath but it was only five inches deep. That was what the Government asked you to do, and what Trix never did. People said even the King and Queen had five-inch deep baths now.

She washed her hair, and rolled it in a towel before going back to her bedroom. The feeling of nerves had not left her, and the prospect of the long night alone, with her father out in the streets and Miggs in the cellar, filled her with a rare sensation of panic. She dressed again, and rubbed her hair dry and set it in the way Trix had taught her. But she had not enough grips. The essential little metal things had disappeared from the shops months ago: it was only Trix who had boxes of them.

Walking down the passage, she went into Trix's room. The place was wild with disorder, Trix had clearly left in a tearing hurry. Her wardrobe door hung open, a pair of satin and lace cami-knickers was on the floor among a heap of silk stockings. Her jewel case was open, its glittering contents scattered among the face powder on the dressing table. There was a box from Harrods on a chair. It contained, half wrapped in tissue paper, some pink French knickers. They were folded to show lines of embroidery in pale blue above one leg. The embroidered words, like a poem, ran:

> Oh please do not do that
> Oh please do not
> Oh please do
> Oh!!!

Raising her eyebrows, Philippa shut the box and the jewel case, and sat down at the dressing table to look for a box of hair grips. She couldn't find any. Her still wet hair was falling from the coiled towel. She sighed, weighed down by a depression like an intense headache.

The make-up drawer was crammed, not only with little pots and boxes, lipsticks, nail files and combs, but with letters. Some of them had H.M.Ships stamped on them. All were obviously from young men. Two or three lay on top of a silver-topped box of face powder, and Philippa picked them up to find the grips. Automatically arranging them neatly, she saw something. A feeling went through her that was so sharp she lost her breath. Swallowing, she looked again.

Among the letters was a bill. It was a hotel bill headed

Amesbury Arms, Buckinghamshire. At the head of the bill in ink was written: 'Room 24. Pilot Officer and Mrs Duval.'

She stared at it. For a while she was so stunned that it did not make sense. Pilot Officer and Mrs –

And then she understood.

But it couldn't be true. Trix didn't know him. It wasn't possible. The two names danced before her eyes, conjuring up such terrible pictures that she couldn't bear what her imagination created. Springing up with a groan, she fled from the room.

Chapter Seven

Philippa lay on her bed like somebody who is bleeding and terrified to move. She did not know how long she lay there. The raid began and she listened indifferently. Hours afterwards came the long level sound of the All Clear with its note of safety. She did not stir. The towel had fallen from her hair which, in untidy spirals, was bone dry.

She had the sensation that there was a stone in her chest, and that was what was making her bleed. When she moved it moved too, falling and crushing her ribs and breaking her veins. She kept thinking, 'I must talk to her. I must know the truth.' But she did know it. She wanted to hear it spoken, to be poisoned and suffer more.

Perhaps Trix would not come home tonight, she so often did not return. That seemed unbearable, and all Philippa did was to strain her ears for the sound of her sister coming into the house. At last, at about two or three in the morning, she heard a noise. It was a taxi stopping in d'Abernon Road. She listened. There was the faint sound of voices. A stifled laugh. A closing door. Then an interval. And then the staircase creaked.

Crawling off her bed, her eyes accustomed to the dark, she went to her door. A pale figure was coming toward her.

'Flip? What are *you* doing up at this hour!'

The whisper was friendly with recent kisses.

'I want to talk to you.'

'Sh! Pa may be home. Come to my room.'

Trix slipped past, carrying her shoes which she swung by the straps. The curtains in her room had not been drawn, and muttering 'Darn it' she tugged them close. She switched on a dressing table light.

'Golly, you're still dressed. Have you been on the tiles too?'

Trix yawned and grinned like an urchin. She wore a short dress of bright green taffeta, a black velvet ribbon trailed from her hair. Her face was pale with tiredness.

Philippa swallowed.

'I came into your room for some grips. I found this.'

Trix glanced at the hotel bill in her sister's hand and made a giggling face.

'Naughty. You shouldn't peek. I know I shouldn't keep things like that, but they do make me laugh sometimes.'

'*Barny Duval.*'

'Oh lor, are you shocked? I've often wondered if I should tell you and Elaine about my odd affairs, but you're both so funny if I mention sex. Are you upset? Honestly, Flip, it isn't important. Lots of girls now –'

'You mean you've done it before?'

'Now you never thought that Yank was my first? I only met him the other night by chance. He came around looking for you and found me instead. He's not bad, is he?'

Philippa ran out of the room to the bathroom and was violently sick.

Trix was surprised when her sister did not appear the next morning. She tapped on Philippa's door and called, but there was no reply. Standing outside the door, Trix wrinkled her short nose. She can't be putting on an act because of what I told her last night, she thought, that really is stoopid. Is she so prim? What an old stick-in-the-mud. Sex is going to rear its ugly head eventually, even with Flip. Why does she take my goings-on so seriously? I don't.

When she trailed downstairs in her dressing-gown, even Trix did not dare to appear in transparent chiffon with *Toi et Moi* embroidered on the naked bosom in front of Miggs, she told the old nurse about Philippa.

Miggs hobbled upstairs and banged loudly.

'Breakfast, lady! You overslept?'

A hoarse voice replied. Philippa said she was ill and would Miggs telephone to tell Mrs Alwynne she wouldn't be coming in to work.

'That's all very fine and large but what's wrong with you? If you're ill, I'll fetch the doctor,' shouted Miggs, offended at the locked door.

Trix went into the morning room, drank some black coffee, she was uninterested in food, and telephoned a girlfriend about the day's entertainment. After another good natured call through her sister's door, she went to bath and dress and left, en route for Harrods.

Miggs donned her white overall, answered the door and the telephone, and took up some tea which she put outside Philippa's door. 'Tea, lady.' The door stayed shut.

Returning to the kitchen and the company of the ginger cat, Miggs stood reflecting for a moment. Then she went to Theo's study. He was reading his morning mail.

'Want a word, Doctor.'

For one alarmed moment he thought she had decided to leave him and join the evacuees in the country. He had changed his mind about her going and had realized how much he relied on her. Then, with sharper alarm from his old childish love for her, he thought she might be ill. But she was her usual solid, if crooked-shaped, self.

'Trouble,' she said.

Relief made him angry.

'What are you talking about?'

'Your daughter's in some kind of pickle. She's locked herself in her room and won't come out.'

'Don't bother me, Miggs. Miss Beatrix is a silly child.'

'*She's* all right. Who's talkin' about her? Miss Philippa's the one.'

He looked astounded. 'Miss Philippa? Is she ill?'

He got to his feet.

'Perfectly all right when she came home last night. It's my guess she isn't ill at all. She's troubled.'

He sat down again, saying with asperity that Philippa was a grown woman and wouldn't thank him to interfere with her private business. It was some young man, no doubt.

'No doubt,' echoed Miggs, giving him a sharp look that Theo had seen when he was ten years old. She realized he was out of his depth. He gave orders and snapped people's heads off, and when the fancy took him he was very pleasant, but the only troubles *he* understood were those he diagnosed. He tapped a patient's chest or looked at the whites of his eyes. He took the pulse and blood pressure, and he asked, 'Where exactly is the pain?' Miggs wondered where exactly Philippa's pain was. She knew there must be one.

'Thought you ought to know,' she said, and left him.

Later that day there was another tap on Philippa's door, a brisk rat-tat-tat.

Philippa was worn out with thinking and sick of the room in which she had imprisoned herself but she still cried hoarsely,

'Miggs, go away.'

'It isn't Miggs. It's Elaine.'

Astonishment made Philippa unlock the door. Elaine, still wearing her camel hair coat with the collar turned up, did not wait to be asked in, but advanced slowly, shutting the door behind her. She took off her coat and sat down.

'Miggs rang Shelton. She said you're in trouble.'

'Why can't she mind her own business?'

'You locking yourself in is her business. And stop prowling about like an animal in a cage. Are you pregnant?'

'What the hell are you talking about?'

'I take it you are not. Then has somebody you love been killed?'

The questions disgusted Philippa.

'It's nothing like that. Nothing like that.'

Elaine examined her sister, whose crumpled clothes, ashen face and manner made her look slightly mad.

'I shan't go until you tell me.'

'It won't do any good.'

Elaine was silent. She saw that Philippa was trying to get the courage to speak. At last Philippa said, speaking fast, 'I went into Trix's room to look for some hairgrips. I found a hotel bill.'

'And?'

'There's a man I know. In the Eagle Squadron. I don't know why I didn't introduce you to him. I suppose I wanted to keep it a secret – being fond of him, I mean. He – he came here looking for me when I was at Shelton. Trix was here instead. She went out with him.'

She was too desolate to hear her sister's unsurprised sigh.

'What you mean is that she went to bed with him.'

Philippa shuddered and said nothing. Elaine leaned back in the chair. She felt tired. How often she had wondered about Trix since the time Miles put the idea into her head. 'I'm not at all sure I approve of your young sister,' he said. Later he spelled it out. Elaine had loyally denied it, but the words had stuck.

'We must talk to her,' she said at last.

'I couldn't bear to.'

'Somebody must. Does she know you're in love with this man?'

'Who said anything about – '

Elaine interrupted with exasperation. 'Of course you are, it's written all over you. Why else are you in this state? I'm sure it's been a horrible shock. But Flip – think! You must see it is not Trix's fault. She didn't know how you felt about him. How could she? Certainly it's her fault if she goes to bed with men. I only hope to God that Father doesn't find out.'

'You're very broad-minded all of a sudden.'

'Of course I am not. I am just facing unpleasant facts. How do you feel about him now?'

'I never want to see him again.'

I don't expect, thought Elaine, when he knows what has happened he will want to see you. In her mind she saw the American arriving here at the house, hoping to see Philippa. Whom did he find instead? A girl modelled on Hollywood, a fair-haired mantrap. Elaine saw that Trix could be irresistible if she set her mind to it.

'I must talk to Trix. Where is she?'

'How should I know?'

'Oh, stop being so *rude*. I came to London to help and that's what I intend to do, so just stop trying to make things worse. Miggs will know where Trix is, she always does. I shall see Trix and hear the whole story. I won't have you two becoming enemies. I refuse to allow it. You'll have to find a way of forgiving her, Philippa, and you must remember that she had no idea in the world how you felt.'

'I suppose she sleeps with everybody.'

'Perhaps she does,' said Elaine with a cold dryness like her father's. 'In which case it's time I knew about it. Apparently it's up to me to do our mother's job.'

She walked out.

She had an effect on Philippa, who washed her face, changed her clothes, and telephoned Jane Alwynne to say she would be at work the next day.

It was true that Miggs always knew Trix's whereabouts. The girl amused her. Miggs saw Trix as the *Belle Dame Sans Merci*, wreaking vengeance on the male sex. Trix's triumphs over men were also Miggs'. Pressed by Elaine, she said grudgingly that Trix would be staying at the Brevet Club off West Halkin Street and would be there 'sure as a gun' by six to change into her party dress. Trix was always at parties.

Elaine telephoned the Brevet, and was told that Miss Tyrrell was a member, and had booked there for tonight. Elaine then rang an uninterested Lady St Aird to say she would be back tomorrow, and would go direct to Blenheim Palace.

The Brevet Club was small and no place to be in a raid. It was a poky eighteenth century cottage that had once been occupied by ostlers. It stood in a cobbled mews. A similar house nearby had disappeared into rubble. There was a notice in the club's narrow entrance hall, 'Best Shelter is Knightsbridge Tube but you're welcome in our cellars. Bring your own blanket.'

The porter told Elaine that Miss Tyrrell was in and would she take the stairs? The lift was out of order for the duration.

Elaine found the door at the end of a narrow corridor and knocked.

'It's Elaine.'

The door opened and Trix, exclaiming, 'Of all the!' put thin arms round her and gave her a scented kiss.

'How did you find me? I bet it was sneaky old Miggsy. Why are you in London? Oh jeepers. You've heard the ghoulish news.'

Guilty and grinning, Trix returned to her dressing table and began to brush her long hair.

'Wasn't it,' she said, 'the damnedest luck?'

'*Trix.* I have not come from Oxford, leaving my job when they needed me, to have a jolly chat about luck. Do you sleep with all your boyfriends? Is that how you usually end the evening?'

Trix made a moue, turning her red lips into a kind of trumpet.

'I wish you wouldn't carry on as if I were the whore of Babylon.'

'Answer my question.'

'Okay, okay. Yes, I've slept with a few guys. You're going to say since when? Since three years ago, as it happens. So it's nothing very dramatic or new, is it?'

'*You were fifteen.*'

'No, I wasn't, it was my sixteenth birthday.'

Now that she was launched on the story, Trix thought she might as well tell it in full. Did Elaine remember all three of them being asked to a party at a house in Bray? A kind of birthday party for Trix, but the people were mostly friends of the parents, most of them quite old. There had been a solicitor. Trix couldn't remember his name. Skipton? Skeffington? He'd made a pass at her and wanted to dance with her all the evening, he had been jolly boring and she had cold-shouldered him. Well, that night very late he'd come into her room. It had not occurred to her to lock her door. She had been quite scared at first because he was so big and so drunk, and he'd caught hold of her and slobbered all over her and ugh! given her great wet kisses and he kept saying 'was that nice?'. When she tried to get away he hit her. She thought of screaming, but he put his hand over her mouth, and then she thought of jumping out of the window, but it was on the second floor and too high, and there was a stone terrace underneath, 'not even a rose bed to fall into'. In the end he'd sort of shoved her on to the bed and was on top of her and before she knew what was happening 'he'd done it.'

'But that is rape.' Elaine was cold with horror.

Trix gave her a candid look.

'No, I can't pretend it was, darling. I thought it disgusting, him grunting and heaving away, and then I began to think it was rather interesting. And I realized that with somebody I liked, someone young, you know, I was definitely going to enjoy it. Poor old thing, he was pathetic next day. And he gave me twenty pounds to buy myself something. After that, of course, there were others. I mean to say, why not? I was quite in love with Alastair. And my New Zealander was wizard. And Canadian Dave, oh, and some others. You mustn't think I let them do it all the time. Only when I like them. Love them, sort of. I know you and Flip think I'm dreadful and I'm sure Flip is a virgin, but I am not dreadful and lots of girls do the same. It's what happens now.'

Elaine said nothing. She was thinking of the middle-aged solicitor coming into her sixteen-year-old sister's bedroom and hitting her and 'heaving away'. What a description for love. The old virtues were falling into rubble too. Men soon to go into danger wanted to make love before the journey. Why shouldn't they take what Trix cheerfully gave away, getting in return the scent and meals and dances and £10 notes?

Trix was looking at her warily, waiting for the row. It then began to occur to her that there wasn't going to be one. She had been right to confess. And it was going to save an awful lot of boring old lies.

'You know I think it is very wrong what you are doing.'

'Sorry.'

'Don't be impertinent. You are not sorry. But there is nothing to be done about you. The harm is done.'

Trix's gardenia cheeks suddenly turned crimson.

'For crying out loud! You talk in a holy voice as if I were a fallen woman. I *knew* you would. I just wish you could hear yourself. What's so terrible about a bit of sex with someone you like? What harm, as you call it, does it do? It's good for the man and for me too. All my girlfriends do it.'

Elaine felt that Trix on morality was more than she could stand. She said coldly that they had talked about it enough. What Trix did was wrong and there was an end to it.

Trix furiously shrugged. She was not used to being told off. Her diet was thick sweet slices of sexual admiration. She began to brush her hair again.

'It wasn't my fault about Barny Duval,' she resumed in a sulky voice. 'You have to admit that. Flip never breathed a word that she knew anyone in the Eagles. He turned up one evening looking for her while she was with you. I didn't know he was anybody special. He just said she was a swell girl, and they'd met on the night of the fire. He hung about, and I gave him what was left of the sherry. Then he asked if I'd like to go for a drive, he'd got hold of a car and some petrol. So off we went. We drove to the country and had supper in a pub – '

She shrugged.

'You know how it is.'

'No, Trix. I don't.'

Trix threw her eyes heavenwards. She had always known that if ever her sisters found out about her sexual adventures they would disapprove and be pious and Victorian. It annoyed her. She found to her surprise that she disliked losing their good opinion. If only Flip had not seen that Yank first. Or if only, more to the point, poor virgin Flip was not so sentimental.

'So we made love. Of course we did. He's a pilot isn't he? He flew over France this week and almost bought it. He had *twelve* Messerschmitts on his tail. Poor Barny,' she said, smiling slightly, 'I don't like him more than other men. He's a bit slow tempo'd for me. Sort of drawling. Only sharpens up when he talks about flying. Do you want me to tell him I won't see him again?'

She looked expectant, anxious to do her good deed.

'No. If he rings simply say you have another date and don't mention Flip.'

'Okay. I bet she never speaks to me again,' she added, sounding like a child.

Elaine could not help marvelling. Everything that Trix believed was anathema to herself and Philippa, just as everything *they* believed she was sure Trix despised and pitied. All they had in common was the Tyrrell nose, a streak of impulsiveness from their father, the past, their parents. When she said goodbye Trix suddenly said,

'Swell of you, coming to town specially.'

While she was waiting for a bus at Knightsbridge, Elaine thought about her sister's life of casual sex with men who were almost strangers. She saw that Trix, who did nothing for the war except embrace its soldiers, had a curious quality of being part of everything that happened. She belonged to this war, moving confidently through the dark days and fiery nights. And she belonged to the men who were fighting. They were not like those chaste admirers who used to take Philippa and herself to Hurlingham. They were lovers. It is Flip and I who are out of date, she thought.

She found Philippa in the kitchen, stirring something in a saucepan, the two crescents of dark hair falling down and concealing her face. She did not look up.

'I saw Trix. She is very, very sorry for hurting you.'

No reply.

'Oh, stop doing that!' snapped Elaine, suddenly exhausted by both sisters. 'I was not supposed to take any leave. It was given to me as a big favour. You can at least be civilized enough to listen when I speak to you. I might tell you that nothing is worse than minding other people's business, it is boring and detestable. And don't say why do I do it. It's no pleasure to me. But Mother is dead.'

Philippa pushed aside the saucepan, and sat down at the kitchen table. The daylight was almost gone. The whitewashed walls, the grey of Philippa's sweater, the shine on Elaine's hair were fading.

'You think me unsympathetic. That isn't true. But,' said Elaine carefully, 'would it surprise you to know that he's by no means the first?'

'She said something about that. I wouldn't listen.'

'You should have. It has some comfort in it for you. It would be worse if she were in love with him. Don't shudder like that, Flip, we have to talk or it will go bad inside you. We're going to have to get used to Trix. She is not like us.'

'She's a tart.'

'What a word. She's eighteen and growing up at a time when nothing is as it was, and nobody believes the things *we* still believe. She's had a lot of lovers.'

'How revolting.'

'Why are you only against her? What about him?'

'It's Trix who catches people.'

'You used to laugh about that.'

Philippa looked down and the two crescents of her hair met across her face. When she glanced up again her face was so strained yet so expressionless that Elaine could have wept.

'I suppose I'll get over it eventually. At present I dread even looking at her. As for all that sleeping with men, I don't think it's right, I don't, I don't! Other girls have men wanting them in this war. They've kept their standards. Why can't she?'

Ah, thought Elaine. Now I understand.

She left St Helen's the following morning. As she was walking down the road she remembered something Miles had once said to her. 'Oh, you! You're the cement of the family.' The cement she'd been trying to spread was pathetically thin between the bricks. Was it any use at all?

While Elaine was on her way to Oxford, and Philippa at work, Trix was in her bedroom in the Brevet Club, drinking coffee and polishing her charm bracelet. She always took a duster wrapped in tissue paper in her suitcase for this purpose. She cleaned her bracelet daily, as a Guardsman did his buttons. The bracelet grew more crowded every week as, added to the gold pigs and horseshoes, the Eiffel Towers and Victorian seals, were buttons gallantly cut off their uniforms by Polish officers, New Zealanders, Frenchmen and Canadians. There was a pair of wings, and a naval crown with curved sails like the petals of an inverted tulip.

She stood up and twisted in front of the long mirror which was inside the old-fashioned wardrobe door. She straightened her stocking seams, added Vaseline to her dark lipstick. Her movements were leisurely but not her thoughts. Jingling and jangling

106

down the stairs, she liked her noisy bracelet, she went to the telephone in the passage and dialled a number. While she waited, she examined the toe of her cyclamen coloured wedge shoe.

'Mrs Mason? It's Trix. You very sweetly said that while Zena's on leave I could stay. Could I really? Today? That's lovely.'

Trix returned to St Helen's, packed a suitcase, gave her address and telephone number to Miggs, and said she'd be away some time.

'The Masons, eh? They're made of money,' said Miggs, approving.

The house had not felt exactly welcoming to Trix, particularly when she went past Philippa's bedroom. It was only when she was in the taxi and it had left d'Abernon Road and turned into Kensington High Street that she began to sing.

> If I only had wings
> One little pair of those elusive things
> All day long I'd be in the sky
> up on high
> Talking to the birdies who pass me by
> How the fellows would stare
> To see me zooming past them in the air . . .

The driver caught her eye in his driving mirror, 'Very nice, Miss. Going to sing for us on the wireless?'

Trix smiled prettily and finished her song,

> I'd be so careless and bold
> That when the story of my deeds was told
> I'd get my picture in the papers
> And it would proudly say
> The RAF and me had had another good day.

Philippa found a letter on her dressing table when she returned from work. The sight of Trix's bold illiterate handwriting made her feel slightly ill. The letter was brief.

Gone to the Masons for a bit, Zena's back and there'll be
parties. Anyway, you want a rest from me being around. It's
rotten and I'm ever so sorry. I do feel ropey about it. Luv – I
mean it –

Trix

It hadn't occurred to Philippa that her sister would swiftly
remove herself from trouble. At first all she felt was relief. She
had been dreading even seeing Trix, and as for hearing her speak
of Barny, it made her want to be sick. But when the relief wore
off, she felt dully resentful. The person who was tactfully absent
somehow put herself in the right. It was the one who stayed
behind who was left to wallow. Philippa hadn't suffered from real
jealousy before, she had no idea what a degrading experience it
was. And it was all the worse because she had been dotingly fond
of Trix, proud of her beauty and her conquests; now she saw her
only in the lurid light of hideous imagining. She saw Trix and
Barny naked together and it made her ill. When she managed to
conquer thoughts which resembled a Victorian engraving of hell,
she was jealous of less unforgivable things; of the hours they had
been together; of Barny looking with frank admiration at her
little sister, the sexy one; of Trix laughing and alluring. She
thought of the food they had eaten and the flirtation starting as
gradually as gentle music, leading at last to the right true end.

Miggs saw that Philippa was silent and self-absorbed, but she
did nothing about it. If Miss Elaine couldn't fix things up, she
certainly couldn't. Philippa looked peaky but she'd recover. She
was young. Miggs was more concerned with today's question –
would the cat eat whale meat?

Philippa made no effort to get over her masochistic jealousy.
Elaine would have done so and even Trix, supposing she were in
a situation where another woman supplanted her, would have
refused to brood. Philippa let herself suffer. She worked exag-
geratedly hard for Jane Alwynne, who merely egged her on.

In the past months, like thousands upon thousands of Londoners, Philippa had learned to sleep through the thump and
thunder of the blitz. People who had never lived through
bombardments had no idea how soundly one could sleep. But
now misery, not fear, kept her awake. The blitz was a background, like the roar of rough seas to a sailor. One night she
scarcely slept at all and when she finally dozed she woke feeling

108

very cold from having unconsciously thrown off a blanket. Her father was standing by the billiard table.

'I am sorry to wake you, Philippa.'

She sat up, yawning, and asked if the All Clear had gone. He said that it had. He had been in Shepherd's Bush where another pub, the third, had been hit. She realized through the haze of sleep that he had come in to tell her something. At this hour? She crawled out from under the table and pulled on her dressing-gown. She saw by the wall clock that it was half past five.

'Yes, Father?' She was awake enough to give her voice a note of resentment.

'When I got back to hospital there was a man in Casualty from the Welsh Guards. He said the Café de Paris has had a direct hit.'

'Oh God!'

'Does Beatrix go there?'

'Often. Oh God! What shall we do?'

She had begun to tremble. He put down his bag and calmly asked where Trix was staying. Philippa went into the hall and found the telephone pad. Her father took it from her shaking hand.

'She's with the Masons,' she said.

He dialled the number.

'Mr Mason? I do apologize for this early call but – yes – the Café de Paris. I see . . . yes . . . thank you.'

He replaced the telephone.

'Beatrix and her friends returned home an hour ago. They had booked a table at the Café de Paris. But changed their minds at the last minute and went elsewhere.'

He looked suddenly quite old.

'I must get to my bed. Tell Miggs to put off any patients until this afternoon.'

Philippa trailed back to the billiard room and lay down. For a few minutes she had believed Trix was dead, and that *she* had killed her. She had not forced her sister to go away, for when was Trix not out enjoying herself? What had made Philippa believe she'd caused Trix's death had been her own jealous hatred which had released the devil from the abyss. But Trix was alive. It was the hatred which was dead.

When she arrived at the office that morning she saw that Jane

Alwynne had been crying. Two of her friends had been at the Café de Paris, young Guards officers, both dead. Her niece had had all her fingers blown off. During the day Jane spoke again about the tragedy. Everybody she knew seemed to have had somebody killed or wounded there. The loss of life had been terrible for the place was packed with dancers. Only one girl at the party of Jane's friends had survived. She had been on the dance floor when the bomb burst, had been hurled across the room, her dress torn off, her hair burned, but she was completely unhurt. Blast was like destiny. It was inexplicable.

It was spring now, the daylight clear and pale, and that evening, saddened and subdued, Philippa walked home down d'Abernon Road. She felt worn out from lack of sleep. She stopped and looked over the gate of an old house. It was roofless now, but friends of the family's had lived there before the war. Children had played among the shrubs, and there had been a swing under the pear tree. Now the garden was going wild and branches were interlacing. By summer it would be a small jungle. On the unkempt lawn, she saw a patch of mauve crocuses. She trailed through the open gate of St Helen's. A figure in Air Force blue was sitting on the front steps. It was Barny.

Chapter Eight

He stood up and gave a mocking salute, his cap at a rakish angle. She thought she was going to faint. She felt giddy, as if she were falling. Before she had taken a few steps he had hurried to her and seized her hands.

'Good to see you! I wasn't sure which of you girls I'd find. I daresay Trix told you we met up when you were out of town. It's so good to see you,' he repeated, gripping her hands and smiling like a boy. She had no time to recover but managed to mutter something about being surprised. He walked up the steps with her to the front door. Still talking, he accompanied her into the hall.

'I've gotten a forty-eight hour pass, I wasn't expecting it, on my honour, that's why I didn't call you first. How've you been? Ages since I saw you.'

'January.'

'As long as that? I suppose it must be. A lot has happened since then. I'll tell you about it, but how are *you?*'

He squeezed her arm.

They went into the drawing room. With Elaine away, it had returned to its wartime state, the dust was thick on the furniture. Some flowers given to Trix weeks ago were still there, roses in a bone-dry vase. Their heads had dropped off, they were mummified.

'Sit down, Barny. I'll see if I can find anything to drink.'

'How about English tea?'

He leaned comfortably back against the sofa cushions.

Escaping into the kitchen, Philippa put on the kettle, thinking desperately – I wish he'd go. I wish he'd go. I can't cope with this farce. Shall I make him go?

The American voice called, 'Can I help?'

When she returned, carrying the tray, he sprang up and exclaimed that she should not wait on him, it was not the way things should be. Back home his sister would be shocked to her soul. He took the tray and put it carefully down in front of her.

She poured tea and he talked about the Squadron being operational at last. Did she know? Wasn't it wizard? They were fighting the real war now. Recently they'd had their first scramble across the Channel towards Calais. It had been strange. There was the sea . . . and suddenly they were over France. But then a Messerschmitt 109 had come towards him and in a moment the sky had just been full of them. 'I had my hands full before I made it for home. I knew then just how green I was.'

He talked on, of his own inexperience and that of the Squadron. It showed up that first time. They'd been lucky to stay alive. Battles taught you something you could learn no other way. Then he said that two months before, while they were still training, one of his friends was killed in a crash. The weather had been dreadful. 'The sky became filthy grey in a few minutes, the clouds came up so thick!' His friend, he said, flying at 20,000 feet had gone into a steep dive. Barny and the others on the training flight had followed him, shouting over the radio transmitter, telling him to pull out.

'He couldn't. Perhaps he fainted or his oxygen failed. We saw him crash. Later we found out what had happened. His plane had gone into coarse pitch.'

'What does that mean?'

'The engine's out of control. You can't get her back again.'

She nodded. She didn't understand, but she understood very well. She wondered if that was what had happened to her. My heart's in coarse pitch, she thought.

He changed the conversation, as if guilty at asking for sympathy, and told her that now the Squadron was on ops, all the letters from home were 'full of hero rot. How we hate it!' Did Flip know that Hollywood was making a movie called *Eagle Squadron*? Could you beat it?

When he passed his cup, he put out his other hand and touched her.

'You look very beautiful. But very pale, honey. Your skin's honey-coloured. It's got just the same golden look of the blossom honey we eat at home. Blossom honey. That's you.'

She put down her cup and it rattled in the saucer.

'Barny. I must say something. Don't interrupt, please, just let me get it over.'

He raised his eyebrows and made a comic face. But Philippa did not look at him.

'What I want to say is this. I know about you and Trix.'

He started.

'Don't say anything yet,' she hurried on. 'Trix did not tell me. I found out by chance. I know it's no business of mine about my sister and you. But I can't pretend I haven't found out, or that it hasn't made me feel different. I can't be your friend any more.'

'How in hell –'

'I told you. By chance. Unlucky chance, you'd say, and I suppose Trix would too. But there it is.'

'She told you.'

'*She did not*. If you must know, and I don't understand why you do, I found the hotel bill in her drawer. It sounds like a vulgar divorce, doesn't it? When I told her she admitted about you and her. She would never have told me otherwise.'

He was horrified. He stood up and went over to the window, standing with his back to her. She wondered with dull curiosity what he would say next. She thought how beautiful his figure was silhouetted against the spring light. She imagined what it would feel like to stand close behind him and wind her arms round his waist.

He turned.

'Is your sister here now?'

'She's gone away.'

'Because of me.'

'I suppose so.'

'What did she say about me?'

Philippa blushed and burst out, 'What did you expect her to say? That you're marvellous in bed? I can't bear any more of this. What do I care if you made love to her? It's nothing, nothing, nothing to do with me except that I won't see you any more. I suppose you're in love with her like everybody else. I just don't want anything to do with it.'

She began to run out of the room but he followed her, caught hold of her and pulled her roughly into his arms. He began to kiss her savagely, forcing open her mouth, putting his tongue between her teeth, pressing himself against her and thrusting forward. Sobbing, she fought him. It was like being raped.

'Don't, don't! You don't care for me, it's horrible of you –' she gasped, and was once again enveloped in the fierce open-mouthed kiss. Bending back somehow she gasped, 'Leave me alone. You're hateful. Hateful.'

She only managed to escape because he suddenly let go of her. She rushed out of the room, leaving the door open. He heard her running up the stairs.

He remained in the empty room, breathing fast. Then, with a fierce grimace, he picked up his cap and left the house.

She did not know what to make of her own feelings. She was disgusted at his taking her in his arms against her will. She remembered how she had fought him. It was indecent of him to embrace her after being Trix's lover. But although she felt a revulsion at his treatment, his brutal treatment, a part of her was excited by it. He wanted her still, in spite of the infinitely more desirable Trix.

The next day while she worked at Chicheley Buildings, staying as late as she dared, she kept wondering what would happen next. He would find out where Trix had gone. They would go to bed again. Apparently everybody who had Trix could have her again. Philippa supposed Barny would find Trix through Miggs.

She tried to envisage a time when Barny would be one of Trix's regular beaux, as she called them. He would appear when he was on leave, take Trix out, and finish in her arms. Suppose Barny were killed? Would Trix grieve much? The thoughts hurt so that she shook her head to and fro as if to get rid of them.

She felt wicked, though, to remember that she must have wounded him yesterday. How shocked and upset he had looked. He was a hero and she had been cruel to him and even now, as she walked slowly home in the rain, he might be over France – or wounded – or dead. How dared she think that her miserable little life was so important? But it was all she had. She had fallen romantically in love with him, and what he had wanted was sex. Trix had given him that. Philippa no longer hated her sister, but she still felt as if she had been very ill and was a long way from getting better.

She turned in at St Helen's gate.

The RAF figure was there again.

She stood rooted to the ground. He did not wave but came down the short drive fast. He said harshly, 'I want to talk to you.'

'Why did you sit on the step?' she absurdly asked.

'Mrs Miggs asked me in, but I wasn't sure you'd want me in the house. So I waited.'

She did not want him in the house and found no way of saying so. Five minutes ago she had thought he was over France – forgetting he was still on leave.

Nobody had been into the drawing room since they had left it the previous evening. The cushions were still squashed where Barny had sat. There was a cigarette end in the ashtray. She shook up the cushions as if to get rid of yesterday. Not asking him to sit down, she faced him, like a cat facing a dog.

'Yes?'

'How hard you look. You aren't, though.'

'What do you want to say? We said it all.'

'You did. I certainly didn't.'

He sat down, although she had not asked him to do so, squashing the cushions she had fussily shaken up. He lay back too far, as if trying to seem relaxed. But his olive skinned face was nothing of the kind. He looked unfamiliar because he did not look easy but drawn and tired. She had to harden her heart against that.

'Listen, Flip. And if you hate me after what I'm going to say, okay then you do and I'll have to put up with it. You said yesterday that I must be in love with your sister. I am not and never could be. Sure, she's glamorous and there isn't a guy in the country who wouldn't be proud to take her around. She's fun. And she's fun in bed too,' he added, staring at her fixedly, 'I can't say she isn't, though I wish in hell you hadn't found out. Do you know whom I'm afraid I *do* start to love? You, for God's sake. You said No to me when we first met, remember? I wanted us to make love but you didn't want me, something like that. I thought – hell, I'm not hanging around if there's nothing doing there. I daresay that sounds filthy but it's the truth. Guys feel like that. My sort, anyway. But then I wanted to see you again although you'd refused to let me love you. I came round here, and I found Trix. Can you blame me? Bud had been killed and I was shocked and unhappy, I guess, and she was good to be with. We got on fine. What we did that night was fine too for both of us, but no more than that. You don't understand any of it, do you?'

'No.'

'I didn't think you would. I don't blame you. But will you see me again? The Trix thing is over. It never started, except that one time. See me again, Flip.'

115

'I don't want to,' she said and began to cry.

He did not touch or go near her but stood up, looking at her in silence with his tired face. He pushed back his hair and said, 'I'll call you.' He walked out without looking back.

She did not go to the window or hear the door close. She sat down on the cushions as if taking possession of his warmth and his body. Leaning back, she closed her eyes.

In the days that followed she thought of him while she worked and travelled and fire-watched on St Helen's roof, with the sky crimson in the distance. Once she was in a daylight raid – it was early evening and the whole heavens seemed to roar with aircraft. Philippa ran into the garden to watch the waves of raiders coming over. Guns were roaring and as she stared up for a glimpse of English fighter planes she suddenly saw what appeared to be four enormous German bombers diving straight for the house. She fled indoors and down to the basement with Miggs. But the bombs that followed were a mile away.

She could not understand why she was no longer afraid for Barny. She had a certainty that she would see him again. Perhaps people in danger had meaningless superstitions and beliefs. She did.

Trix rang Miggs to say she would not be back for another week.

'Your sister,' Miggs told Philippa, 'is having a rare old time.'

'Good,' said Philippa, almost meaning it.

What she waited for happened. Barny telephoned her.

'I'm in town. You alone?'

'Yes, but – '

'Trix back yet?'

'No,' she said, deeply shocked at his mentioning her.

'Better if she isn't. Can I come round now?'

'I'm not sure.'

'See you in half an hour.'

She would not receive him again in a dirty room and hurriedly cleaned it before going to wash and change. With Trix away, Philippa's make-up had run out. She had no lipstick left and almost no face powder. She brushed her hair, looked at her face and remembered her mother's phrase. 'You look dingy.' I don't care. That's what I feel.

She heard the bell and ran to the top of the stairs, but Miggs was already in the hall, wearing her creaking white overall.

'I'll answer it. It's for me,' gabbled Philippa.

Giving her a look of sharp curiosity, Miggs disappeared.

Barny said, 'Hi,' easily enough, but they went in silence into the drawing room. It smelled clean. One of the windows was open and a bush of flowering currant, budding outside, sent in a smell of early summer. Philippa asked him calmly to sit down. She was slightly trembling.

'I keep turning up,' he said, taking his usual place and giving an automatic smile. He stretched out his long legs and looked at his black RAF shoes. They were dusty.

'How did you manage to get leave again so soon?'

'I haven't. I hopped on a lorry and must hop back in an hour or so. We're not supposed to play hooky but I'm not on call tonight. I wish,' he added without moving, 'you wouldn't look that way.'

'I wasn't aware of looking any particular way.'

'But you do. As if somebody had knocked you down. Hell, I suppose it was me. Don't you love me any more?'

The question made her desperate.

'I never said I loved you.'

'Oh, but you did. With your eyes. And the way you kiss. I suppose I can't kiss you, can I? I've only got an hour.'

'I'd rather you didn't,' she said, and stood up as if expecting him to go. But he got up and came to her and began to kiss her, passionately, differently, gently, strongly, holding her against him so that every part of their bodies touched. Moving away after what seemed a long time, Philippa said in a broken voice;

'Do you still want me? Then the answer's yes.'

What is the use of virginity, she thought, I could keep it and Barny might die. Better, oh so much better, to love him now.

He did not answer, but went on kissing her, breaking off to mutter indistinguishable words. After a while he picked her up and carried her to the sofa where they fell rather than sat.

Lying on the cushions she thought – will it be now? She wanted it to be now. But all he did was go on kissing her, hold her breasts, rub his cheek against hers so hard that his face scratched hers. Then he sat up and looked at his watch.

'Christ. I must go. Well . . . do you love me, then? I have a funny feeling that you do. What shall we do about it? I know what I want to do. Make love to you until we drop dead.'

117

'So do I.'

He wiped his hand over his face.

'Yeah. But we're not going to. What am I doing, feeling this way? I always said falling in love was for the other guy. I know I slept with that sister of yours. Don't look so frightened, I am not going to hurt you, I swear it. But I'd come to find *you*, and you were off God knows where and I hadn't heard a word.'

'But I wrote to you! I thought you didn't want to see me because you never answered.'

'I didn't get the letter. Hell. So what next? I'm not going to make love to you, Flip, though you so beautifully said . . . not to a girl like you. There's only one thing for it. We must get married.'

When he had gone and she was free of his physical presence, no longer the slave of her own helpless body, she knew the idea was mad. You couldn't marry a stranger. It was wrong. It was miraculous. She looked at the prospect, trying to grasp it. Barny, husband, lover, next of kin. Would he have asked her if she had gone to bed with him that night at the Wings Club? Or if she had not found out about Trix? She could remember nothing of what they had said after the extraordinary 'we must get married'. All she recalled was a haze in Barny's arms while she felt she would die of desire. What would become of her if she did marry him? Hopeless to ask the question. To try and use her head even now felt like coming into a room where a raving lunatic sat in a corner. You sat down very calmly and you took the madwoman's hand and you said, 'Let us be logical. Let us be practical'. All the poor lunatic could do was laugh and babble.

The moment that he had asked her to marry him, she had started so violently that he burst out laughing.

'Is the idea so terrible?' he said. Was it any different from an Englishman asking her?

'You might say we are made for each other or some damn thing.' He told her that marrying a pilot would take guts. And the other way round, because it took guts for a pilot to marry. Many of them wouldn't. In the RAF he'd heard pilots say it wasn't fair on the girl. Flyers buy it sooner or later, and then the girl would be a widow. Why store up misery for her in the future? But he was not one of those. He wanted her for keeps. Even if the keeps was to be short, it was all that they'd got.

Before he left, he told her she must break the news to her family.

'And that is going to take guts too.'

It was never wise to speak about anything but the weather and last night's blitz to her father during breakfast. Silence was the best way to escape a glare over the top of *The Times*. But Philippa had never been a diplomat. She had the Tyrrell impulsiveness more than any of the three girls. During the meal she was too excited to eat, and waited for the non-existent right moment. She chose a time when Miggs was pouring the tea – Miggs might give her some moral support.

'Pa. Sorry, Father. I hope you'll be pleased,' she began idiotically, 'I am engaged to be married.'

Theo, who had been turning the pages of the newspaper, put it slowly down.

Miggs became frozen with interest.

'What did you say?'

'I'm engaged.'

A pause.

Her father said contemptuously, 'What tosh is this? And who is the man, pray?'

'You've met him. Months ago,' said Philippa. Her father looked pinched as well as angry; and why was he so thin?

'His name is Barny Duval. He is in the Eagle Squadron. He is an American,' finished Philippa bravely.

'An American?'

'Yes, Father.'

He seemed at a loss for words. 'Who knows about this? Your sister?' he finally said, meaning Elaine.

'No. I wanted to tell you first. Barny is very anxious to meet all the family. He did catch a glimpse of you on the night of the fire. But of course you don't know each other yet.'

He glared at her and Philippa added with more sang-froid than usual, 'He is looking forward to meeting you, Father.'

Ah, thought Miggs, a bit of gumption at last.

'This is no time to discuss the matter,' said Theo, with a haughty look at Miggs, as if she could be kept out of any family row. 'Come to my study later and explain yourself. I will make

119

one thing clear. I will not allow this marriage to an *American*. Make up your mind to that.'

Philippa walked out. But only as far as the kitchen where she sat by the boiler. A moment later Miggs joined her.

'You're a sly one. I thought that young feller was one of Trix's hangers-on.'

Like a man who knows that if he doesn't jump the precipice he is doomed, Philippa went at it. 'He only took her out once because I wasn't here. You'll like him, Miggsy. You always said the RAF is marvellous.'

'Doesn't mean you've got to marry one, does it?'

'Yes, Miggsy. It does.'

'Really goin' to marry him, then?' said the old woman with her intense, interested curiosity, 'That's a turn up for the book. You were always reckless. Miss Elaine works things out and Trix knows where she's goin' too. But *you*. That hot head'll get you into hot water one of these days.'

Miggs chuckled at her own joke.

'The doctor's goin' to carry on somethin' chronic, we can make up our minds to that. Think we can persuade him to give you away?'

Blissful, excited, Philippa burst into all kinds of happy nonsense about love at first sight. Miggs listened and nodded and thought that if she did manage to throw a drop of cold water on the burning words it wouldn't do a bit of good. The fire would just go on, hotter than before. The girl looked as if she believed she could never be unhappy again. The very war seemed forgotten. Drenched with happiness, Philippa was like somebody hit by an enormous wave, lying on the sand ecstatically waiting for the next.

Miggs, making herself a fresh pot of tea, listened to the story. She noted it contained no more reference to Trix. Miggs admired Trix's success with men, but for once it looked as if Philippa had got what she wanted. Talk of engagement rings made it sound real. There was no point in recalling that Philippa's chap had cast a quick eye over Trix first.

Drinking her tea and listening to the romantic story, Miggs reflected that the girl had not changed since she was a child. This was the Philippa who had made passionate school friendships, written appalling poems which she used to read aloud to Miggs, who had been bored stiff. Philippa was the one who had given

Elaine for a wedding present the only good piece of jewellery that she owned, a ring of her mother's. The jewels, diamond, emerald, amethyst and ruby, spelled 'Dear'.

It was exactly like Philippa to fall into marriage with a foreign pilot she had clearly only met a few times. People didn't change.

'Tell you, somethin', lady. Your sister had best come to town. You'll never get to organize your own weddin', sure as a gun.'

Even Philippa saw the sense in that.

Before she left for work she telephoned Shelton. Lady St Aird was very cold. Yes, Elaine was here. She would get her. The moment she heard her sister's voice she poured out the news, punctuating the story with laughter and 'I'm so happy.' 'You won't disapprove, will you?' she added eagerly. Elaine laughed too. She did not say it was very sudden and certainly rash. She simply said how glad she was and that she looked forward to meeting Barny and of course would get some leave and help with the wedding.

'Will it be soon? He'll have to get compassionate leave.'

'He calls it passionate leave,' was the maundering reply.

Elaine let her talk on. When Philippa was beginning to run out of steam she asked the only question not tied with white ribbons.

'Flip. What about Trix? I gather she is still away. Would you like me to tell her?'

'Oh. Would you? And – and I'd be so glad if she'd come home.'

'You might like her to be bridesmaid,' said Elaine. She thought wryly what a dreadful suggestion she had made. What would Miles think? An American stranger would soon be walking up the aisle, having had one Tyrrell girl in his bed and about to have the second.

'Oh yes, she could, couldn't she?' came the dazed, happy and boring reply from London.

'One last thing, Flip. Don't let Pa upset you.'

So he could have done at any other time. Philippa loved her father, whom she had so often tried to approach, always failing. He awed her. But another male figure dominated her thoughts, a graceful, lounging, youthful figure. Another voice replaced her father's abrupt English syllables, with a drawl and an accent of unexpected elisions, 'gotta', 'kinda', 'helluva.'

Her father was sitting at the old-fashioned desk in his study, which since Philippa was a child had always been heaped with papers which never seemed to grow less. The room had its wartime changes. The strengthened metal sheet fixed to the ceiling, and a pile of government health leaflets in a clip. On the wall in a rectangular frame were three photographs of his daughters. Elaine, at fifteen, was at the top, dressed in tennis white, smiling. Below her in the centre was Philippa, at eleven, sitting in the garden swing, serious. At the bottom was Trix, seven years old and wearing gingham. She was looking down at the toy dog in her arms. The frame had been there so long that every one of Theo's patients knew it, and his daughters were so accustomed to it that they no longer noticed it was there. But Philippa looked at it now. She saw for the first time that it was a symbol of paternal love.

Sitting facing him, she looked at him with her candid eyes. He returned the glance stonily. His conscience lately had been rather like a subdued recurring toothache. There had been some trouble with the girls, God knows what it had all been about, he had preferred to avoid a scene, and had deliberately not enquired into it. When Miggs tried to tell him, he had shut her up. She had then, high-handedly he considered, sent for Elaine. His eldest daughter had not informed him what had happened, which had been a relief. She was the one to tackle such problems, after all, it was up to her to take Mary's place. He had presumed things were settled. It now occurred to him that Elaine must have come to London to try and prevent this harebrained marriage scheme.

'Well?' he said, swivelling round in his chair to face her, 'Try to tell me quietly what this is all about.'

She did try. She kept her voice as reasonable as she could manage, and with difficulty she avoided superlatives when mentioning Barny. She also attempted to make the decision to marry appear carefully thought out. Barny was writing to his sister and her husband, and so on. He had his pilot's pay, and his Squadron Commander had actually said that when Barny was married, Philippa would be allowed to live near the station. It was unusual, but permission had been given.

When she finished, Theo said, 'I'm afraid all this is out of the question. What do we know about this man? A foreigner. An American from God knows where.'

'Louisiana.'

He ignored that and went straight on.

'For all I know, he may have a wife in the United States. Things like that happen with men overseas. What you are suggesting is impossible. You are simply behaving like a young woman with a head full of nonsense. I refuse to give my consent.'

She was sorry for him, because he had used his authority.

'It's no good, Father. I don't want to cause you pain, and I know this will upset you, but Barny and I are going to be married. We really are.' She swallowed the words, 'And you can't stop us,' but they both heard it.

'I hope you will give me away on my wedding day.'

She went out of the room then without looking at him, sure that she had hurt him.

Trix had been the family pet for so long that finding herself cast in the role of villainness was very uncomfortable. She had pangs. Sometimes, remembering the look on Philippa's face, she felt quite miserable. It must be awful, she thought, to feel like that about a man. She never had. When Elaine telephoned from Shelton with the news, Trix was astounded and very amused. Wartime romance put everything right.

Unless she was pretty crazy about a man, which happened rarely, Trix soon forgot about the lovemaking. She had enjoyed her night of sex with Barny Duval, who had been energetic and enthusiastic and he'd had a lot of stamina she remembered with a grin, but he was definitely not very exciting. She vaguely recalled that he had woken her twice during the night for more. But she hadn't thought of that again and only about him because of Philippa. There were new men around who excited her far more.

What now filled her thoughts was the coming wedding. When Elaine had married in the winter of 1939 it had been unfashionable to wear white, it showed lack of patriotism. White satin and French champagne were definitely discouraged. Poor Elaine had worn a suit and carried some violets. It had all, thought Trix, been definitely dreary. But now it was not a question of patriotism but of practicality. Brides were delighted to wear white if they could borrow old wedding dresses preserved from before the war. Churches, of course, were boarded up. Confetti and rice were illegal. Trix considered the worst feature of wartime marriage parties was the cake. Iced wedding cakes were now banned and everybody getting married had elaborate cardboard covers looking like the three-tier traditional cake, covering whatever poor rationed sponge could be offered. Trix had attended a wedding the previous month where, surrounded by wine, whisky or gin, the cake had stood in its glory, decorated with artificial flowers. Then the cardboard cover was whisked off, and underneath was a poor eggless thing tasting like sawdust.

Flip, thought Trix, wasn't going to have anything so phoney. The thing to do was to beg, borrow or steal extra sugar. Always part of the present, Trix turned overnight from immoral sister staying away from home to kindly bridesmaid planning to help a wartime marriage in the family.

Returning to St Helen's the day after she had heard the news, Trix rushed into the house, found Philippa upstairs and flung her arms round her.

'Delightful! Delicious! D'lovely!' she exclaimed, quoting a song. 'I've got some wizzy ideas for your dress and what do you think? We can have a *real cake*. Mrs Mason gave me two pounds of granulated sugar. You put it through the mincer and behold – icing sugar.'

Philippa had dreaded actually seeing Trix. What she had not realised was that Barny's kisses had healed her and wiped the jealousy away.

Barny had a special licence; the marriage would be in the same church, St Barnabas, where Elaine and Miles had married two years ago. Trix was up until three in the morning, finishing a dress for Philippa. It was cream-coloured silk, and had a pocket cut out of a piece of mink in the shape of a heart.

'She's wearing her heart on her hip,' said Trix.

Elaine, on special leave and at home doing the arrangements, was almost awed by her younger sister. She isn't sorry in the least either about all the other lovers or about Barny, she thought. She is simply glad we know the worst. But she *is* sorry to have hurt Flip and is doing her best to show it. Wheedling sugar rations from friends and making clothes is Trix's best. She is like the tumbler who did back somersaults in church, thought Elaine. It was the only way he knew how to pray.

The first thing Miggs told Elaine when she arrived from Oxfordshire was that Theo was not only refusing to give the bride away, he was also not coming to the wedding. Yes, he had met Barny. A pleasant-enough young man. It did not make an iota of difference to his decision that the marriage was totally unsuitable, hurried, and something he considered wrong for his daughter. He would not attend.

Elaine went into his study. He looked up from his desk, but neither greeted nor spoke to her. He was grim. She bent forward calmly and kissed him. As always, his expression changed. Something in her soothed him.

'I've told Philippa that I will not sanction it.'

She made a noise of sympathy. He began to tell her what he must have said many times before, to friends, to Miggs, to poor Philippa. He would not have had moral support from Miggs. She was enjoying the drama.

'You had met Barny before, you know, Father,' Elaine said mildly. 'Didn't he help put out the fire months ago? And Philippa said you and he got on perfectly well when he came to see you. Were you unwelcoming?'

'I didn't put out the red carpet.'

'But you liked him?'

'I know nothing of Americans.'

'You soon will. Now, darling,' she said – it was a rare endearment to him – 'You must come to the wedding. You must give her away for everybody's sake. For ours. For Mother's. Even for your own.'

There was a long silence.

'I don't know how you have the gall,' he said.

Despite the dark church, the wedding was a cheerful affair. Four members of the Eagle Squadrom, rangy Americans with easy manners, were present. Marjorie Flower managed to get to London and brought her cousin, Miles' friend Dick Polglaze. The two French Λ's had not yet been sent abroad and they arrived with a remarkable amount of beer bottles. Annette Ghilain came too, looking very elegant. Elaine saw her father's face brighten when he spoke to the French girl.

Philippa looked quite beautiful in the creamy dress made for her by Trix, and a little wreath of yellow roses. During the ceremony she was so pale that Elaine thought at one moment she was going to faint. Trix looked like a bluebell, even to a hat made of petals. At the reception she was surrounded by men.

Barny was taking his bride to spend their first and only night's leave at the Savoy. They left St Helen's in a taxi. As Philippa leaned from the taxi window Trix sprinkled her hair with fragments of torn-up silver paper, and Philippa laughed and threw her bunch of roses to Trix, who neatly caught it.

'My third this year!' called Trix, 'I'm sure to be next.'

Chapter Nine

It was breathlessly hot that June. Trix sang to herself as she dressed to go out. She could not remember the last time she had been to Kew Gardens: probably not since Miggs took her in the bus when she was a child. They used to walk for miles, in what Miggs called bluebell time or lilac time. Miggs knew the names of every flower they saw.

Dick Polglaze had suggested he should take her there, and afterwards he'd drive her down to Wargrave to punt on the river. Goodness knows, thought Trix complacently, where the petrol was coming from.

The sun poured through her open windows and she fastened the shoulder buttons of a new white dress she had made from one of her mother's evening petticoats. It was very short, and had a blue silk sash. Her idea was to look about twelve.

She had first met Dick Polglaze at Philippa's wedding and had taken a fancy to him. But the Eagle Squadron had demanded her attention, and all four had declared that after the wedding she must come dancing with them. 'We will teach you to jitterbug. Know how? Good, we'll show you.' After Philippa and Barny had driven away, Trix, flushed with American compliments, had gone in search of Dick and found him in the dining room, quite alone and unselfconscious, sipping a final glass of champagne and looking at the garden.

'I'm being swooped away by the Eagles to the Dorchester. You come too.'

'Thanks, but I don't think I will.'

'Bother, you have another date. Cut it and come with us.'

'No date. Too much American competition.'

Trix pouted and looked at him languishly. But that did not work either. He bade her a smiling goodbye.

The Eagles all flew away after that. But Dick Polglaze wrote to her. He was at Greenock doing trials for a new ship, and he might be able to wangle some leave soon.

He telephoned her from Scotland, and Trix rearranged her

dates. She found that she liked him, although they had spoken so little at the wedding. It rather surprised her that she was looking forward to seeing him so much. The war had been on, it seemed to Trix, a very long time. Trix had been only sixteen when it began and when she had decided to be beautiful. From the moment she came out of her chrysalis she had collected men. She never expected not to be admired, given presents, telephoned, pursued, asked out and asked to bed. She did not necessarily say yes to the sexual invitation, and she had a rare talent for keeping as admirers the men she did not sleep with; she was so promising that perhaps they still hoped.

When her men went abroad, others appeared at once. Now Dick Polglaze had, as she put it, hove into view.

He was unlike other men she had known. To begin with he was short, scarcely five foot eight, and she liked her men to be tall, regarding it as a sort of compliment. He did not treat her seriously and she was accustomed to every man being at her mercy. He was teasing, highly-sexed, and tough. They went to bed after they had met once or twice. He had been lent a dilapidated flat over a gymnasium in Orchard Street. When they went up the stairs he remarked that if there was a blitz, they would not have a chance.

'Concrete is best,' he said, 'there's some stuff called vibrated concrete, whatever that is. Even your billiard table is all right. Sure you want to risk your lovely self in this rat-hole?'

'Certain,' said Trix blithely.

Up in the shabby flat they fell into bed. He was an exciting lover, quite silent, strong, and she sharply enjoyed him. He never said he loved her.

The omission piqued her. All her men declared their love, some in terms so extravagant that she smiled inwardly. When she thought about Dick, she was determined to make him fall in love with her. He ought to do so. Sometimes when she was in her room at St Helen's, she took off every stitch of clothing and dispassionately studied her naked figure. Her breasts were small and pointed, the nipples the colour of wild roses. Her waist was only twenty-two inch, her hips swelled out well and at the top of her long silky legs was a fuzz of hair a dark gingery gold. Really, she thought, looking critically at herself, I am not bad. Then, going close to the mirror, she stared at her nose, and turned sideways to catch a glimpse at her profile. Why didn't Dick say he loved her? Everybody else did.

Trix's taste in men until Dick came on to the scene had been predictable. She liked them big and tall, with heavy shoulders and what she called 'lovely muscles.' She preferred the sort of man who, like Rhett Butler, could pick her up as if she were a feather and rush upstairs to the bedroom to rape her. But it would not be rape with Trix. Dick was only an inch or so taller than she was, and although he was sturdy she very much doubted if he would make the stairs with her in his arms. More annoying still, he would not want to. She had an idea that he was not the man drawn to the big romantic gesture.

Elaine told her he was a friend of Miles' and that his parents lived in Cumberland and were quite rich.

When he was talking to her about his family once, he said vaguely that his father owned two companies in Lloyds.

'Lloyds of London? I saw a movie called that. Tyrone Power was in it.'

'Yes, featherhead. Lloyds of London. Nice work if you can get it but I am not at all sure it's my kind. However, not much point in bothering about that just now.'

'So your Pa is rich?'

'You could say that. Come and kiss me and stop asking silly questions.'

She liked Dick Polglaze. She even liked the fact that he was short. He was attractive. His looks were curious, he might have been an actor, his cheek bones were so high and his face was triangular. He had slanting eyes which were never serious. Very sexy, she thought his eyes were. His mouth was too thin, and when he set it in a certain way, she knew there was no point in wheedling. He was the first man to say No to her. She found that sexy too.

Sitting on bar stools at the Ritz – he liked expensive hotels – holding hands at the films – he liked funny ones – Trix learned more about him. His father was apparently a tycoon. His mother had been an actress but gave it up when she married. 'She was not very talented but had a pretty singing voice. My father was a sort of stage door Johnny really. He buzzed round backstage and asked her out. Rumour has it, I don't know if I believe the story, that he gave her some flowers with a diamond brooch popped inside.'

'Jolly romantic.'

'You don't think that at all. If it was your sister Philippa – well, yes. But there is not a romantic bone in your body, Trix Tyrrell.'

On the hot June morning she was ready long before he arrived. When she heard the bell, she tripped down the staircase to pose at the corner, her hand on the staircase nob, her head slightly on one side. Miggs opened the front door and Dick stood looking at her. With a sniff and 'leave it to you' Miggs disappeared through the kitchen door.

Dick grinned as he took Trix's hand.

'How glamorous you look.'

'Do I? Good. I've made us a picnic. Did you bring some drink.'

'Will champagne do?'

'Where *did* you get it? I won't ask.'

They went out into the blazing midday. A small car, a pre-war MG scarlet as a poppy, was at the gate. Dick settled her beside him, remarking that the way she did her hair was like Veronica Lake. 'But you're much prettier.' As they drove away through the deserted roads in the direction of Kew he asked her teasingly what she had been doing since he last saw her.

'Making the men suffer, I suppose.'

'Stoopid. I'm their ray of sunshine. Actually I was in bad with my father last night. Quite a row. I was so relieved when my date turned up to rescue me.'

'And what had you been doing? Unsettling the male patients? Any of them threatening suicide again?'

'All I did,' said Trix, opening her eyes wide, 'was to use some of my father's beastly gin. Well, it was the last drop in the bottle but honestly, so *little*.'

'My dear Trix, I had no idea you liked the stuff or I'd have – '

'Silly! It was to clean my diamond ring.'

His laugh was sudden, infectious, and sounded like a burst of machine-gun fire.

Trix liked to make men laugh. Looking at him from under her curling lashes, she wondered if she were falling in love? A new experience. Flip had once told her that there was an answer to that eternal question. Her sister had been talking about love. Trix had been scarcely fifteen, and Philippa was mad about some man or other who later vanished from her life. 'My theory,' said Philippa, 'is based on Watford Station.'

'What do you mean, Flip!'

Philippa explained that it was a test one could set oneself. If a girl was willing to take a slow, stopping and crowded train to

Watford Station, knowing that when she arrived the person she was meeting would only have five minutes on a draughty platform to talk to her – and if she eagerly went on the journey – that was love.

I can't see myself on the Watford train for you, Dick Polglaze, thought Trix.

They parked the car outside the high walls of Kew and went into the gardens. Dick carried the picnic basket.

'You are not supposed to carry anything when you are in uniform,' said Trix, 'the command's quite right, it ruins the way you look. A Naval officer, too. Let me have the basket. I shall look okay with it. I shall be little Red Riding Hood.'

'And I'm to be the wolf? Don't tempt me. The basket is too heavy, I can't have you with bulging muscles.'

'I have beautiful muscles.'

'Then we must keep them that way.'

The gardens still had some flowers, roses, scenting the air as they went by. The grass had been left to grow long, for hay. There were beds of symmetrically planted, curled green cabbages. None of the great glasshouses had been bombed – so far, and they shone like giant diamonds which had been cleaned with Doctor Tyrrell's gin, winking and sending back rays to the sun. In the distance in the blue sky, swimming, floating, was a long line of motionless barrage balloons.

'Come paint the dawn with dainty elephants
To graze upon the pastures of the sky,' quoted Dick.

'Do you like poetry, Trix? Somebody should write a poem about you.'

'Oh, they have,' she said, and he laughed again.

They picnicked under feathery trees more exotic than any English oak or beech. They drank the champagne. Trix took off her shoes and the sun warmed her long bare legs and pretty, narrow feet. She lifted up her face, thirsty for the golden light.

Propping himself on one elbow, he looked at her with his narrow eyes. His senses were stirred. The great gardens were empty and very still. No figure crossed the grass or walked under the trees. They could have been in Arcadia. He leaned over, put his arms round her and kissed her. She returned the kiss. He said nothing when they drew apart.

In the afternoon they drove down to Wargrave. At the river's edge by an old hotel there was a boathouse. Dick, who had come

131

often here, went to a cottage and persuaded an old woman to unlock the boathouse for him. For a pound she allowed him to drag out a punt.

Trix climbed into the long narrow craft and they set off along the river. Cows stood up to their knees in the water and stared mildly at them from the other bank.

Using a paddle, Dick steered his craft skilfully past deserted houses sleeping in the sun, and gardens where weeds grew among the delphiniums. He turned into a backwater, overhung with trees. There were forget-me-nots at the water's edge and little flotillas of moorhens. It was a world empty of people and smelling of flowers, filled to the brim with summer. Trix lay back on water-stained plush cushions and trailed her hand in the water.

The backwater at last joined the broad sweep of the river, and he finally moored the punt under an enormous willow tree. It was more than fifteen feet across, high, green, an ancient tent whose hanging branches swept the water. Tying the punt rope to a tree stump on the shore, he stepped back into the punt beside her. They were in a dim, green, watery light. The river gently slapped against the craft now and then.

'Shall we make love?'

She giggled in reply, excited. Lying down together, their movements rocked the punt. They made love for a long time. He was fierce and silent in lovemaking and when she opened her eyes to look, she saw a tranced expression on his face. Excited, melting, she was not as tranced as he. When it was over, he said, putting on his clothes, 'you're a luscious piece of female flesh.'

Still naked, she put her arms behind her head.

'I thought you were going to say that you loved me.'

'Did you?'

When he drove her back to St Helen's, gave her a brief kiss and said he would write when he was at sea – 'Lord knows when you'll get the letter, though' – Trix smiled airily. She waved, watching the short sturdy figure walking, with a light step, towards the gate. He turned and gave a salute.

She made up her mind to marry him.

After Philippa's marriage and its excitements, Elaine returned to the unchanging pattern of her life in Oxfordshire. She worked at

Blenheim six days a week, every evening was spent at home. She lived for Miles' letters. Apart from Marjorie Flower, she had made no friends. And her mother-in-law was far too busy to notice that.

Claire had joined the WVS before the war on the week that it had been founded. It was started with the aim of specialising in air raid precautions, but the Service's work since 1939 had steadily extended. Claire wore her WVS green tweed suit on every day except Sunday, it was as much her uniform as Miles' navy blue was to him. In the evenings, however, she still changed into pre-war lace dresses, floor length, and her string of pearls. But it was in the uniform, which she named her battle dress, that she looked her angular and energetic best.

She had learned to drive a lorry; she delivered food and baby clothes. She cooked (not very well) and knitted (excellently) and organized work parties. The WVS wanted salvage of every kind. Claire was one of its most pitiless collectors. She would cajole or shame women into giving up their precious aluminium saucepans, their children's metal tea sets, and sackfulls of magazines. Nobody in Claire's district had a spare blanket in the linen cupboard. She collected blankets and clothes, packed them and sent them to the bombed cities. Her work took her all over the country, and often when Elaine came home, the old house was empty. Lord St Aird, of course, was in the stable studio. Sometimes Elaine's heart would give a jump: there would be a letter on the hall floor. *On Active Service. H.M.Ship. Passed by Censor.*

Miles had been sent to Canada after the bombing of Liverpool, as part of the expedition crossing the Atlantic to collect the US destroyers. Roosevelt had offered Britain forty or fifty elderly ships in exchange for British bases in the Atlantic and the Caribbean and Churchill had accepted immediately. The destroyers were sorely needed.

Elaine received a letter from Miles when he had arrived in Quebec. Letters from him were usually written in pencil, at sea, on scraps of paper torn from notebooks. But this time he used rich-looking writing paper, at the top of which was the engraving of a gothic Quebec hotel.

The ship, he wrote, had been crowded to the gunwales with women and children, evacuees travelling to Canada. Praise be the sea had been calm, and the journey safe. There had been a lot of nervous faces. He had played deck tennis, walked for miles round the deck to keep in training and made a lot of friends. 'We subs hit it off pretty well,' wrote Miles in his optimistic way. 'And you'll be amused to know, darling, that the drinks really *are* duty free.'

Elaine read and re-read the letters. Sometimes she could not decipher a particular word, and was glad. It meant puzzling it out later on, and so getting something more. She was like a man half dead with thirst, licking the inside of his water-can.

Miles' parents received letters from him about the same time: he never wrote to his wife without writing to them.

Claire read paragraphs from his letters during dinner, including a description of Quebec.

'I simply can't imagine how he can like Canada, can you, Edmund? We couldn't stick it.'

'I recall that my grandfather enjoyed the salmon fishing,' said Lord St Aird.

He sounds, thought Elaine, exactly like an American's outdated idea of an Englishman. She was glad one of Philippa's Eagle friends was not present. Philippa had told her about the American prejudices about the English.

'I know it sounds ridiculous, but they come from so far away – most of the boys have never travelled before, and their ideas about us are archaic! They think all Englishmen are reserved, frigid and never see a joke. Worst of all, they are convinced the English feel deeply superior to boorish Americans. Of course I keep telling them they're wrong.'

Are they? thought Elaine. Perhaps the St Airds preferred the caricature. Her father-in-law put all his paintings with their faces to the wall.

The summer days were bright, and one early morning as Elaine was leaving for Woodstock, the telephone rang. Claire was in the fields at the back of the house feeding the chickens. Elaine answered it.

'Shelton Manor?'

'*Miles.*'

'Darling, what luck. I thought you would have left. I'll be home tonight, or tomorrow at latest. I must fly. Did I remember to tell you that I love you?'

Elaine ran. Her feet scarcely touched the ground as she flew out into the blazing sunshine. In the distance she saw Claire surrounded by a sea of brown chickens. She was sprinkling corn.

Dragging open the farm gate, tripping as her shoe caught in a rut, Elaine yelled, 'Lady St Aird. Miles rang! He's coming home tonight or tomorrow. Isn't it wonderful? Oh, isn't it wonderful?' She was running and gasping, out of breath, radiant.

Claire stood with one hand spilling corn. The brown feathered sea eddied round her.

'Good. Please don't shout, Elaine. I've told you that before.'

That day, her intense happiness scared Elaine. Her nature was balanced and preferred a chosen calm. The wave of feeling which kept seeping over her was so violent that she felt as if she were drunk. And in between a terrifying happiness she felt cold and her stomach ached. She told Marjorie the news at lunch time. Marjorie beamed, laughed, exclaimed with pleasure, patted her shoulder. She did the things needed by a person suffering from bliss. She then looked observantly at her friend, and suggested they should go for a walk after lunch.

'Why not now? I couldn't eat a thing.'

'Elaine St Aird! I am starving. You come and watch and I'll eat anything you don't want.'

After the meal they went out into the hot sunshine. The fields were full of marguerites and a breeze made the forest of white flowers shiver. The palace towered. The lake had turned blue.

'I know how it is,' said Marjorie, 'pretty awful, hmm?'

'Awful and wonderful.'

'Of course. But you mustn't stare at the hour glass when he's with you. *Enjoy* his leave. My cousin Elizabeth was with us recently during her husband's leave. Elaine, she was frightful. She kept wailing 'only two days more' at breakfast and thoroughly depressing everybody. Her husband Ted is a cheerful soul, he loves a joke and a gin, and he looked positively hunted. You must find the way to enjoy Miles, at the same time blocking off the thought that he will soon be gone.'

'I suppose you know how to do it.'

'Of course I don't. Doesn't mean, because I know what is right, that I'm capable of doing it.'

* * *

135

The evening bus stopped on the corner by the Wheelwright pub. Elaine had a quarter of an hour's walk to Shelton. Miles hoped to be with her tomorrow. In twenty-four hours she would see him again. She gave a sigh of happiness. But as she climbed out of the bus she saw something that made her feel as if the blood was draining out of her body. Standing on the green by a gnarled tree which had a bench built all round it, was a figure. Tall, dark clad, narrow shouldered, a man with a brown face, wearing a shabby naval cap.

She began to run. He opened both his arms and she threw herself into them.

That evening St Aird brought out the 1912 burgundy, two cobwebbed bottles taken from the Shelton cellars. He poured out the wine slowly into heavy eighteenth century glasses.

Miles was delighted and astonished.

'Not the 1912. Really, Father, you shouldn't!'

'I can't think of a reason why not.'

Punctuating stories of his life in the Navy with bursts of laughter, Miles was full of talk. Dinner was festive. It was odd, thought Elaine, to see Claire actually smiling, to hear her short amused laugh. Her mother-in-law was in her best lace, and Elaine wore a new dress that Miles had bought for her in Canada. It was made of crêpe, very clinging and soft, the colour of a geranium.

'I forgot to tell you,' said Miles, drinking his third glass of brandy with relish after the humble dessert of stewed apples and custard. 'You are all going to laugh. I've been put up for a gong. A civilian one. For the shindig in Liverpool.'

His father's lined old face beamed.

'A decoration? You told us nothing of what actually happened in Liverpool, did he, Claire?'

He referred every question to his wife.

'Oh, I couldn't say much because of censorship,' said Miles, grinning. 'It was nothing to make a song and dance about. I told you on the telephone, remember, Mother? About the fires. There was a big blitz over Liverpool and I was on my way to barracks. I'd been to a movie. Hellish boring in Liverpool. The blitz was roaring away and as I was going down the road, carrying a totally unnecessary torch, suddenly I heard a voice – very loud and absolutely furious. It was a warden shouting "Put out that bloody light." That was a laugh, because the fires had really got going in the docks, it was so light you could have read a newspaper by them. The sky was crimson.'

'I remember that at Amiens,' Claire said.

Elaine did not speak.

Miles said – 'I bet you did, Mother. I must say, it did look exciting. So I turned back and ran down to the docks. There were some ships burning, one worse than the others. Apparently it was just about to explode. There were two matelots still on board, both of them had been wounded. I got hold of the rope they'd used to pull off the others, and said I'd shin up it. Somebody shouted to me that I'd fall off – the men were on the top deck. I said, what the hell? I'll only get a wet shirt if I do fall. So up I went and got 'em. First one, then the other.'

'And came down the rope, carrying them,' said Claire.

'Yes, poor beggars. They both died later.'

'Worth a try, though,' said Claire.

St Aird sipped his burgundy.

'Good show. Nice try,' he said.

Elaine had never felt so distanced from them. She even felt separated from Miles. *She* wanted to cry out, to exclaim, to ask questions and let her feelings burst out like stars. She didn't dare. Instead, she managed to say with nearly as much coolness as Claire,

'What about the gong?'

Miles laughed again. 'Rumour has it that it's to be a George Medal. Look rather nice, won't it? White and purple. A bit like an MC.'

The evening seemed very long to Elaine. And Miles was so very nice to his parents. He went out in the dark to the studio to see his father's new painting. He admired his mother's WVS work charts.

'Good lord, Mother, you're going the pace. You're the one who should get the gong.'

Elaine jangled with nerves. To be alone with him. To have him in her arms. To make love.

At last they went up to bed. The old house settled down into its thrall of country silence, and she was in bed with Miles, close to him, feeling his warmth. They made love over and over again.

'Being away from you, sweetie, makes me very sexy.'

When they separated, he lay and held her hand. Letting his hand go, she got out of bed and pulled the curtains. The

137

moonlight of early summer washed into the room. There he was, really there, she could see him in the shadows, a dark shape in her bed.

'Sleepy, poppet?'

'Oh no. Do you want to talk?'

'A little. I've got some news. I wanted you to hear it first and I've been saving it up. Best bit is that it looks as if I'm going to get quite a lot more leave. How you started! The fact is that the old destroyer we just chugged back over from the States is not exactly used to the rough Atlantic. She was happier in warmer seas. She is not, distinctly not, in good shape. She's in dock for repairs and our skipper's guess is that this is just the start. We'll be in and out of dock after every trip. So – more leave.'

Elaine looked at him. She could just make out the prominent bumpy forehead, two dark hollows for eyes, a thickness of black hair.

'Second bit of news. I'm taking you away for a naughty weekend.'

She was dumbfounded. Since when had Miles wanted to be anywhere but Shelton?

'It sounds wonderful. But are you sure, my darling? What about your parents?'

It cost her a lot to say that.

'Oh, I suggested it to Father this evening in the studio. He agreed. We ought to get away by ourselves.'

Oh did he, thought Elaine. Or was it that he would agree to anything asked by his son.

'I thought Brighton,' Miles said. 'We had fun there when I was at King Alfred. We must recapture the first fine careless rapture. Except that we've just done that.'

Elaine had to go to work the next morning. On her journey to Woodstock her thoughts kept returning to the astonishing fact that Miles was taking her away from Shelton for three whole days. How would his mother like that?

Yesterday evening, his first at home, when they had had dinner, and sat afterwards in the drawing room, Elaine knew very well how self-conscious and inhibited she had been. She found it impossible to be natural with Miles when his mother was there. Any sign of affection to him, even a 'darling', would be despised. Elaine knew Claire would think it very vulgar. She did not even dare to touch his hand. Was Claire jealous? Elaine had had a strong sensation last night, as if there was a kind of invisible grabbing coming from Claire, a pulling of Miles towards herself whilst pushing Elaine away. Perhaps Miles had felt a little of that too.

Marjorie promptly said she would exchange some leave with Elaine to make the Brighton trip possible.

'Don't bother to thank me. You just wait until Bob comes home!'

'Then you can take all my Sundays.'

'You're right. I will.'

While she was packing, Elaine heard Claire and Miles talking on the stairs. Claire laughed, sounding like a girl. But when the taxi arrived, and Elaine came down the stairs, she saw that her mother-in-law was displeased. Her manner to Elaine was very cold, ridiculously so. She was all smiles to her son, who gave her a smacking kiss.

As they drove to the station the morning was grey. Summer was hiding in a white blanket and the wind was cold. By the time they arrived in London the day was drearier still.

'Do we care?' said Miles, giving her arm a pinch.

But when the train drew in at the station at Brighton and they stepped out, everything was blue and gold. The transformation was dramatic, it was as if they had walked inside a pre-war poster for the Cote d'Azur. Brighton was teeming with troops. There seemed to be regiments marching down every street, the pubs were so filled they overflowed, and troops went by in lorries. Miles and Elaine walked down the street towards the sea.

As they came to the front they saw that it was full of block houses, there were huge rolling barricades of barbed-wire, gun emplacements, and notices saying succinctly, 'KEEP OFF!'

They stood looking at the stretch of shingle, grey, white and brown. It sloped down to the almost waveless sea. They were both thinking of their wartime honeymoon. All they had had was twenty-four hours. But they had crept out of the hotel at midnight and swum. The water had been as warm as a bath. All the mysterious future was ahead of them, sprawling across the horizon. They had been too happy to look at it.

Miles glanced from the menacing beaches to his wife. She stood quietly, a small elegant figure, fairish hair curled under a hat shaped like a little wreath. Elaine's appearance, he sometimes thought, was a work of art as much as his father's pictures

139

were. Everything about her was perfect, the result of thought and design. He had never seen her look messy, or caught her with a smut on her face or a laddered stocking. She glowed with a kind of interior colour, as if the painting were lit from behind the canvas, her skin like a peach, her eyes steady shining blue. He marvelled at the difference between Elaine and her impulsive rather untidy sister Flip, whom he liked but did not admire. As for Trix, she was a chorus girl. But Elaine was his ideal. She was beautiful and collected, passionate when he wanted her, reserved at other times. She continued to fascinate him and continued to belong to herself.

As for Elaine, behind the cool façade she was hiding the very emotion Marjorie had warned her about – a consciousness of time running away like the sand in the hour glass. Its neck was so narrow that you thought nothing could get through it: yet the sand seemed alive, rushing downwards to the growing heap of yesterdays.

'What do you want to do this evening, sweetie? The cinema's only a step away from the hotel. I *think* it is a Will Hay.'

'Oh, do let's.'

The film finished on the stroke of ten fifteen. A notice on the screen announced To Patrons that the curfew began at half past ten, and would they please return home as quickly as possible.

Walking back to the hotel, they met only two soldiers, both hurrying, and a policeman.

'I never liked Brighton so much,' Elaine said.

The night was so quiet that after they had made love, when Elaine lay wide awake looking into the dark, she could hear the sea washing the shore. The waves broke and made a gentle, dragging noise. She wished it did not make her feel sad. 'Forlorn, the very word is like a bell, Tolling me back from thee to my sole self.'

'Are you awake, poppet?' said Miles in the dark.

She moved so that her shoulder pressed against his bare chest. He folded her in his arms.

'You smell delicious. Expensive. There is something I have to tell you. It won't happen just yet, there'll be more life on the ocean wave in that poor benighted US destroyer. But. I am thinking of volunteering for submarines.'

The silence was only broken by the sound of the sea.

'Well?' he said, pressing her close, 'are you going to ask me not to?'

'Of course not, if that's what you want to do.'

It was the most difficult sentence she had spoken in her life.

'You are wonderful, know that? I was afraid of a scene.'

'Since when, my darling, have I made one of those?'

'Never. There are never any at Shelton either, thank Allah. I had a girlfriend before the war. Very glamorous. But she enjoyed scenes. They made me curl up.'

'I've always known you felt like that.'

'It's strange. You know everything about me. Much, much more than Mother, and I always thought she and I were the same kind of people. Now I see the differences. Anyway, back to being a submariner. It's a grand life, you know. Interesting and difficult and technical. Fascinating stuff. I'm mad about going into submarines. A friend of mine, Allardyce, you haven't met him, you'd like him, has already volunteered. He tells me one gets danger money.'

What answer was there to that?

She heard the smile in his voice as he said, 'So at last I can buy you a really decent naval crown, with good-sized diamonds, not those chips you wear at present. Something worth looking at.'

Once before the war when she had been playing tennis and the game ended, she had jumped the tennis net. She had tripped at the top of the net and fallen forward, winded. She had the same intense stomach-ache now.

'When shall you go, Miles?'

'Oh, not for ages. First there's the next Atlantic trip. Then all the papers have to go through, and then there's the course at *HMS Dolphin* at Portsmouth. Allardyce said it's a pretty intensive course with lots of hard work. It will take three or four months. I shan't be going for a while, sweetie. You'll have to wait a bit before your husband is a hero.'

He talked for a while longer, and then he kissed her. Soon, with a gentle sound not unlike the waves outside, a kind of sigh, he fell asleep. She lay awake, her head against his chest, eyes wide open, in pain.

141

Part II

Chapter Ten

During the late autumn of 1941 the Tyrrell sisters saw nothing of each other. A giant hand had come out of the sky and shifted them, as it moved everybody in Britain, pawns in the game of chess.

Miles returned from the Atlantic and was sent to Portsmouth on the course for submariners. Elaine was not allowed to live near him, the area was prohibited. When he was given leave, which was seldom, she set off on one of the slow wartime journeys by train and cross-country bus to get to the village which was nearest to the line over which civilians must not cross. Here she and Miles met and stayed at the village pub – often only for a single night.

He had never seemed happier or looked more handsome. He retained a tan from months at sea, to his own surprise. 'I don't know how I manage it, we were below decks most of the time in the most filthy weather.' His grey eyes were so clear that the whites were blue, and his figure was as springy as steel. When she walked with him, she had to run to keep up. He was, he declared, a hundred per cent fit. It was his favourite joke, after making love to her a number of times during the night.

The course was taxing and some of it was technical, but it was also a big sharpening up, he said, of seamanship. Submarines were 'sensitive beasts'. They were difficult to handle and the seamanship underwater was more advanced than for a big ship. He learned of deep sea pressures, of keeping the submarine on course – a strangely difficult task – and of many kinds of attack and escape. He praised his fellow officers. He always did that.

When the hoarded leaves were over, she returned to Blenheim and Marjorie's acerbic company. Her friend reminded Elaine of the sweets that she and Philippa used to buy as children called Refreshers. They fizzed when you bit into them.

Elaine could never get to London now, since her time off had to be saved for when Miles was granted leave. She had to content herself with telephoning St Helen's. She rarely managed to get Trix or her father, but Miggs gave her the news. The doctor was taking out 'that French girl Gilling or whatever she calls herself' to dinner sometimes. Trix 'had her picture in the *Mail*, dancin' with some young chap.' Miggs's cat 'turns out to be a gentleman, so no kittens.'

Telephone calls were unsatisfactory but reassuring. Her family was still there, well, busy. And at last the blitz on London had stopped, so she need not worry over the night raids.

The member of her family most in Elaine's thoughts was Philippa. When she rang her at the cottage where her sister was now living, Philippa sounded happy. Elaine wondered how true that could be for a girl newly-married to a pilot on operational flying. Sometimes in the background Elaine could hear the sound of men laughing. Philippa said gaily, 'That's the boys. They've all just come charging in.'

Elaine's guess was right, Philippa's happiness was an act – in a way. When she had walked up the aisle on her father's arm and had seen Barny waiting for her, it had been like going towards paradise. She had scarcely been able to believe the wonder of it. Here he was, the man she adored, and she was to be his wife.

On her wedding night Barny made love to her, taking her virginity not gently but roughly. When he was asleep at last, lying against her naked body, his face buried in her neck, he breathed as peacefully as a child. And it was then that she saw for the first time what she had done.

When Barny put the ring on her finger that morning she had taken more than a husband. She had accepted ghastly company. From today it would sit down at her dinner table, stalk her, grin at her. When she was alone it would come up behind her and blow its icy breath on her neck as Barny now breathed his warm one. Her father had known all this. So had Elaine. Philippa never had. But now as clearly as the skeletons grimacing in plague paintings, she saw it. She had been given what her body longed for, a winged hero for a lover. In a dreadful exchange.

She was unlike other women married to fighting men. She was not destined to wait, to dread a telegram, to sleep with censored letters under her pillow, to live for a few pathetic days of leave. Compared to Elaine's life, Philippa's was infinitely better and terrifyingly worse. In many cases the officers in the RAF were not allowed to have their wives living near the station. CO's thought this pyschologically wrong. Other pilots without women envied them. And the closeness of wives made the pilots themselves more conscious of danger, unsettled, uneasy. But Barny had been given permission, and Philippa lived ten minutes away from the Eagles' aerodrome.

They had arrived in the evening following the day of the wedding. The sun was setting as Barny unlocked the rickety cottage door. Just then there was a noise in the sky growing into a roar. Barny and Philippa ran into the overgrown garden and looked up at the sky – there they were, six, seven, eight Spitfires in tight formation, flying low, then steadily rising.

'They're off on the daily bus service,' Barny said. He looked at her and gave her a kiss. 'You don't know what I am talking about, do you? We fly over to France every day for a sweep. That's the bus service. Your husband will be up there tomorrow.'

And so he was. And Philippa must learn to bear it.

Within a week of her arrival at the cottage, Barny had brought all the members of his Squadron to meet her. Eighteen pilots visited her at odd hours, sometimes in a crowd which made the cottage bulge. When she heard voices, she threw open the front door and there were the Eagles, walking through the nettles towards her.

She was instantly and uncritically fond of them. They came from all corners of the United States – from Texas, Florida, Georgia, New England, New York. She could not distinguish which accent matched which State, although she could hear one lilt differing from another. At first she was hard put to it to recall who was Tex or Pete, who was Buzz or Andy. They had short names or nicknames, and they called her Flip the first time they met her.

They were Americans who described themselves as 'part of Lease-Lend.' Civilian pilots in American could earn thousands of dollars a year, but the Eagles were paid seven pounds a week. They belonged to the RAF, wore its blue uniform, and had adopted its lore and language. RAF slang coloured their talk. To be shot down in flames meant to be crossed in love, sprog could be a new uniform or a recruit, putting up propos meant being promoted. A favourite topic – it was the same with all RAF pilots – was the subject of gremlins. These were creatures of the upper air. One or two of the Eagles swore they had seen them – they looked like elves, or demons, or goblins. One English fighter pilot, the story went, had his own gremlin covered with fur like a

147

mole. If stroked the wrong way, it rolled on the floor of the plane in rage. Gremlins plagued pilots. They shifted flarepaths, guided planes to the wrong aerodrome. One ground-based gremlin lived in the Central Registry and hid the files. It was agreed that the gremlins' greatest pleasure was to get pilots into trouble. The WAAFs disagreed. *They* loved the gremlins and said the little creatures protected pilots, cleared away frozen snow and sat on the wings of bombers to prevent the wings from shuddering.

Listening to the talk, Philippa was only half amused. Pilots were superstitious and she had already caught the feeling. To be lucky you must be cautious about invisible things. Who was to say that there were not elves, malicious or well-wishing, living in the icy regions of the upper air?

She did not know how she was going to manage when Barny was flying. She had dreaded discovering that she was too weak to bear it. But she found that she could. It was exactly the same as living through the blitz.

Barny was concerned at her being alone during the days or nights he was flying.

'But I'm sure I can get some kind of work,' she said vaguely.

He tenderly agreed. But he agreed to everything that she said, and she found his American way of spoiling her both beautiful and shocking. She wondered puritanically if it was bad for her.

She had scarcely settled to her life as a pilot's wife when the telephone rang one day.

'My dear Philippa, or do I say Mrs Duval?' said an energetic English voice. It was Jane Alwynne.

Philippa had left Chicheley Buildings in a daze a few days before her wedding. She was too far gone to notice that Jane had asked for the address of the station, and written it in a small note book on the cover of which, in her bold hand, were the words *Do Something*.

They exchanged politenesses. Philippa thanked Jane for her two wedding presents.

'Quite an interesting combination, didn't you think?' said Jane complacently. She had given Philippa an electric iron, and a copy of *The Forsyte Saga*.

'Well, now. Do you suppose you could find a typewriter somewhere?'

'A *typewriter*, Mrs Alwynne!'

'Certainly. There's usually an elderly one knocking about somewhere. Try the WVS. Or perhaps your husband might buy you one as a present. Americans are richer than we are,' said Jane. 'I wonder, you see, if you might consider working for the hospital again? I daresay there are times when you will be glad to be busy.'

An ancient upright typewriter was discovered in a junk shop; Barny bought it for her, and one of his mechanics put it in order. After that, with Barny away and her thoughts on him every breathing moment, Philippa once again began to work for Jane. She worked hard. She kept files, sent weekly reports to London, and thumped away at begging letters. Now and then she looked at her watch. At last the Squadron was due back.

She went out into the garden to watch for the planes.

Occasionally a girl called Joan Monteith, a WAAF at the station, called round. When they heard the sound of the planes they would go out and watch for them together. They always began to talk nervously and too much as the planes appeared, tiny dots in the sky. When they could make out the individual planes, Joan would say,

'There's Buzz.'

'That's Tex.'

'There's Barny.'

Both girls would relax and talk more slowly then.

Death did stalk the farmhand's cottage which was now Philippa's home. But she could face it. Sometimes she was strong enough to drive it out and slam the door. It was not only Barny's love which filled her with joy despite the spectre in the house; it was also being with the Eagles in a kingdom of the young and brave. They seized her in their arms and danced with her. They taught her to jitterbug, picking her up and throwing her round. They played Fats Waller until the record wheezed. They shouted with laughter and sprawled on the floor. She was one of them. She loved them.

'You know what you're turning into,' said Barny. 'A Yank.'

'Oh good.'

'It isn't good at all. I married a Limey. I can't have her losing the lime.'

At the time of her marriage, the Eagles had at last flown in battle, welcoming the chance with an eagerness amounting to

149

desperation. Wasn't that what they had come for? But before they flew on ops, two of their pilots had been killed in air accidents. The deaths had confused and depressed the Squadron. Suddenly, death was real. Barny told her about the effect this had had. It sounded crazy, but he thought none of the Eagles had faced it until then. They had come to England for the big show. What they all had in common was being in love with planes, speed, excitement – and danger. That was what being in the RAF meant. Quite a number of the Eagles, Barny said, had wanted to fly in the American Army or Navy, or in the Marines, but they could not pass the tests.

'Here in Britain it is a darned sight easier to get in.'

'That's because we need you.'

He smiled at the reply, but gravely. He returned to the death of the two Eagles. It was decided to give them State funerals. The coffins were draped in Union Jacks, and the Eagles marched behind the gun carriages to the eerie wail of the Funeral March.

'A lot of VIP's from the Air Ministry were there,' he said, 'And the whole Squadron. Officers lined up by the sick quarters, and we were all in service dress with black armbands. It was so odd, Flip. We marched in slow time behind the gun carriages and the music made the hairs stand up on the back of my neck.'

'I suppose it was a gesture to Anglo-American friendship.'

'Oh, sure. But it didn't seem to be anything to do with our buddies, you know. They would have laughed their heads off at the solemnity. One of the guys from Texas is an Indian, you know – you've met him – well, he just couldn't move to that slow tempo. He loped along the way the Indians did across the plains. Of course we were impressed by the British giving our guys a send-off. But – a State funeral, for God's sake.'

The farmhand's cottage, Philippa's first married home, was uncomfortable and poky. The front room was airless and hot in summer, its small window overlooking the garden full of nettles. The kitchen shelves were covered with cracked oilcloth, the brick-floored scullery was so narrow that three big Americans could not fit in it at the same time.

Being married to the Eagle Squadron was a revelation to the conventional English girl. She had only known life at St Helen's, with its middle-class formalities. Now she found her home treated as open house. Nobody telephoned, they simply turned up, called her Pal and gave her a hug. They brought American

150

magazines, Coke and packets of Lucky Strikes and shouted from the door, 'Hey, Flip?'

If she was washing her hair, they sat on the bath and talked to her. If she was ironing, or darning her precious silk stockings, they sprawled beside her on the carpet. If they found her busy with her hospital work, they demanded to help.

'Give us a job. Folding letters? Sticking on stamps?'

Nothing about these Americans was in the least like Englishmen. They thought it right to help in any domestic chore and enjoyed it, saying it reminded them of home. They had no ceremony, and would not know it if they met it. They were as casual as brothers. Sometimes they were rough and boisterous, at other times they quietly talked of their homes on the other side of the world. Of cattle ranching or growing timber, of days in the saddle and nights in the open. They told her stories of beaver dams and young pumas – they called them mountain lions – of raccoons and rattle-snakes, the howl of coyotes, and the slow walk of armadillos.

One of Philippa's closest companions was Chuck Greenfield, whom she had met with Barny at Christmas. Chuck was the youngest member of the Squadron, popular, shy and much teased. His family was wealthy and when cheques arrived from Rhode Island he spent the money as lavishly as the two penniless French A's who had decreed that money was meant to roll. Philippa was at home with Chuck. Yet she was as strongly drawn to the wildest of the Eagles. 'You like Chuck because he's like an English guy,' Barny said, smiling, but it was not so. She loved his candid face and truthfulness and a sort of innocence.

Barny did not share Philippa's admiration for Joan Monteith, a WAAF officer with whom Philippa had things in common – a widowed father and two sisters. Joan was too serious for Barny's taste. She must have guessed that, because Philippa often noticed how she made an effort to be bright when Barny lounged into the cottage and found her there. Philippa admired her – she was stage-struck about the WAAFs and envied her job.

The autumn weather, gold upon gold, went suddenly. The skies grew overcast and there were heavy rainstorms. When Barny woke one morning he went straight to the window, pulled back the curtains, looked at the sky, and returned to bed. Bad weather meant that fighter pilots were grounded. He loathed inaction. He was irritable all the morning, and when the duty

151

officer telephoned to say there was a Recognition lecture, Barny left with alacrity.

Philippa settled down to her hospital cards. How quiet the cottage was. Petrol had become almost impossible to obtain now, and life in the country had returned to an early nineteenth century existence – it might have been Jane Austen's time. Nothing went by in the lane outside but the occasional clip-clop of a horse-drawn farm cart or pony trap.

She was surprised when the front door bell rang. Eagles ignored bells. The thin uniformed figure of Joan Monteith stood on the step.

'I did telephone but the number must be out of order. It was engaged for ages.'

'That was my boss, Mrs Alwynne, giving me orders. She goes on forever. How nice to see you. Let's have tea.'

Joan gave her curious almost embarrassed smile which made her look as if she might cry. When Philippa brought in the tea, they sat down in the stuffy front room on a sofa as hard as a stone. Joan talked of the bad weather – how the Eagles hated it – 'Eagles need clear skies' – she spoke as if of a flock of birds. Thank heaven for the lecture, otherwise they would simply hang round the mess playing poker or shove halfpenny, and getting steadily more jumpy and picking at each other.

'When I look at the boys sometimes,' she said, 'I think about all those American girls who write to them and send them photographs of themselves. They can't know what it's really like.'

'I don't know what it's really like either. I envy you. Being part of it.'

'But you're married!'

'That's not it, Joan. You know it isn't. Barny married me and I know he sometimes thinks he shouldn't have done. So many CO's think it is bad for morale to return from night fighting to home comforts. They don't believe a man with something important to do in the war should have the responsibility of a wife. Of course I never think we shouldn't be married. But some of his friends do. There are things they think and don't say.'

Joan looked at her for a moment.

'I suppose I do see. It's true you aren't part of it, on the station, working with them. For them, really. But don't envy us. We know them and we love them, although we try not to fall in

152

love with them. That's true. We try. The Eagles come into our mess, you know, just as they come here, and they sit and drink beer or grab us and dance. When that happens, they're just the same age as we are, they call us kids, but so are they. Then there's a call. And they go off to "receive further orders in the air" as it's called. Maybe the afternoon bus service to Abbeville or Lille. They go to the dispersal hut and into their planes, and we stand on the roof and count them as they set off. We wave. They might be setting off to some air circus to do aerobatics.'

'I don't think I could bear to stand on the roof and count.'

'We can't help it.'

Joan sighed. She said that she had disliked Americans before the war without knowing a thing about them. Her father still did. He hated foreigners and nothing would budge him about it. He'd been horrified when she was posted to the Eagle Squadron. She remembered that she herself had not been too pleased. She was ashamed to remember that.

Philippa wondered whether Joan's 'we try not to' really meant that she was in love with one of the Eagles. Which one? Did he also love her? She had the strong impression that Joan was already regretting having said too much. That happened. You said what was in your heart and then you wished you hadn't. Saying it aloud made it worse.

Barny was still the sweetest-natured man Philippa had met in her life, the most spoiling, the kindest. But the very times she thirsted for – when he was out of danger – were what made him very nervous. There was nothing he would not do for her, yet the only part of his life that truly mattered to him she could not share. For the first months of their marriage he told her almost nothing about flying and she knew she could not ask. The weather cleared, Barny kissed her, and swung away in the early morning with a 'goin' huntin'.'

But one night he came home in a state of exhausted excitement, his eyes blazing in a grey face. He took her in his arms and made love to her fiercely – she had the feeling that almost any woman would have done just then. But after he had slept, he woke and told her what had happened.

He had been over St Omer. The Squadron had been sent to escort the bombers, and after the bombs had been dropped Barny saw a dog-fight going on behind him. He turned to join battle, attacking a Messerschmitt which dived vertically towards the ground. Barny dived in pursuit, but a second enemy plane came after him, firing in hard bursts. In a few moments Barny was at ground level, flying at 500 miles an hour right over the St Omer aerodrome with the enemy planes still hunting him. He was flying below the level of the trees and only glimpsed the enemy now and then in the plane mirror. He waited until the first enemy was in firing range, pulled the stick back and turned as tightly as possible – only to realize with horror that the enemy was turning too, inside his turn, and Barny was now the target. He couldn't climb . . . the Messerschimtt was above him.

'Suddenly I knew I was fighting for my life. It was a weird sensation, realizing if I didn't do something in that split second, I'd never see you again.'

By now he was a mere five feet from the ground, almost skimming the grass. He pulled the stick back so hard that he blacked out – it must have only been a second but it seemed like terrifying hours. When he came to he was twenty feet behind the enemy plane. He gave the plane a burst of fire and the enemy began to do extraordinary aerobatics, weaving, climbing, then streaking back to the aerodrome with Barny chasing him right down to the hangar, then across the flying field and back. The enemy was trying to get the St Omer ground defences to shoot Barny down. The whole thing was so wild, so quick, the planes moving so impossibly fast, and as the enemy plane in desperation turned on its back, Barny gave it a long burst – and found his guns were empty. He turned frantically for home, pursued for a while, and losing his hunters at last. He flew at hedge level all the way to Le Touquet, only rising when he reached the sea.

Philippa could say nothing when the story finished. She kissed him.

But the description of the fights stayed in her imagination and now her dark opponent was harder than ever to combat. She worked for Jane Alwynne when Barny was flying. She ran out of work and telephoned for more. Jane, delighted, asked if she could manage to do the hospital's financial records? They were in an appalling mess and she would be so very grateful. The trouble was the time it would take . . .

Philippa agreed. She would have agreed to dig the foundations of a new hospital wing single-handed, providing the work could be done near the cottage. She welcomed anything which kept her from seeing visions of planes skimming the grass, attacker and pursuer, both with death in their hands.

Now when she heard the planes coming home she ran out to count them. And if one or more was missing she sat, dry-eyed and sick, until Barny came home.

Often he returned to say they had flown on two patrols and seen nothing, nothing at all. The sea had been flat, visibility good, the patrol boring. Dreary.

'When damn all happens, patrolling is just hell. Battles are different. They're exciting.'

Days went by. Winter days when lovers in another world would have walked in the bare woods or climbed the low brown hills, or sat by fires in English pubs, eating bread and cheese. She couldn't believe there had ever been such a time, free of the dark companion. What was real was her life now, her life close to Barny, who lived in the sky and returned unwillingly to earth, an eagle well named.

'More patrols. Nothing bloody happening. Some of the boys swear they'll get out of the goddammed Air Force and I don't blame them.'

It was evening, and she went across the room and knelt down beside him. He put his hand up to her cheek. But his eyes were looking inward.

'Long spells without action do get us down, Flip. I know I griped when the weather grounded us, but patrolling is almost as bad. We want to be in battle. That's our job.'

'I know.'

'Do you realize that when I first met you that time I'd never been in a dog-fight? And nor had any of my pals. And even after our first go, when we were jumped by some Messerschmitts, we were so wet behind the ears, it was difficult for us to realize there was an enemy actually trying to kill us. Some guy up there stooging around waiting for the chance to give it to us if we weren't quicker on the draw and got him first. I remember the first plane I shot down. I was so excited and het up and everything happened so fast and I thought – Christ, it's him or me. It was a bomber coming straight at me. I fired a half second burst at about a hundred yards. I saw the bomber burst into flames and head straight into the drink. God, it went so fast, and it hit the sea and I reckon I killed the lot of them. I couldn't help thinking about it. Everybody at the station congratulated me, and the story was written up in the personal combat reports. The bomber was seen going down. I'd scored officially. But do you know, I couldn't help thinking about how that bomber had been *there*, in the sky ahead of me, and its crew had been alive and full of hope and excitement, just as I was. And the next minute there were flames and the huge splash, and a sort of mess on the surface of the sea. It's still the only one I remember.'

He had taken her hand and was examining the palm. She knew he couldn't see it.

'I suppose fighting men have always felt like that, Barny. If they had hearts, I mean.'

'We mustn't have them. That's the point.'

When the Squadron was moved – this happened three times – Philippa moved too. The cottage among the nettles was left behind, and she packed and travelled on, and quickly learned how to make a ramshackle lodging comfortable. She became a practised camp follower.

Months had gone since her marriage. The Eagle Squadron was extended from one to three, with more pilots, more Spitfires, more action. There were losses. Andy was shot down. Tex was missing, believed killed. He was never traced. And there were others. Young men who had hung round in the cottage, called her 'Pal' and sat drinking Coke or danced to the old records with her. They vanished as if they had never been, and more young Americans replaced them.

The Eagles talked of the dead pilots as if they had been posted abroad, matter-of-factly, without emotion. 'Isn't that Andy's favourite song?' somebody said, and 'Tex never believed that story of yours, Buddy.'

Philippa also lived in the present. She loved the Squadrons with a passionate partisan love. They were proud of their identity, wore English uniform, and were utterly, movingly, American.

Towards the end of the year it was bitterly cold. The fields were sprinkled with frozen snow and the skies were so low that the pilots were grounded. The Squadrons, and Philippa, were back at Martlesham Heath, where she had come first after her marriage. Barny managed to get back the same cottage, which had stood empty since the Eagles had been gone. It was odd to find herself back in the poky rooms where she had lived what seemed now to be years ago. She tried not to think of the lost friends who had filled its narrow rooms.

When Barny came home one bitter December night, she knew he was going to be gloomy and difficult. She left him to himself. She had lit a fire in the sitting room, and after giving her a perfunctory kiss he went to sit by it and listen to the wireless. From the kitchen, she could hear a measured English voice. It must be the nine o'clock news.

Suddenly there was a blood-curdling yell.

With a pang of sheer terror she rushed into the sitting room. He was staring at the wireless in stupefaction. He began to stutter –

'The Japs have attacked Pearl Harbour – they've b-b-bloody well attacked – *we're in the war!*'

Leaping up, he picked her up and swung her round.

'You were in it anyway, stupid Yank!' she cried, laughing.

'But this is different! The US *is in the war!*' he shouted back.

He hadn't stopped exclaiming when there was a thunder of knocking on the door which burst open and in pelted Chuck Greenfield.

'It was on the radio in the pub – what do you know – the Japs – '

It was a night of drink and song.

After the extraordinary news the Squadrons' spirits were irrepressible. They teased Philippa.

'It's our war now.'

'When wasn't it yours? You're in the RAF, aren't you?'

'Yeah, but now it's different.'

It never occurred to her, sharing their gaiety and the euphoria of the 'Here's to the good old USA drink it down, drink it down' that it was indeed different. Later news came from across the Atlantic that the Eagles were going to be disbanded. That was not the word used – it was called 'transferred'. The three squadrons were to be transferred out of the RAF Fighter Command to the United States Air Force.

When she heard that she knew that part of her life was over. She had, in truth, taken on Barny's life as if buttoning herself into his blue tunic, and because she wore it she had accepted the never absent dread and the more terrible visitor. But it had been a fair exchange. She had had Barny in her arms, and she had

157

lived among men who made Englishmen seem tame. When she first married, the Eagles had been boisterous and uncontrolled, keeping no rules, forgetting to salute, blowing off steam by crazy forbidden flying when on test flights. She'd seen them flying upside down over the tops of trees, or skimming the fields as if cutting corn. They had been excitable and excited, lovable and maddening.

But fighting had changed them. They'd started by thinking they had a birthright to behave as they damned well pleased. Weren't they individualists? Weren't they American? But they painfully learned that the old myth of the solo ace shooting his way through the sky was a dangerous myth indeed. They had to become professionals, to work and fly in formation. The very thing they resisted, discipline, was what brought them safety. They were veterans now. Danger had changed them, and the death of friends. During one terrible ten days, the Squadron had lost five pilots.

Barny had altered too. He was quieter and older. Philippa had a pain in her heart to remember the young man of last year who had been in the London fire raid with her. Would that young man ever come back? She didn't think so. Sometimes in his sleep he started and shuddered. Or he woke groaning 'Oh Christ.' And when he was sitting with her during the day, he would suddenly flinch.

She knew that *he* must speak about it and that she could not. Then one evening when he returned from a sweep over France and came into the cottage, his teeth were chattering in his head. He said he felt icy cold. She made him sit down, she fetched a blanket, and hot coffee laced with rye whisky. She knelt by him and rocked him in her arms.

He couldn't speak.

He leaned against her in the silence of the hideous little room. At last he drank the coffee and said, 'It's the flak. I dread it so. Even on the ground I keep thinking about it, imagining it, thinking I can see it. I'm not afraid of meeting the enemy planes, Flip, it's not that. It never has been. It's the flak barrage, seeing the shells exploding round you like – like giant black flowers all over the sky. And then the plane shivers and rocks about from the explosion and you can't control it. And while you're trying to get it back on course, the flak gets worse. There are explosive shells that the gunners shoot at the planes, which can burst in the middle of the formation. They knock holes in the wings or the fuselage, or they hit the pilot, or the plane catches fire. Then you're trapped. It isn't the enemy,' he said again, 'You can see him and fight back. Flak feels like a hand reaching up to pull me out of the sky.' He paused and shivered again and said, 'Tonight there were shell holes in my wings.'

But he went on flying. And although his nightmare recurred, he never talked about it again. Philippa did not dare. Perhaps speaking of it would raise it like a demon.

Chapter Eleven

'Flip? It's Pa's birthday next week. I really think we both ought to make the effort to get home. He'll start thinking he only has one daughter. And I shouldn't imagine he sees much of her, would you?'

Elaine was speaking on the public telephone in one of the ground floor corridors at Blenheim. It was difficult to hear her sister's reply, there were footsteps and voices going by.

'Sorry. There's such a noise here. Did you hear me about Pa?'

Raising her voice, Philippa agreed that they should come to London. They arranged to meet at St Helen's on the day of their father's birthday which was in mid-January.

Elaine went back up the staircase from the Great Hall to her office. She sat down at her desk, on which reports lay waiting to be typed. Sensual-lipped eighteenth-century women in silks and pearls looked down at her from the walls. Things at the palace had changed since their day. Sighing, she began to work.

The Submariners' Course had ended and now, after more leaves than she had dared to hope for, Miles was gone. He was at sea. She found it hard to know nothing. When he had been on convoys, horrible though the Atlantic was, she had at least been able to imagine something of his sailor's life. But it was different now. Where had he gone? Husbandless, she was glad to work for more than nine hours a day. She had said that she wanted an 'eating up' job, and the description applied to her work at Blenheim. It consumed the uncounted days as if it were a dragon.

She still worked for the well-mannered and silent Captain Goodier. His reserve towards her was total. She could not remember him ever asking her a personal question. She supposed it was a change for him after the exhausting interrogations which were part of his work.

The one bright spot in Elaine's dull life was Marjorie. To Marjorie she could admit how painfully she missed Miles. Her friend's attitudes were her own. She could tell Marjorie things about herself that she would never tell her father or her sisters.

'You really hate Shelton, don't you?' remarked Marjorie, on the day Elaine had telephoned Philippa. 'I don't know why you stay. You could think up some straightforward lie, as we used to call them at school, and get digs at Keble. You could live with me, come to that. Why not? We'd have a lot of fun. You are an unnecessary martyr, you know. What can Miles possibly gain from you being stuck with those parents of his?'

She glanced at Elaine, who was walking beside her under the huge bare trees, the collar of her coat turned up. A scarlet scarf was tied round her neck, it trailed on to her breast. Marjorie said, laughing,

'You're a robin. Oh look! There's another.'

Elaine was not looking. She said humourlessly, 'You know quite well why I'm at Shelton. Because the *idea* of my being at his home makes him happy. He so loves it.'

'And you detest it.'

'The house is very beautiful.'

'Pooh. You know I mean your in-laws. What is the good of a mansion and crests on the family silver when you have a stone-faced mother-in-law behind the teapot?'

'She liked you when you came to see us,' said Elaine perversely.

'Stone-faced,' repeated Marjorie, 'I am middle-class and so are you, and the upper classes really make us feel it, don't they? They can't let go of their superiority. They have to grind down us peasants. Do you remember how Lady St Aird asked me about the Flowers when I came to tea. She positively grilled me. And then she discovered one of the Flower cousins nine times removed was related to that St Aird bishop. One had the feeling she had found an excuse for giving me tea. What it all boils down to is that if you're one of them you're fine, and if you are not, then you are out. Well, you married one, so you are in.'

'But she doesn't like me any more than I like her. And then there is Miles' father.'

Marjorie couldn't help laughing. St Aird, who had only appeared at the door at tea time and then, seeing her had promptly vanished, had taken her fancy. He was a kind of mad Mrs Rochester, wasn't he, she said. Except that he was in the stables and apparently knew how to paint.

'Or so you say. I wasn't asked to look.'

161

'He did look funny, standing in the door so suspiciously,' said Elaine, beginning to laugh too.

Elaine did not feel disloyal, smiling over the St Airds with Marjorie, because what her friend said was true. Elaine tried with all her heart to see with Miles' eyes and think with his thoughts, but now that he had gone it was becoming more and more difficult. There had always been differences in his way of thinking and her own; but his enchanting presence removed them or perhaps veiled them. When she was with him, she could see nobody else. She knew he was a snob: that made her smile. She knew that money – or to be exact the stylish signs of it – pleased him. Why shouldn't he look at things in that way? Miles was convinced, quite wrongly, that she would eventually love his parents and Shelton as he did. It was part of his deep family affection that he believed it, and Elaine stayed in his home just because of that. Sexual love between Miles and herself formed a kind of glue, which mended the ship and held it fast and made it seaworthy. Now that he was far away, there was the danger that the glue would melt.

Life at Shelton told on her nerves. There was the farce, every night, of changing for dinner when there was not a servant in the place. Claire was no cook, and the food was as bad as Miggs', but there was much less excuse, for in the country such treasures as fresh eggs and vegetables were commonplace. Elaine offered to cook the meal once or twice, but Claire had been so patronizing at the result – Elaine cooked beautifully – that Elaine realized it simply counted against her. To cook well was middle-class, or even common.

Usually serene and with a gentle philosophy, Elaine discovered in herself a temper she had not known she possessed and which needed to be kept in check. She lived in an ancient house with a dreamy English feel about it which soaked into the very walls. The bedroom smelled of lavender, the windowsills were broad enough to sit upon, the parquet floors were the colour of honey. From every window she could see a garden overgrown and wild, but lovely yet. In the dining room enigmatic St Aird faces looked down at her during the ill-cooked meals. How much more did she prefer the Blenheim portraits, all of them sexy, some positively vulgar. If it were not for Miles, she thought, I wouldn't stay here for five minutes.

The St Airds had few visitors. But the weekend Elaine had

arranged to go to London for her father's birthday she heard that Claire had invited her elder sister to stay.

Breaking the news of her coming absence, Elaine felt very guilty. Who would help to cook for Lady Agatha, she wondered.

At Elaine's hesitant and anxious manner, Claire raised pale eyebrows, 'My dear Elaine, of course it is convenient for you to go. Edmund and I are taking my sister to dine at The Bear at Woodstock.'

Never once since Elaine first came to Shelton had they taken her out for a meal, despite the Government positively encouraging people to eat out as a way of improving the meagre weekly rations.

Lady Agatha arrived before Elaine left for the station. She was older and plainer than Claire, very stout and slow. Even during tea she had begun to drone family litanies.

'I saw Cousin Robert at Eastbourne, Claire. His three boys are at Eton now.'

'Rachel is in the Wrens. She's engaged to a lieutenant commander, one of the Eynshams. You remember Michael Eynsham? He married . . .'

Refusing a second cup of tea, Elaine escaped to finish her packing. The round winter sun had begun to set. It shone through her bedroom windows, and when she looked out, the gardens were lit with a dying orange light. The yew hedges which had been shaped like peacocks and urns when she came to Shelton in peacetime summer had lost their identities now. They were simply green bushes. The lawns were like winter fields.

There was a tap on her door, and Claire walked into the room. 'The postman has just come. Two letters from Miles. One for you.'

She handed Elaine the letter with *On Active Service* stamped across it, and stood in the doorway, reading her own letter.

Elaine tore hers open. And found something in the envelope which was not a letter at all, but a square about five inches in size; Miles' letter had been photographed. His writing, never easy to read, was rendered miniscule.

'My darling. Here I am and this will be a dull letter due to dull routine only enlivened now and again by moments of happy oblivion due to the local drink. You'll be amused to hear that it

163

is cheap and very plentiful. Do you remember in Brighton, my darling, what a great event it was for us when we actually got hold of a bottle of white wine? Here it flows like a river . . .'

Elaine gave a little gasp.

Claire looked up from her own letter and said sharply, 'What is it?'

'He's in Malta.'

'So he says. Well?'

'Oh,' said Elaine weakly, 'it seems so far. I wonder when on earth he will be back.'

'Very likely not for a year or even two,' said Claire in a voice of an admonishing headmistress. She put her own letter into the bead handbag which she carried about with her, like a girl going to a ball. At the door she turned and looked at Elaine. The last sunlight shone on her, making her handsome and old.

'Our submarines must be based at Malta to patrol the Med. They are needed and the more there are of them the better. I trust,' she said, turning to go, 'we are not going to be sorry for ourselves.'

Marjorie was in Oxford on a shopping expedition, and she arranged to meet Elaine and see her off. She was in good spirits.

'Keep your eyes peeled for a lipstick for me, *please*! Any colour, any price, and as black market as you like. My face is looking khaki now my lipstick is down to the metal edge. And it's jolly painful putting it on, I might add.'

Elaine had been prepared for London to look dirty, but her country-accustomed eyes were shocked by its battered, dusty, wrecked appearance. It was a city of ruins which had not settled to be just that. There was a thin fog in the streets and it was nearly dark though not yet blackout time, when she walked up the short drive to St Helen's, letting herself in with her key. She put down her suitcase, pulling off her hat which had flattened her hair. The kitchen door opened.

'You're back, then. Like a cuppa? Sailor and I are havin' one.'

Wondering what matelot was sharing Miggs' strong red tea, Elaine followed her into a pleasantly warm kitchen. The split in the boiler was wider and through it she could see coke glowing almost white. It made a dull roar. There was nobody in the kitchen but Miggs and the ginger cat. It, too, had grown considerably.

'I call him Sailor because of the way he strolled in here. Casual-like. Quite settled down, he has.'

'How does Father take him?'

'Pretends not to see him, of course.'

Nothing in the kitchen had changed. On the mantelpiece so high that Miggs had to stand on a chair to reach it, was a black marble clock with a brass plaque: it had been presented to Miggs' great-uncle in the Royal Engineers when he left the army. Its chime, on the quarters, was like Big Ben's and it was the only clock in the house to keep good time. The dresser was built against the wall, and stacked with white china patterned with red, blue and yellow plums, a design called Imperial Fruit. It had been a wedding present to Theo and Mary – thirty-six of everything. A surprising number of the dishes still remained, considering how many Miggs smashed, shouting, 'God damn it!' as yet another soup plate crashed to the ground.

On the bottom shelf of the dresser was a large basket for Sailor. Miggs's sewing box was on the table, with some socks of Theo's. The three ration books were nearby, fastened with an elastic band.

Pouring tea, Miggs looked approvingly at Elaine. She had a soft spot for the eldest daughter, often remarking that Miss Elaine didn't let you down. And she liked Miles. Miggs had finally grown accustomed to Philippa's Yankee husband, but still sometimes remarked 'How do we know there isn't a wife in Hollywood or wherever he comes from?' Her prejudices had not died because America was now an ally.

'Up for the doctor's birthday? I hope you're not plannin' a dinner at home. There isn't a blind thing in the larder.'

She gazed into her teacup.

'Blow me down, another stranger. Must be a new young fellow of Trix's. That'll be no surprise. Who keeps an eye on her now, I ask you, Miss Elaine? Nobody. Not your job or mine either. It's the doctor's and he's too busy to see what goes on under his nose. Not that I blame her,' added Miggs with a swerve of attitude, 'for makin' the young chaps dance. But nobody could say she's doin' her bit, could they? Ah. There goes the surgery bell.'

She donned her creaking white overall.

Upstairs, Elaine thought how small her bedroom looked after the high-ceilinged spaciousness of Shelton. She was unpacking

165

when she heard her sister's voice and called out, 'Is that Flip? I'm in here.'

A second later Philippa rushed in headlong, to throw herself at Elaine and hug her tightly. Elaine, embarrassed at any emotion except between Miles and herself, laughed.

'Oh, darling!' cried Philippa, 'What an age! I've sure missed you – let me look at you! Glamorous as ever.'

Elaine was wearing one of the suits she had had made for her before the war; it was a milky brown and with it she wore a white silk blouse. As the nearest thing to uniform, such clothes were fashionable. Philippa was dressed in a purple, green and white checked shirt like a cowboy's and a pinafore dress of dark brown with metal clasps on the straps. Her hair was glossy and fell in its two crescents as always, but her eyes were too large for her face.

'Flip, you're very thin. I am not sure it suits you.'

'I measured my waist. It's nearly as small as Trix's. Less than twenty-three inches – imagine.'

'Sure you get enough to eat?' said Elaine disapprovingly.

Philippa laughed. Of course she did, more than enough. Why the Eagles were sent lovely boxes of American food, chocolate and biscuits and a wonderful cake made of things called pecan nuts and great big sticky cherries. It was a miracle that she was not as fat as a pig.

'By the way, Barny sends his love. He's got a weekend pass and please God will be here on Saturday.'

'How lucky you are to have him in England!' Elaine exclaimed without thinking.

Her sister did not answer but sat down on the bed and asked about Miles, about Blenheim and Shelton. The questions were perfunctory, and soon she began to talk. She had so wanted to see Elaine, she said. She had so much to say. She had tried to write, but somehow things looked melodramatic when you wrote them down.

The summer had been tough, she said. The patrols had been sent out over France every day. Then the offensive had begun and the bombers went out in large numbers and of course they had to be protected by the squadrons of Fighter Command, which included the Eagles. Big groups of fighters always guarded the bombers. First there was the advance guard – 'Their job is to try and sweep the enemy fighters from the sky,' she said. Then came the bombers with their escorts, fighters who flew

166

beside them and in the rear and above, making a kind of protective wall. Escorting was the hardest job for fighter pilots, they were not allowed to leave the bombers, they had to stay in their exact positions.

'You see,' said Philippa carefully, 'they must not break away and attack the enemy, even if he's trying to get through the wall. The only action an escort fighter ever gets lasts for an instant – it's never a real fight to the finish. Escorts can't have the fun of the chase. The position they *do* like is being above the bombers, it's like the man in the crow's nest of a ship on the lookout. Pilots prefer that job because there's the chance they'll be ordered down to attack.'

She talked on. Of the comradeship between pilots and their technicians, the signal operators, the engineers. Of how on duty most pilots drank nothing and 'ordinary people' didn't know that, and thought them hell raisers. She talked of battles, chases, of planes hunting and planes vanishing, of baling out and landing in the sea, of a bullet hitting Barny's compass, and how one of his friends flying to France lost his way and came home and how horrified he was. The air was filled with Spitfires in her talk, the sea with ships. The Eagles often said 'A Spit's more sensitive than a dame.' And the other thing they were always telling her was 'Those Krauts sure can fly.'

Her language was littered with slang unfamiliar to Elaine who knew nobody in what Miles called The Royal Advertising Force. Philippa talked of stooging and weaving, peeling off, snaking about, hedge-hopping. To parachute into the sea was to brolly hop into the drink. The slang was flippant, her sister's face tense.

'One of the Eagles wrote a love song to a WAAF I knew,' she said, 'it was called "You Shot me Down in Flames".'

She sang the refrain in her hoarse voice.

Then suddenly,

'I'm so selfish. Why do you let me go on like this? Forgive me. It's just so good to be able to talk. Not to have to watch my tongue.'

'With Barny?'

'With everybody, Elaine. They're so different now. The war has changed them. Changed Barny. When I first got married and met them all, they were just a bunch of wild boys. Their CO told Barny he thought they would never make a proper squadron, they just didn't know how to think as a team. That's very

American, you see. Not toeing the line, no obedience, things like that. They changed because you have to. They're experienced pilots now and they're tough. They joke about getting killed, about who'll be next. I think they make themselves feel that death is for the other guy. It won't happen to them.'

'Do you manage to feel like that?'

'I only pretend, Elaine. And there's something else. The three Eagle Squadrons are to be disbanded. Not right away, but it is going to happen when the Americans come over here. All the Eagles are quite excited about it, really, even Barny. I mean, their own people here and not on the other side of the world, not understanding a thing that's going on. But I *hate* it. Knowing the Eagles won't be in the RAF.'

She sighed and stood up, saying – an old panacea of hers – that she would go and wash her hair.

As she left the room she said, 'Do you like my pinafore dress? It's called a lumberjack. Barny's sister in Louisiana, Mary-Lou, sent it to me. Wasn't it swell of her?'

Elaine, who disliked it, agreed about the kindness of the American sister-in-law. For a moment she imagined Claire St Aird, in her trailing pre-war lace and pearls, faced at dinner time with a girl dressed as a lumberjack.

Miggs was doing the blackout. Theo was still at the hospital, and there was an hour before the family would be leaving to dine out. The girls went into the drawing room and sat by a miserable one-bar electric fire, talking of small things. The food at Blenheim, served by the duke's daughters, Philippa's hospital work which had recently raised two hundred pounds.

'Elaine? Flip?'

A metallic little voice called. In darted Trix.

'Together at last!' She ran over to kiss them both, squatted on the floor between them radiantly smiling. Her hair seemed longer and fairer, she still wore it in the Veronica Lake style, hanging on her cheeks and hiding one dark eye. Her pale blue skirt was short and pleated like a kilt, and a fine silk blouse was of a darker blue, with antique silver buttons engraved with daisies. Her smile was as gamine, her face as flawless as her sisters remembered. But it was more secret.

'Fun to see you,' she said, 'I begin to forget that I've got two big sisters. Of course I tell everybody about you both, but I don't think they believe me any more. I suppose you're up-to-the-minute with each other's news, and all I shall get is the fag end. Well, girls? What's been happening?'

She looked charmingly from one to the other.

Philippa glanced towards Elaine, almost for rescue. She hoped Elaine would speak, for she herself still found it quite difficult to talk to Trix about Barny. It was foolish and unsophisticated, and she had been married for nearly a year, but there it was. Trix and Barny had made love. Why couldn't she forget it? Elaine, always quick, began to talk about Miles and Malta and Blenheim. She also described the St Airds and Trix listened and laughed.

'Flip will fascinate you about the Eagles later,' finished Elaine casually, 'but what we both want to hear is about *you*.' She sounded like their mother when she added, not without severity, 'You never write to us. And when we telephone, where are you?'

'Dynamiting the West End, I guess,' said Philippa.

Trix gave her a friendly look.

'That's Yankee talk. I like it. Yes, I do a bit of dynamiting but lately perhaps not as much as usual. The fact is – '

She paused for effect. She wound a lock of hair round her finger, and then arranged it on her shoulder.

'The fact is, girls, I am married.'

Chapter Twelve

'You're what?'

Two horrified voices spoke at once. Trix looked delighted.

'I thought I'd knock you out. Yes, I am a married woman. Have been for two whole weeks. We were married by special licence at Caxton Hall. I told Pa I was at the Masons as per yuge, but actually I was ˜with my *husband* at the Ritz. He got passionate leave to marry me and then after a glorious night of love, off he went back to his ship.'

'To his ship,' repeated Elaine who had gone pale, 'Who is he?'

'Wouldn't you like to know?'

'Trix!' shouted Philippa, as red as Elaine was white, 'You are under age, you had no right – poor Father – '

'Poor fiddlesticks. What does he care? Particularly now that boring French girl is hanging around. You remember her? Mademoiselle from Armentières. One of the two French A's stupidly brought her here, she's Alain's cousin. Miggs simply can't stick her and neither can I. Anyway, if you must know, I married a guy I met at your wedding, Flip. He is a friend of Miles' and *you* know him, Elaine. You invited him as a matter of fact. I am married to Dick Polglaze.'

'Marjorie's cousin!'

'That's right. He often tells me about the Flowers in Oxfordshire and says I must go down and meet them. Well, he's had a bit of leave, not much, his ship was due for a boiler clean and . . . and . . . off he took me to Caxton Hall. I must show you our wedding photographs.'

Elaine and Philippa stared at her. She had never seemed so much a stranger, so far from the little girl who had sucked sweets and failed examinations, the child whom Elaine had worried over and Philippa had petted.

Both sisters continued to look at her, as if waiting for something she was not going to give them. Philippa automatically put her hand into the pocket of her pinafore dress and pulled out some Lucky Strike cigarettes. Elaine refused, wrinkling her nose, but Trix accepted. They smoked for a while in silence, the room filling with the foreign scent.

'Do you love him,' asked Philippa at last.

'Of course I do, stoopid.'

'Are you having a baby?' said Elaine suddenly.

Trix really laughed at that.

'How old-fashioned you are. Why should I be preggers if I don't want to be? Not that Dick would object, he said I'd look quite sweet, one baby pushing the pram of another. But of course I am not.'

'Then I don't understand and I'm sure Flip doesn't either. Why rush into marriage exactly as if you *were* pregnant and didn't dare to leave it another week? Why the haste and secrecy? Dick Polglaze is a nice man. I can't imagine what he was thinking of.'

Trix stretched her legs and wiggled her toes in the toeless pink and blue shoes. She seemed as if she were reflecting, a rarity with Trix. Philippa saw that although Trix had expected their reaction, and had been prepared for it and even amused at it, she still found her sisters hard to cope with. She might be casual and airy about them at a distance, but Elaine in particular impressed her. Far more than their father did. Perhaps, thought Philippa, that is because Elaine loves her. Trix is not sure that Father does . . .

'Dick's ship is back on Atlantic convoy now,' she said, 'we thought we'd take the jump while we had the chance.'

It was a sentence to move the hardest heart, and it certainly reached Philippa's. She looked kindly at her little sister.

'Are you very happy?' she said in a soft voice.

'It's lovely fun being married,' said Trix, seizing on the sympathy and affection, 'Why didn't you tell me what a lark it is? I would have rushed to Caxton Hall ages ago.'

'Scarcely with Dick Polglaze, since you only met him at Flip's wedding. And he must have been at sea most of the time since then,' said Elaine very coldly. She had no sympathy at all, and Trix was getting on her nerves.

'Oh Elaine! What I meant was supposing I had met Dick sooner, of course. Anyway, it was love at first sight. Isn't my ring wizzy? Little sapphires, because Dick likes me in blue. It's an eternity ring, of course; he got it at Asprey's. He's going to get me a diamond one next, he is *so* extravagant.'

171

Turning her black eyes on her elder sister, she said in a wheedling tone, 'Elaine . . . one thing . . . '

'I know what you are going to ask me. About Pa.'

'Darling, it *would* be better if you told him.'

'Trix!' exclaimed Philippa, sympathy oozing away, 'That is pretty monstrous of you.'

'Oh I know. But I am.'

Elaine did not know what to answer. She saw in Philippa's face as well as Trix's the belief that she would do it. They were as bad as each other. They leaned on her as if she were quite old. They demanded that she would take their mother's place. You are the strong one, their silence said. She did not feel strong. Miles's absence had weakened her. She had the sensation that it would be easy for anybody to pull her down. She had lost the certainties of peacetime, the old moralities and standards. She resented her two sisters looking at her like puppies waiting for a biscuit.

'Very well,' she said, after a pause, 'I will do it. But not for your sake, Trix. If you are old enough to marry, you are old enough to do your own dirty work. I'll do it for Dick. Because he is Miles' friend.'

She walked out of the room.

Free of Elaine's coldness and disapproval and seeing how passionately interested Philippa had become, Trix told her in colourful detail the story of her wedding. She had worn a new dress from Harrods (she wasn't going to say how much it cost), and Dick had bought her white orchids to carry. They had had champagne cocktails, and the best man had been somebody from Dick's ship, he was called Lofty because he was six foot five, and he was *so* funny. They had had a lovely party, the three of them, at the Ritz after coming back from Caxton Hall.

'It was just gorgeous,' finished Trix.

A strain of impulsiveness, of precipitate haste, ran through the nature of all three Tyrrell girls. It had been in Theo when he was young: it was in Trix and in Philippa. They let theirs rip. Elaine had hers under control, but this evening she gave way to the Tyrrell lust to get things over. She marched straight into her father's study when his last patient had left. She met Miggs sidling out, unbuttoning her white overall. Miggs whispered, 'So she's told you.'

'*You knew!*'

'She never said. I found out,' said Miggs succinctly. 'I suppose you've got landed with the job of tellin' the doctor. Typical.'

Theo was at his desk, taking the wrapping off a weekly medical journal. He looked his usual immaculate and tired self. When he saw her, he stood up.

'Father.'

She did not, this time, back away from his kiss but stayed close to him and shut her eyes. He smelled of eau-de-cológne and disinfectant as he had always done. She liked it.

'A happy birthday, Father. We're going out to dinner, you know. *We* are taking *you*.'

'That's very nice of you, Elaine.'

He gave her a kind smile.

She sat down, drew a breath and said,

'Before we go I have a shock for you.'

Theo stiffened. He thought – it can't be Miles, she is too calm.

'Trix is married,' she said baldly. 'It was my idea to break the news to you before we go out. I think you should know right away. But I don't want you to quarrel with her. Listen, please! She is impulsive and hotheaded and all the rest of it, but people do things like this now. The man she has married has rejoined his ship and is in the Atlantic. God knows when she'll see him again. They didn't tell their respective families, they simply didn't have time. They just upped and went to Caxton Hall.'

'*Caxton Hall*. Why not a church?'

He actually looked angrier at that than when she first broke the news.

'I know, Father. A civil marriage of all things. I dislike it as much as you do. I suppose they chose it because it was quick.'

He looked, she thought, as hard as Claire.

'And who, might one enquire, has she married?'

'Someone you know. A friend of Miles' who was at Flip's wedding. Dick Polglaze.'

Hearing the name, a faint change came over her father's flinty face. I'm through the worst, thought Elaine. And perhaps he will get closer to Trix now that she is married to a man he likes. She remembered her father's pleasant way with Dick at the wedding; there was no mistaking it when Theo liked somebody.

He asked one or two questions, sounding calm. He even smiled, a sign that ordinary life had returned. From now on, she thought, he would think of Dick Polglaze as a son-in-law and

173

when Dick finally appeared at St Helen's, Theo's imagination would have turned him into a member of the family.

'You will be nice to her, won't you, Father?' said Elaine, sensing an advantage.

He replied with a dry smile that it did not look as if he was going to be given much choice. But her advantage was not so very strong after all. When she suggested that they should open the bottle of champagne he had been saving for the end of the war, he refused.

He did not speak to Trix about her marriage when they all left for their dinner in Knightsbridge. During the meal she kept darting expectant looks at him. He did not meet them. With their father present, there was the usual constraint on conversation between the sisters. Elaine talked of Miles in Malta, and Philippa told her father about the Eagle Squadron's exploits at Dieppe.

'Do you know, Father, nearly one-third of the pilots whose planes were shot down at Dieppe were saved. Barny said that's because the designers of the Spits had planned a proper exit.'

Trix, competitively, weighed in with something about Atlantic convoys. Her father merely nodded. Apart from offering her a second glass of white wine, he did not address a word to her. Trix was not sure whether to be relieved or annoyed.

When they came home, their father thanked them warmly for the dinner and bade them goodnight. The girls exchanged glances. Trix and Philippa wandered into the kitchen to make a final cup of tea. But Elaine, also saying goodnight, went up to her room. Her sisters' company oppressed her. Philippa was foreign and sentimental and Trix, the moment her father had gone, would start to show off again.

Elaine felt slightly sick. Her period was a fortnight late. Could it be herself and not Trix who was pregnant? She certainly did feel sick and rather ill. She had not wanted to go out to dinner, and had had no appetite.

She was already in bed, trying to read and feeling wretched, when there was the ghost of a knock. A grizzled head came round the door.

'Have a nice time, did you?'

'Very nice, Miggsy, thank you.'

'And how did things go with the doctor and the news, lady?'

'Not too bad. Better than I hoped.'

174

Miggs stood in the doorway, her hands in the pockets of her red dressing-gown.

'She can thank her stars that you were here, that's all I say. You're the only one with a bit of tact.'

Miggs turned to go, but suddenly gave a laugh which sounded like the snort of a pony.

'One thing I will give Trix. She knows when it's wise to look slippy. But she cut it pretty fine, didn't she?'

Elaine did not know what she was talking about, unless it was pregnancy again. She said shortly that there had never been any question of her sister *having* to get married. She did not spell it out. Miggs had offended her.

The old nurse impatiently shook her head.

'I'm not talkin' about bein' in the family way, Miss Elaine. She's a sight too smart for that. I'm talkin' about the call-up. You surely heard of *that*, down in the country? Girls in the Food Office told me today that it's the first time it's happened in history, callin' up unmarried women between the ages of nineteen and thirty. They got to go into uniform, or they got to go into factories. Well. Your sister wouldn't have liked either, would she? Not with those long finger-nails.'

Elaine went to see a doctor when she returned to Oxfordshire. He was the St Aird's doctor, who lived within walking distance of Shelton, a sharp-featured elderly man with a faint Irish tang in his voice, and a surgery out of a Victorian novel. He was very kind to her and confirmed that she was pregnant.

The news made her deeply, overwhelmingly happy: so much so that when she told her mother-in-law she almost felt she would enjoy being kissed. But that would be going too far.

Claire smiled, refusing to be surprised, and said excellent, excellent. Miles would be delighted and it would be sure to be a son. There was a 'preponderance of boys' in the St Aird family. She ignored the fact that Elaine was one of three girls. Claire also added that she would inform her husband. Elaine was not too starry-eyed to miss what Claire meant, which was that if Elaine told him St Aird would have been shocked to his soul at such middle-class lack of propriety.

The feeling of bliss, not unlike that which drenched her after Miles' lovemaking, did not last. She was regularly sick every morning before taking the Blenheim bus, and sometimes sick again during the day. There was a lavatory at the end of the corridor near her office, to which she gratefully retired, returning – just like the old days of proposals of marriage – with a rosy face. Captain Goodier surprised her by saying she looked well. She had not told him yet.

'Suppose,' remarked Marjorie, 'you were working in the despatch department. They have to walk miles. You'd never make it.'

Marjorie made up for Claire by her unaffected delight at Elaine's news. She was knowledgeable about pregnancy, lent Elaine a brown smock with a pale blue collar, and offered a wardrobe-full of baby clothes which she was keeping for her own next child. When would that be arriving, she said. She hoped she would not be too old to conceive by the time Bob came home from the Far East.

The girls also talked over Elaine's other piece of family drama – Trix's marriage to Marjorie's favourite cousin. The suddenness of it was not what surprised Marjorie who said Dick Polglaze was a man who made up his mind and then carried out his decision without hanging about. It was his marrying at all which was so unexpected. Marjorie had never thought he would: he had too many affairs.

'How do you know?'

'Because he's told me about them. What a face, Elaine! I do believe you are a prude. He doesn't go into the details, you know, but he always confides in me because he knows it makes me laugh. He says I do as a sister. There was a girl in Cumberland who worked in a factory. Very tarty, she was, I have a vague notion she was his first (he wasn't hers, which was the point). They made love in a boat on the river. Dick likes boats. For about a year there was a Wren, Rosy Whitlock, he said she was lovely. They spent bits of his leave at expensive hotels: Dick's a great one for hotels as well as boats. He took his wife to stay at the Ritz, didn't he? He runs true to form. There were others too, only I forget their names. Dick is a sexy old thing.'

'My sister is not exactly the virgin bride.'

'That must be what they have in common. Sex is the strongest bond.'

'In the long run?'

176

'What long run have we, Elaine? Any of us?'

Marriage had apparently changed Trix for the better. She telephoned Elaine two or three times to report that she had received letters from Dick. She also described the appearance in London of Mr and Mrs Polglaze who had come down from Cumberland specially to meet Theo and herself. Mr Polglaze, she said gaily, was short and grizzled and exactly like an old bear. And his wife had a big bosom and a huge diamond brooch which she assured Trix would be hers one day. They had had dinner at Brown's, and Trix had dressed for the part in her dullest clothes. They had been very nice to her, so she thought she must have been a success. Elaine, who had seen Trix put herself out to charm, was sure of it.

Marjorie was eager to meet Dick's wife. When Elaine said this, Trix sounded pleased. She obligingly travelled to Oxford one Sunday in the usual unspeakably crowded train, and met both girls for luncheon at The Mitre. Trix had enjoyed the journey. She had sat, all the way, on the knee of a Scots Guard sergeant.

The lunch went well, but Elaine did wonder if Marjorie had expected anybody quite so startling to look at as her younger sister. Everybody in the dining room, everybody male, that was, stared. Trix seemed unaware of the sensation she caused. She was friendly to Marjorie, talking about Dick and asking lots of questions. Did Marjorie know what was his favourite food? What did Marjorie think was positively the best Fortnum's parcel to send him? She had forgotten to ask him if he liked dried figs: she had been given a whole box of them.

When Trix was once more on her way to London, perched upon another stranger's knee, Marjorie saw Elaine to the bus stop.

'She's gorgeous looking. Do you think she'll stay the course?'

Trix enjoyed being a married woman. There was a song she often sang, 'Kiss the Boys Goodbye'. Before Dick went to sea he had told her that she could 'kiss the boys hello', as long as that was all she did. She had agreed solemnly. And when she was out and about in London now, expertly keeping susceptible men in order, she often said to them, 'Of course, Dick always comes first.' 'Of course,' they agreed. With Trix, they agreed to anything. She no longer went to bed with the boyfriends who attracted her, but their number did not grow less. She was wonderful company besides being the best-looking girl in a restaurant, and the lightest dancer on a dance floor.

Her twentieth birthday had come and gone. It was the summer of 1942. To Trix, London was home. It was a city which she could never remember as not dusty and shabby and crammed with troops. There were the Commandos in their green berets, the Poles rakishly wearing their dark blue ones. There was English 'khaki and Naval blue with gold lace, and Wrens wearing hats which made them look like Nelson, and Land girls, and Philippa's beloved RAF with their romantic silver wings.

Suddenly, quite suddenly, London was invaded. The Americans arrived. Pearl Harbour had been months ago, and of course everybody knew they were coming. But when the American troops actually began to pour into London it was very extraordinary. They appeared overnight in their thousands. It was impossible to estimate how many Americans there were. London was engulfed.

Americans were not strangers to Trix. She had had one or two admirers in the Eagle Squadron, had gone out with them now and again, and lost touch with them. She had no close American friends. There had been the incident, conveniently forgotten with Barny. But Trix liked Americans and Canadians. She liked their accents, familiar from the films, and she also liked the idea of America. That summer – there they were wherever she looked. When she walked down Bond Street, or danced at Hatchetts, or glanced from taxi windows she saw them. They had done something no other foreign troops had done. They had changed the face of London.

They sat on the steps of stuffy antiquated houses which had been the guarded mansions of the aristocracy. They lounged at Rainbow Corner in Piccadilly where the American Red Cross had set up a club for GI's, including a canteen and a theatre. At the back of Knightsbridge, the Berkeley Gardens hotel, shut since the outbreak of war, was opened. The Stars and Stripes hung outside it – it was now a club. American troops went in and out of its swing doors in a stream of pale coloured khaki.

If Trix was conscious of the young men now swarming over the great dirty city, the Americans were even more conscious of

Trix. Before they had arrived in England, a place which apart from the language, and there were pitfalls in that, was as foreign to them as Peking, they had been given instructions by the War Office in Washington. These had been in the form of an 'Introduction to Great Britain' and began 'YOU are going to Great Britain as part of an Allied offensive – to meet Hitler and beat him on his own ground. For the time being you will be Britain's guest. The purpose of this guide is to start getting you acquainted with the British, their country, and their ways.' It did not mince words. The British were reserved but not unfriendly. There were differences in the language that it was necessary to remember. British people did not say bum or bloody and a GI must never say that the USA won the last war. They must not brag. US pay was the highest in the world. They mustn't say so. 'Don't make fun of their accents, you sound just as funny to them but they will be too polite to show it,' said the instructions severely.

The instructions were actually orders. Having had them dinned into their heads, the Americans were wary. In many cases they found their worst fears confirmed. British people *were* stuck up. Their accents *were* ridiculous. Their food *was* filthy. And a large number of British troops resented them. It was not long before the Americans heard the jealous joke against them, that they were over-decorated, over-paid, over-sexed and over here.

And then, as their eyes wandered through the mass of uniformed or drab strangers, they suddenly saw Trix. She was the epitome of the beautiful blonde. She was Betty Grable and Veronica Lake and Alice Faye. She was a knockout. It seemed impossible that she could be British.

'Aren't you really an American?' was the question that Trix was asked daily. She smiled delightedly, lowering her eyelashes over her black-treacle coloured eyes. Did they really think she was? Surely she looked like a Londoner, for that was what she was. There would follow more admiration and more assurance of the positively American style of her good looks.

Trix met them on dance floors, they stood beside her and her friends in the bars of expensive hotels. Sometimes, like the two French A's now vanished from her life, she picked them up on the tops of buses. But 'Dick always comes first', and she did not invite them home. Yet they fascinated her. She would have

179

liked a passport into the new American world of occupied London.

Of all the people to provide such a passport, her father proved to be the man.

The blitz was over. The sound of the Alert was rarely heard now and Theo had returned to concentrating on his private practice. Many of his patients who had fled from London had come back, and his telephone and waiting room were busy. He was also seeing something of the young French girl, Annette Ghilain. She was working as a secretary at the Centre d'Acceuil. He took her out sometimes for a meal in the West End.

Trix did not like Annette much. She thought her a gold-digger which Trix herself had never actually been. She certainly wouldn't go out with somebody her father's age just to be given a meal. But she did not wish Annette ill and had once said to a shocked Philippa, home on a brief visit, that anybody who could make their father spend his money was jolly clever.

'Of course most of it is Mother's money, but still. I take my hat off to her. They went to the Dorchester twice. Imagine that.'

'Do you think he may be in love with her?'

'For Pete's sake, Flip. He's over sixty.'

Refreshed from undisturbed nights of sleep, enjoying the summer and the occasional company of someone young and attractive, Theo was quite pleasant nowadays to his married daughter Beatrix. One evening he found her watering her row of lettuces in the garden. She was still a fervent follower of the Dig for Victory campaign.

Her father stood watching her. The air was filled with the smell of wet earth and birds were singing in the pear trees. For the moment he remembered his youth; he had brought Mary to see St Helen's before he had bought the house and Mary had said, 'Why, look at the pear tree, Theo. All that blossom. Just like a bride.'

Now the tree was hung with small greenish-brown fruit.

He pulled up a deck chair and sat down in the deckled shade under the tree. Behind him was the skeleton of the conservatory which had never been pulled down, but had become a part of the landscape, a familiar ruin. The burned frame was green with moss and lichen, weeds grew in the cracks. and a buddleia with long purple flowers had managed to take root in the roof.

Trix finished her watering and sat back on her heels.

'Have you *seen* how many Yanks there are in town now, Father? They're simply everywhere. Poor things, I bet they are homesick. We ought to ask one or two of them round for a meal,' she added, remembering a brief flirtation on the top of a Number 73 bus.

'It would be better if you did some work for them,' replied Theo. 'Do you remember Mrs Alwynne? I met her recently at a dinner party. Philippa still works for that children's hospital, you know. But Mrs Alwynne has taken on some new tasks, it seems. She is working for the Americans. Apparently there are clubs for the American troops opening up all over London. And they're crying out for help.'

He was accustomed to Trix, although he never used the idiotic name. He scarcely noticed his youngest child's dyed silvery hair, her strong scent, or heard the little voice quacking on the telephone. He was used to seeing her dart through the house busy on her own devices. In a way he loved her. She was his child. And she did not need him: she was a married woman and an adult. He was glad to give her a home while her husband was at sea, but she was Dick's responsibility. Looking at her with slight irony, he waited for her to refuse to do some war work. Even unobservant Theo had noticed that Beatrix never worked.

She put down the watering can and clasped her hands, exclaiming eagerly that she would love – simply love! – to do war work for the Americans. Could he possibly arrange it?

Theo felt the same unfamiliar fatherly satisfaction which had come to him when he helped Elaine to get to Blenheim Palace.

Anyone willing to work for Mrs Alwynne had no chance to change their minds. The telephone rang next morning while Trix was in the bath. Miggs shouted for her. Trix dashed down in a négligé so transparent that Miggs averted her eyes and retreated to the chaste company of Sailor.

'Mrs Polglaze?' said a lively commanding voice, 'Jane Alwynne here. Your father tells me you have most generously . . . know your sister, of course . . . sterling work . . . the club is at Knightsbridge. Yes, I shall be here. Could you come at six this evening?'

Unlike Philippa, Trix did not realize that when she agreed to meet Mrs Alwynne at the club, she had taken on the job.

She dressed thoughtfully for what she believed was an interview. She decided on a new clinging crêpe dress. It was white,

181

one of her favourite colours, and had the fashionably large padded shoulders embroidered with gold beads. She blued her eyelids, brushed her hair energetically, and when she was ready picked up a flower made of stiffened white lace. She put it on top of her head and looked at herself. Yes.

The evening was still hot and sunny when her taxi drew up at the Berkeley Gardens hotel. The Stars and Stripes hung limply from its pole without stirring. The hotel's flight of once-white marble steps was so dirty it had turned almost black, and all the way up were soldiers, sitting like debs at pre-war dances. All the way up Trix was given whistles of approval.

A harrassed woman at the reception desk said that Mrs Alwynne was in her office, the second on the left. And – 'Yes, Lieutenant, what is it that you want?' to a young man waiting to catch her attention. Four others waited behind him.

Trix found Jane Alwynne sitting in a small office crammed with baskets of clothes and box files. She was dictating to a cowed-looking girl.

'Oh, sorry. Am I interrupting?' said Trix, knowing that she was.

'You must be Mrs Polglaze. Come in, come in. You can run away, Betty, I will send for you when I need you.'

Jane looked at Trix and hospitably patted the vacated seat.

Inwardly, Jane was having a good laugh. Who would have credited Philippa Tyrrell with having a sister like this one? If I had knelt down to pray for a helper in this place, thought Jane piously, I could not have been sent anyone more fitted for the work.

'Well?' she said briskly, 'One night or two?'

'Oh, more if you really want me.'

Trix had enjoyed the wolf whistles.

'Shall I put you down for four? You can shout if you find it is too much. The hours are six until midnight, if you can keep awake that long.'

'I'm sure that'll be okay.'

Jane paused diplomatically. 'Of course you know that it is voluntary. This is war work, so there is no pay, naturally.'

Trix, who had vaguely imagined generous pay since it was for the Americans, replied that she had never imagined being paid.

'Good, good. I'll get Betty to take you along.'

'What would I have to do, Mrs Alwynne?'

Trix spoke in the conditional tense. She felt she was being rushed. The lace flower had become unpinned, and she made a dab at securing it.

'All the girls here are cooks and bottle-washers. They dish out the Coco-Cola and the coffee and the fruit juices and so on. Not demanding work, you know. But it is important to look after our Allies, isn't it?'

Trix most earnestly agreed.

Jane's cowed secretary, who looked as if she could do with a good night's sleep, took Trix down the corridor. A group of girls far less pretty than Trix were hard at work in the hotel's big kitchens which were filled with steam. Three girls at the sink were standing on the wet linoleum floor.

'Thank goodness, more help,' said a lanky girl with spots whom Trix thought should be introduced to that wizard lotion from Harrods. 'Take this tray out to them, will you?'

She picked up the heavy tray and put it into Trix's hands. 'The boys sitting are waiting for hamburgers. The ones by the bar want Coke. All right?'

The tray was excessively heavy, thought Trix, but at least she was escaping the steam. The smell of cooking was unpleasant, and she recoiled at the prospect of having to put her clover-tipped hands into water slimy with soda. But she liked Americans.

The room into which she carried her tray had been a spacious hotel dining room. Now it was the club room and had a dance floor. Two GI's at two pianos were playing a duet of 'Kiss the Boys Goodbye'. Hearing it, she grinned. At her entrance, thirty or forty pairs of eyes looked across the room. And thirty or forty men thought – so they make 'em this way over here after all.

She moved among the tables, smiling at the compliments, stooping to put down plates, then shaking back her glittering hair. Wherever she went there were the wolf whistles again. She was enchanted by her success, and was at her most fascinating and confident when a tall man put his hand on her arm.

'Good to see you again, Trix.'

She looked up, surprised. She did not recognise him but saw that he wore wings.

'Again? We haven't met, have we?'

'Sure we have. At Flip's wedding and afterwards we took you dancing, remember? I'm Barny's buddy, Chuck Greenfield.'

'One of the Eagles!'

She turned the full ray of her smile on him, to the envy of a tableful of admiring GI's.

'Will you dance with me, Trix? I'd like that.'

'But I can't, Chuck. I am working,' said Trix for the first time in her life.

'Not allowed to say No to an ex-Eagle, didn't they tell you that?'

She stood holding the tray, tempted and tempting. He lingered beside her. He had a most particular smile, it was mischievous and intimate and trusting. It was as if he loved the world. Trix had known many men. Conceited men and clever ones, sexy men and shy ones, confident Frenchmen and serious Dutchmen and Guards officers with handsome faces and not a word to say and wild New Zealanders. She had never met anybody as innocently friendly as Chuck Greenfield.

He gently took the tray out of her hands and put it down on the table. Then he led her to the floor where a few couples were dancing. The music changed to a slow tune. 'That Lovely Weekend'.

'"The two days of heaven you helped me to spend,"' sang Trix, and he put his arm round her and danced in the swaying American way, cheek pressed against hers.

When the dance ended he said, 'You're like a leaf.'

'Thank you, kind sir.'

'Don't you dare dance with another guy. They only just got here. I had a claim on you when I arrived in 1940.'

'Were you in the Battle of Britain?'

'Not quite, but we were *here*, weren't we? Waiting to join in.'

'Flip says all the Eagles were heroes,' said Trix winningly.

'Don't know I can live up to that!'

The music began again and they danced again. He told her he had already been transferred, he called it pitchforked, into the US Army Air Corps. They'd made him a temporary instructor. The job was 'all talk and no do.'

'I bet you're a swell instructor.'

'I do my darndest,' he said, looking down at the sympathetic beauty in his arms, 'but teaching's so dull. We study air battles, analyse mistakes that were made on both sides. That's called learning tactical awareness. I sure would prefer being in the old squadron dispersal hut, waiting for a scramble signal.'

He told her that it only half amused him to receive letters from home complaining of the terrible privations they were now suffering. All they were allowed now was a pound of sugar a week, just imagine that. And forty-six gallons of petrol a month, how did they manage?

Trix listened and smiled and liked him. She thought it very attractive that he wore two pairs of wings, the RAF wings on the left of his tunic. He was a prize and she wanted to go on dancing with him. She also wanted to avoid the kitchen but thought it wiser to be seen there, at any rate tonight. So, with a lingering goodbye to Chuck, she returned to the kitchen to carry more trays and to help with the disgusting washing-up. At midnight the club closed. When she came down the hotel steps, her face freshly made-up, the white flower bobbing on top of her head, she was not even surprised to find Chuck waiting for her. He had a driver and a jeep. Trix had never ridden in a jeep before, and stood for a moment admiring the great heavy automobile. It was painted dark khaki, built like a tank, and on the bonnet was WHATAGIRL!! in thick pink lettering. Stepping over the word, wearing French knickers and nothing else, with enormous breasts crimson-nippled, was the figure of a girl. She wore high heeled ankle-strapped shoes and carried a parasol.

'The boys call her Rita Hayworth. She's not near as pretty as you,' said Chuck, giving Trix his hand. She climbed into the jeep, showing yards of silken leg.

When they stopped at St Helen's it was dark and moonless. Telling the driver he would not be long, Chuck walked with Trix to the steps of the sleeping house. She turned to say goodnight. For a moment or two he hesitated, taking her hand and pressing it. But something in the way she stood, something in the very air made him know he could kiss her. He put his arms round her and kissed her so passionately that she could scarcely breathe.

'Beautiful. You're beautiful. Don't you forget me, now. I'll call you.'

Chapter Thirteen

Summer was hot. Day followed cloudless day of blue skies, and when the clouds did appear they were fine weather mountains of gleaming white. In the park at Blenheim the hay was cut – it was bone dry in a few hours. When Elaine walked home in the evenings, the hedges were alive with birds and the strong-smelling meadowsweet had grown four foot high.

She used to love the summer. But her pregnancy was not easy, she felt rather ill most of the time and although she determined to go on working, the journey to Woodstock and back was long and made her ache. She had another worse pain. She found that she missed Miles more than ever before. Was it because she was pregnant that she felt this dreadful and unceasing want, a yearning that never left her? How long was it since she had seen him – seven months, twenty-nine weeks. Marjorie had not seen her husband for over two years. I suppose it is what Claire calls my condition that makes me miss him so, she thought. She wondered where her serenity had gone.

He wrote to her as often as he could and he was overjoyed at the news of the baby. But the letters did not bring her very much comfort for there was not the least chance of his being posted home. Watching the ebb and flow of the war, she saw that for Miles to come home from the Mediterranean now was impossible. The war was going badly, the Eighth Army in the Western desert was in retreat, and the terrible Russian war did not abate. What could *she* expect? She was one near-invisible dot on the huge bloodstained map of the world.

Sometimes Miles's letters had references to his work, vague references, but she never managed to create what his life was like in Malta. He had no gift of description. He said the job was hellish difficult and very absorbing. He said he'd made good friends. Miles always made those. She tried to imagine the life of a submariner. But she had been afraid of the world beneath the sea since she was a child. When she learned to swim she would never swim underwater. The thought of Miles, fathoms deep, scared her. Everybody needed courage now. The families who had faced the blitz, the troops sweating in the desert, the men in Japanese prison camps, the friends like Dick Polglaze sailing the cruel Atlantic. But soldiers, sailors, pilots, civilians, could at least use their eyes. They could *see*. The world Miles had chosen was in the dark.

Every day and every night of her life she thought about him. The child stirred and jumped in her womb. Would it be a son? Would he have Miles' grey eyes and that dent in his chin? Miles's face, arrogant and movingly young, came to her. There was a photograph of him in a silver frame in the drawing room, and a badly-painted portrait in the dining room. It had been one of his father's failures: St Aird was no portrait painter and had done the picture entirely because Claire asked for it. St Aird had painted Miles in uniform, with an almost black sky above him, and the dim shape of a surfaced submarine in a dark sea behind his shoulder. Elaine disliked the painting. The man looking out with painted eyes was not Miles but a waxwork hero. There was no mischief or humanity in the face. It was a poster for a flag day.

Avoiding the eyes of the portrait and the stiff photograph, Elaine took Miles with her, as she took his child, wherever she went. He was part of her. She had a real photograph of him in her room. Theo had taken it at St Helen's just after Miles had gone into the Navy. He wore matelot's uniform and was laughing like a schoolboy.

Captain Goodier actually referred to Miles one day. As he never said anything personal to her she was very startled.

'I gather your husband is a submariner in the Med., Mrs St Aird.'

Elaine wondered what was coming next.

'They're doing important work out there, you know. Now that Crete has gone, we are using Malta as our bastion. As a matter of fact, we ourselves are using the island for some of our work at present. I mention this because you will see it in my next report. It is Operation Ali Baba.'

He gave her a dry smile.

'The submarines are running our agents into the Middle East at convenient moments. It is a most useful way of delivering them,' he added. He made the submarines sound like suburban trains.

The weather grew steadily hotter, and Elaine in her eighth

month felt the heat more than ever. Her hands had become slightly swollen and so had her ankles. She did not mention this to anyone, even Marjorie. Talking about aches and pains embarrassed her, she had always been physically reserved. She supposed the swelling was usual when one was dragging about with so much extra weight.

One evening which seemed hotter than the rest she walked back to Shelton after the oppressive bus drive. She was sweating. She kept thinking about the river which lay behind a distant row of willow trees. Months ago before her pregnancy she had asked Claire is one could bathe there. Claire was dumbfounded.

'Good gracious. Only factory girls do that.'

Elaine hadn't the spirit to disobey. Probably Miles would think it common too.

But now the idea of the river, across the hot fields of dusty stubble, haunted her. She imagined what it would be like to be immersed in the cool water. She could feel the silky mud as she waded in, and smell the green scent of rushes . . .

One day Miles and I will take a punt from Oxford and go down the Cherwell, Miles promised he would take me there. We will have strawberries and champagne, and then we'll swim, and then we'll lie in the punt under a tree and kiss and kiss.

The old house dozed. Its stones were hot to the touch, the rooks croaked in the high trees behind the house – caw-caw-caw. The St Aird retriever lay prostrate under a crab apple tree. When he saw her he raised his head and lazily thumped his tail, not bothering to come and welcome her.

In doors there was a cool spell of silence. Nobody was about, and she supposed that Claire was out on her unending work for the WVS. She automatically looked at the salver in the hall where Claire left her letters, but there was no envelope with HMS Ship on it. The drawing room door opened. Claire stood there.

She had a piece of paper in her hand.

'Miles's submarine is missing,' she said.

Elaine stumbled up to her room and slammed the door and fell on the bed. She began to cry violently, her sobs a dreadful sickening kind of cough as she groaned aloud like a woman in her death agony. Oh Miles, Miles, dearest, dearest, you can't be dead, I won't believe it. I want you, I need you for always, I need you now. There's a baby inside me, you can't have left me, you never would, you never would. How can I live if I'm never going to see you again? Never. Never. Never. They don't only sail in the dark, they die in the dark. If you're in a ship and you're hit there's a chance, but not in submarines, and nobody knows whether it's quick or slow or where the ship is somewhere in the black water, fathoms, fathoms deep. Miles's submarine is missing.

Lying on her face, coughing and groaning, she did not hear the door opened so roughly that it hit the wall.

'*Stop that.*'

The voice was so loud that Elaine did stop for a second, losing her breath, rising up and turning a face distorted with crying.

Claire walked over to the bed and took her by the wrist.

'*How dare you have hysterics?* How dare you behave like this? And in your condition too. What would Miles think if he saw you howling like a servant dismissed for stealing? If my son is dead, and I don't think there's the least hope he has survived, then he's done his duty. Died for his country like other men before him and other men will do in the future. In the last war they were cut down in their hundreds of thousands, left to drown in the mud. Do you suppose their women acted like you? You make me sick.'

She walked out, slamming the door so hard that it reverberated through the house. The sound of Nemesis.

Elaine began to vomit in the night, and could not stop. It went on all night long and the whole of the following day. Claire finally telephoned the doctor, and when he arrived said contemptuously to him that she presumed it was shock. The doctor took one look at Elaine and rang for an ambulance.

At dawn, in a Banbury Road nursing home, Elaine went into labour and the child was born. She had been suffering from toxaemia for some time, which explained the swollen hands and ankles. She had never visited the doctor while she was in that condition and it had worsened. The child was born dead. It was a boy.

Philippa sent her flowers. White roses whose petals dropped in the heat of the bedroom, making it smell of their sharp scent. The nurses were jarringly kind. Elaine asked the matron to telephone her family to say she wished to see nobody. And would she please give the St Airds the same message. The matron tried to dissuade her, but Elaine was perfectly calm and perfectly cold. She looked dreadful. A priest called to see her, but she would not see him either.

She lay in the hot room, with the blinds pulled down but still blazing white from the sun outside and wished that she was dead too.

When she was well enough, she returned in a car to Shelton. Neither of the St Airds spoke to her about the loss of the baby. Claire avoided her as much as she could without making it too obvious. Elaine knew she had not been forgiven. She felt that Claire also blamed her for the death of the child, believing – although the doctor would have told her otherwise – that Elaine's paroxysms of grief had brought on a stillbirth.

The week after she came back from the nursing home, Elaine received a letter from Miles. She had been expecting one and through her dulled misery it was the only thing that she thought about, the only thing to live for. But when she actually saw it on the salver in the hall, she could scarcely pick it up. She thought she was going to faint.

The house was empty. She took the letter and walked out into the gardens and up to the coppice at the top of the hill. Here alone she groaned aloud as she opened it, her voice making the same hoarse sound she had made in labour.

It was not a photographed letter. That might have kept him at a distance and have been easier to bear. But the letter was real, it was a piece of paper that Miles' hands had touched, scrawled in pencil on a sheet torn from a Services notebook.

'I have,' he wrote, 'for some unaccountable reason a desire to write to you, my darling, and keep on writing as if to rid myself of an intangible sadness that seems to be all round me. I keep feeling that I'm being prepared inside for something to happen. That I must lose something. It can't be you, the best and dearest thing I have, I know it can't be you. And surely it can't be my life because I don't care a damn about that.'

She read with the tears pouring down her face and when she saw that sentence she sobbed 'How could you think that, write that? How could you not care for your life when it was all I had to live for?'

During the two months that she remained at Shelton the loss of the submarine was confirmed. There was no more news. Perhaps they would never be told what had happened. Had there been a sea battle? Had the submarine hit a mine? The

190

Admiralty might know or not know: they would tell the St Airds nothing and the St Airds accepted that in silence. Miles went so quietly. And took his son with him.

Claire was unsurprised when Elaine told her she would be giving up her Blenheim job and returning to London. What went on in Claire did not show, even in her pale eyes. Sometimes when Elaine looked at Claire she had a kind of longing. She is Miles' mother, she thought. She is his flesh and blood, all that's left of his reality. Why can't I love her and feel a shared sorrow? But it seemed to Elaine now Miles was dead, and she was no longer carrying his child, that in an extraordinary way she had evaporated as far as Claire was concerned. She had been turned into a ghost. The St Airds now thought she was nothing to do with Miles any more. There would be no child to carry on the name and title. It would go to a cousin, towards whom Claire now began to offer an interested friendship. Elaine still had Miles' name but she was not a relative: merely a widow.

On the afternoon that Elaine was finishing her packing, Claire came into the bedroom. She had not entered it since the night of the telegram. She stood for a moment in silence, looking vaguely round the room which was filled with Miles' possessions, school photographs, books. Glancing up at her, Elaine could not see a trace of grief. Perhaps she had learned that in France in the 1914 war, she thought. Perhaps it is the only way she can bear things. It is brave and it makes me shudder.

'I've been wondering if you would like anything of my son's, apart from things that he himself gave you.'

'I have all I need, thank you, Lady St Aird.'

'Do you want this?'

Claire held out a small cardboard box. When Elaine opened it, she saw it contained a child's metal watch of the kind that small boys wear at school. The strap was worn, the holes much enlarged, and the back of the watch badly dented.

'We gave it to him when he was at prep school. For his tenth birthday. I found it just now among some old things. Well?'

'Can you spare – '

'I was going to give it to the WVS jumble sale.'

Elaine took the watch and fastened it on her right wrist. She already wore on her left the gold watch her father had given her. She wound up Miles' watch and put it right. It didn't go.

The day that she was leaving Shelton dawned hazy and

191

autumnal, the leaves had begun to turn and fall, many of them were already scattered across the unkempt lawns, yellow, brown, crimson. Claire had lit a bonfire in the field and the pungent smoke floated in bars upon the still air. When she was ready, Elaine went to the stable studio and knocked.

Her father-in-law opened the door, said nothing, and stepped back for her to enter. She saw that he was working on a landscape: it was the river scene he had painted often before. But in this new version the water seemed to have no light, and the dark sky was filled with rain.

'I am sorry to disturb you, Lord St Aird. I came to say goodbye.'

He wiped his hands on a paint rag. He stood looking down at her, his bearded face guarded. He stooped more than he used to do.

'Going to London, are you?'

He never called her by her name.

'Yes, I've asked to be transferred. They say it can be arranged.'

He nodded, saying, 'Good.'

She wished, suddenly, passionately, that he looked like Miles. He put out his hand and shook hers formally, as if they had only just met. Then he saw the child's battered watch and a grimace of pain went across his face.

'Goodbye, Lord St Aird,' she said.

Elaine was ready long before the taxi was due. She wandered into the dining room to look at the painting of Miles. It was as meaningless as it had always been, the painted face was not his. But the prophetic menace of the submarine behind his shoulder made her look away.

When the taxi drew up at the door, and Elaine had shown the driver where her suitcases were stacked in the hall, Claire walked in from the garden. She stood watching the driver stow the cases into the taxi. Elaine hesitated for a moment.

'Goodbye,' said Claire, 'I hope the train journey won't be too tedious.'

'I don't expect it will be.'

Claire did not shake hands.

She stood, in her green uniform, with Shelton a painted manor behind her, watching as the taxi drove away. As it turned at the gates, she called the dog and went indoors.

* * *

192

Philippa's heart went out to Elaine. She kept thinking about her sister. She wrote to her. But she did not telephone Shelton. What could one say? And in a dreadful selfish way that she despised in herself, Elaine's loss frightened her, as if destiny were whispering 'your turn next'.

The autumn had its own blow for Philippa too. When she had first heard the news that the Eagle Squadrons were to be disbanded, she had felt a chill as if a splinter of ice had entered her breast. She had been part of the Eagles. She had secretly been proud of the fact that all the time she'd been with them, even though she was only a civilian, she had done the Squadrons credit. She had almost seen herself as an Eagle too, having known and loved them all and borne their sufferings as stoically as they did. She had the sensation that she herself had been with them on their sorties over Germany and France.

And now the three proud Squadrons were to be disbanded. They would no longer be part of RAF Fighter Command, they were to join the United States Army Air Corps.

She began to dread the day when all this would become official, and found herself saying 'it's over a month before it will happen', and then 'a week' and then 'a whole day.'

But at last on a day of pouring September rain, only two weeks after Elaine lost her child, the Eagles mustered at their aerodrome. They stood smartly to attention together with a unit of the RAF Regiment, lined up in a hollow square. Philippa and other RAF wives watched from the barrack window: it was raining much too hard for them to stand out in the open.

On the platform were Sir Sholto Douglas, the C-in-C of RAF Fighter Command, and two commanding generals of the American Air Force. And there in front of them were the three Eagle Squadrons 71, 121 and 133, on their final day as members of the RAF.

Sir Sholto made a wonderful speech, Philippa thought. He said that during the two years they had been flying, the Eagles had destroyed the equivalent of six squadrons of the Luftwaffe, and probably many more.

'There are those of your number who are not here today – ' he said – 'those sons of the United States who were first to give their lives for their country.' He went on to say that the Eagles who had fallen would remain the honoured dead of two great nations.

'Goodbye. And thank you, Eagle Squadrons of the Royal Air Force.'

Behind the pilots were the ranks of English mechanics, riggers, fitters, radio-men and armourers who had kept the planes flying, who had shouted 'Good luck' as the Eagles set off, who had run across the airfield to greet them when they returned.

Philippa looked at the Eagles standing to attention, camouflaged buildings behind them, forming a quadrangle round the parade ground. There they stood, the young men who had meant everything to her, the Americans who had come over to join an English war.

The rain hammered down on the figures in blue. The Stars and Stripes was slowly hoisted next to the RAF's blue flag. The two hung side by side, but there was no breeze to make them shake out their bright colours and snap and stream.

'Good hunting to you, Eagle Squadrons of the United States Air Force,' said Sir Sholto. The Eagles marched slowly in review – out of the RAF.

Barny and Pete Jansen, one of the 1940 friends, wandered back into the mess when the ceremony was over. They were very wet. New uniforms had been laid out for them – brand-new uniforms, of fine brown twill with a gold US on the lapel and wings on the breast.

They stood staring at them critically and Pete scratched his nose. He glanced from Barny's shabby tunic to his own. The elbows were patched with leather, the wings were worn and dirty.

'Know what these need?' Pete said, pointing at the perfect uniforms, 'a bit of mud.'

Barny returned to the cottage in his unfamiliar uniform, and Philippa – waiting eagerly – hugged him. Her face shone with the determined optimism she had burnished all the morning. The ceremony had been wonderful, she said. She did not admit she had wanted to weep. She had convinced herself that now she would give her love and loyalty to the American squadron. Why not? Many were friends. All were Barny's countrymen.

But it did not happen like that. The US Air Force recognized the value of seasoned veterans. Some of the Eagles were posted. Some had already gone, including Chuck Greenfield who was a temporary instructor to new pilots.

194

Philippa guessed that the new squadrons with the Eagles' name would be moved – it always happened like that. Some weeks after the handing-over ceremony Barny told her that the Squadron was going elsewhere.

'This time we've had it, my honey. You won't be allowed to come too.'

He put his arms round her tenderly. But she could not relax and lean against him. She was stiffened in pain.

'Darling Flip, you mustn't mind so much. Your days as a camp follower have been good, haven't they? Now kiss me and stop being so brave and quiet.'

Her eyes brimmed as he gently said that it was not as bad as all that, she mustn't fret. There was a town near the aerodrome, and he was sure she could 'put up at a hotel' now and then. There would be leaves. Even sleeping-out passes.

'Isn't that what we need, my honey? Lots of sleeping-out passes?' And he laughed.

She longed to burst into passionate argument. To say it was unjust to send her away, and that she had proved her worth in the dangers of the past.

But she didn't dare to.

Chapter Fourteen

There had been too little sympathy for Elaine at Shelton – but there was too much at St Helen's. Miggs and Theo were unnaturally kind to her, and she caught them looking anxiously at her when they thought she was unaware of it. They got on her nerves. All her clothes had been dyed black while she was at Shelton, and although they said nothing about that, she knew that the sombre figure she made startled them. Nobody went into mourning now.

She was listless and easily tired, had no appetite and slept badly. Her father did not need to be told any of this and suggested she should postpone going back to work, at least for the time being. She must get back her strength.

Ignoring his kind advice, she went to MI5's offices in St James' Street. The tired-looking woman who received her and knew of her work at Blenheim said they were no longer recruiting in Counter Intelligence. The direction of the work was changing, she said. But Elaine could work in Special Operations.

It was the other side of the Intelligence coin. At Blenheim they had been combating enemy agents in Britain. At SOE the job was to send allied agents into enemy-occupied Europe.

Elaine went to the headquarters near Baker Street and to her own dulled surprise was given a job. I wouldn't employ somebody looking like me, she thought. But she knew people were needed, even widows as thin, unimpressive and indifferent as she was.

Drifting home, and trying to keep her mind on the idea of working again, she thought about Marjorie. She missed the only real friend she had made in this war. At St Helen's there was her old sardonic nurse and there was Trix – neither replaced a dear friend. Her young sister's sympathy had been demonstrated by a hug, a kiss, and a promise to make Elaine a new dress.

'Oh golly, you're in black. Never mind, I can make you a

marvellous black dress with lace round the neck. I've got some white lace. I'll dye it.'

Trix made clothes for people in a way a child offers a loan of his teddy bear.

The offices where Elaine now began work were in an ugly pre-war block; the rooms were the usual wartime jumble of partitions. She compared the place to Blenheim. Here were no panoramas of the changing seasons outside the office window, no flash of lakes, no sulky Marlborough beauties pouting from the walls. She no longer arrived through vast gates to see the ponderous building floating in the mist of its curious past. And there was no narrow-faced, teasing friend to walk with her under the trees.

Her new boss, Giles Seton, had been wounded at Tobruk and invalided out of the army. He was lame and like many crippled people contrived to walk fast with a sideways swing. He had ginger hair and a curling handlebar moustache and despite being ex-Army, used the kind of RAF slang Elaine had heard from Philippa. When Elaine arrived at the office every morning he would say 'Good-oh. Now we can get weaving.' Sometimes he suggested they should 'bale out for coffee'. His highest praise, of course, was wizard, and his lowest disparagement was ropey. But despite the affectations he was tough.

Seton's office was next to the operations room, on the wall of which was an enormous map of Europe. The map was covered with flags, each representing an agent working underground. When the map was explained to her, Elaine asked why there were no flags anywhere in Holland. Seton looked grim. Recently the entire Dutch Resistance had been penetrated by the enemy. Every one of the agents was dead.

It was through Seton that agents were despatched to training centres where they learned the strange craft of being a spy; they were taught to parachute, to use short wave wireless, their skill at language must be faultless, their knowledge of the country to which they were bound must be full of the most elaborate detail. When the agents left London and were dropped into Europe, it was often too dangerous for them to contact London. They were on their own.

From the first day that she began to work there, Elaine found the atmosphere as matter-of-fact as an office in peacetime. Seton and his officers sent men on missions as if they were dealing with a team of door-to-door salesmen. There was no sense of danger. SOE had an enormous – and odd – staff working in and out of London. There were people skilled at creating false passports, craftsmen who knew how to make specially constructed suitcases, deliberately seeming old and battered, to contain wireless transmitters. Seton had an office drawer filled with lethal pills which he gave to the agents before they left London. If an agent was caught and felt that he might betray his friends, he could use one. In one corner of Elaine's small office was an old sewing machine. It was stuffed full of American dollars and was destined to be dropped by parachute for an agent in France.

Lysanders took off at night to ferry the agents to the remotest districts of France, returning with news of the Resistance. Giles Seton called the flights 'our Lizzie Landings.' Secret armies lay waiting for the Lysanders. They set out lights in deserted fields, in a pre-arranged pattern for the pilot to recognize. The Lizzie landings were mostly in France which was large and in places wild and uninhabited. Holland, Belgium and Italy were harder to penetrate.

Staff at Baker Street office were a motley crew, markedly different from the officers and upper-class girls at Blenheim. There were men and women of many nationalities and countless curious realms of knowledge, from those who knew precisely what labels to sew in an agent's clothes if he were to be dropped in Marseilles to the correct cigarettes a workman would smoke in Antwerp. RAF pilots came to the office too: their job was flying the Lysanders across the shrouded darkness of Europe.

Elaine was good at her job, which was demanding. At night she returned home, listened to the wireless, went to bed early to read and not to sleep. Marjorie telephoned and invited her to Oxfordshire. Elaine lied, saying she could not get away. She shrank from being forced to behave like a real person again. She fended off affection and got through her life like an automaton.

In January the London raids began again. On the news there was triumphant talk of huge waves of bombers over Germany. Twenty-four hours later when Elaine was home from work she heard the unfamiliar banshee wail over London. Hearing the sound of planes, she ran to look out.

'Quite like the bad old times. You just come indoors,' shouted Miggs on her way to the cellar.

Elaine ignored her and stood watching the enemy bombers

going over, and the flares in the sky, and hearing the thunder of explosions.

During the January raids she never slept under the billiard table. Totally lacking fear, she did not care if she were killed. She went to bed and lay thinking of Miles. Sometimes the thought was so clear that she could see him, young and beautiful and sexy and brave. She could remember just how he made love, once, twice, three times. She saw his large grey eyes shining as he lay with her. Once, after they had made love, he was silent for a long time and Elaine snuggled up to him, tenderly asking what he was thinking about.

'I was thinking what I'd choose for breakfast if peace suddenly broke out. I decided. Haddock kedgeree and coffee with cream.'

She slapped him.

'What was that for? No, on second thoughts, I'll have bacon, eggs and fried mushrooms. Or kidneys. Bulldog Drummond always had those.'

He rolled over and leaned on his elbow and said, 'Want to hear a joke?'

'Must you?'

'Yes, I must. There was a Polish general and he said to one of his officers "Have you any children?" "Oh no, sir," was the reply, "my wife is unbearable".'

'Miles! That's as old as the hills.'

'Ah, but there's more. "Surely, Lieutenant" said the general, "you mean that your wife is inconceivable". The officer answered, "No, no, General, I do not say it right. I mean my wife is impregnable."'

Miles burst out laughing. He liked the silliest jokes. Sometimes in the beloved lame letters he sent her, he copied out new ones to amuse her. When the Americans had begun to arrive in England last summer, Miles put a *P.S.* on his letter.

Have you heard the new description for Utility knickers? One yank and they're off.

That night, there was no raid. Elaine lay reading and re-reading her packet of letters, and the joke caught her eye. For a moment all she thought about was Miles' mischievous face. Then for the first time since he had died, the selfishness of grief left her. She thought about somebody else. Trix. Trix had left this evening as always for the Berkeley Gardens club and what she now called 'my war work'. Trix was on her way to show her paces to a hoard of susceptible and lonely Americans. Trix had yanked off some far-from Utility knickers often before her marriage – once for the man whom Philippa had later married.

Trix talked fondly of Dick. Sometimes she fished letters from her handbag and read aloud boring passages, punctuated with 'Isn't he sweet?' Whenever she went out with a man, she earnestly said to Elaine before leaving the house, 'Of course he understands completely that with me Dick always comes first.'

The man about whom Trix now talked, rather more often than about Dick, was Chuck Greenfield, the ex-RAF Eagle and friend of Barny and Flip. Trix quoted Chuck a good deal. She used his expressions – his friends were 'a bunch of palookas'. When she came home with spoils, they were always gifts from Chuck.

Coming home one snowy night, Elaine found Trix playing a record. It was 'Whispering Grass', and Chuck had bought it for her. Singing with the music, Trix was on the floor by the electric fire, surrounded by tissue paper.

'Chuck wrote to his folks in Rhode Island,' she said, 'Look what they sent! Have you *seen* these stockings? They're the newest thing, made of nylon. Look, they absolutely float if you blow them. Chuck asked for four pairs. And ciggies for Pa and candies for Miggsy. I thought you and I could share these!'

Scrabbling in the paper she held up a squat, striped box tied with shiny ribbon in the shape of a twelve-inch high lipstick. She opened it to show eight lipsticks arranged in colours, from pale pink to crimson.

'Aren't they wizzy? Which will you have?'

'Trix. I want to talk to you.'

The girl's face clouded. She took the lipsticks out one by one and painted them in stripes on the back of her hand. She looked up warily at Elaine.

'Chuck Greenfield seems to come into your conversation a good deal.'

'He comes into the club a good deal. Whenever he has a bit of leave.'

'You know perfectly well what I mean.'

Trix continued to stripe her hand with crimson. She sniffed it and said, 'Delicious.' Then, irritably, 'Give a dog a bad name. Sure, I see Chuck. I can't very well avoid it, can I? I'm at the club and he asks for a Coke or a dance or something. Anyway, Dick *said* it was okay because I asked him before he went to sea. Could I go out occasionally, I said.'

'Occasionally!'

Trix opened her black eyes very wide.

'Yeah, that is what I said, occasionally. Dick just laughed. What he said, if you must know, was "you can kiss the boys hello". He knows me. He doesn't expect me to stay home and die of boredom. *Or* watch my father with that French witch cluttering up the place.'

'There is nothing wrong with Pa taking Annette Ghilain out now and then.'

'I never said there was. She's *his* war work, isn't she? Anyway, she was supposed to like Alain. What happened to him? Imagine preferring an old man.'

Elaine ignored the rudeness, and returned to the point which she saw Trix was trying to avoid.

'Your husband is away. When he does get leave – '

'Then I'll be thrilled to bits,' was the snappish reply. Picking up her parcels, Trix flounced out.

After her sister had left for the club, Elaine went up to her room, passing Trix's. The door, as usual, gaped open, and she noticed that there was a very new, very large photograph in a white leather frame on the dressing table. She recognized the young man, she had met him at Philippa's wedding. He was very young, wearing his Mae West, flying boots, and holding his helmet. *All love, Chuck* was scrawled across the picture. He looked as insouciant as Miles.

Elaine scarcely remembered him, she had only spoken to him for a moment of two at the wedding. And, although he came so often into Trix's conversation, he never appeared at St Helen's. She decided that Trix was keeping him out of the range of sisterly disapproval.

Spring came. The wild flowers on the bomb sites began to blossom in mauve and white, their leaves and buds thick and healthy. On the bomb site near Bruton Street, Elaine saw that a little poplar was growing, it was nearly three feet high. There had been a jeweller's shop where the tree flourished now – Miles had taken her there to buy her a naval crown. It was the same all over London. You looked at a place which had been a friend's house, and the burned wreckage sprouted with flowers. In the place of a familiar shop there was a reservoir. Trees and weeds had turned dead places green.

The raids had not stopped, and one April evening when Elaine had just returned home after a long and hard day of work, the Alert was wailing. Miggs was nowhere to be seen. The brown teapot and tea caddy and the cat's basket were missing. Her old nurse must be in the cellar with Sailor for company. Listening to the raid tuning up, Elaine sighed. *Must* she shelter? The idea bored her, but when her father returned from his rounds he would only scold if she did not.

As she went through the drawing room, on her way to the billiard room, she heard an unfamiliar sound. It was her father's laugh.

'Is that you, Elaine?'

Theo was installed under the table. The scene was festive. A half bottle of gin, two glasses, lime juice, American cigarettes, and a plate of digestive biscuits. Keeping him company was Annette Ghilain.

'Coming to join us?' he asked.

'But of course you must shelter, madame, or your papa will be anxious,' from Annette.

Elaine could scarcely refuse. She was hospitably offered a gin and lime.

'Share my glass, madame. On this side I have not drunk.'

It was, thought Elaine, rather like being offered a sip from a loving cup.

She made an effort to be pleasant to the French girl, whose narrow foxy face resembled a Delacroix painting of the figure of Revolution. She only needed to grasp a tricolour and wear the cap of liberty.

'Have you seen anything of Alain and Alexandre?' asked Elaine. 'It is such a long time since they've been here.'

Annette's expression which had been pleasant enough, changed. She looked as if she resented the question.

'Alexandre is with General de Gaulle. For my cousin, I cannot say.'

'Surely he is with the General too?'

'I do not know. He wished to join the British. There was some dispute about it.'

She was brusque enough to be almost rude and Elaine said nothing more. But Theo, smoothing things over, said that

Annette had heard arguments between the two men. General de Gaulle wanted all Frenchmen to serve under him. Some, Alain among them, chose to go with the British.

'He told Annette it was from gratitude.'

Changing the conversation, Theo began to talk to Annette. His manner was doctorly. Was she sure she had enough to eat at the Centre? She had lost some weight. A good diet was essential, and even in wartime not difficult to obtain. 'The nation's health has never been better,' he said sententiously, 'and strain is more easily borne on a full stomach. Your work is taxing, my child.'

Annette's smile was forced.

'I am thinking of my silhouette, *Monsieur le Docteur*. The empty stomach is flatter than the full one. It is the same with warm clothes in winter. You scolded me because I shivered. But at least I do not wear clothes so thick that I do not look *bien*.'

'My dear child, I have never seen you look anything else.'

Raids or no raids, Annette was a constant visitor to St Helen's. Sometimes Elaine heard her voice coming from Theo's study. Sometimes, on raid-free evenings, she met them leaving the house to go out to dine. Occasionally Elaine found Annette seated in the drawing room as if she owned it, reading a French novel, with her feet up on the sofa.

When she had first seen Elaine after she returned from Shelton, Annette's manner had been solemn. It was as if the French girl had hurriedly pulled on a black armband and a face to match. But seeing that Elaine never cried, and talked of Miles in a normal manner, Annette relaxed and became her real self. She criticized everything.

'This dried milk that the Americans send us, it is *dégoutant*.'

'How can one dress well when all one's coupons buy but one pair of silk stockings?' exhibiting a thin leg. If was a waste of breath to contradict her or resent her attitude to her host country. She was more scathing about France. It anyone mentioned Occupied France, she exclaimed, '*Lâche, Lâche*'. When there was a reference to the Free French, she remarked that they were all sex mad, which Elaine took to mean that she was constantly fighting for her virtue at the Centre. Even her Breton home came in for no praise. 'It smelled of fish.'

Theo heard her pronouncements with exaggerated laughter

and a flushed face. Elaine disliked seeing her father excited by a girl who was two years older than Trix.

Summer came. The Allied victory seemed nearer, the dark mood of last year was fading. But not for Elaine. What happened to grief? You grew used to it. But it did not leave you, and you did not want it to do so. What else had you?

It was late one summer evening when Elaine went upstairs to find Miggs doing something very unusual, she was giving Philippa's room a desultory flick with a near-bald feather duster.

'Haven't seen Miss Philippa for a month of Sundays,' said Miggs in a disgruntled voice. 'Why can't she get home to see her own folk now and then, that's what I want to know? Those Eagle Squadrons, they've been disbanded, haven't they? Doesn't that give her a bit of time to come up? Anyway, she rang today, wonder of wonders. Said she'll try and come this weekend. I'll believe that when I see it.'

She continued to flick the duster here and there along the top of Philippa's bookshelf. Her back was turned to Elaine. It looked more crooked than it used to do.

'What's the matter, Miggsy?'

'Dunno what you mean.'

'Yes, you do. You're worried. I wish you'd say why.'

'You got your own cross to bear.'

'Like thousands of other women. It's Trix, isn't it?'

Miggs turned round in plain astonishment.

'What's *she* got to do with anythin'? Yes, I'm worried and so should you be. Know what the doctor wants to do? Give that Frenchwoman my job. Miggs, he said, Miggs, I think Miss Whatsit will do very nicely as my receptionist. The practice has picked up since the big blitz, and a lot of patients have come back to London. Miss Whatsit hasn't enough to do workin' where she is. (Why hasn't she, I ask myself? Isn't there a war on?) She's been good enough,' finished Miggs savagely, 'to say she'll work for us. *Us!*'

Elaine was as dismayed as her old nurse.

'He can't mean it.'

'Oh, but he does. And a foreigner. Takin' away an Englishwoman's job. And more than that. You've seen the doctor with her. Gigglin' like a silly kid. There's no fool like an old fool. Beg pardon, lady.'

Elaine was not sure whether to make matters worse by agreeing.

'But Miggs, what can we possibly do about it?'

'I can do somethin' and pretty sharp too. I'll go to my niece in Ditchling.'

'*Leave us?*'

'That's about the size of it.'

Annette's constant presence continued to disturb Elaine. And there was now a new visitor to the house, who up until now had been kept out of the way.

Chuck Greenfield was being what was called 'rested up' after working as an instructor for some months. He was due to go back to active service, and in the meantime had been given generous leave. He had time to call, now, very often in the hope of finding Trix. Nowadays she was always in. He collected her and bore her away for a day, or an afternoon, or an evening. Returning, Trix was in the sunniest of tempers. Elaine never remembered hearing her sing as much as she did now.

Elaine could not stop herself from liking Chuck. He was the friendliest and most uncomplicated man she had met in her life. When she compared him in her thoughts to Miles she saw that her husband had had tensions, paradoxes and reserves. From the little Elaine knew of Barny, he was not easy either, despite an American openness. But Chuck was a man of simplicities.

He never arrived at St Helen's empty-handed. She sometimes thought that Chuck would consider not arriving with gifts an impossible discourtesy. He simply had to give. He epitomised the extraordinary, unaffected American generosity. He took Elaine's breath away. He brought tins of coffee and butter, real oranges the peel of which Miggs later preserved to flavour cakes and puddings. He brought boxes of every kind of chocolate bar, which he called candies. There was scented soap for Elaine, tinned jam for Miggs, Bourbon whisky for Theo. He never came without a long pack of cigarettes under his arm – Lucky Strikes marked *For the United States Services Overseas*.

He reminded Elaine of a boy at school, a prefect or the head of a cricket team. His figure was loose-limbed and young, his eyes filled with tears when he laughed. His hair sprung up in a wave above his forehead, he couldn't make it stay down no matter how much he slicked it with a wet comb.

Sprawling in the house or on the burned-dry grass in the garden during the hot early autumn weather, he could not take his eyes off Trix. He had the look of a man seeing a vision. When she was near him, he linked his arm in hers or held her hand, her long thin fingers interlocking in his own. Every now and then they looked at each other, their eyes half drowned, and it struck Elaine that it was possible to kiss without moving a muscle.

She was moved and disturbed by the emotion there seemed to be between them. Aware of his eyes, Trix went through her paces, dancing on the lawn, sitting on the arm of his chair, playing records and singing all the words.

When he spoke about Trix to Elaine, Chuck sounded as if he were talking of royalty. He seemed more American when he spoke about Barny for whom he had a boyish admiration. Barny sure was a brilliant flyer, just brilliant; there was nothing that guy couldn't do with a plane, he could make it sit up and beg for him.

Who could resist Chuck? Yet Elaine found her sister's intimate manner with him hard to bear. Trix knew she was being disapproved of and put herself out to please her big sister, using a coaxing charm.

On the last day of his leave Chuck managed to get some petrol, and he and Trix planned to go out to the country. They were going to lunch at the Compleat Angler at Marlow. Giving Elaine a scented kiss, Trix left with Chuck, her long hair shining in the sun, a new handbag with TRIX in gilt letters slung over her shoulder.

It was a day for couples to leave the house. Theo and Annette also went, they were bound for luncheon in Soho. The sight of them did not worry Elaine as much as seeing Chuck and Trix, although the behaviour of her father did put her teeth on edge. As Theo had come downstairs he had seen Annette waiting for him by the front door. She was wearing a navy blue dress with a broad sailor collar and a pleated skirt, and a little straw hat perched over her eyes. Seeing the fresh pretty figure, he had blushed the colour of a beetroot.

There was no escaping the fact that the point of command at St Helen's had moved. Annette had left the Centre, and now sat during the week at a desk in the hall – the desk, a handsome

Sheraton piece, had been moved from the drawing room specially for her use. Miggs said no more about leaving, and at present satisfied herself with a war of attrition. She omitted to tell Annette if a patient telephoned when she was absent. She hid the tea. The threat of her going was not overt, but Elaine could hear it rumbling like thunder on a sultry evening. She wondered what St Helen's would do without its spirit, its grudging laconic witch with cat? She could not imagine life without Miggs, or think how to prevent losing her.

Alone in the shabby old house, with the sun unpleasantly hot, Elaine went out into the garden and found a deck chair. All the garden chairs were pre-war and had begun to split. She sat down gingerly under a tree. The garden was dull with no flowers but a few seeded michaelmas daisies. The freshest things were Trix's lettuces standing in crisp green rows: her sister always watered those. Sitting in the shade, Elaine closed her eyes. Birds chirped. Next week was the anniversary of the day the telegram had arrived: a whole year since Miles' death and the birth and death of their little son.

1943 had changed the spirit and feeling in England. There had been the conquest in North Africa, victories in Italy, and now the great US raids on Germany. Sometimes in broad daylight the planes flew over London in their hundreds, squadron after squadron of huge dark Flying Fortresses filling the air with their roar like enormous birds. People in the streets stopped and looked up and admired. There they go, good luck to them.

There was a feeling of hope now. But not for Elaine. With her eyes shut she thought of Miles. Thinking, loving, longing, grieving, ah, those were the things that made her weak. What had Marjorie said before they parted in Oxford. That grief was not like an illness, it *was* an illness. You were sick and you had to wait until you got better. I am not better, Miles, and I don't want to be.

There was a sound on the terrace by the French window; she heard it through her reverie and slowly opened her eyes. In a terrifying moment like an ecstasy she thought she had raised a ghost. It was a man in naval uniform.

Dick Polglaze came running across the grass.

'Elaine!'

She sprang up and he took her in his arms, holding her close and kissing her. He had never done such a thing before and she understood everything he meant by the embrace.

'Beautiful sister-in-law,' he said after a moment, as he let her go. 'It is so good to see you. And where is my beautiful wife?'

'Oh, Dick. Why didn't you let us know? How awful – she's gone out.'

She was still shaken by that first moment of seeing him, and now a feeling of desperate anxiety flooded through her.

He laughed.

'Silly of me to imagine she'd be home. I did try to ring but I couldn't get through. From Scotland.'

He threw his cap aside, and the sun shone down on his cropped curling fair hair. He was sunburned and he looked handsome and confident. He met her eyes just then, and said matter-of-factly that he had never written to her about Miles. He hadn't heard for a long time, letters arrived in batches. And by the time he had known, it was too late.

'It would only have been one of those letters.'

'I liked those letters.'

'Hell. You're right. I'm sorry, will you forgive me?'

'I expect so.'

Leaning on his elbow as he sat on the grass near her, he began to talk about Miles. He talked of when they had been in the Lower Deck together; of Miles' astonishment at having to do his own washing, and the 'make do and mend period' when the NCO would shout 'Settle down, you men,' and huge stokers would begin painstakingly darning their socks. He made Elaine laugh. For once she felt that the hideous word 'widow' was not pinned to her like a label on an evacuated child. He seemed unworried by Trix's absence, saying how he had wished he could let them know. His ship was having a refit.

'Glorious, isn't it? Nearly two weeks' leave'. But he had thought he was going to be duty officer for the first couple of days.

'I rang, as I say, but no luck. It's my fault, rolling up without warning. Of course she's out. Is she as beautiful and run-after as ever?'

'Oh, you know Trix,' said Elaine, smiling. She thought – but do you? He smiled back at her with his narrow eyes. His English voice sounded unfamiliar, after Chuck's drawl.

He talked about the recent months at sea. He was in a Hunt

Class destroyer, and they had been on convoy, bringing ships over from America and Canada. He couldn't tell her where except that the ships had come to Scotland.

'It was so strange, Elaine, this huge sheltered bay filled, packed, crammed with liberty ships. I went fishing in the loch for mackerel with some mates – we dragged pieces of silver paper behind us on lines and we got scores of fresh fish, delicious. When our boat went near an American ship, the Yanks leaned over the side and threw us chocolates.'

'That's so exactly like them.'

'Yoo-hoo? You in the garden?' called a voice gaily.

Elaine went cold. She waited to see Trix appear in the French window hand in hand with Chuck. Trix was alone.

'*Sweetheart!*'

Dick sprang to his feet, rushed across the garden and picked her up, to swing her round like a child, pressing a kiss to her mouth as he did so. He was laughing as he set her on her feet.

'Dick, where on earth have you sprung from?'

'Leave! Isn't it marvellous? Our ship's in trouble and needs a refit, poor thing, I've got *days*. Let me look at you.'

Grabbing her hands, he held her at arm's length, taking in the extraordinary beauty.

'More gorgeous than ever, isn't she, Elaine? Two lovely Tyrrell girls. Are you both coming to dinner with me at the most expensive place in town? I've months of pay to waste.'

To Elaine's nervous relief, Trix behaved just like a wife whose husband has returned from the wars. She let herself be kissed a good deal, and waited, smiling, while he fetched his bag and produced presents, scent and soap and silk stockings. The gifts were less than those Chuck brought, and Elaine's heart hurt her.

Trix opened the bottle of Jean Patou scent, rubbed it on her freckled arm and said that it was her favourite. And what wizzy soap. Did Dick know the beastly government had rationed soap now? They wanted us all to be filthy.

Sitting on the grass with him, she looked calm enough when he put his arm round her.

Elaine refused the invitation to dinner. She thought Trix insisted too much, but she stood firm. It was Dick who accepted her refusal, saying affectionately that there was lots more time and lots more pay. He gave her hand a casual kiss before he and Trix left in the evening.

She watched them walking towards the gate, Trix with her long-legged strut, her skirts short and full as a ballerina's, her legs in American nylons. Dick whispered something to her, and Elaine saw her sister slightly move away.

They did not come home. Her father returned late after supper, yawning and saying he was going to bed. She was not inclined to ask him if he'd had a good time: he wore a most self-satisfied expression. When she told him Dick was home on leave, he said 'good, good', scarcely listening.

Elaine did not go to bed. Dick was staying the night at St Helen's and she told herself that there was absolutely no reason for her to sit up for them, as if she were a maiden aunt. Trix was with her husband and everything was as it should be. At last, tired out with her own anxiety, she went to bed.

She woke suddenly, knowing somebody was in her room. A faint greyness came through the drawn curtains. It was dawn.

'Elaine?'

'What is it?'

Her voice was frightened and she heard Dick say, 'Sorry.' It was not an apology. 'I woke you.'

'I was awake,' she lied. 'Don't put on the light. Pull back the curtains.'

He went quietly over to the windows, a dim figure, and pulled the curtains gently as if anxious to make no noise. More grey light came into the room. He was in uniform. Already dressed? Still dressed?

He stood at the foot of her bed.

'No,' he said, meeting her eyes, 'I have not been to bed. Trix has. She is asleep.'

He had the look of exhaustion which makes a face appear dirty, as if smeared with dust.

'She wants a divorce.'

Elaine gave something between a gasp and a shudder.

'Surprised?' he said in derision, 'I imagine you have known about it for months.'

'What do you mean! Of course I didn't know.'

'About Greenfield, the American? She's sleeping with him. Don't tell me you didn't know *that*, because I shan't believe you.'

'I don't care if you believe me or not. I didn't know.'

He shrugged and folded his arms.

'I don't see that it matters. She wants a divorce. "I don't love you any more".' He mimicked the metallic voice. 'She's made up her mind. And as you know, when Trix wants something, she sure in hell gets it.' This time he mimicked an American accent.

Something in him, cruel and savage in its pain, dried her sympathy.

'She's overwrought. She's only a child still.'

He gave a violent laugh.

'Don't laugh like that!' she said angrily.

'Why not, don't you think it's funny? You expect me to behave well, don't you? To agree that she's a child. I don't agree and why in God's name should I behave well? Oh, of course, the Flight Lieutenant is a hero, a pilot, and what is more a fully-fledged Eagle, an American who came here to fight our war. Nothing's too good for him. He must help himself to my country, my hospitality, and of course my wife. Indeed, why not. She's common property.'

'*Stop it.*'

'Why?'

'Because all you are doing is revenging yourself on me. I won't have it. What did you say to Trix?'

'A good deal.'

'Surely she saw reason?'

He gave another imitation of a laugh.

'Oh yes. She cried and carried on. I suppose I agree with you in a way, she was like a child, a disgusting spoiled child. A greedy child who isn't used to being called names. She makes me sick.'

'And the divorce?'

'Let her have it.'

Elaine was shocked to the depth of her soul.

'But you've only been on leave a few hours. How can you and she decide anything so – so terrible. She is twenty, Dick, not thirty. The Americans have gone to her head. Yes, she is spoiled. We've spoiled her. You have. But she is your wife.'

Putting up both hands, he pulled his hair, viciously tugging it. She scarcely recognized the enchanting man who had sat on the grass this afternoon. He looked merciless.

'She is not my wife and now I think about it I see she never was. It was her idea that we married. She got it into her head and I agreed. I was in love with her. I thought her the most

211

beautiful sexy thing I'd seen in my life. And I believed she was in love with me.'

'So she was – don't laugh like that, I hate it – and will be again.'

'Oh –' he stopped himself, and then went on, 'I won't swear in front of you, I'm sure you've never heard bad language in your life but there's a dirty word for Trix. I was the sucker who married her, so it's my own bloody fault. However. I'll fix up the divorce. It'll take time, as I'll be at sea, but I don't suppose that will worry her much since she is fu-sorry, making love with that American anyway. I just came to tell you,' he said, turning away, 'that I don't expect I'll see you again.'

He walked to the door.

She climbed out of bed, ran across to him and caught hold of his arm. For a split second she felt his body react towards her. It was as if by touching him she had made him human again. But when he looked at her, his face again wore a vicious smile.

'Please give it time, Dick! Give *her* time.'

'Trix doesn't want me to give her time. She doesn't want me to give her anything. Except the certainty that she won't set eyes on me again.'

He looked at her for a moment with his iron face. Then went out, closing the door so carefully that she thought she would scream.

When Elaine arrived at the office she telephoned St Helen's. She rang twice, but both times Annette told her that Trix was asleep. On the third call Trix answered, yawning.

'Yeah?'

'I want you at home when I get back tonight. Don't go to the club. I have something to say to you,' snapped Elaine.

'It won't do any good.'

Elaine had been growing steadily angrier all the morning.

'I shall expect you there when I get back.' She slammed down the receiver. She would have liked to box her ears.

When she came home, Trix was in the sewing room. The battered nursery table was covered with yards of slithering oyster satin. Trix was cutting out a pair of cami-knickers. As Elaine walked in, Trix looked up. She, too, was in a temper.

She went on cutting out.

'Stop that and pay attention.'

Trix gave an exaggerated sigh. But she put down the scissors and sat waiting, and there was something, even in her way of sitting, which made it impossible to be angry with her. She looked so young and so absurd. As swiftly as a puppy knows its mistress has stopped being unkind, Trix lost her ill temper. She put her chin on her hand.

'I know what you're going to say, but it truly isn't my fault that I've fallen in love again. How can you control a thing like that? I'm just unlucky not to have met Chuck sooner, before I married, I mean. You were absolutely right,' she added solemnly, 'I never should have rushed into it.'

'Now you propose to rush into something worse.'

'Oh no! Chuck and I are wonderful together. I can't tell you what it's like, Elaine. Him and me.'

It was only too clear she was talking about sex. 'You know, he's really honourable,' she went on. 'That's rare, isn't it? He believes in behaving well. He is a guy who wouldn't do a dirty trick to a living soul – '

'But he's breaking up your marriage,' interrupted Elaine, finding it hard to listen.

'That's the *point*, Elaine. He feels the way I do. That this is it. Love.'

Trix gazed at her across the table covered with bride-like satin.

Elaine answered carefully, trying to explain that what Trix wanted to do was mad. Sudden, mad and cruel, and she would regret it. It was Trix's turn to look as if she could not bear to listen. She fidgeted and sighed and tried to interrupt, while Elaine who was out of her depth droned on, using cliché words like infatuation.

'You must see what you want is impossible,' she finished.

'You don't understand anything!' was the sudden fierce reply. 'I told you. Chuck and I are getting married. I shan't listen to another word.' Putting her fingers in her ears, Trix began to hum. Elaine leaned over to unstop her sister's ears, but Trix dodged, humming more loudly. Deeply offended, Elaine stood up and began to walk out. The humming abruptly stopped.

'Don't go!'

Trix began to talk very fast, words of resentment and self-justification tumbling out in a flood. In her voice Elaine heard the frantic selfishness of passion. How *could* she stay married to a man she didn't love? If she went to bed with him she'd be sick. Dick had taken her out to dinner last night and the moment they sat down she told him right away. She hated lies and couldn't go on acting. She had said she was in love with Chuck, and Dick must give her a divorce. It had been awful at first, because he had thought it was a joke and burst out laughing. But then he saw she meant it, and when she was explaining about Chuck he took her by the arm, really hurting her, and sort of dragged her out of the restaurant, paying a lot of money although they hadn't had a single thing to eat. He walked her round and round St James' park arguing and pleading until she thought she would go mad. Then he pushed her in a taxi and brought her home.

'He made me creep up the stairs and he kept sh-sh-ing me and saying we'd wake everybody. *Stupid.* What did it matter if we had? Then when we were in my room he started all over again, going on and on about staying married and loving me and then he began to kiss me,' said Trix shuddering, 'and begging me to do it with him, do it *now* and it would all be okay, and then when I said I wouldn't he slapped me across the face.'

'Trix, stop. I shouldn't hear all this.'

'Why not if it's true?'

'I can't listen. I'm sorry.'

Elaine left the room.

She stood staring down the passage at the staircase and thinking of Dick walking so quietly so as not to wake the sleeping house, and shutting her door this morning in the same awful, careful way. And she thought of his life in his ship facing the fatal seas where many men drowned and ships sank in flames and smoke. She thought of the cold and danger, and how all the time he had carried Trix in his thoughts as a beautiful secret. And here instead was a girl with a white face and black eyes who looked like a witch.

The Tyrrell passion to get things over, even if doing so was idiotic, was strong in Elaine during the weeks following Dick Polglaze's dawn exit from St Helen's. She knew it was her duty to tell her father – or to be exact it was Trix's duty to do so, and the sooner the better. But Trix was keeping out of her way. When Elaine saw her she was pale and snappish, only brightening up when Chuck managed to get some leave. He was now back on ops. If the telephone rang Trix ran to it so fast that Elaine pitied her, and pitied her more when the call was so often not from Chuck.

He came to the house one day expressly to see Elaine. At breakfast Trix had said abruptly, with a warning glance in her father's direction, 'Chuck may drop by this evening. Shall you be around?'

'Yes. Why?'

'Could you look after him for me. He surely wants to see you,' said Trix whose vocabulary became more American every day.

Another look towards her father, who was deeply engrossed in *The Times*.

Chuck arrived early in the evening. The weather had been muggy and there had been a slight fog all day. Now the temperature dropped sharply, and the fog thickened. From the window Elaine saw a tall figure in uniform looming out of the mist. Why did Americans move so differently to Englishmen? Everything about them was easier and looser. Was that, she thought – displeased at the idea of the coming interview – the trouble with them?

She went to the front door to let him in. He greeted her with his pleasant politeness, and left a package in the hall for Miggs. Elaine wished he had not done that. He followed her into the drawing room in silence, and sat down, placing his hands on his knees.

Elaine looked at him earnestly, trying to see why Trix found him irresistible. There he was, handsome in a clean-cut boyish sort of way, with his shining hair and beautiful unmarked skin fresh with youth and health. He still made her think of a school prefect, or perhaps the head of the school team. He was like an eager boy who was ready to run faster and jump higher and win the most games. Yet he was as eager to make the loser feel it was only a game after all. Chuck was nothing if not gallant. But he was neither as odd nor as fascinating as Dick Polglaze; and it was for this pleasant boy that Trix was behaving with such cruelty.

'Are you very sore at us, ma'am?'

'I am afraid I am.'

'Of course you must be. I respect you for it. I can't apologise

215

for loving your sister or be sorry that she loves me. But I sure don't think,' he finished sadly, 'I play an honourable part in all this.'

'Trix plays a worse one.'

He was shocked. He was an American and his girl was perfect. He begged Elaine's pardon but he must disagree. She should not put the least blame on her sister who was wonderful, and most unhappy over what had happened.

He did not say that what had happened was simply that Trix had fallen into his bed and in his turn Chuck had fallen passionately in love. She was the girl desired by all men and married to an Englishman fighting the war at sea . . . yet she had chosen him. It was miraculous. He told Elaine how much he loved and longed for Trix, adding gravely, had Trix mentioned that he had re-named his plane TRIX?

'No, she didn't tell me.' Elaine could not think what to say to that.

As she listened to him talking of Trix and himself, it was as if he were talking of two people struck by an act of God, an earthquake or an avalanche, in which the helpless victims were hurled down by the force of mighty Nature. But just as Trix had some spell which weakened and finally erased condemnation, so had Chuck. Hers was caused by beauty, his by honesty. He talked of Trix with love and simplicity. His voice was reverent. Against her will, Elaine was moved.

'Of course you know we're out of the RAF now and part of the US Air Corps. It makes a mighty big difference,' he finished.

'Flip told me things had changed.'

'That's what I'm coming to. Now that Trix and I are engaged – '

Is that what they call it? thought Elaine.

'She won't be able to follow me around. They just won't allow it. Flip made a fine job of it when we were in Fighter Command, but that's all over. Maybe for the best. I know I couldn't fly as I should if I thought of Trix hanging around near the station, miserable and at a loose end. Maybe Barny's getting to feel the same. Flip's being sent home. Did she tell you?'

'She wrote something about it.'

'Well – '

He gave her a beseeching look.

Elaine said slowly, 'You mean that you want Trix to remain here at home.'

'Please, ma'am.'

The cement of the family, thought Elaine. What have I got myself into now?

'But my father is against divorce and she hasn't told him anything about all this yet. I should think she daren't.'

'Trix mentioned that your mother was a Quaker. Some of my folks are too.'

'My father isn't. He is scarcely an active member of the Church of England,' she said dryly. 'He only goes to church about twice a year. But his principles are those he grew up with. They are there. Immovable. He detests divorce and will not accept it.'

'Yeah. She said.'

'The point is,' said Elaine, meeting the serious eyes fixed on her, 'there will be an almighty row when my father finds out what is going to happen. It *is* happening, is it? I mean you have both quite made up your minds to marry. I know she said so, and her husband told me the same thing. It all seems very reckless and sudden.'

'No question. We are going to marry as soon as she is free.'

'But you want her to remain here.'

He was leaning forward, his elbows on his knees, his large graceful body anxious and unrelaxed. They treat me as if I were their mother, she thought with resentment. Trix. Dick. Even this American. Now that Miles is dead, is this all I am to be for ever? Somebody who minds other people's business.

She said, after a pause,

'If you are not allowed to have Trix with you, and I understand that when you're on ops, I suppose there is nothing for her but to stay. But I don't think my father should be told anything about the divorce.'

He looked surprised. Relieved and surprised.

'Are you sure you can manage that?'

Now you are going to be dreadfully grateful, she thought, and resented him more.

'It seems underhand to conceal the divorce,' she added, 'but if Father found out he could refuse to have her here.'

'Some people back home are like that.'

217

She had an irrational desire to exclaim, 'Then why don't you see that this is as a disgraceful mess and you are as much to blame as Trix. And what about her husband, for God's sake?'

But instead she stood up and so did he, looking about for his cap which, like his uniform, was too crisp, too smart. She preferred the old shabby RAF blue. Putting out his hand, he gripped hers painfully. He muttered something about it being impossible to thank her, she was the soul of kindness, and other things she did not exactly catch. She thought there were tears in his eyes. She even thought she heard him say she was like a mother to Trix. That, as Annette Ghilain would say, was *le comble*. Elaine did not want to hear any more of the muttered speech, and went to the door with him, bidding him a most matter-of-fact goodbye.

Turning at the gate, he gave her a salute.

There was a jeep waiting.

Chapter Fifteen

Knowing that her father was safely out of the house at the hospital, and Annette had gone shopping in Kensington, Elaine telephoned Philippa the moment that Chuck left. She began by asking if Philippa were really coming home.

'I'm glad you called up, I keep meaning to,' Philippa said. 'But there's such a short time left. And it goes so fast. Bloody, having to leave him, isn't it?'

Elaine scarcely paused to be sympathetic before she gave the bad news.

'I've had one of your ex-Eagles here today. There has been a lot of drama. Trix is getting a divorce from Dick and marrying Chuck.'

She waited for her romantic sister to be astounded and fascinated. Philippa was furious.

'*Chuck Greenfield.* Do you mean to tell me . . . and divorcing Dick. How disgusting.'

'Isn't he a friend of Barny's? You are not going to be beastly about Chuck, I hope. Everything is bad enough at this end, and I haven't dared tell Pa.'

More than Elaine had done, Philippa had absorbed her parents' attitude to divorce. Divorce happened to film people and in 'Society', about whom ludicrously snobbish gossip was dished out in the Sunday newspapers. Philippa thought divorce a dreadful thing: she also thought it *déclassé*, despite it being usual among the aristocracy.

'Chuck had no right to break up the marriage.'

'Flip. What's the good of being censorious? You know what she is like. Dick has been away so long and London is swarming with Americans. She's been mad about everything American since she was ten years old, She fell in love with it when she started going to the films.'

Just as you, thought Elaine, fell in love with flyers. She remembered the old scandal of Barny and Trix. Of course, Barny had been Trix's first lover from the United States . . .

219

Both her sisters had a strong sexual urge towards an idea which excited them. They had had preconceived images in their heads. It was as if the men they chose stepped into canvases in which the background had been painted in advance. She remembered the horribly black sky and surfaced submarine in Miles' ugly portrait. For Philippa the background had been a sky full of vapour trails, bursting shells and Spitfires. For Trix, the vast sprawling continent of America.

'Barny will be as shocked as I am,' said Philippa in a grating voice.

Elaine tried to keep her temper. She wanted to be rude, but it would do no good. She had lost her influence over her sister now – Philippa was in a world she knew nothing about, with different laws and a different language. Leaving aside Philippa's declaration that the divorce was Chuck's fault, which was patent nonsense, Elaine said coldly that she had decided to keep their father in the dark.

'The child must live somewhere. And she won't be allowed to join him when she *is* married to Chuck, just as you are no longer allowed to stay with Barny.'

'She isn't a child and she isn't married to him yet. All I can say is I hope his CO doesn't find out. There'll be a God almighty row if he does. Americans are not encouraged to break up British marriages.'

'Stop talking in that disagreeable voice, and stop being so unrealistic! Just speak to Barny quietly. Chuck is a nice man and a vulnerable one, and he is behaving as honourably as he knows how. Talk to your husband. He'll tell you to shut up,' said Elaine and rang off.

Still red with anger, Philippa sat by the telephone in her hotel bedroom. She was going to ring back and go on arguing: when furious she always did that if the quarrel was on the telephone. But the door of her room opened, and Barny put his head in. She had expected him, but some hours later. She rushed to him, filled with the bad news and her righteous indignation.

But before she had said three words he told her that he knew. Chuck was back with the Squadron. He'd talked to him yesterday about it, and asked him not to mention it yet to Philippa.

'He was going to see Elaine and he wanted to get that settled. He's very fond of your elder sister. I'm sure she was good to him. You must be the same.'

'Good to him!'

She was just going to burst into a long righteous speech about men stealing the wives of other men away at the war. She was going to flay wives who were unfaithful. Old resentment flooded through her like a poison. But Barny looked so tired. He sat down on the bed.

'Do you think they'd bring us up some horrible English tea?' he said, and then he added, 'You must do as I say, Flip, my honey. Be kind to Chuck. Feelings are the devil, they can throw you right out. Feelings can affect your flying.'

It was the sentence which frightened her most.

Philippa did not receive her marching orders for a while. Barny and his friends had become part of the American Air Force and the operational experience of the Eagles was very valuable. But it had not occurred to Philippa that, for that very reason, some of her friends would be transferred. She had simply imagined them in a different uniform, continuing the Eagles' tradition.

A few days after the transfer, Barny came home to the hotel where she had been living for some weeks, and told her that he was being sent into another Fighter Group.

'I have to retrain,' he said, walking round the hotel garden with her.

'Retrain. How absolutely ridiculous. You're more experienced than any pilot they've got. They're lucky to have you.'

He squeezed her arm.

'What a partisan you are. I have got to retrain, Flip, because I'm not to be in Spits any more. I shall be flying a P38 Lightning fighter in the new squadron. They tell me it's very much faster.'

Retraining was to be at the same station, so Philippa need not leave just yet, he said. 'I guess learning the new plane will take a couple've weeks.'

She did not see him at all during the course, but he managed to get a sleeping-out pass when it was finished. He looked tired and pale, he had had his flak nightmare again.

Determined to switch his mind away from that, she eagerly asked about the new plane.

'Well. It has advantages. It's a lot bigger, twin-engined, and it's mighty fast. Utterly different to fly. The trouble, for me anyway, is that it isn't as nimble as a Spitfire. I miss that reaction of the Spit's, the way it answers to you – as Chuck used to say, you can make it sit up and beg.'

221

He would be back on active service again at the end of the week, his Squadron's job was escorting the Flying Fortresses into Germany and back. Late that evening, lying in bed beside her – they had not made love – he began to talk of how it felt to be in the American Air Force.

'My God, Flip, it's different to the RAF. Much more different even than the Lightning and the Spit. All our pilots are fully trained, of course, and real keen. That's the trouble. The mess is full of guys all talking at once, just screaming for action. They keep saying how they can't wait to start knocking off the enemy, and how those Krauts aren't going to believe their eyes when *they* come zooming in.'

He was silent, and then added.

'If only they just wouldn't talk so big.'

'The Eagles used to be like that.'

'Yeah. I know. Sometimes they're uncannily like we were. It's as if I hear us talking. But I keep thinking how they've seen nothing, and can't know what it's going to be like. They've had no fighter experience, never seen their pals going down in flames, never had flak through their wings. Do you know what they call the Battle of Britain? The last war.'

He knew he sounded old, faced with the spirited young. Had he caught something of the English reserve, the much-mocked stiff upper lip? Yet there were times, he told her, when he felt at home with the noisy young pilots and the very sound of their voices was a marvellous relief after the clipped tones of the RAF. But then the innocence of his companions would suddenly irk him. They hadn't lived with death.

'But they will, Barny. That's what is so awful. And so inevitable. It's all in the future for them. Don't grudge them a short time of ignorance now.'

He sighed and took her in his arms, looking down at her sweet, familiar, vulnerable face.

'What would I do without you?'

'Get another girl. Much prettier.'

'Don't fish.'

Two days later he telephoned her from the station to say that he had received his posting, and that she must leave.

'I don't know if I can make it tonight or tomorrow, but I'll be along. Just get packed.'

It was brilliant October, sunny crisp days following each other in that autumnal beauty which pretends it will never end. Philippa began to pack up her few possessions. She felt extraordinarily bereft to think she must leave him.

On a sunny Saturday morning, lovelier than the rest, Barny's Squadron went out on a daylight patrol in advance of the big bombers. At 12,000 feet over the Channel they met a flight of enemy fighters coming straight at them. Barny's plane was hit. He managed to climb out before the fire was too fierce: he parachuted into the sea. A rescue boat spotted him and reached him. But the Messerschmitt which had shot down Barny's plane suddenly dived downwards over the boat as Barny was being hauled on board. The deck was sprayed with bullets.

They thought he was going to die. He was in a coma from loss of blood, wounded in leg and hip in four places. They managed to get him to a coastal hospital, he did not die on the way, and was operated on at once.

Barny's section commander was his old friend Pete Jansen, who came to the hospital to tell Philippa.

He took her in a jeep a long way across country, into an area forbidden to civilians. When they arrived at the hospital he couldn't stay, he was on duty that night.

'I'll be thinking of you both, pal.'

He pressed her shoulder before striding away.

She sat in the hospital corridor. She did not know how long she waited, she was told later that the operation had lasted for four hours. At last a small man with grey hair came towards her through the swing doors. He wore a white coat.

'Mrs Duval? I'm John Murdoch, your husband's physician. He stood up to the operation pretty well, pretty well. We'll just have to see. We had to limit the anaesthetic we gave him, you understand. Because of the condition.'

Philippa did not understand. And could not ask.

The weeks that followed for her were spent in limbo. She was allowed to move to a seaside hotel, it was almost empty and within reach of the hospital. One night, returning after sitting with Barny, she had looked up 'limbo' in a battered dictionary she found in the lounge. It said that limbo was a region on the borders of hell.

Taking limbo with her, she travelled every day from the big, shabby hotel where only some servicemen were staying, to the hospital six miles away. A taxi came for her at the same time every day, driven by a taciturn old man who said nothing but good morning. Each day she was allowed to sit by Barny's bed.

He was still in a coma and she knew, although they did not tell her, that there was a possibility he would never emerge from it. Comas were, in a way, inexplicable things. People could remain unconscious for weeks, even for years. It frightened her. The hospital was big and full, for although the area was forbidden to visitors, people living on the south coast, the old and the very young, were patients here, and there were two wards of American casualties, ground staff and pilots. Philippa did not know any of the men who lay in the rows of beds. Sometimes they smiled at her.

Barny's bed was at the end of a ward containing forty beds, twenty on either side, arranged in lines so straight they could have been drawn with a ruler. The green screens round his bed made it into a sort of private room.

The weather had suddenly turned freezing cold, it was getting on towards November, and the wards were also very cold. There was not enough coal to keep the radiators comfortably warm. Nurses rustled up and down, carrying hot water bottles and scarlet blankets which they offered to the patients.

'Now are you sure you are warm enough?'

Each of the Sisters was named after her ward. Barny was in David Ward, and every morning Sister David sent a nurse to Philippa with a scarlet blanket. She was instructed to wrap herself up well. If she caught cold she would not be allowed to visit her husband. The nurses also brought a mug of hot cocoa.

Sitting in her blanket, watching Barny, Philippa did not feel strong enough to ask Sister David any questions. Her moral courage had deserted her. Elaine would have done so – she couldn't. Besides, they would never tell her, would they? that Barny was going to die. And in any case they did not know. Nor could Sister David or the doctors tell when he would emerge from that sleep so like the sleep of death. They would only give her half truths and cheerfulness. But she knew that the longer he stayed unconscious, the more he was in danger.

Every morning she walked down the aisle of David Ward between the rows of beds, where pyjama clad men lay patiently, and she went behind the screens, and sat in the chair by Barny's bed. The nurse arrived with the blanket, and Philippa thanked her, and wrapped it round her waist. She always said, 'How is he?' and the nurse answered, 'Not too bad,' with an upward note in her voice.

When she was alone with him, Philippa leaned forward and looked fixedly at the unmoving figure, and touched the dark hair so tidily combed, and took his hand, and wondered if she was ever going to look into his dark eyes again.

The only person she spoke to during her lonely ordeal, apart from the nurses, was Pete Jansen. He was a tall rangy man, older than the other Eagles who had been Philippa's friends, Pete was twenty-eight. He had thick hair that was so fair that it was almost white, and large blue eyes. Everything about Pete was on a big scale, his hands, his voice, the country he came from, Wyoming. Now and then, with a few brief hours of leave, he drove out to the seaside hotel to have dinner with Philippa. She was desperately glad to see him and – since the news of Barny was not good and limbo was around her – she forced him to talk about himself. She would listen with concentration, keeping her mind away from the bed at the end of the ward behind the screens.

'You cetainly make a fellow talk,' Pete said one evening, smiling at her thoughfully. She knew he guessed why and that *he* knew it was a way of helping her.

He told her about his State, which was 3,000 feet up, bitter cold in winter, roasting in summer. In the distance, he said, there were mountains with snow caps, and names like Cloud Peak and the Big Horns. In the deserts huge cactuses grew, 'big as houses. No, castles more like.' Pete's family bred horses.

'We breed 'em, train 'em, and sell 'em,' he said. Once a year he and his father rode into Cheyenne to the fair to sell their horses. It was the year's great event for the Jansens. Peter had grown up in an enormous and lonely country – sometimes his family did not see their neighbours for a month.

'When I got to England, Flip, I thought I'd never seen so many people in my life.'

She was glad to see him. She leaned on him. He was tough and had a stubborn kindness and even his silences were comforting. He was the only person she wanted to be with: she scarcely telephoned her family.

In December it began to snow. The snow looked dirty as it came flying down across the grey waste of the sea. When

Philippa came down to breakfast in the hotel dining room, where a few officers at the far end of the room talked in low voices, she saw that the snow was already lying thickly on the bushes in the hotel gardens. Suppose the taxi could not come. Suppose the road to the hospital was blocked. Her anxiety was out of proportion, for she knew it made no difference to the poor sleeping figure if she was there or not. But being with Barny was all she had. She could not eat, but kept going to the window to look at the snow.

The old driver did arrive after all, somewhat late and looking disagreeable. He drove at five miles an hour to the hospital, grumbling. The snow was slushy on the road but still piling up on gardens and hedges. At the hospital door, he said he would return in an hour. 'Can't leave it more than that.'

She went into David Ward and behind the screens and sat down. The nurse gave her the blanket. When she was alone, Philippa leaned across and took the pale clean hand lying on the bedcover. It was inert in hers. She looked at Barny's hand. It was thinner, and had the fineness of a sick person's hand, it felt like silk. This hand, she thought, has touched me in sexual love, and it has controlled the guns of a plane and it has killed people. It looked like a child's.

Very faintly, it moved.

She had a wave of something as sharp as fear. She could scarcely look up. His eyelashes were fluttering, and then, drowsily, he opened his eyes and said so softly that she only just heard it, 'Honey.'

When she returned to the hotel she rang Pete and Elaine – Sister David had been so pleased! – it was a wonderful sign! But her joy was short-lived for although he had now returned to consciousness he was very ill. His foot had been badly burned. Fighter pilots wore long leather gauntlets and knee-length boots for protection against flames, and their large goggles were shatterproof and covered their foreheads below their helmets to protect foreheads against fire. But while he had struggled to escape he had literally not known that his foot was burning, he had lacked the automatic violent physical reaction against the flames. So they were worse.

When he was well enough to travel by ambulance, he was moved to East Grinstead, where an operation was carried out on his foot. Another followed. Philippa left the hotel by the sea and tried to find somewhere to live near East Grinstead. She finished up in a guest house full of middle-aged women preferring to be out of London in a place where there was good food and a few luxuries. She missed Pete Jansen more than she could say.

She was not allowed to visit Barny daily or sit with him for hours. Nobody wrapped her in a scarlet rug. She had to make the best of an hour three times a week. Barny was feeble and quiet, and although he held her hand sometimes and smiled when she kissed him, he slept most of the time.

It was deep winter now, and dark at four in the afternoon. On a day darker and colder than the rest Barny told her he had seen the surgeon who was 'quite pleased' with his wounds. He was to be sent to an American convalescent home in Surrey.

'So I'm moving again. It's getting to be a habit with us both,' said Philippa, touching his arm. She had learned to use the upward lilt which was always in nurses' voices.

Lying against a high pile of pillows, he frowned.

'I'd like for you to go home, Flip.'

'Of course I won't, darling. I want to be near you and see you every minute I can. All the time until you're back flying. Then, since they say I can't be a camp follower, I must lump it.'

'It's swell of you . . . spending all these weeks . . .'

'Darling, I wanted to!'

'But I don't want you to,' he said in a fretful tone. 'Sister says the place is about thirty miles from London. You can come by train sometimes.'

Love made her obtuse. She bent towards him, her face alight with energy and devotion, her good health an exhausting loud presence in the room. She laughed and argued. It was so like him to think of her, as if she'd care about moving to another dreary hotel. Nothing mattered but Barny, his health, his convalescence, she would love to live in Surrey! Even her eyes looked hot to the man lying in the bed.

It took her a long time to realise the bald truth. He did not want her with him. Her absence would be a release.

He did not suggest that she should come down during his first days there. It would be better if she waited for him to settle. A week, maybe. Or two.

Before she left the hospital that afternoon, Philippa was called into Sister's office. This lady, her name was Glenn, was quite

227

unlike the fat and motherly Sister David who had sent Philippa blankets and cocoa. She had no easy smile and apparently no sympathy. She was thin and small and looked like an elderly nun. A mass of stiff organdie frills was anchored on the top of her head, her starched blue dress reached just above her ankles.

'Mrs Duval. Sit down, please. Nurse has made us tea.'

Philippa sat down obediently. She was wearing a dark fur coat which Barny's sister Mary Lou had somehow managed to send from America at Barny's request last year. The rich glossy fur emphasised her pale face.

'Flight Lieutenant Duval tells me you are returning to your family in London,' said Sister Glenn, pouring tea with a rock-steady hand. 'That's sensible of you.'

'But Sister, I don't want to go at all!' burst out Philippa, imagining she had found an ally. 'I *tried* to explain that I don't mind a bit staying near the convalescent home. He wouldn't listen.'

Sister Glenn had interviewed many service wives in the last three years. It was not only patients who suffered from shock. There were young women who took bad news like dumb animals in stupefied silence. There were silly girls who had hysterics if she allowed it, and brave ones who seemed already practised at a kind of art of suffering. There were women who were so aware that you needed to tell them nothing. This dark young woman was none of these. Apparently she had character but no trace of instinctive understanding. A sad lack. If a person does not see for herself, she thought, you had to make her.

'You wish to be with him, Mrs Duval. I realise that. But he needs time to himself. He has not only been very ill, but the pace of his life has stopped, perhaps for good. He realises that he will be grounded.'

Philippa drew a breath in shock and shame. She had never thought of that.

Sister Glenn read her face.

'You've been too worried to realise that would happen, I expect. But the wounds in his legs and thigh are considerable. He wouldn't be passed fit as a pilot, let alone as a fighter pilot who needs every bit of co-ordination of hands, feet, eyes – every instantaneous reaction. He realises all that. He is deeply depressed.'

The elderly woman went on talking. She'd known many pilots

228

and nursed them, and their life as fighters was intense, a strain which they themselves did not realise was almost impossible to maintain. Barny had survived 'a long, long time'. Even without the crash it had been catching up with him. Hadn't Philippa noticed that? He had lived at top pitch, going into battle day after day. Philippa must have lived at top pitch too. The pace stopped pilots from thinking about life and the risk of death. 'If they did, they wouldn't be able to fly. Now he's being forced to think for the first time.'

'I suppose I ought to be grateful that he will be safe.'

'Perhaps one could say that,' said Sister Glenn politely.

St Helen's comfortable old presence welcomed Philippa but she no longer thought of the house as her home. Miggs had given her room a winter clean. Elaine put some bare twigs from the garden in a vase on her dressing table. Trix added a small bottle of *Moment Suprême*.

Her sisters were kind to her. At first Trix rather avoided her, she was expecting to be reproached about Chuck. But Philippa was miserable, and aware of her own empty heart, and had no stomach for moral issues she had once been fierce about. She was pleasant enough to Trix and Elaine. But gloomy.

Elaine considered she was behaving badly. She disliked Philippa's silences and her inward-looking expression. Philippa had grown thin and looked rather plain: it was also the first time that Elaine could remember her being totally selfish.

I was supposed to be the selfish one, thought Elaine, who had believed it. In their adolescence the sisters had acquired labels pinned on them by their mild mother, Miggs, and each other. Elaine was selfish, Philippa was sentimental and generous, and Trix was an addle-pate, an antique expression of Theo's.

Nobody's label suited them any more. Philippa was wrapped in her own anxieties, Elaine had been forced to take their mother's place. Even Trix laughed and sang less. Elaine missed the metallic little voice, word perfect in the newest dance numbers. The most recent one was 'Don't get around much any more.' It was true, even for Trix.

Phillipa knew she was not behaving well and longed to stop, but Barny filled her thoughts. She had seen the Eagles change, and gone on loving them. Now she had lost them. She was not thrown into the desolation of widowhood like Elaine – but she was in a wingless land. She did not know what to feel or think. She'd realised that Sister Glenn had seen and despised that. She was ashamed that she had actually felt angry with Barny, and had in her thoughts used schoolgirl adages. He must stop being sorry for himself, pull up his socks, make an effort, show some backbone. The phrases were those she and Elaine had used when playing netball. And it came to Philippa with a sense of pain that *she* was the one who should do all those things. Not Barny who lay like a wounded bird fallen from the sky.

When she had been at home for about a week, Elaine suggested one evening that she should telephone Jane Alwynne.

'You mean you think I ought to work.'

'That is exactly,' said Elaine, with a level glance 'what I mean.'

Philippa turned her head away. She wanted to be angry because Elaine had coldly refused her sympathy. But in her heart she knew she hadn't the right to that weakening comfort. She said, with a visible effort, that she would ring Jane in the morning. Elaine said nothing to that.

Jane Alwynne was enthusiastic.

'My dear Philippa, good to hear your voice. Your young sister is doing such excellent work at our club, you know.'

Actually Trix, with kindly tact, had said nothing about it. 'She's one of our stalwarts,' went on Jane, 'so willing. There is nothing she won't do for our American friends. Well, now, are you free tomorrow? Could you come to a little mews off Berkeley Square on the left? Thurston Mews, and I am in Thurston House. Did I tell you poor old Chicheley Buildings had a direct hit some months ago? Nobody killed, thank God, just a heap of burning rubble. My poor files!'

Jane sounded as powerful as a river in spate.

Thurston House was a small block of flats built in the 1930s on the site of a seventeenth century garden. Philippa found Jane installed in an office which had been the bedroom of a flat. Rosy and plump, and wearing her usual expensive style of suit, Jane pressed Philippa kindly to her bosom.

'I am so glad to see you, child.'

Jane was not alone – she never was. A stooping man, skeleton thin, was busy with some box files. After politely shaking Phillipa's hand, he left the room.

'Dear Andrew,' said Jane, when the door had closed on him, 'a treasure. The poor fellow was invalided out, he's had consumption. On the mend now, and we must be thankful for his misfortune. Well, that's not very kind, let us say we must be grateful that in his misfortune he came our way. He is magnificent with my charities.'

Jane inquired kindly about Barny. Philippa had not told her that Barny had been shot down, but Jane's information service was always efficient. Philippa was determined to sound cheerful about his convalescence. Jane asked one or two questions – there was nothing she did not know, apparently, about pilots in hospital, even to the names of the doctors.

Having made sure Philippa had no other work and could therefore belong entirely to Jane, the lady rattled off her requirements. Her kingdom was spreading. There were American charities, the problems of evacuated children, war widows, a club for the Poles, and of course, a new one for the Americans. 'We have to keep them amused, poor things, so homesick.' As an afterthought she spoke of the Princess Victoria Hospital.

'You'll be pleased to hear that what with your splendid efforts and my own little contributions we can relax. They have just come into a considerable sum of money.'

Jane described Philippa's new job as 'a secretary on all fronts'. Ever the opportunist, Jane said, 'Take your hat off, and be comfortable. We may as well get through a letter or two.'

She handed Philippa a fresh notebook.

When Jane was preparing to leave for a meeting at the American Embassy in Grosvenor Square, she wrapped a fur stole round her shoulders and said, 'The old Eagle Squadrons are quite famous now, aren't they? I dined with Sir Sholto Douglas the other night. He said that the RAF couldn't have asked for better companions.'

Not missing a certain brightness in the girl's face she added, 'The American and British squadrons are flying together now. When we watch them going over, we can't tell which is which.' Then, changing the subject with wartime briskness, 'It's really first rate of you to work for me again. I've missed that pretty smile, let alone the excellent typing. I'll see you at the end of the week. My taxi, Andrew? Many thanks. And if you find yourself running out of work,' she said, turning at the door to look at Philippa, 'just telephone Andrew. He will always find you a little bonne-bouche.'

The next day Philippa was going to visit Barny at the convalescent home for the first time. It was dark, foggy and freezing hard. She squeezed herself into the usual crammed train which travelled at what seemed like five miles an hour. She thought she would never get to Guildford. She had told Barny on the telephone that she would be with him by midday, but it was after half past one when she crawled out of an antiquated taxi at the door of the convalescent home. The fog was very thick, muffling the grounds and turning a high barrier of rhododendrons into a looming cliff. The driver ground away into the obscurity.

Through the swing doors she was again in the only world Barny now knew, a world which separated him from her more completely than the silent fog outside. The hospital echoed with voices and smelled of antiseptic and furniture polish.

Men in dressing-gowns went by. One gave her a lopsided grin. He had the lumpy, shiny, crimson face of a pilot who has been burned. Another, on crutches, said 'Hi.' Philippa smiled brightly. When she got to Barny's door, she gave the six raps she always used. But before she could open the door it swung wide, and a figure in brown American Air Force uniform threw his arms round her and kissed her as the Eagles used to do. It was Chuck Greenfield.

'Pal! Barny told me you were coming. That husband of yours kept looking out at the fog every darned minute!'

He gave his boyish grin and said, twice, 'Sure good to see you.'

Oh, thought Philippa, her heart filled with emotion, you were an Eagle and I love you. Just for a moment, just while you stand there, dear dear Chuck, it's like it used to be. How could I have been angry *at* you, as you'd put it?

She ran over to kiss Barny, who was at the window, dressed and in uniform for the first time.

'Do I look okay?'

'Wonderful!'

'It's hanging off me. It'll need tailoring.'

'I *like* you so thin. It's romantic!'

Chuck's presence changed the feeling, the very scent of the room, it smelled of Camel cigarettes and hair lotion and crowds of people and reality.

'What do you know?' drawled Chuck, 'I brought that palooka a great bunch of pink carnations. I felt pretty silly carrying the thing, and of course, I left them in the jeep.'

'I never liked pink anyway,' said Barny, laughing.

The trio talked a little. Chuck said he had a packet for Trix, would Philippa give it to her? He hoped to be able to call her tonight, 'if she can wait up that long.' While he was there, Barny was almost natural. But when she touched his hand, it was cold with sweat.

Chuck finally said that he must go. He kissed her again.

'You have forgiven us, haven't you? Trix said you've been real nice to her. And here's the packet. Two. One for Trix, and one for you and Elaine. Nothing much . . .'

He went over and put his hand on Barny's shoulder, using an expression Philippa remembered.

'Well, old buddy.'

He left them.

The silence which followed was like looking down a precipice. She lifted his cold hand and kissed it.

'How are you, my darling?'

She was never sure what he would say and she was always afraid.

'The doctor says I can work again.'

In a moment of unthinking joy she blurted it out,

'Fly again!'

'Hell, no,' he said furiously, and she dropped his hand; he clutched at it as if he would fall.

'The medic report has gone to the CO in charge of my old squadron – Pete Jansen. But it'll go further up than that. Chuck didn't come here on a sick visit, he came to tell me the news. I'm to be grounded. You must have guessed, although you've never said. They're putting me into Intelligence.'

'Is that so bad – '

'What do you think? Hell, what do I mean, I talk to you as if you were a flyer yourself. Yeah, it's bad. A wingless wonder. Christ.'

Chapter Sixteen

Two days after the 1943 Christmas, Elaine went to Shelton. She had told herself that she would never go back but this proved to be untrue. Two or three times a year she telephoned Claire, and then made the weary journey, returning home tired and oppressed. Neither of the St Airds had the least idea why she came. They accepted her visits with an adequate politeness and never suggested that she should come again. But she did.

When she telephoned Claire to ask if she could come, Claire said 'Of course', and re-arranged her WVS appointments. But after giving her tea, Claire would glance at her watch and excuse herself. She would go out to feed the chickens, or to make a telephone call. Later when Elaine said it was time for her to catch her bus, Claire obligingly walked with her to the bus stop; sometimes she even managed to get a friend to give Elaine a lift to Oxford. St Aird in the stable studio was less crudely pleased to see her leave.

Elaine did not go to Shelton to see the St Airds. She went because the beautiful old house had been Miles' home. When Claire left her, Elaine always went up to Miles' bedroom. The house was very quiet, in winter the silence seemed to ring. And if Elaine kept very still, sitting on the bed and waiting, she could hear Miles laughing. Miles' things were in their unchanging places: a shelf of silver cups for cricket and boxing, small cups engraved 'Miles St Aird, Egg and Spoon Race', 'St Aird, Monkey Race'. They were dazzlingly clean, almost blue. Did his mother clean them? The cap he won as a member of the school cricket team hung on a hook. It was red and white velvet beginning to turn yellow, and had long silk tassels.

Elain had not taken Miles' books with her when she left, and now they had become part of the spotless room. They looked as if they had been glued. *Swallows and Amazons. Kim. The Seven Pillars of Wisdom.*

In this room, keeping very quiet, she could still hear him. Perhaps it was wrong to go to Shelton and listen. She could not help it.

The end of December journey had been at Claire's invitation for the first time. She telephoned to say that Miles' trunk had finally been sent back from Malta. Would Elaine come and cope, as she put it.

Elaine had sometimes wondered about Miles' possessions. She thought it impossible for them to be returned. Why should the Navy take precious ship-space to send back the pathetic things left by men who were dead? News that the trunk had come home was a painful shock.

When she arrived at Shelton in the little winter afternoon her mother-in-law was not there. The trunk had been taken up to Miles' room. It was locked, and the key was on the dressing table.

There it stood, a black tin trunk painted with his name. She knelt down as if to pray and opened it. She began to tremble. The contents of the trunk were in a perfection of order, everything skilfully folded and packed. There were a dozen white shirts, silk pyjamas, black socks, and his uniforms. The arms of one of his jackets was creased on the inside by the elbow. There was shaving tackle in his initialled leather box and two photograhs of herself – looking very young. And at the bottom of the trunk were all her letters. He had kept them in date order, fastened by rubber bands which the Maltese heat had rotted.

She knelt in front of the open trunk, his clothes round her, and crouched down and put her face into the creased uniform. It smelled of him. She burrowed into it and there it was, faint and clinging, the smell of Miles, of his skin and his hair . . .

The journey home was long and cold, and she was glad to toil up to the blacked-out shape of St Helen's. Dazzled by the lights as she walked into the drawing room, she found Trix on the floor, hunched by the fire. Elaine asked why she hadn't gone to work at the club tonight. But she knew why. The pattern of closeness between the sisters had shifted: Trix often sought her out. She had been waiting for her.

With Tyrrell suddenness, not bothering to ask Elaine about her day, Trix wailed, 'Oh Elaine, I couldn't work, I feel so low. I wish, I wish, I *wish* the divorce would at least get started. Dick said I could have it. But he's at sea and you have to go through all that faked rubbish about being seen at a hotel. Chuck was so glad when Dick said he'd do his stuff. He hated me being the guilty part – you know how Chuck is about women. He *respects* them so. I went to see that stupid solicitor and he said he can't do a thing. He kept mumbling, "it's up to your husband, Mrs Polglaze." I hate that name, it isn't me. And there's another thing. The silly fool rang here this morning and Annette took the message. Pa gave me a funny look when I came home this afternoon. Do you think he knows?'

'How could he?'

'I wouldn't put it past that nosey French bit to listen at doors. Imagine doing such a thing. Disgusting.'

'Trix. You know quite well Miggsy has listened at doors since we were born. Anyway, why should Annette bother?'

'Because it would put him against me. She's that sort. Oh, what a worry everything is. If I were Chuck's wife it would be so wonderful. I'd be safe.'

Elaine had never heard her speak with so much feeling – certainly not when she'd startled them with her sudden marriage, like a conjuror merrily producing a bouquet of paper flowers. Now she was anxious, vulnerable, and real.

'You know when Chuck was rested up and he took me away for a few days? I was jolly ill actually, I had a kind of miscarriage.' Elaine gave an exclamation, and Trix, satisfied at getting an effect, went on, 'Chuck was off his head with worry. He's so loving. Swell. Just marvellous. I was ill and my stomache has ached ever since. Do you think there's something wrong with me? It still hurts.'

'You must see a doctor.'

'I did. Today. Chuck sent me to the best specialist in Harley Street. I didn't like him too much. He said my stomach ache is nerves. Lots of girls get it now when their men are in danger, you see.'

Listening, Elaine thought, it's as if my darling Miles had never existed. She has utterly forgotten. Is that how it is with all my family? They just forget the dead.

Trix went on talking about love. She had never felt like this before. It sounded like the words of one of the tunes she used to sing. She'd always been fond of the men she slept with, she said earnestly, but it had never been like this. 'Why, when Chuck

and I meet, we've got to have each other right away. Like that!'
She clicked her fingers.

She went to the country sometimes and stayed at a pub near the Squadron's aerodrome. It had to be a secret because girlfriends and wives weren't allowed. It was bad for the pilots. She didn't like to say where she was going, in case Philippa heard. It might depress her because of Barny. Trix's voice had no trace of triumph, she felt for Philippa. Sometimes Chuck got away for an hour, she said, and couldn't Elaine guess how they spent *that*. The other night he'd been able to stay with her until five, he was on a dawn patrol. After he'd gone, Trix lay in bed and listened to the planes leaving for Germany. It had been rather wonderful. And awful.

Bending her head so that her hair covered her face in a golden curtain, she played with her bracelet, moving the charms round to find Chuck's US button. She looked like a man counting money – but Trix was counting pigs and horseshoes and buttons cut from young men's uniforms.

January was bitterly cold. One evening when both her sisters had stayed up late to hear a play on the wireless, Trix returned from the club looking brighter. She announced that she had been given a part in a film.

'There's a guy at the club, a real film director who's making a movie at Pinewood. It's called "They Flew into Danger" and – guess what! – it's about the Eagle Squadron. Chuck was so embarrassed when I called him up. Flip, do you remember the Hollywood movie, "Eagle Squadron", which made all your buddies squirm with embarrassment because they loathed being called heroes. Didn't they all boo? This one's going to be good. I'm to be a Waaf like the one in John Pudney's poem. "The Ash-blonde Waaf makes tea". I'm being paid twenty-five shillings a day.'

'But how can you get out of doing your work at the club?' asked Elaine innocently.

'Stoopid. London's crawling with girls just begging to wait at table for the Yanks.'

Considerably more cheerful than she'd been recently, Trix pranced into the kitchen to ask Miggs to wake her at half past five. A car was coming for her. It was the first time since she had been born that Trix was willing to wake at such an hour.

Miggs was old and found no difficulty in rising on the dot.

Wearing her flannel dressing-gown, she hobbled into Trix's bedroom. It was cold and pitch dark. She cruelly switched on the lights, and when the girl did not budge, took a sadistic glee in shaking her.

'You gotter get up for this lark of yours.'

Trix, groaning, dragged herself out of a deep sleep. She washed her face and dressed and stumbled down into the blackout where a car was waiting. Round her weary head she tied a pale blue and pink scarf on which was printed *We shall fight on the beaches, in the streets, and on the airfields*.

She came home that night exhausted. She was not the girl who strutted off every evening to the American club. Her face was plastered with brown make-up as thick as mud, her eyes painted purple, and she was too tired to eat. For the next ten days she left at the same ungodly hour and returned, said Philippa, looking as if she'd been put through a mangle. Trix hated filming. The hanging-about fretted her, she was unused to being patient, she disliked the boring repetition of her few little scenes. For a show-off, filming simply did not interest her. Star-struck about everything American, there never was a girl less film-struck than Trix. On the last evening she came into the drawing room at St Helen's, waving an envelope.

'Never again. But I've earned thirty pounds. That'll buy this baby three new frocks.'

While her sisters worked, each chained as she slightingly described it, to a typewriter, Trix chained herself to the family sewing machine.

The life Elaine and her sisters now led at St Helen's was not a natural one. Married women who returned home to their parents never comfortably settled. Elaine could not go back to the old, easy, submitting and daughterly frame of mind. She was independent and had only lived at Shelton because it was convenient, and would have hurt Miles had she not done so. Disliking her in-laws, she never felt imprisoned.

Now it was different because she was forced to live at home. She had little money, her salary was meagre, and she certainly couldn't afford a flat of her own, unless she was willing to make do with far less comfort than at St Helen's. Her nature disliked the idea of deliberately choosing to be poor. Besides, she would be lonely. Who had she, apart from her family? Her few girl friends in London were not close to her. Her dearest friend, Marjorie, was in Oxfordshire. The Baker Street job, despite its strangeness, was monotonous. And she discovered with a chill of the heart that she was not attracted to men since Miles had died. She supposed that happened with some women. It was a kind of psychological suttee.

There was a flu epidemic in January, and just after her birthday she caught it from someone in the office. She had to spend three days in bed. She had not been ill since she lost her baby, and a temperature and solitude combined made her feel low-spirited.

The fever was gone by the weekend: she would be well enough to return to work on Monday. On Sunday evening she was alone in the house, as she often was nowadays. It was dark and cold and very quiet, except for the noise of rain. She was dressed and lying on the sofa in the drawing room, trying to read. The family were off on their own devices. Miggs was in Sussex with her relatives. Theo had taken Annette to stay the weekend with his friends in Hertfordshire. Trix had gaily left on Friday night.

'I won't kiss you, darling. Suppose I caught it and gave it to someone we know!'

And Philippa was with some American friends at the Embassy in Grosvenor Square. She would not be back until midnight or later, she had said.

Elaine felt melancholy, listening to the rain. Is it the noise, she thought, which makes me feel so sad? She picked up her book again as the telephone rang. She gave a sigh. It would only be an American from the club, Trix collected them from habit. They were so friendly, and they deserved better, thought Elaine, than talking to me.

'Is that Elaine?' said a voice with a distinct actorish pitch.

'Dick! Are you on leave? I'm afraid Trix isn't here.'

She heard him laugh.

'I'm not ringing for my ex-wife. As a matter of fact I hoped it would be you. I'm in town. A very short leave. I couldn't persuade you to come for a drink, could I? Now?'

She opened her mouth to refuse. But didn't. He must be coming to talk about the divorce and since Trix was so anxious about it, Elaine supposed she must see him. She did not want to.

She hadn't forgotten their last interview, when he had come into her room in the small hours of the night Trix threw him over. Elaine had been desperately sorry for him, but his behaviour had shocked her. Jealousy and anger made him vicious. He wasn't a man who believed, as Miles had done, that there were standards, and in bad times you owed it to yourself to be civilized.

Hearing the taxi, she put out the hall lights and opened the door to the pouring wet night. Dimly, she made out a figure running towards her. When he was indoors and the door was safely shut, she switched on the light. He laughed, pulling off his greatcoat and cap. Rain shone on his clothes and curling hair.

'Hello, Elaine. Long time no see.'

She gave an embarrassed smile. He was tougher and more formidable than she remembered.

'There's nothing to drink in the house except what Father locks up in his study. I'm so sorry. Will coffee do?'

'But I'm taking you out, remember? Great luck, finding you at home when I rang.'

'I usually am at home,' she said with a little meaningless laugh.

In the drawing room they stood by the fire, and Dick looked at her appraisingly. Something in the look reminded her of an expression she often saw on Miggs's face. Disapproval.

'I see you are still in black.'

Nobody remarked on this, and if they had she would have shut them up. He put one foot on the brass fender.

'When do you plan to come out of mourning?'

'I don't know. I like it.'

'Miles wouldn't. He was all for you looking beautiful.'

'I'll get the coffee.'

She had forgotten that he had refused it. Then she remembered, but still crossed the room to get away. He reached her before she was at the door.

'Elaine. Don't be angry. You mustn't mind, you know, if I tell you the truth. Would you prefer a lot of stupid stuff you couldn't believe? Don't run away.'

He did not say he was sorry, but took her hand and led her to a chair. Then he sat down, his arms along the top of the sofa, looking at her with his fascinating eyes. His face was like a satyr's. It was hard and laughing.

'Trix is away,' she began but he interrupted.

'I told you. I didn't come to talk about her. I'm not avoiding the subject, but the divorce has only this minute started because I haven't been able to do a thing until now. Your sister's solicitors (which mine call 'the other side') have been asking if we can hurry it on. Is she pregnant?'

'Of course not.'

'Don't be uppity. I wouldn't put it past her to make sure of her American lover. Of this one, anyway.'

'How cold you sound.'

He scratched his nose.

'Do I? Well, I am not cold. Not at all. It is simply that I'm not one to hang about when not wanted. One refusal, and you don't see me for dust. I'd like to hurry on the divorce myself. What is the American like, by the way?'

'Very nice. Very gentle.'

'Poor old him.'

'Sour grapes.'

Instead of being annoyed, he burst out laughing, with a rat-tat-tat as sudden as machine-gun fire.

'You must believe me, Elaine, I am quite recovered. It was like getting over a bad go of measles. There was a big depression for a while and I needed a tonic, Navy rum did the trick. It's wonderful stuff, thick and dark and strong. Delicious. We have a ration every morning. We line up and are given a tot in a pewter measure. My heart wasn't broken, you know. Just bruised. I was more furious than sad.'

'You certainly were.'

He looked at her with friendly eyes.

'I was rude, wasn't I? So unkind. Why was I unkind to you, when all you did was to be your sweet self? I felt a beast later. I wanted to write and apologise, but then I thought you had enough to cope with at home. You would only have written back, saying I hadn't been rude at all. We both know that was not true, but you're a girl for the courtesies.'

He seemed to know a lot about her.

'What happened with your father?' he went on curiously. 'I remember Trix told me that he is serious about religion and dislikes divorce.'

'He doesn't know.'

'What!'

'We have managed to keep it from him so far.'

He looked as if he found it hard to keep a straight face. He annoyed her. It was one thing to be good to a broken-hearted ex-husband, quite another to be faced with a spirited man trying not to laugh at the family's troubles.

'You can't keep his daughter's divorce a secret for long, Elaine. He is certain to find out. Then he'll be angrier still at being made a fool of. This sounds like one of Trix's dotty ideas.'

'It wasn't,' said Elaine coldly, 'it was Chuck Greenfield who asked me to let her stay. It is true, Father does disapprove of divorce. He might even refuse to let her live at home. He can be very difficult and where would she go then?'

'Aren't all Americans rich? She could live in some luxury hotel somewhere.'

'I have no idea if Chuck has money or not. I am simply looking after her until he can.'

Dick continued to regard her with his odd, slanting eyes. He remarked that keeping secrets was the devil. She replied that she was used to it, because of her job. He shrugged. Those were official secrets, we all kept them. Family secrets were something very different. They were to do with hurting people. Being forced to keep them made one nervous.

'Trix is very nervous,' admitted Elaine, calming down now that he had stopped looking as if he were laughing at her.

'I daresay she is. But the reason *you* feel anxious is from family affection, whereas Trix just wants to stay put while it suits her. Hell, am I being rude again? She is lucky to have such a champion,' he added. 'I salute you.'

Later, sheltered by one of Doctor Tyrrell's pre-war black silk umbrellas, Dick accompanied her out into the blackout on their way to the Hogarth. The rain hammered on the umbrella, the darkness was complete. It was, he said, holding her arm, like swimming. They ran, arriving breathless and dripping at the pub.

The Hogarth was in a square of old houses. On the winter's night, it was loud with voices, most of them American. The place was crowded with United States officers and their girls. Dick bought the drinks and took her over to a window seat in a corner. The pub was dark, panelled and old, and the walls were covered with the Hogarth cartoons. Above Elaine's head hung the dying gallant in *Mariage à la Mode*.

Dick looked round at the girls roosting on bar stools and flirting with their escorts. He observed dryly that all the women in London appeared suddenly to be blondes.

'I suppose American men choose girls with fair hair.'

'Charitable Elaine. What about peroxide on the black market? *You* are the only natural blonde in the place. Your hair's so pretty. Like golden feathers.'

She wasn't used to compliments any more, and did not know what to say. She smiled nervously.

He talked about the Navy. He was on Dover patrols now, the weather vile, the job boring. Then they began to talk about Miles. Not the dead hero, but the young man whom Dick had known before the war. Once after a party, when they were both driving home, Miles had said to him, 'Tell you what. Let's go to Scotland.' They had driven all night up the A1, stopping at Scotch Corner for porridge and bacon.

'Miles said we were characters in the first chapter of a John Buchan book.'

'Oh, he told me about that. It sounded such fun. It was before I met him, and he said we'd do the same thing, just drive and drive until we got to Scotland!'

A warmth went through her, sitting with this man. He had a kind of magic because he had known Miles. In his mind, as in hers, Miles still lived. He had not shuddered away from his loss, but sat there with her remembering him. She smiled, and Dick took her hand and give it a casual kiss.

When they walked back to St Helen's the rain had almost stopped. They went up to the house and he lingered for a moment, as boys used to do with her in innocent peacetime.

When she said goodnight in her resolute little voice, he suddenly said, 'Elaine. I forgot. I meant to ask a favour. Would you think it very unattractive if I asked for a book which I lent Trix ages ago? If she still has it, I really would like it back. It's my illustrated *Treasure Island* which I had when I was twelve. When I lent it to her, like a fool, I believed she would read it.'

'Perhaps she has,' said Elaine automatically.

'Don't kid us both, Elaine. You know she only reads *Vogue*. Well? Do you think we might at least see if it is in the bookcase?'

'Of course.'

They went indoors. She was pretty sure he would find his

book, for Trix's shelves were crammed with books lent to her by young men and never read. They remained there like trophies.

They climbed the stairs. Elaine put on the light as if to chase ghosts.

They went into Trix's bedroom. It was in its usual mess, drawers gaping, the wardrobe ajar to show dresses as bright as the costumes at a carnival. The air was filled with strong, evocative scent.

'Same old Trix,' he said, stepping over a pair of pink wedge-heeled shoes.

Elaine did not reply. There was no point in pretending Trix was not appallingly untidy. He went to the bookshelf, raised his eyebrows and said 'Henry James! What simpleton thought she'd read him? Ah. Here it is. Good-oh.'

It was a large handsome book lettered in gold.

'I'm really glad to have it back. Such an old friend. Thank you, Elaine.'

They walked down the passage. He stopped at the open door of her own room and peered in as if amused at the comparison. The room was spotless, tidy, a bunch of jonquils on the dressing table beside a photograph of Miles and Elaine at their wedding, looking at each other and laughing.

'I've never seen that before.'

He went over to pick it up, smiling at the smiling faces.

'How pretty you are.'

She gave a little empty laugh.

'I was.'

Putting the photograph carefully back, he turned to her.

'That's a silly thing to say. *You are* just as pretty now. Changed, yes, but it only makes you more beautiful. Surely you must know that?'

He pulled her gently towards him.

For a second her body stiffened, she resisted. But then, ah then, something inside her which she believed was made of iron and fated to keep her always imprisoned seemed to break. Her whole body melted. Not letting her go, he moved her towards the bed.

'No, no, I mustn't.'

'Of course you must. You're so lovely. So sweet. So beautiful. Don't waste it – '

Scarcely knowing that she was lying down, that his body was

urgent against hers, she only felt his racing heart. When she opened her eyes, his were closed and his face was changed, almost as if he were in pain . . .

When he had gone she lay in the bed where they had made love and fell into a dreamless sleep. She awoke late the next morning, and for a moment forgot what had happened to her. She was only conscious of a delicious sweeping languor that she had not felt for two years. And then she remembered.

Chapter Seventeen

'Elaine?' said a voice on her office telephone.

She answered in a low voice, 'How on earth did you get this number – '

'You gave it to me.'

She heard the laugh.

'I – I don't remember.'

'It's true. You were very sleepy.'

Alone in the little dark office, she blushed a miserable burning red.

There was a pause.

'Elaine? I'm standing in a freezing telephone box at the other end of nowhere. You are there, are you? You haven't died?'

'I'm here.' Another pause. 'Did you – did you want anything?'

'There's a question. I rang to say goodbye again. I keep having a funny idea you are feeling guilty this morning. Are you?'

'I can't talk now.'

She tried to collect herself, but couldn't.

'You see. You are feeling like that. Well, don't, Lovebird. For my sake. I'll write, I promise. Well? Are you going to say goodbye nicely?'

'Goodbye, Dick.'

'Do you never say "darling?" It's a shame to tease you. Goodbye, *darling* Elaine.'

When she thought about the conversation all that day, she did not know what it – or he – had meant. She did not know him at all – except in the flesh. She had never made love to any man but Miles. Now she had been unfaithful to him. She felt guilty and deeply shocked at herself. She had not known it possible to want a man again, as she had wanted Dick. When he had taken her she had thought she would die of physical bliss. He had made love strongly, fiercely, tenderly, for a long time. He had even stopped before it ended and said – 'Let's wait. Lovely torture to wait', and so they had, but it had been impossible to stay apart for more than a few minutes.

Now he was gone.

I suppose he rang me because *he* felt guilty too, she thought, and remembered the laughing voice and knew that was nonsense. She could think of no other reason why he should bother to speak to her from that freezing telephone box. And why had he called her by that sweet, stupid name?

She did not tell Trix about his visit. He had not asked her to, had twice said he hadn't come to talk about Trix. Elaine was glad she need not mention him, and ashamed of the pleasure of thinking about him. It couldn't be right to feel like this about her sister's soon-to-be-divorced husband. But when he came into her mind, so often! her heart still turned over. She remembered his face, narrow-eyed, clever and alluring. She remembered her sexual joy, and longed, literally longed, to see him again. Perhaps I never will. Is that what happened in love affairs? She was ignorant of the way men behaved who made love to you outside marriage. She wondered if quite often they never returned.

Trix was still gloomy at times about not yet being Chuck's wife, but one morning her whole manner changed. She was radiant. She had received a letter from the solicitors to say that the divorce was being given priority 'under the circumstances'. Chuck, she said, must have pulled strings.

'His CO doesn't approve of him being worried over *me*.'

She took to singing again, left for the club with her old swing and spring, and actually wrote to Chuck every day. She brought him tediously into every conversation, using American words. Petrol was gas, leave was furlough, and nobody was annoyed, they were fased.

During the bitter winter, Philippa once more had reason to be grateful to Jane Alwynne. When she had been part of the Eagle Squadron, the banging at the ancient typewriter had almost drowned the noise of the planes leaving for France. Now once again, Jane's shameless use of every moment of her time stopped Philippa from brooding. Barny had begun his work as an Intelligence officer, and telephoned her whenever he could. But she knew she must not ask when they were going to meet. She had discovered the curious truth that courage only grows if you nurture it.

Elaine and Trix were matter of fact about Barny. They asked how he was getting on, but never if he was due for any leave.

247

Trix, who had moments of perception, made encouraging remarks about his new work.

'That's a real tough job he's taken on. Specially when the pilots get back and report, and one of them really *believes* he's scored. And the Intelligence guy finds out that he hasn't. Imagine going up to a pilot and having to tell him. That takes guts.'

At last Barny telephoned to say he had some leave and she could come to Sussex for the weekend. 'I've booked us a room at The Dolphin. I'm just longing to see you, honey.'

There was fog at Chichester station. Muffled in her fur coat and an old knitted Eagle Squadron scarf, she shivered with cold and nerves. Carrying her suitcase with numbed hands she walked down the platform. The smoke from the train made the darkness deeper. There were only thin beams of torches, figures dimly seen. Had Barny not been able to come? Where could she find a telephone?

Suddenly a voice said, 'There you are,' and she was lifted off her feet, and hugged so tightly that she lost her breath.

He shepherded her out of the station, saying that the hotel was only a few blocks away. He held her hand tightly as they walked through the unlit fog where figures loomed and vanished like ghosts. Philippa tried to hear in his voice if he were himself again. She thought he sounded strained, although he laughed now and then. She was so nervous that she was still shivering. As they crossed a blank mass of fog which was a street, he put his arm round her shoulder.

'You're very cold. Never mind, we're here.'

A moment later they were in the dazzlingly bright woodsmoke-smelling hall of the hotel.

Barny took her straight to the bar and ordered them some rum, drawing up a bar stool for her and sitting facing her.

'Now drink that up. It's good for that old unheated train feeling. And that old unheated train feeling's good for nothing.'

They looked at each other then. He saw how thin she was, and that there was a shadow on her charmingly-shaped face. He thought she looked *triste*. The thinness made her more beautiful, in a way. She was no longer the plumpish candid English girl whom he had married, she looked as if she had secrets. But everybody did now. She wore the old pinafore dress his sister had sent her, and the bushranger shirt, and her Eagle Squadron brooch. He bent and kissed her cheek. She smelled of scent and of her own smell which he always thought was like biscuits. She moved him. He was the reason for that thinness. He felt guilty and resented the guilt. For one terrified moment he wondered if he could bear so much love – and was the more afraid that she might guess what he was thinking.

As for Philippa, she looked at his olive-skinned rather triangular face and black hair, at the new lines under his serious eyes. He was more like the Barny of old.

'Let's go upstairs,' he said, after he had made her drink a second rum because of the cold night.

They walked up the stairs, passing ancient walls that bulged, and stooping under low ceilings in the quiet deserted corridor. We're going to make love she thought. She was nervous, because it had been so long since they had. Before his crash his lovemaking had been violent, exhausting, almost impersonal. She had had the recurring thought that any woman would have satisfied him.

Unlocking the door, he took her into a room with walls crisscrossed by black beams, and an oak floor which sloped. There was an ancient double bed, with slots at its four corners where the posts of the four-poster had been. Locking the door behind him, he looked at her with heavy eyes.

They began to undress in silence, throwing their clothes on the floor. When he began to make love to her, it was slow and delicious. She did not feel violated, she gazed up to see the face above her tender and lost.

It was over and they separated. Barny was wet with sweat. He bent across her to find a cigarette. Then, with his arm round her, for the first time since the crash he began to talk. It was as if he had been under a spell, literally struck dumb until now. He described how the plane had been hit, and the sound of the Messerschmitt diving towards the ship, and the moments of excruciating pain before he had fainted. That pain returned in nightmares.

Then he began to speak of what he said had been worse.

'Being grounded. It was as if I'd been a goddammed bird, you know? As if I'd grown wings and they'd hacked them off. I didn't want to see you when they did that. I was maimed and useless and no good. Even when I began to work again, I felt ill, not being able to get up there with the rest of them, having to stay *here*, on earth. The aerodrome was bombed one night. There was a hangar on fire, and a lot of stuff coming down, and I was pretty well in danger of being killed. I remember thinking "this is life." Isn't that something? This is life.'

He covered her with the eiderdown, carefully tucking it in.

'I didn't want you with me when I was like that. Who was it talked about the dark night of the soul? Mine was black as pitch. Well . . . I've gotten used to my job now. I don't do it badly, and I can help the guys I look after, because I've been there. I still want to fly, but my reactions are too slow. *This* machine,' he looked scornfully at the long scars on his body, 'isn't in flying order. But the work – Intelligence officer – means I can make the boys go out to battle with confidence. That matters, doesn't it?'

He described how he briefed the pilots before they went on ops. They met in the Intelligence room where wall maps were set out and the course drawn. He showed each man how to fly on a certain course, how to avoid ground batteries, telling him to fly around or in between the ack-ack guns. He briefed the Squadron about the purpose of the flight. Sometimes they were escorting the big bombers, at other times sweeping out over Occupied France to challenge the enemy to come up and do battle. 'Lucky beggars – that was the job I liked best.'

When the planes returned, he was on the field waiting. 'I have to look at the planes after they've taxied down on the runway, to see which of their guns has been fired. Remember I told you that, Flip? There is adhesive tape across the muzzles to keep out the dust while the planes are on the ground. How it used to bug me when the Intelligence guy came looking at the muzzles of *my* guns. Didn't he believe that I'd fired them, for Christ's sake? Now that's my job. So there I am with the boys, listening to their stories, hearing about battles and narrow escapes – they're so excited – '

'You always were.'

'Was I? I don't remember. They all talk at once, swooping and turning their hands about to describe the flights, and I have to wait to quiet them down. Finally I write up the account of the day's fighting. The official report.'

He put out his cigarette, looked at his watch and exclaimed that she had had nothing to eat, she had been travelling for hours, and all he'd done was to make love and talk for too long. They must go down to supper.

His leave lasted two days. They met some young pilots at the Dolphin on the following day. Barny was glad to see them. It was very strange how the boys treated him with deference. Nobody called her Flip either, and that was strange too.

In the afternoon, with the fog thinning and a hard frost Barny took her for a country walk. Now and then the sky overhead roared with planes. They stood and watched the great dark flocks which filled the air with their steady roar before vanishing towards France.

'Fortresses, Flip. Did you ever see so many?'

'Never.'

'Things have changed a bit since the Battle of Britain, eh?'

Yes, she thought. And so have we.

When the sound of the Fortresses died away, they walked on in silence. The hedges were bare and thorny, the grass thickened and flattened by the frost. Along the edge of the road were little pools which had frozen, and she ground her heel into one to see it turn into stars. He watched her unsmilingly, and then said, 'There is something I want to tell you. No, don't look scared. Just give me your hand. When I was at East Grinstead there was a doctor called Wheatley. I told you about him.'

He had not told her, but Philippa said nothing. She thought with anxious love that he was like a sick animal, who will only eat and drink if you hold the dish with a motionless hand.

'Wheatley talked to me a lot. That's not true, I talked to him, because he wanted me to. About my parents dying. How they'd hated for me to fly. The Eagles. You. The future. I thought it pretty dumb, talking of the future slap in the middle of a war but he said that was the time to talk of it. He wormed out of me that I'd always wanted to write. I even showed him those poems I wrote when the Eagles first began to fight. Remember those?'

'They were beautiful.'

He looked at her and just for a moment he seemed young again.

'Honey. I'm glad you remember them. So – I've started to write again. I've done about a third of a book. You needn't ask what it is about. You know it can't be anything else.'

'The Eagles.'

'Got it in one.'

251

'Oh Barny! I suppose you wouldn't let me see it before it's finished?'

'How did you guess?'

Quite suddenly the blitz started again over London. Once again people heard the whistle and thud of bombs. Red hot shrapnel poured into d'Abernon Road, hitting and splitting the tiles on roofs. The February raids were heavy and so was the thunderous barrage of the guns. The night skies were full of the rapiers of searchlights and the sudden violent flash of flares. On one night in late February, a power station was hit and St Helen's – and miles of London homes – were plunged into blackness. But Miggs knew where the candles were.

Nobody in St Helen's, nobody in London, had the heightened energy and courage which had come in the 1940 blitz. The war had changed. It had become a vast conflict all over the world and there had been victories, and would be more. There was strain and resentment during the new blitz, instead of the old stubborn patriotism. People flocked down into the Underground again. There were many horrible fires burning in the streets.

By far the most nervous person at St Helen's was Annette. She would not go home to her lodgings a few streets away, but spent hours under the billiard room table, and usually refused to accept the All-Clear. 'Another wave of bombers will come. They always do.' Sometimes she was right.

Her exaggerated fear surprised Elaine, for the French girl must have been very courageous to escape from Brittany and make her way across the Channel. Elaine was sorry for her. Philippa, nervous because she knew the blitz alarmed Barny for her sake, pretended to be cool. But like the rest of Londoners she was not as strong as she had been the first time around. As for Elaine, she felt nothing but curiosity. Often she crept out of the house in the cold dark to watch. Now and then the old house trembled when a bomb fell. When she looked up at the sky, it was filled with golden-white flares and the stain of fires, it was split with flashes or the unearthly glow of phospherous bombs. Curious flaming blobs, like the stars of the most expensive fireworks hung suspended in the air. She thought of all the people in danger, and of those who would be killed tonight. She did not care for her own safety. Perhaps Dick, her fascinating

252

lover of a single night, might be sorry if she were killed. But she herself was like Siegfried, immune because he had bathed in the dragon's blood.

The blitz went on until March and when it ended, and sirens no longer wailed, London was filthy. Dust was everywhere. Dust from fires, explosions and the wrecks of houses. Everybody developed a sore throat, and Elaine's was so bad that although she went to work, she could scarcely speak.

Spring came. The nights were peaceful again and one sunny weekend Trix, all smiles, told Elaine that Chuck had rung and she was allowed to visit him for a twenty-four hour leave 'somewhere in England.' Everything was very hush hush, she couldn't say where. It looked as if the divorce would soon be final.

'Imagine. I'll be Chuck's wife. Oh brother.'

When Philippa came home from work that evening, the sun was still shining as Trix was walking through the open gate. She wore a new black and white striped dress, and a tiny hat with a spotted veil was balanced on her blonde head.

'Hi. I'm off to see Chuck. Shall I give him your love? He's always telling me how much he misses Barny. They were real buddies, weren't they. I'm sure they'll be together again some-time soon.'

Trix, happy, flowered with generosity.

Philippa couldn't help smiling.

'Give him both our loves,' she said and meant it.

Trix waved and tripped away on the lookout for a taxi.

Philippa sighed as she went indoors. She often envied Trix these days. There was an extraordinary quality about her young sister. Who else had the ability to walk, light as a feather, through the war? But Trix had known no other adult life but this; she grew up to the song of sirens. She had adapted to food shortages, air raids, dirt and danger, to divorcing an English husband and acquiring an American one. She was up-to-the-minute even when the world she lived in was a terrible one. When she talked of air battles and death at second hand, what she spoke about was often, almost always, tragic. Did she listen to what she herself said? Her voice rang with more reality when she spoke of her own magical knack of having fun.

The next day was still sunny, and Philippa brought home some of Jane Alwynne's work to finish on her father's typewriter. The telephone rang. Annette was out, and Philippa heard Miggs answering with the old familiar chant, 'Doctor Tyrrell's residence.'

There was a pause.

The old woman spoke again.

'My poor child. Come home.'

Philippa's heart turned over. Miggs came into the drawing room.

'That young chap of Trix's was killed this morning. Poor kid. Sobbin' her heart out.'

Both her sisters were waiting when Trix came home. They heard the taxi, the slam of the front door. They both wanted to rush out. Neither moved. When Trix came into the room she looked as if she were in a trance, and her face was so pale that it looked green. It was blank until she sat down, when she grimaced.

Elaine said, 'Is your stomach hurting?'

'Like hell.'

Philippa sprang up and ran over to clasp her in her arms. Trix clung. They broke away and sat down, and Trix slipped to the floor, where she crouched with her arms round her shoulders as if she were freezing cold.

'Isn't it awful? Oh, isn't it awful? Do you know he was with me until half past five this morning. I had him *in my arms*. We were together all last night, making love over and over, and when he left this morning he gave me a huge kiss and said he'd see me tonight and we'd fix the wedding for when he had his next rest period. Then he went and I fell asleep after I'd heard the planes go over. I don't know how long I slept but there was a banging on my door, and the porter was there and said someone wanted to see me. I was so frightened my legs gave. He came into my room, one of Chuck's friends, Ray. Oh, he was so upset. He could scarcely speak and we both began to cry even before he'd told me. He saw Chuck's plane go down near Amiens. In flames. He hadn't parachuted. There wasn't a doubt that he was lost.' She repeated, 'Not a doubt about it.' And rocking to and fro 'What a bloody war. What a bloody, bloody war.'

She was ill for two days, doubled up with stomach cramps and unable to eat or sleep. Sometimes in the night she slept for an hour and then woke crying and trailed into Elaine's bedroom in the dark. Elaine woke to find her standing beside the bed, just as she'd done as a child with earache.

She looked dreadful, she scarcely spoke a word. Neither Elaine nor Philippa, one widowed, the other knowing the anguish of a wounded husband, considered that Trix should not give way to sorrow. They put no time limit on her behaviour, as they would have done on themselves or each other. They gave her no stoic advice or fierce despising, as Claire had thrown at Elaine and that she, in turn, had pitched at Philippa. It seemed there were different rules for Trix. Just as in the war, where every other woman, even those over sixty were working, Trix never did a thing.

For Philippa, Trix's loss was a dreadful kind of bond. She suffered with her because she loved and understood pilots and their brief dangerous glory. Philippa's old protective love for her young sister filled her heart when Trix talked of Chuck. It was only then that Trix's dull eyes brightened. Chuck had taken her to dance to Glen Miller. He had asked his mother to send her a whole box of real nylon stockings. Then there was a faint light in her lightless face.

Her father did not ask her what ailed her. He sought out Elaine.

'The girl looks ill. I think I should take a look at her.'

Elaine was reminded of Miggs's proverb that the shoemaker's children were the worst shod in the village. She said that Trix had caught some kind of flu, and wanted to go to the country.

Theo, relieved, agreed and asked no more questions.

One of Trix's girlfriends in the ATS, who had heard the news, invited her to stay with her and her parents in Leicester.

'I may as well go,' Trix said indifferently.

When she said goodbye to Elaine, she began to cry.

After Trix was gone, Elaine noticed something very odd. The young men whom her sister admired began to disappear too. There were no longer crowds of GI's lounging in Piccadilly, or sprawling on the steps of what used to be the mansions of the aristocracy. The Americans seemed to drain away from the great wartime city. One day they were as familiar as the scarlet buses. The next day they had vanished from London.

There was a nervousness in the air as summer began. People bought more newspapers and switched on the wireless more often. They were waiting for news of the Second Front.

Philippa was not allowed to see Barny again, but he telephoned her whenever he could. He had been stricken by Chuck's death and had written to Trix. But Philippa knew that her sister had not opened any of the letters about Chuck. When they spoke on the telephone, Barny said very little. How was his book, she asked. 'Okay, but I can't get around to it now.' Philippa told Elaine that it felt as if their conversations were censored.

'Everything is a secret now,' said Elaine who lived in no other atmosphere. 'He can't tell you where he is or what is happening. But how did he *really* sound?'

'Staccato.'

One warm June night the sisters woke to the roar of thousands of aircraft. They both ran down in their nightdresses out into the garden. The sky overhead was thick with stars, and against them they saw line after line of powerful winged shapes in formation. The planes never seemed to end.

Next morning Miggs heard on the eight o'clock news that the BBC were quoting German reports that the Second Front had started. By half past nine, it was official.

Theo said, 'Thank God.' Philippa said, 'At last.' Elaine said nothing. Curiously, nobody was excited. When Elaine travelled to work, nobody talked eagerly in the bus or the Underground. And at the office it was the same.

She thought about Dick and wondered if he would be part of the great new movements of the war. When she thought of him her heart ached. She told herself she was being foolish. I meant nothing to him, so I suppose I must find a way of making him mean nothing to me.

She began to type the bills of lading. They were for guns, plastic explosives and ammunition. Yet it was like typing lists of tinned foods, she thought. She was told nothing about the work and was not allowed to ask. This morning she suddenly decided to risk it. Her boss was in his office talking in French about the daily list of messages broadcast to the French resistance. The messages always intrigued Elaine – who invented them? They were in the oddest kind of code. Giles Seton was repeating 'Yes . . . the umbrella dies of love. I've got that. The umbrella dies of love. Good. What? Ah, yes. The kangaroo has five children. The kangaroo has five children.'

'Wizard show,' he said as usual, seeing the coffee.

'Captain Seton,' said Elaine after a moment. 'Won't our job soon be finished?'

He daintily wiped his ginger moustache.

'One of these fine days, Mrs St Aird. It will all be mopped up, tidied away and finished.'

'But surely – '

'While there is a single enemy remaining in France, we've got a job of work here for the partisans. Which reminds me. There's a batch of new complaints about the equipment being too heavy. One of our SOE chaps is over and insists on seeing me. Stall him a bit, will you? He's due soon and I've some calls to make.'

Elaine left his office resentfully. Keeping official secrets was one thing. But now the Second Front had begun, the partisans must be joining the allies, area by area. She saw the invasion as a flood, with the resistance fighters scattered across France like small rivers and lakes waiting to be engulfed in the huge victorious tide.

She returned to her own desk in her box of an office which overlooked the well of the building. She was collecting her lading bills when the door of her office burst open. A man came in. He wore shabby foreign civilian clothes, patched and dirty. It did not need more than a glance to see he'd come from France. He carried a revolver and a canvas bag.

'I have a rendezvous with Captain Seton, mademoiselle – '

He stopped.

She stared.

Without a word they rushed into an embrace.

It was Alexandre.

They hugged and laughed and kissed, both filled with the sharp, intense joy of wartime reunion. It was as if they had both returned from the dead. When he released her, he held her hands and looked at her at arm's length. They looked at each other. Both saw faces that the war had changed. With his sharp eyes he saw that she must be a widow. There were new lines in her face and round her mouth, and her glow was gone. Elaine saw more dramatic changes. He was as thin as a skeleton, his bones stuck out, his lustrous eyes were staring and smudged with shadows. He looked dirty – and there was something dangerous about him.

They had only just started to talk when Giles Seton came in, to find his secretary and the French partisan holding hands. He ignored that, and breezily invited the visitor into his office, observing that he gathered there was a little matter of an official complaint. Alexandre caught Elaine's eye and winked.

'Yes, Captain, I have a strong complaint to make. But excuse me – ' he broke off and turned to Elaine. 'May we lunch? It has to be today.'

She nodded, and he turned back to Giles saying loudly, 'We know all about your tests on the weight of our equipment, Captain. We are told that it is *not* heavy and that we make a great fuss. We are absurd. You tell us that an officer here in London wore the equipment for an entire day and declared it perfectly satisfactory. Light as a feather. You did *not* tell us that this man was *un arrimeur*.'

The door closed. Elaine couldn't help grinning. It was true, there had been a man here doing the test – a huge man who in peacetime had been a stevedore.

They lunched in a small deserted tea shop in a mews near the office. Alexandre was in excellent spirits, having won his argument. With a touch of his old boasting he told her he had recently escaped from a German prison hospital.

'I had appendicitis. I escaped with the stitches still in my belly! The good British sewed me up.' He had been a partisan in Burgundy in the forests, and it had been there that Elaine's containers with their guns and explosives had been flown on some of Giles' Lizzie Landings.

Alexandre talked about himself in the old expansive way.

'I was sent to train as an agent. Parachuting. Ugh, that I detest. Combat. *That* I enjoy. For a time I flew a plane. You remember never had I flown one? I am,' said Alexandre with simplicity, 'a natural pilot. But our Halifaxes were crude. They were carcases of raw ironwork menacing our heads. Utility planes, cheap as the cheapest cigarette lighters. Two days ago, Elaine, I saw an American Liberator. Never had I seen such a thing. Engines that never break down, ash trays, leather seats, even soundproofing. Gadgets to bring cold or hot air to suit each man. Combat helmets. Bullet-proof vests to protect against flak. I was envious.'

'Were you, Alexandre?'

'You are perceptive, Elaine. No, I did not envy them. I feel that our planes are more in the spirit of the poverty of my nation than if I flew in one of those luxurious weapons of war. Our merit is not diminished. We will not achieve less than our American friends.'

He leaned across the table saying how quietly she listened and how glad he was to see her.

'You have suffered and you, too, are in the spirit of combat. After this war, perhaps I shall fall in love with you. You are very beautiful. Your sisters were lovely, it is true. You, the loveliest.'

When he left her at the door of the office near Baker Street, he kissed her. She stood and watched him swinging away. An invisible cape still seemed suspended from his shoulders.

Chapter Eighteen

There was no out-of-the-sky victory after the Invasion started. At home Philippa was very quiet, for Barny had been posted with his Squadron to France. Elaine lived through the first days after the Invasion with the curious sensation that she was gradually coming alive. Was it a process which had begun on the night Dick had made love to her? She felt like a creature protected for a long time by a repulsive chrysalis who was now crawling out of it. She felt weak and curiously lonely.

Returning home after a day at SOE she thought – what am I doing here at home? She was a widow of thirty-one with no future and nobody to care for. Even when Trix had been struck down by sorrow she had not needed Elaine.

The following morning a letter arrived for her. The stamped words on the envelope were hideously familiar – HM Ships. When she opened it, Philippa, sitting opposite her at the breakfast table, began to giggle.

'That isn't a letter, it's a doily.'

The thin blue paper was perforated with holes, varying from a slit or a small circle to a gap two inches wide. The censor's scissors had reduced the letter to paper lace.

'It's from Dick.'

Their father had left the room and Philippa murmured, 'I suppose the divorce is through. Not that poor Trix will care.'

Elaine began to read.

'Yes. He says it is. But he has not heard that Chuck has been killed. I must write and tell him.'

Philippa scraped margarine on her toast.

'Do you realise something odd, Elaine? They could re-marry. Trix does need a man. It is not impossible that they might get together again.'

'It sounds like a stupid Hollywood film,' said Elaine, upset to find how much she minded the idea. The doily had said little enough in between its gaps. The sea was hellish. Dick had bought her some French scent. He had thought about her a lot. At the bottom of the pierced page was scribbled, *I hope you are out of black*.

It was not an important letter and she did not know why she carried it all the time in her handbag.

Trix had been away for weeks. When she telephoned, she sounded unlike herself.

'But she won't grieve for long,' said Philippa after one of the telephone calls.

'Surely you don't want her to?'

'Elaine, what a thing to say. I want her to be happy.'

'Trix is like a boxer,' said Elaine, after a moment, 'she knows how to bend when the blow comes.'

'She's been so lucky until now. I always thought her luck would hold. She hasn't been like some of us – spending our lives expecting our man to be shot down.'

She did not add – or whose man was drowned, and Elaine thought again that her family had forgotten Miles. Or was it that Philippa remembered, and set herself up in a sort of contest of courage, with Elaine recoiling from the sea, while Philippa dared not look up at the sky?

Trix arrived home unannounced one hot evening. Her beauty had returned. She still talked of Chuck and smiled over things he had said. Sometimes her black eyes brimmed. His photograph in flying jacket and Mae West was on her dressing table. But she began to work at the club again, and she spent a good deal of time polishing her charm bracelet.

Later that week all three sisters were at home and in bed when there sounded the old familiar wail of the Alert, followed by thundering guns and distant, shattering explosions. As Elaine sighed and pulled on a dressing-gown, Philippa stood in the doorway.

'Boring. I suppose we'd better go down. I'll call Trix.'

'I'm here. Back under the old table. Golly, I thought we'd had all that,' said Trix, floating in clad in one of her indecent nightdresses. She looked aggrieved when Elaine sharply told her to fetch a dressing-gown: but obeyed.

The trio trooped downstairs, carrying pillows. They settled under the table.

'Elaine?' Theo peered round the door, grey hair on end like the crest of a parrot. 'Do you notice anything curious

261

about the noise? It sounds different. Want to come and have a look?'

Elaine scrambled out and followed him. Across the summer sky was a long straight trail of smoke stretching from the direction of Earl's Court. It was followed by what looked like something belching smoke and flames. There was a loud clattering sound.

'What the devil's that?' muttered Theo. A few moments later there was a loud explosion.

'Good,' said Elaine, 'They hit it.'

The raid went on all night. The girls were asleep when the All Clear finally sounded at half past seven, and when they saw the time, Elaine and Philippa rushed to bath and dress. Before they were ready another Alert wailed out.

'Damn and blast,' said Philippa, as she and Elaine both ate their breakfast standing up. Miggs waited on them.

'Doctor's out. House in Strickland Road's been hit, the milkman said. He told me somethin' else. That wasn't an ordinary blitz last night. They're usin' planes without pilots. Robots, they're shootin' at us now.'

Like the rest of the Londoners, the Tyrrells detested the flying bombs. The war had been on a long time and they had become like soldiers in the trenches – war-weary. The Second Front had given everybody a great surge of hope and a look towards the extraordinary possibility of peace. Now the flying bombs sputtered over London. They sounded as loud as airborne lorries and their tails flamed. In the House of Commons it was announced that if a bomb was overhead, the moment that the light in the tail went out, an explosion followed between five and fifteen seconds later.

In the past the civilians under bombardment had known they were being attacked by living men who risked their own lives and were in mortal danger from the defending guns and fighter planes. But now nothing could be done when the robots came over, except to wait until the light in the machine's tail went out before throwing oneself to the ground.

During the first two weeks the bombs, called variously buzz bombs, doodlebugs, fly bombs or bumble bombs, flew over London night and day. Anti-aircraft defences were ordered not to fire on them. If the gun did hit one, it would do just as much damage as if it simply landed.

262

In SOE headquarters, in Philippa's Mayfair office, in Trix's club – now noticeably thin of US troops – nobody talked of anything else but the bombs: there were stories of dreadful damage and there were jokes. Londoners finally became used to the things. Elaine heard one sputtering overhead when she was at the hairdresser's. Trix went shopping in Bond Street with one eye on the sky, where the familiar shape was whirring with its tail aflame. She waited for the light to go out, but it didn't. The bomb sputtered away towards Regent Street.

Rumours also flew across London. It was said that the RAF planes could get close enough to the flying bombs to tip the angle of their wings so that they fell harmlessly into the sea. The bombs, said some people, were radio controlled. Other said they were jet propelled. Most dramatic was the rumour that the Germans had discovered a way to use the earth's magnetic field, and that *we* must hurry up and find a way to upset that.

During the new blitz hundreds of thousands of houses disappeared into black smoke or were damaged beyond repair. There were no official figures given of the dead and wounded.

Both Elaine and Philippa acquired steel helmets in which they went to work, and Trix looked enchanting in her GI's helmet, her fair hair flowing from below the chin strap. There was an advantage to the bombs, she said. She'd been to Harrods and – imagine! – had been offered a choice of *four* different bottles of French scent. Elaine watched her young sister returning to her butterfly self. She envied her; it must be wonderful to be so resilient.

After thinking about it a great deal, Elaine made up her mind that she must tell Trix that she had seen Dick. One evening during an All Clear she found her sister in the garden. Trix was on her knees on the parched grass, admiring her row of well-staked and ripening tomatoes.

'If you pick this little bit in the crook of the stem, see? you get another tomato. How gorgeous they smell.'

Elaine sat on the grass. She wore a turquoise coloured pre-war silk dress which suited her. Her black clothes had been packed away at last. Trix was in white cotton, polka-dotted with scarlet. A ribbon trailed from her hair.

'I had a letter from Dick the other day,' began Elaine casually.

'Oh lor. Ropey news,' sighed Trix. 'What does *he* want? It would be the limit if he expects parcels from Fortnums from me now we're divorced.'

'Of course he doesn't. His parents can do that.'

'I should say so. They're filthy rich,' agreed Trix amicably. 'It was jolly nice, me not asking for alimony. I could have done but Chuck said no. I said – but American girls do, and *he* said "Stay as sweet as you are". Darling Chuck,' she added and returned, tearless and pretty, to the tomatoes.

'Dick didn't write about you, as it happens. And he called round some time ago.'

'Did he? And you coped? Good-oh. I s'pose he was hoping to see me?'

'Not particularly.'

'Wanted to know if I'm okay, so round he comes to see Little Mother Kitty. Remember that bit in Angela Brazil that Flip used to quote? "Little Mother Kitty, What would we do without you, You're the salvation of our family, she said with a happy sigh." If you do write, you can tell him that Chuck bought it. But I absolutely don't want to see him, per-leeze.'

Summer went by. News of the war in Europe was of victories but the flying bombs went on. And now the V2's were a new fear. They were mysterious rockets and did more terrible damage. People said they came down from the sky coated with ice.

The person who took the blitz the worst was Annette. She was plainly terrified, rushed out the moment an Alert sounded to listen to the distant putt-putt-putt, then ran to the billiard room to shelter. She would not answer the telephone to patients. The more nervous she grew, the more smug Miggs became, again wearing her creaking white apron. Annette was too alarmed to notice how often Miggs took over the telephone and showed patients to the waiting room.

Matching the raids, another kind of bomb burst inside the sheltering walls of St Helen's. One afternoon, with Miggs out shopping and Annette under the billiard table, Theo himself answered the telephone.

It was Trix's solicitor asking if Mrs Polglaze could call at the Temple about some matter concerning the decree absolute.

The moment Miggs came in through the back door, Theo stormed into the kitchen. He had had an hour to get steadily more furious. His face was a dull crimson.

'Do you know what I learned on the telephone!' he shouted. 'That there has been *a divorce* in my family without my knowledge.'

He continued to rant. Nobody had told Miggs about the divorce but she had known from the first. There was nothing about the family she didn't know, and what she did not gather from listening at doors she seemed to absorb through the pores of her skin. She filled the kettle.

'Hadn't you best calm down? You don't know the half of what happens to your children, and you never did.'

He went out, slamming the door.

Miggs waited. She knew the three separate ways that the girls opened the front door and when she heard Elaine come in, she bobbed out into the hall.

'Game's up, lady. The doctor's found out.'

'What on earth are you talking about, Miggs?'

'Save your breath, Miss Elaine. I know all about the divorce. Knew the marriage wasn't any good long before the poor Lieutenant came on leave and she gave him the boot. The one who looks like gettin' the boot now is Trix. Unless you stand up to the doctor. He's fit to be tied.'

Why, thought Elaine, should we imagine she wouldn't know about it? The old nurse then told her, not without a relish at the drama, of the solicitor's telephone call.

Theo was in his study dictating letters. Annette only incompetently wrote them in longhand, but he was patient with her. He was smiling. His face changed when he saw Elaine.

'May I have a word, Father?'

'I will leave you,' said Annette, showing by her expression that she, too, knew what had happened.

As Elaine sat down, her father looked at her as if at an enemy, and went into the attack.

'It appears that you decided to keep me in ignorance of the disgusting matter of my daughter's adultery with some American or other.'

He had at last put two and two together, she thought.

'You know very well that Trix was fond of poor Chuck Greenfield who was shot down last month.'

She hoped to shame him into charity. She failed.

'Very tragic. What has that to do with Beatrix? Where is her husband?'

'Dick is at sea. You know that too. He's been away almost continuously for two years. Anybody could see they were becoming estranged. Trix is so young.'

'Indeed. What you say appals me. You condone your sister's adultery, I take it.'

'I do not. But I can understand that it might happen – that it does happen, because of the war – '

'Don't use that excuse to me,' he interrupted savagely. 'I saw scores of people die in the last war, and I've seen them die in this one too. Brave men and respectable women. You are saying that separation turns women into whores. I am sorry the young man was killed, but I feel no more, perhaps less, than for any man dead in the blitz. What I do feel is disgust at Beatrix. I won't have her living under my roof.'

'Father!' cried Elaine, scarcely able to believe the iron prejudice and lack of pity. 'You can't mean you'd refuse to have the poor child here. Where would she go? She has nobody but us.'

'To my recollection she had a husband. Make up your mind to it. I won't have her here.'

She ran out of the room.

Both her sisters had come home and Miggs must have told them, for they were waiting in the drawing room, their faces wearing the same tense large-eyed anxiety.

Trix said, 'He wants me to get the hell out of here.'

'He'll come round,' said Elaine.

'No he won't. Okay. I'll go.'

Trix was white. She said, staring to the ground, 'I'll find somewhere. I could write to Chuck's parents for some money. Or there's a guy in the club who – '

'Trix!'

Both Elaine and Philippa burst out at the same time.

'I suppose he called me a whore,' said Trix, 'I don't care. He always hated me.'

'He is angry because he is fond of you, for heaven's sake,' said Elaine. 'Of course he won't turn you out.'

Philippa was looking fixedly at Elaine. Her loyalty and love were all unswervingly with Barny, and now because of Chuck's death, Trix belonged to the old lost Eagle world.

'Pa can't turn her out, Elaine,' she said carefully, 'because he is doing exactly what he blames her for.'

266

'What are you talking about?' said Elaine sharply. Her sister's voice sounded ominous.

Philippa hesitated, then said in a rush, 'I wasn't going to tell anybody about it, but now I must. Annette was coming out of his bedroom the other afternoon. She didn't see me, because I dodged behind the door. And once I'd seen that I suddenly realised that they were having an affair. It is written all over them.'

Trix burst into an angry triumphant laugh. Neither Elaine nor Philippa smiled.

Elaine gave a long sigh.

'What a thing to speak of to my own father.'

All three sisters knew that the task would be hers.

But Theo did not send for Elaine and demand that Trix should pack her bags. There was no showdown. He was brusque with all three girls, and spent his time when not at work trying to soothe Annette who, hearing the rattle of flying bombs, was hysterical. Perhaps Theo realised that something in the atmosphere had changed. Or perhaps Annette did not want any trouble and consequent attention shifted away from herself. Trix was allowed to stay.

The flying bombs continued to land, people became fatalistic. The summer crawled by, the invasion news was good. Paris would soon be liberated. 'And when,' said Miggs, complaining that the milk ration had been cut, 'are we goin' to be liberated? That's all I want to know.'

One Sunday, weeks after Theo's discovery of the divorce, he asked Elaine to come to his study. Her heart sank. It was all going to start up again, and faced with the degrading prospect of counter attacks against her own father, Elaine felt a revulsion against them all. Why, she thought, must it always be me?

But Theo, looking unusually stylish in a new shirt with a thin blue line, and a blue silk tie Annette had clearly chosen, asked her to sit down quite pleasantly. He was in the old swivel chair, which twisted and turned for a moment. As she waited, she thought that her father's Julius Caesar face looked relaxed. Perhaps there would be no trouble after all.

Finally he said, 'Annette is very upset over the flying bombs. One understands it with such a highly-strung temperament. She's a Latin lass.'

'Yes.'

'The strain is bad for her. Very bad. I've decided she must go to the country. Remember Colonel Pendleton who gave you the introduction to Blenheim? He and his wife are living in Hertfordshire and most kindly say that Annette may stay with them until things have quietened down.'

'Miggs can help you while she is away.'

Her father was not listening.

'I have some further news. Annette has agreed to be my wife.'

Elaine had a moment of sheer astonishment. Her mouth fell open. Her father was marrying a girl of Trix's age. A French girl who did not like his daughters any more than they liked her.

'I know it must be a surprise to you,' said her father boyishly, 'but you must have seen that I admire her. We have grown very attached.'

He began to talk of Annette and himself. He used language which dated back to the time when he was young, to the romantic years of Edwardian courtship. It was odd to hear him. He said he was deeply honoured at her consent, that her character was exceptionally fine and he considered she had true nobility. He made the match dignified, even serious. Elaine produced some clichés about being sure they would be happy. He gave another of his boyish smiles, saying he had told Miggs, but would Elaine tell the girls?

'We will be married in Hertfordshire, I think, from the Colonel's house. Annette does not wish me to wait for her for long.'

You haven't, thought Elaine, waited at all.

With Tyrrell impulsiveness she ran straight up to the sewing room where Trix was helping Philippa shorten a dress.

'Pa's marrying Annette!'

'She got him in bed,' said Trix. 'He's nothing but a dirty old man.'

'*Shut up!*' exclaimed Philippa. 'He's our father, for God's sake, but what do we know how he feels? He's never been close to any of us, even you, Elaine. He doesn't understand us, and I'm sure it isn't his fault. He's reserved, sort of closed with us and always has been. When have we tried to understand *him*? Perhaps she does.'

Trix's pale face had the witch-like look which Elaine had seen before.

'How can she bear to marry somebody old. It's because of Mum's money.'

'But it is left to us in trust,' said Elaine.

268

'Pa's got it until he dies. She'll make the best of it while she can,' said Trix. 'She might even get the will changed. French-women are clever.'

Elaine might have guessed how her sisters would take the news. Philippa had returned to her romantic self. Trix was spiteful with revenge.

But what of Miggs? Among the family, it was Miggs who loved him and had known him since he was born. She was not all that much older than Theo, sixteen years was less of a gap between people of their age. And she could not stand Annette. But when Elaine went into the kitchen, Miggs did not even scowl. She was squatting by the giant basket which contained Sailor, listening to him loudly purring. She looked up.

'He told you, then.'

'And you too.'

'Didn't surprise me, lady. I know him like the back of my hand, daresay I knew what would happen before he did himself. There's no fool like an old fool, Miss Elaine, and that's a fact. We don't need to be botherin' about the orange blossom, that's a blessin'. She's off to the Colonel's and she'll be livin' the life of Riley.'

'Pa says they will marry soon.'

'He's not the boss any more, is he?'

Miggs stood up, grimacing at the pain of her rheumatism, and limped over to lay a tray. The Alert had begun to moan.

'The day she comes into this house as missus, I go out. Miss Philippa said I can go with her when peace comes. To America. Don't fancy it, but it's a sight better than puttin' up with that sharp little madam.'

One of Theo's patients had an appointment on the morning that Annette was leaving London. She had arrived from her digs with three large suitcases which were left by the front door. Theo was taking her to the station. Elaine came down earlier than usual, to say goodbye to Annette. She was surprised to find her in her white overall, at the desk in her old place.

Annette smiled.

'Old Lady Leveaux is coming to see Theo this morning, and she is very fond of me. I shall work until she has gone. It will please her.'

'That's kind of you,' said Elaine since it was expected of her. 'We haven't talked much lately. I'm not sure that I have congratulated you.'

Annette fiddled with a ring on her left hand. Elaine saw that it was one of her mother's, the emerald and diamond half hoop.

'Theo will make me happy, I am sure,' said Annette.

The comparison between her and Elaine was very marked. Annette looked young, handsome, confident. Her hair shone like the black wings of a bird.

She said suddenly, 'Alexandre told me he saw you at your Bureau. We dined that night. He always sees me when he is in London. He gives me news of my village. He obtains it through his secret work.'

'He shouldn't tell it.'

'To me. *Tiens*. I left France as Alain did.'

'I was very grieved when I heard that Alain was dead,' Elaine said impulsively. It was something she had known, through SOE, months before. 'I felt unhappy that I could not tell you.'

The serious young Breton had been a partisan. He had been shot.

'But I knew of it. I knew when it happened,' said Annette flatly. 'It is for him that I wear the cross of Lorraine. I have told Theo that it will stay on my neck until I too am dead.'

The words were dramatic, the tone the opposite. Annette tidied some papers on the desk.

'Did Alexandre tell you that Alain and I were betrothed? No? He could have done. Alain kept it a secret at the Centre d'Acceuil, he did not wish people to know of our love. That was why I came to England. Because he did. Not for patriotism, what is that? For love.'

It was impossible, thought Elaine, to say anything to the girl now wearing her mother's ring. And besides, Annette preferred to talk than to listen.

'Alexandre gave me the news that my parents are dead. They were killed in a British raid. How stupid the British are, what did the bombing of our village achieve? We did not even have a factory. I have some cousins who live there, but I do not like them. That is all. There is no reason for me to return when victory comes. Your father and I need each other. I do not believe in attaching myself to the past.'

270

'I am sure you will be happy,' said Elaine, and there was a faint tone of wonder in her voice.

'I will make him a good wife. We will have children. Theo needs a son.'

Thinking about Annette after she had gone, Elaine could not find a single thing that she and her sisters had in common with their future stepmother. Annette's affection for their father was probably genuine now, but it was based on commonsense, and when had any of the Tyrrell girls loved for such a reason? Annette was conceited in her polite way, and even Trix, the beauty of the family, had not a trace of conceit. She shared her beauty with people as if it were a kind of gift.

What the sisters did have was something in common with their father. He had fallen in love with a young girl over thirty years his junior and he had not hesitated. He asked her to be his wife. The family impulsiveness was in him still.

Elaine gathered, talking to the omniscient Miggs, that Annette was settling down well with the Pendletons. Perhaps she had decided to use some Gallic charm for a change. It seemed that she had taken over the cooking. The Pendletons were delighted with her, and thought the unsuitable match most suitable. Theo travelled to their Hertfordshire house to spend every weekend.

With Theo away a good deal and Annette gone, a blitzed calm descended on the old house. Elaine received more letters from Dick. Fortunately, Trix was rarely up at breakfast time and always missed the arrival of the morning post. She would not have cared that Dick was writing to her sister, but she might have laughed. Elaine was glad she did not know.

The letters were friendly and funny. They began *Lovebird*, and ended *All my love, Dick*. She read them over and over again. She was like a woman searching in her lap for a needle. She did not find it.

Chapter Nineteen

The war was dragging to a kind of close, but the foggy 1944 Christmas came and went, and it was not ended. The blackout was lifted. It was called a dim-out, and should have been cheerfully welcomed. But after five years in the dark, the lighting seemed abnormally bright to dazzled Londoners. Trix disliked it, it was unromantic. 'What about goodnight kisses now?'

Paris had been freed at the end of August, while London was still under bombardment, and the stories and pictures of its joyful liberation told on Londoners' nerves as they went their stubborn way to work through new ruins. Now in the winter the tales filtering through from France were of Paris, already its brilliant self, with money spent like water, not a single ruin from bombs, people dancing until four in the morning and cafés full to bursting point. That did not please Londoners either. They were envious and irritable.

Philippa had seen nothing of Barny. He had not stayed long in France after the first months of the invasion, he was back in England. But every time there was a big American raid, and the never-ending Flying Fortresses blackened the London sky like giant birds, Philippa wondered which of the planes were protected by Barny's fighters. Sometimes he managed to telephone. Telling her nothing.

One evening the telephone rang, and Miggs came into the drawing room.

'Your husband, lady.'

Philippa flew.

'Honey? Like to come up for a couple of nights? It's permitted.'

'*Would I!*'

'Grab a train to Chichester. I'll have a jeep meet you. And bring a party frock. It's Pete Jansen's birthday, he's thirty, would you credit it! Another thing . . . I've been thinking. Howsabout bringing Trix with you?'

She was very surprised.

'We're short of pretty girls,' he said. 'And besides . . . Chuck would've liked it. Okay?'

When Philippa told Trix, it was the first time she'd ever seen her young sister blush.

A heavy open jeep, with RITA HAYWORTH on the bonnet, was waiting for the girls when they arrived. It was already January and freezing cold. But the girls were too excited to notice the knife-sharp air as the great automobile thundered down frosty roads. There was a winter moon, and the headlights were now only half-masked. They shone on high glittering hedges and stretches of fields hard under the frost. Trix chattered gaily. But Philippa thought the metallic little voice sounded unnaturally hard. She wondered if the thought of being at an American air station again, seeing pilots again, would hurt. Yet Trix had accepted the invitation almost feverishly.

The girls were set down at the entrance of a big rambling old house round which a series of ugly army huts had been built. The Stars and Stripes hung above the doorway, stirring in the icy winds.

Through the door, they found themselves in a high-ceilinged entrance hall, facing a double staircase. Portraits hung on the walls. This had been somebody's home, once upon a time. Now it teemed with American troops; the noise of men's voices was loud. Every soldier going by stared at Trix who automatically shook back her long pale hair.

Suddenly Philippa saw Barny. How long it was since she had seen him, weeks, months. She simply ran, and he put out his arms and caught her and kissed her as if they were alone in the house, in England, in the world.

'Flip. Honey.'

'Oh, my dearest!'

Then he drew away from her and said, 'Is Trix around?'

Still holding her, he looked beyond her and Philippa saw him give an odd smile. She turned round.

There was her sister looking curiously small, despite her high wedge heels. Her head was tilted upwards. And, fairer than she, looming over her like a giant, was the broad figure, wings on his breast, of Pete Jansen.

* * *

Elaine was the only one to stay at home in St Helen's on the day which was called VE Day. It was not a complete peace, for there was still war in the Far East. But in Europe it was over.

'Our war's finished,' Philippa said, and it set Elaine's teeth on edge to hear it given the kindly pronoun.

In the house, in the garden, she could hear bells and car horns. Now and then laughter went by in d'Abernon Road, and somebody sang. Or there were shouting voices. London had turned into a river of people, arm in arm, arm round neck, slowly drifting towards the West End. They were bound for Downing Street to cheer Churchill. Then to the Palace to cheer the King and Queen. Londoners always went to the Palace when they felt happy.

Miggs had tried to persuade Elaine to go too. The old nurse never missed being part of a celebration.

'I remember the old Queen's funeral, all those kings walkin' behind the coffin. And I was in Trafalgar Square for Armistice Day. Then there's all the Royal weddin's and funerals. I can't miss this,' said Miggs, who had fished out a pre-war white straw hat, with daisies round the brim, from a box under her bed. After vainly trying to get Elaine to join the jollifications, Miggs left the house alone. Probably, thought Elaine, to get a lift to the Palace in somebody's taxi.

Philippa and Trix had risen in the dawn to walk to the Wings Club where Barny and Pete were supposed to be arriving as so on as they could. 'We must,' declared Trix, 'be there first.' Trix was quite out of herself, as Miggs described it, since Pete had asked her to be his wife.

'I always knew,' said Trix to Elaine, waving a hand decorated with yet another (larger) sapphire, 'that I'd marry a Yank in the end.'

Since Philippa had taken her to the American air station in January, Trix's recovery had been complete. Like a child at the edge of the sea waiting to tumble in, she had fallen in love again. Her sisters congratulated her, Elaine was introduced to Pete, and an atmosphere of romance – Trix was shopping again – invaded St Helen's.

Philippa and Elaine had supper one night at home, and afterwards went into the sitting room to sit by the fire. The day had been cold. Trix's plans, Trix's bliss, Trix running up and down stairs, waving new satin petticoats for admiring approval, talking on the telephone to girlfriends, playing new American records, had occupied the entire week. A kind of lull had fallen as the two sisters sat looking into the fire.

Elaine finally said,

'I like Pete Jansen very much. But . . . do you think they are going to be happy, Flip?'

She turned to Philippa for enlightenment. Her sister understood Americans.

Philippa made a rueful face.

'Barny and I are slightly bothered. Barny more than me, really. You know Pete's from Wyoming. It's such a *huge* state, really enormous. Some of it is nothing but a great desert. Barny says there's nowhere else like it in the whole of the United States. Pete's family live their entire lives in the open.'

'But Trix knows all about that.'

'Yes, Elaine, but has she really grasped it? Has she actually realised that there is not a city for four hundred miles from their ranch?'

The sisters looked at each other. They had a vision of frivolous little Trix setting off blithely towards a life about which she had not given one serious thought. Elaine with her steady soul, Philippa with her full heart, might just have made so extreme a choice and succeeded by sheer love. But how would Trix endure such a life? Not because she wasn't young and strong, but because she wouldn't try. What Trix thrived on, what made her beauty glow, was pleasure. At present, with an American flyer making passionate love to her, she was in a dream. When she finally arrived in Wyoming, that fierce sexual bond between Pete and herself must hold for a while. Even the land itself, with its vast and harsh simplicities, might touch her imagination. But for how long?

Elaine and Philippa arrived at more or less the same moment at the same conclusion.

'Oh Flip. What will happen, do you think?'

'I suppose she'll leave. She'll never stay the course. Poor Pete . . .'

Elaine reflected.

'Perhaps he'll be relieved in the end.'

'That's what Barny said. He said any girl who marries Pete had just better come from a farm.'

There was a little pause.

'I'll tell you what,' said Philippa suddenly, 'I can't imagine her ever coming back to England, can you? If she leaves Pete she'll pack up, and she might even go so far as to buy her ticket. But she'll never come home – '

'You mean because she'll find somebody else.'

They were silent again, thinking of their sister.

'I suppose we ought to be grateful,' said Elaine finally, 'that whatever happens, she will be all right.'

'I don't know why we're so certain of that. But I agree.'

Trix herself talked knowledgeably of Wyoming and the ranch, for some mysterious reason called a spread, and the breeding of horses. She was sure Elaine knew how she'd always longed to ride again but Pa had refused to pay for it after that time she used to ride in the Row. He'd said it had become too expensive.

'Pete says I'll be able to ride again in three hours. He says you never forget and that I'm naturally graceful. But he also said the only way for me to ride *there*, quite different from here, is to learn from him and that I've got to do what I'm told. He makes me behave,' she added, speaking as if she and Pete were united in controlling a horse or a dog which was out of hand.

A month after Trix had 'met up' with Pete, as she called it, and Elaine supposed they must have gone to bed, Trix grew noticeably quiet for a few days. She was very pale and looked stricken. One night her colour and vivacity were back. She came into Elaine's bedroom. Remembering her sister's dislike of her naked nightdresses, she wore a modest négligé of white organdie threaded with blue ribbons.

'Oh Elaine. I'm so relieved I could cry. I had to come and tell you. I thought I'd lost him.'

'*Flying?*'

'No, no, he's not flying just now. It isn't anything to do with that, it was something I did. Oh, it was awful. God, I'm glad it's okay again.'

And out came the story in Trix's now completely American voice.

'It was last weekend when he called me up and said I could come to the station, and he'd gotten hold of a flat over a boathouse on the river. Well. Pete took me there. We had a night together. It was . . . well, it was just so wonderful, he's the most marvellous lover, oh Elaine, he's the best. Then Pete said next day why didn't we have his Captain over for tea. I thought it would be good because although he'd seen me around, and must have guessed Pete and I were crazy about each other and everything, I'd never met him properly. I'm sure he is fond of Pete. After all, Pete's a star flyer, DFC in the RAF and all that. Anyway, the Captain (that's what they call them in the US Air Force) came to tea. I bought some buns,' said Trix solemnly.

Listening, Elaine could not imagine what was going to come next.

'He was swell, I sure did like him. He was funny and relaxed, you know? We talked about English antiques, and I told him how I'd bought a chest of drawers, you know the one, when Chuck and I – well, I didn't mention poor Chuck but I said that when Pete and I married, I was going to take it with me to the States. And I was dying to live in the US of A.'

She sounded uncannily American.

'The captain laughed, and then he said how he'd have to get back. I was quite glad. Because Pete was looking at me in a kind of way and I knew what *he* wanted and so did I. Then I had a brainwave. I was nice. I mean, I *can* be, can't I?' she said earnestly. 'I said something like Oh, Captain, there's one little thing I'm dying to say and that is – isn't it time Pete was rested up? He's pretty tired, and he's done ten sorties and his squadron and his folks keep writing me to know if he's okay.'

Elaine stared.

Trix made a face.

'It wasn't so terrible, was it? He had done more flights than a lot of other guys. But the Captain looked murderous. He didn't say a thing. As for Pete, he practically jumped out of his skin and he just said "*shut up*" and then said something to the Captain about me acting hasty and he didn't know what had gotten into me. Then he and the Captain went down the stairs, it was a kind of ladder thing leading into the garden, and Pete saw him off.'

She fidgeted with her bracelet. It clinked.

'When he got back, Elaine, he was *awful*. He yelled at me. He said I was nuts and he hit me. I don't expect you remember, but Dick slapped my face that night we parted. I mean that stung. But Pete hit me real hard, and I spun across the room and fell against a chair and banged my head. I saw stars. Then he picked up his jacket and walked out and didn't come back. I called up the station four times. They said he wasn't there. I didn't believe

277

them. I had to come back to London. I hung about at home, you saw me, didn't you? I was so scared. I was sure I'd lost him. He's the real one, you know. The real one. In the end it was me who called him again – I've never done that before. I thought he'd refuse to speak, but then this time he did. He just said "never interfere with my job again or I'm through. I'll never see you again." Wasn't it awful? I'm still frightened, sort of. But I swore I'd never do it again, and then he let me come down to the station and we made love. And it was all wonderful again.'

'It was all wonderful again' was also the burden of Philippa's song. The book that Barny had written about the Eagles had been sold to an American publisher as well as to an English one and, Philippa said with shining eyes, Barny knew what he was going to be. A writer.

'We'll be going to the States pretty soon – there are no more U boats, haven't been for months, so we'll be getting a ship. Oh Elaine! I shall miss you! But I can't help being excited, you do understand, don't you?'

What answer was there to that?

Philippa continued to talk in her old, impulsive, romantic way. She talked of Louisiana where she would be living and of the letters she had received from Barny's sister Mary Lou. How kind everybody was! She showed Elaine photographs of a white house set among strange, drooping trees. Wasn't it wonderful to think that Barny was going home, and she would be with him, and – imagine! – Miggs had agreed to come too.

'Of course Miggsy is very funny about America. She keeps saying she is sure they won't like her, when what she means is that she won't like them. But she and Barny get on so marvellously. He spoils her and she pretends to think he is silly when really she's thrilled. Barny did say the other day that he was dreading going home. In a way, you know, because nobody there knows what it has been like. But we have each other. And Miggsy will be our bit of England. And maybe we can have a baby soon.'

Philippa gazed at her sister, seeing only joy.

Trix. Philippa. They had become part of the American invasion, thought Elaine. And then she remembered Alain and Alexandre, and the girl now married to her father. They had brought a French invasion to the old house, and changed her father's life.

It rained heavily last night, and VE morning was dull, damp and grey when Elaine went out into the garden. The coarse unkempt grass which had once been a lawn was drenched. She fetched a raincoat, and spread it on the wooden bench by the syringa tree where her mother used to sit and sew before the war.

All over London, all over England and France, and the great map of Europe pinned to the wall in the Baker Street office, people were running into each other's arms. They were laughing and kissing and dancing and making a noise. Happiness makes people want to bang drums and sing, she thought. They want to be part of a crowd, and sharing. Even Miggs.

What is there for me? She remembered talking to Dick at the Hogarth on that wet evening. He was so very fond of Miles that she had felt she could tell him almost anything. She had said how she had often thought that a dreadful day might come when she would wake up and find Miles did not love her any more.

Dick had given her an odd look with his slanting eyes.

'Yes. Lovers always think that. But it would be much much worse, Elaine, if you woke up one day and found you couldn't love.'

Perhaps that has happened, she thought, and even if I could, I'd be afraid to love. She pushed the thought of Dick's lovemaking away. Thinking about him hurt her. She began to think, instead, of Miles. In a wave of sorrow she heard his voice, felt his thin cheek pressed against hers. Is Claire feeling like this? On a day of such happiness, this is when it is worst.

She leaned back against the seat, looking at the tangled grass and hearing the distant tumbling of church bells. Suddenly in the garden a blackbird began to sing his heart out. He sounded just as her sisters did – free and blessed.

Philippa and Trix shared all the joy that was flooding through London, and soon they, and the Americans, would be gone. They would cross the Atlantic and become part of the country which had grown so close to England during the long, long war.

Father will sell this house. Annette doesn't like it because we all lived here together before she came. Miggsy will be gone.

She shut her eyes, listening to the blackbird, and did not hear the footsteps on the wet grass. Somebody touched her hand and she opened her eyes.

'Dick!'

'Elaine!' He took her hands and stood looking down at her. A rush of dismay, of love, of embarrassed love, went through her. She returned his look with her old bright reserve. Even her voice was brittle when she said,

'What a surprise.'

'I couldn't get to a telephone. The queues! I thought it quicker just to come. I'm ridiculously optimistic,' he went on lightly, 'I kept hoping you hadn't gone out to celebrate.'

'I suppose you thought I wouldn't want to.'

'Something like that,' he said, still looking at her very thoughtfully.

He had not kissed her. He sat beside her on the bench. Then, after a moment he said,

'Will you answer me something?'

She did not know why she was frightened.

'What?'

'Don't look like that. Answer me bravely. Did it worry you – that we made love?'

She was so embarrassed that she could not answer. He leaned towards her, and she recoiled.

But he ignored that and put his arms round her.

'Lovebird. Don't move away from me. Stay close. Now listen. I know, I knew, even when I left you after all that beautiful sex, how you'd feel. Sweet girl. You never had an affair, did you? Only Miles whom you loved. When we were in bed, and you were so gorgeous, I did remember that. But you thought that for me it was just one night of love, didn't you?'

'I don't know. I – I suppose I did. Marjorie once said you have lots of affairs.'

He laughed at that.

'My lovebird. How could *you* be an affair? Don't you know I worship you? That night was like stars. Dear love. Beautiful Elaine. Come closer. That's right. That's right.'

By the author of
THIS SIDE OF HEAVEN

Street
Song

EMMA BLAIR

Susan's parents had wanted a son . . . and they did
little to hide their disappointment with her. As soon as
was decently possible they packed her off to boarding
school.

If only they could have known . . .

Because in the tradition-bound Scotland of the 1920's
there was no place for a woman like Susan. But she was
determined to find one – even if it meant beating her
wealthy parents at their own game . . .

STREET SONG – Emma Blair at her best . . . a
passionate saga.

GENERAL FICTION   **0 7221 1941 0**   **£3.50**